THIRST
NO. 2

ALSO BY
CHRISTOPHER PIKE

THIRST NO. 1

THIRST

NO. 2

INCLUDES
PHANTOM
EVIL THIRST
CREATURES OF FOREVER

Christopher Pike

Simon Pulse
NEW YORK   LONDON   TORONTO   SYDNEY

This book is a work of fiction. Any references to historical events, real people, or real locales are used fictitiously. Other names, characters, places, and incidents are the product of the author's imagination, and any resemblance to actual events or locales or persons, living or dead, is entirely coincidental.

SIMON PULSE

An imprint of Simon & Schuster Children's Publishing Division

1230 Avenue of the Americas, New York, NY 10020

This Simon Pulse paperback edition January 2010

Phantom copyright © 1996 by Christopher Pike

Evil Thirst copyright © 1996 by Christopher Pike

Creatures of Forever copyright © 1996 by Christopher Pike

All rights reserved, including the right of reproduction in whole or in part in any form.

SIMON PULSE and colophon are registered trademarks of Simon & Schuster, Inc.

For information about special discounts for bulk purchases, please contact Simon & Schuster Special Sales at 1-866-506-1949 or business@simonandschuster.com.

The Simon & Schuster Speakers Bureau can bring authors to your live event. For more information or to book an event contact the Simon & Schuster Speakers Bureau at 1-866-248-3049 or visit our website at www.simonspeakers.com.

Designed by Mike Rosamilia

The text of this book was set in Adobe Garamond.

Manufactured in the United States of America

10 9 8 7 6 5 4 3 2 1

Library of Congress Control Number 2008940563

ISBN 978-1-4169-8309-5

These titles were previously published individually.

CONTENTS

PHANTOM

For Scott, who loves female vampires

ONE

Someone knocks at the door of the Las Vegas home where I stand. It is late evening; the living room is dimly lit, four walls of blurred shadows. I don't know who this person is. For that matter, I'm not sure who I am. I have just awakened from a dead alchemist's experiment. My mind is foggy and my nerves are shot. But before I embarked on the experiment, only hours ago, I was a steel-willed vampire—the last vampire on earth. Now I fear—and hope—that I may once again be human. That I may be a young woman named Alisa, the humble offspring of a five-thousand-year-old monster called Sita.

The person continues to knock.

"Open the door," he says impatiently. "It's me."

Who is me? I wonder. I do not recognize the voice, although it does sound familiar. Yet I hesitate to obey, even to respond.

Of those few I call friends, only Seymour Dorsten is supposed to know I am in this Las Vegas home. My other friends—well, a couple recently perished in the Nevada desert, in a nuclear blast. A lot has been happening in the last few days, and most of it has been my doing.

"Sita," the person outside the door says. "I know you're in there."

Curious, I think. He knows my ancient name. He even says it like he knows me. But why doesn't he tell me his name? I could ask him, but some emotion stops me. It is one I have seldom known in my five thousand years.

Fear. I stare down at my hands.

I tremble with fear. If I am human, I know, I am practically defenseless. That is why I do not want to open the door. I do not want to die before I have had a chance to taste mortality. Before I have had the opportunity to have a child. That is perhaps the primary reason I employed Arturo's alchemetic tools to reverse my vampirism—to become a mother. Yet I am still not a hundred percent sure the experiment has succeeded. I reach down with the nails of my right hand and pinch my left palm. The flesh breaks; there is a line of blood. I stare at it.

The wound does not immediately heal.

I must be human. Lord Krishna save me.

The knocking stops. The person outside takes a step back from the door. I hear his movements, even with my mediocre human ears. He seems to chuckle to himself.

"I understand, Sita," he says. "It's all right. I'll return soon."

I hear him walk away. Only then do I realize I have been standing in the dark with my breath held. Almost collapsing from relief, I sag against the door and try to calm my thumping heart. I am both confused and exalted.

"I am human," I whisper to myself.

Tears roll over my face. I touch them with my quivering tongue. They are clear and salty, not dark and bloody. Another sign that I am human. Moving slowly, striving to maintain my balance, I step to the living room couch and sit down. Looking around, I marvel at how blurred everything is, and wonder if the experiment has damaged my eyesight. But then I realize I must be seeing things as a human sees, which means to see so little. Why, I can't even distinguish the grain in the wood panel on the far wall. Nor can I hear the voices of the people in the cars that pass outside. I am virtually blind and deaf.

"I am human," I repeat in wonder. Then I begin to laugh, to cry some more, and to wonder what the hell I'm going to do next. Always, as a vampire, I could do anything I wished. Now I doubt if I will ever leave the house.

I pick up the remote and turn on the TV. The news—they are talking about the hydrogen bomb that exploded in the desert the previous night. They say it destroyed a top-secret military base. The wind was blowing away from Las Vegas so the fallout should be almost nonexistent. They don't say anything about me, however, even though I was there and witnessed the whole thing. The experts wonder if it was an accident. They don't connect it to the mass police killings I committed in Los Angeles a few days earlier. They are not very imaginative, I think. They don't believe in vampires.

And now there are no more vampires to believe in.

"I beat you, Yaksha," I say aloud to my dead creator, the vampire who sucked my blood five thousand years ago and replaced it with his own mysterious fluids. "It took me a long time but now I can go back to an ordinary life."

Yet my memories are not ordinary. My mind is not either, although I suddenly realize I am having trouble remembering many things that hours ago were clear. Has my identity changed with my body? What percentage of personal ego is constructed from memory? True, I still remember Krishna, but I can no longer see him in my mind's eye as I could before. I forget even the blue of his eyes—that unfathomable blue, as dear as the most polished star in the black heavens. The realization saddens me. My long life has been littered with pain, but also much joy. I do not want it to be forgotten, especially by me.

"Joel," I whisper. "Arturo."

I will not forget them. Joel was an FBI agent, a friend I made into a vampire in order to save his life. An alteration that caused him to die from a nuclear bomb. And Arturo, another friend, a hybrid of humanity and vampires from the

Middle Ages, my personal priest, my passionate lover, and the greatest alchemist in history. It was Arturo who forced me to detonate the bomb, and destroy him and Joel, but my love for him is still warm and near. I only wish he were with me now to see what miracle his esoteric knowledge has wrought. But would the vampire blood—obsessed Arturo have still loved my human body? Yes, dear Arturo, I believe so. I still believe in you.

Then there was Ray, my Rama reincarnated. My memories of him will never fade, I swear, even if my human brain eventually grows forgetful. My love for Ray is not a human or vampire creation. It is beyond understanding, eternal, even though he himself is dead. Killed trying to kill a demon, the malignant Eddie Fender. There are worse reasons to die, I suppose. I still remember more than a few of them.

Yet, at the moment, I do not want to dwell on the past.

I just want to be human again. And live.

There comes another knock at the front door.

I become very still. How quickly frightened a human can become.

"Sita," this person calls. "It's me, Seymour. Can I come in?"

This voice I definitely recognize. Standing with effort, I walk to the front door and undo the lock and chain. Seymour stands on the porch and stares at me. He wears the same thick glasses and hopelessly mismatched clothes of the high school nerd I met in a stupid PE class only a few months before. His face changes as he studies me; his expression turns to one of alarm. He has trouble speaking.

"It worked," he gasps.

I smile and open the door all the way. "It worked. Now I am like you. Now I am free of the curse."

Seymour shakes his head as he steps in the house and I close the door. He liked me as a vampire, I know. He wanted me to make him a vampire, to poison him through the metamorphosis, an act that was strictly forbidden by Krishna five thousand years ago. Now Seymour is upset. Unable to sit, he paces in front of me. There are unshed tears in his eyes.

"Why did you do it?" he demands. "I didn't think you would really do it."

I force my smile wider and spread my arms. "But you knew I would. And I want you to be happy for me." I gesture for him to come to me. "Give me a hug, and this time I won't be able to squeeze you to death."

He hugs me, reluctantly, and as he does so he finally does shed his tears. He has to turn away; he is having trouble breathing. Naturally his reaction upsets me.

"It's gone," he says to the far wall.

"What's gone?"

"The magic is gone."

I speak firmly. "It is only Yaksha's blood that has been destroyed. Maybe you don't like that. Maybe your fantasies of being a vampire are ruined. But think of the world—it is safe now from this curse. And only you and I know how close it came to being destroyed by it."

But Seymour shakes his head as he glances at me. "I am not worried about my own personal fantasies. Yeah, sure, I wanted to be a vampire. What eighteen-year-old wouldn't want to be one? But the magic is gone. You were that magic."

My cheek twitches; his words wound me. "I am still here. I am still Alisa."

"But you are no longer Sita. The world needed her in order to be a place of mystery. Even before I met you, I *knew* you. You know I knew you. I wrote my stories late at night and your darkness filled them." He hung his head. "Now the world is empty. It's nothing."

I approach and touch his arm. "My feelings for you have not changed. Are they nothing? Good God, Seymour, you speak to me as if I were dead."

He touches my hand but now it is hard for him to look at me. "Now you will die."

"All who are born die," I say, quoting Krishna. "All who are dead will be reborn. It is the nature of things."

He bites his lower lip and stares at the floor. "That's easy to say but it's not easy to live through. When you met me, I had AIDS. My death was certain—it was all I could see. It was like a slow-motion horror film that never ended. It was only your blood that saved me." He pauses. "How many others could it have saved?"

"Now you sound like Arturo."

"He was a brilliant man."

"He was a dangerous man."

Seymour shrugs. "You always have an answer for everything. I can't talk to you."

"But you can. I'm a good listener. But you have to listen as well. You have to give me a chance to explain how I feel. I'm happy the experiment has succeeded. It means more to me than you can imagine. And I'm happy there's no going back."

He catches my eye. "Is that true?"

"You know it is true. There is no more vampire blood, anywhere. It's over." I squeeze his arm and pull him closer. "Let it be over. I need you now, you know, more than I needed you before." I bury my face in his shoulder. "You have to teach me how to be a nerd."

My small joke makes him chuckle. "Can we have sex now?" he asks.

I raise my head and plant a wet kiss on his cheek. "Sure. When we're both a little older." I shake him, but not so hard as I used to. "How dare you ask me a question like that? We haven't been on a date yet."

He tries hard to accept the loss of his world, the death of his magic. He forces a smile. "There's a vampire movie in town. We could see it, and eat popcorn, and jeer, and then have sex afterward." He waits for an answer. "It's what most nerd couples do every Saturday evening."

I suddenly remember. It has taken me this long. There

must be something wrong with my mind. I turn away and swear under my breath. "Damn."

"What is it?" he asks. "You don't like popcorn?"

"We have to get out of town. We have to leave now."

"Why?"

"There was someone here a few minutes ago. A young man—he was knocking at the door."

"Who was it?"

"I don't know. I didn't open the door. But this guy—he called me by name. He called me Sita. He kept insisting I open the door."

"Why didn't you?"

"Because I didn't know who he was! Because I'm human now!" I pause and frown. "His voice sounded familiar. I swear, I knew it, but I just can't place it."

"What makes you think he's dangerous?"

"Do you have to ask that question? No one alive, except you, knows me by the name Sita." I stop again. "He said he would come back. He laughed as he said it. He sounded so sure of himself."

"What else did he say?"

"He called himself my darling."

Seymour was thoughtful. "Could Arturo have survived the blast?"

"No."

"But he was a hybrid. Half human, half vampire. It's possible. Don't dismiss the possibility."

I shake my head. "Even Yaksha could not have survived that blast."

"But you did."

"I floated away at the last minute. You know, I told you." I turn toward the kitchen, my car keys. "The sooner we leave the better."

Seymour grabs my arm. "I disagree. You have said there are no more vampires. What do we have to fear from this person? Better we stay and find out who he is."

I consider. "The government must have known Arturo was using this house. Such records were probably kept somewhere else besides the army base I destroyed. The government might be watching this house now."

"But you said you knew this person."

"I'm not sure about that. There was something in his voice, though . . ."

"What?" Seymour demands when I don't finish.

I strain to remember through my newfound human fog. "His tone—it gave me a chill."

Seymour acts like a wise guy. "In the real world not everybody who comes to the front door wants to kill you. Some guys just want to sell you a vacuum cleaner."

I remain stubborn. "We're getting out of here now." Grabbing the keys off the kitchen table, I peer out the back window and see nothing significant. In the distance, the lights of the Strip come alive and shimmer, colored beacons in a desert wasteland. A nuclear bomb just exploded but human vice will not be postponed. Of course the wind was blowing the other way, but I do not judge. I have always been a gambler. I understand better than most why the atomic dice did not betray the city of sin. Why the fallout fell the other way. Still, I swear again. "Damn. I wish I had my old vision right now. Just for a minute."

"And I bet your old hearing." Seymour comes up at my side and pats me on the back. "You're going to make that same wish a lot of times in the next few days."

TWO

I own houses all over the world, some modest places to relax when I enter a foreign country in search of fresh blood, others so extravagant one would think I was a princess. My home in Beverly Hills, where we drive after leaving Las Vegas, is one of the most opulent ones. As we enter the front door, Seymour stares in wonder.

"If we stay here," he says, "I have to get new clothes."

"You can have the clothes, but we're not staying. Ray's father knew about this house, so the government might as well. We're just here to get money, credit cards, clothes, and fresh identification."

Seymour is doubtful. "The government knew you were at the compound. They'll think you died in the blast."

"They'll have to know for sure that I died. They were obsessed with my blood, so they'll research every possible lead concerning me." I step to the window and peer outside. It is the middle of the night. "They may be watching us now."

Seymour shrugs. "Are you going to get me fresh ID?"

I glance at him. "You should go home."

He shakes his head firmly. "I'm not going to leave you. Forget it. I mean, you don't even know how to be human."

I step past him. "We can discuss this later. We don't want to be here a minute more than we have to be."

In the basement of my Beverly Hills home, I pick up the things I mentioned to Seymour. I also take a 9mm Smith & Wesson equipped with a silencer and several rounds of ammunition. My reflexes and vision are not what they used to be, but I believe I am still an excellent shot. All my supplies I load into a large black leather suitcase. I am surprised how much it weighs as I carry it back upstairs. My physical weakness is disconcerting.

I don't let Seymour see the gun.

We leave Beverly Hills and drive toward Santa Monica. I let Seymour drive; the speed of the surrounding cars disturbs me. It is as if I am a young woman from 3000 B.C. who has been plucked from her slow-paced world and dumped into the dizzyingly fast twentieth century. I tell myself I just need time to get used to it. My euphoria over being human remains, but the anxiety is there as well.

Who was at the door?

I can't imagine. Not even a single possibility comes to mind. But there was something about that voice.

We check into a Sheraton hotel by the beach. My new name is Candice Hall. Seymour is just a friend helping me with my bags. I don't put his name down on the register. I will not stay Candice long. I have other ID that I can change my hair style and color to match, as well as other small features. Yet I feel safe as I close the door of the hotel room behind me. Since Las Vegas, I have kept an eye on the rearview mirror. I don't believe we've been followed. Seymour sets my bag on the floor as I plop down on the bed and sigh.

"I haven't felt this exhausted in a long time," I say.

Seymour sits beside me. "We humans are always tired."

"I am going to enjoy being human. I don't care what you say."

He stares at me in the dimly lit room. "Sita?"

I close my eyes and yawn. "Yes?"

"I am sorry for what I said. If this makes you happy, then it makes me happy."

"Thank you."

"I just worry, you know, that there's no going back."

I sit up and touch his leg. "The decision would have been meaningless if I could have gone back."

He understands my subtle meaning. "You didn't do this because of what Krishna said to you about vampires?" he asks.

I nod. "I think partly. I don't think Krishna approved of vampires. I think he just allowed me to live out of his deep compassion for all living things."

"Maybe there was another reason."

"Perhaps." I touch his face. "Did I ever tell you how dear you are to me?"

He smiles. "No. You were always too busy threatening to kill me."

I feel a stab of pain. It is in my chest, where a short time ago a stake pierced my heart. For a moment the area is raw with an agonizing burning, as if I am bleeding to death. But it is a brief spasm. I draw in a shuddering breath and speak in a sad voice.

"I always kill the ones I love."

He takes my hand. "That was before. It can be different now that you're not a monster."

I have to laugh, although it is still not easy to take a deep breath. "Is that a line you use to get a girl to go to bed with you?"

He leans closer. "I already have you in bed."

I roll onto my side. "I need to take a shower. We both need to rest."

He draws back, disappointed. "You haven't changed that much."

I stand and fluff up his hair, trying to cheer him up. "But I have. I'm a nineteen-year-old girl again. You just forget what monsters teenage girls can be."

He is suddenly moved. "I never knew the exact age you were when Yaksha changed you."

I pause and think of Rama, my long dead husband, and Lalita, my daughter, cremated fifty centuries ago in a place I was never to know.

"Yes," I say softly. "I was almost twenty when Yaksha came for me." And because I was suspended so long between the ages, I add again, "Almost."

An hour later Seymour is last asleep beside me on the king-size bed. But despite my physical exhaustion, my mind refuses to shut down. I can't be free of the images of Joel's and Arturo's faces from two nights earlier when I suddenly began to turn to light, to dissolve, to leave them just before the bomb was detonated. At the time I knew I was dead. It was a certainty. Yet one last miracle occurred and I lived on. Perhaps there was a reason.

I climb out of bed and dress. Before leaving the hotel room, I load my pistol and tuck it in my belt, at the back, pulling my sweatshirt over it.

The hotel is located on Ocean Ave. I cross over it, and the Coast Highway that separates me from the ocean. Soon I am walking along the dark and foggy Santa Monica Beach, not the safest place to be in the early morning hours before the sun rises. Yet I walk briskly, heading south, paying little attention to my surroundings. What work it is to make my legs move over the sand! It is as if I walk with weights strapped around my ankles. Sweat drips in my eyes and I pant audibly. But I feel good as well. Finally, after thirty minutes of toil, my mind begins to relax, and I contemplate returning to the hotel and trying to sleep. It is only then that I become aware that two men are following me.

They are fifty yards behind me. In the dark it is hard to distinguish their features, but it is clear they are both Caucasian and well built, maybe thirty years old. They move like two good ol' boys, one dark featured, ugly, the other bright as a bottle of beer foaming in the sunlight. I think these boys have been drinking beer—and stronger—and are feeling uncomfortably horny. I smile to myself as I anticipate the encounter, even imagine what their blood will taste like. Then I remember I am not who I used to be. A wave of fear sweeps through my body, but I stand and wait for them to come to me.

"Hey, girl," the one with dark hair says with a Southern accent. "What are you doing out at this time of night?"

I shrug. "Just out for a walk. What are you guys up to?"

The blond guy snickers. "How old are you, girl?"

"Why?" I ask.

The dark-haired one moves slightly to my left. He flexes his fists as he speaks. "We just want to know if you're legal."

"I'm old enough to vote," I say. "Not old enough to drink. You boys been drinking tonight?"

They both chuckle. The blond guy moves a step closer. He smells of beer, whiskey. "You might say we've been looking at the wrong end of a few bottles tonight. But don't let that worry you none. We're still fully capable of finishing what we start."

I take a step back. Perhaps it's a mistake that I show fear. "I don't want any trouble," I say. And I mean it, although I feel as if I can still take them. After all, I am still a master of martial arts. A series of swift kicks to their groins, their jaws, should settle any unpleasantness. The dark-haired guy steps off to my left, and wipes at his slobbering mouth with the back of his arm.

"We don't want trouble either," he says. "We're just looking for a good time."

I catch his eye, and really do wish that my stare was still capable of burning into his brain. Seymour was right—my wishes have already settled into a pattern of wanting what I have lost. Yet I do my best to make my voice hard.

"Sometimes a good time can cost you," I say.

"I don't think so," the blond guy says. "You agree, John?"

"She looks like a freebie to me, Ed," John responds.

They've used their names in front of me. That is a bad sign. It means they're either too drunk to know better, or else they plan to kill me. The latter seems a distinct possibility since they clearly intend to rape me. I take another step back, and am tempted to reach for my gun. Yet I don't really want to kill them, especially since there is no need for their blood. Knocking them unconscious is my preference.

Actually, it is my second preference. Surviving is my first.

"If you touch me I'll scream," I warn them.

"No one's going to hear you down here," John says as he reaches out to grab me. "Take her, Ed!"

They go for me simultaneously, John close on my left, Ed three feet in front of me. But it is John who reaches me first. He has pretty good reflexes for a drunk. Before I can twist away, he catches me in a bear hug. Briefly I struggle, and then go limp. When Ed closes within two feet, however, I shove back against John and jump up, lifting both my feet off the ground. Lashing out with the right, I catch Ed in the groin. He shouts in pain and doubles up.

"The bitch got me!" he complains.

"Goddamn it!" John yells in my ear. "You're going to pay for that."

In response I slash backward and up with my left elbow. The blow catches John square on the jaw and his hold on me loosens as he staggers back. In an instant I am free. Since Ed is still bent over, I do him the favor of kicking him in the face, breaking his nose. He drops to his knees, his face dark with blood.

"Help me, John," he moans.

"Help him, John," I mock as John regains his balance and glares at me with death in his eyes. I gesture with my little finger. "Come on, John. Come and get your good-time girl."

John charges like a bull. I leap up and lash out with my left foot in order to kiss his jaw with the heel of my boot. The only trouble is that my timing and balance are all off. I have not risen far enough off the ground. Instead of striking him in the face, I hit him just above the heart, and the blow has not nearly the power I anticipated. John is a big man, over two hundred pounds. He grunts in pain as I strike but he doesn't stop. The momentum of his charge brushes aside my leg and now it is me who is suddenly off balance.

Frantically, I try to bring my left leg back in beneath me before I land but I am too late. With a thud, I topple on my right foot and hit the sand with the right side of my face. John is on me in a second, grabbing me from behind and pinning my arms midway up my spine. He's strong. My upper vertebrae feel as if they will explode. With his free hand he smacks me on the back of the head.

"You are one nasty bitch," he swears as he presses my face into the sand. Straining, I twist my head to the side so that I can breathe and see what is going to happen to me. "Ed, give me a hand with this whore. She looked like a good sport to begin with but I'm afraid when we're done pleasing ourselves we're going to have to bury her in this spot."

"We'll let the crabs eat her," Ed agrees as he staggers over, still bleeding profusely from his smashed nose. Behind me, John reaches around for the button on my pants. That is something of a break because if he had just tried to pull my pants down from behind, he would have found the gun. Also, reaching around as he is, I realize, John is slightly off balance.

Digging in with my right knee and pushing off with the tip of my left foot, I shove up as hard as possible. The move catches John by surprise, and I momentarily break free and roll in the sand. But my freedom will be measured in fractions of a second if I don't take drastic action. Squirming onto my back, I see both John and Ed staring down at me with stupid grins. They look ten feet tall and as ugly as highway billboards. Together they reach for me.

"Wait!" I cry as I move my right hand slowly under my lower back. "If I lie still and cooperate will you please not hurt me?"

They pause to think about that. "You better lie still, bitch," John says finally. "But you've messed up my friend too much to just walk away from tonight."

"But we might give you a chance to crawl away," Ed says, wiping at his bloody face and picking at his broken nose all in the same move.

"I won't leave here crawling," I say in a different tone of voice as my hand finds the butt of the gun. Leaning slightly to the left I whip it out and point it at the good ol' boys. They stare at it, frankly, as if they have never seen a gun before. Then they both take a step back. Maintaining my aim, I take my time getting back to my feet. I speak gently. "That's right, boys," I say. "No sudden moves. No screams for help."

John chuckles uneasily. "Hey, you got us, girl. You got us good. We give you that. But you know we didn't mean you no harm. We just drank a little too much and didn't know what we were doing."

"We weren't going to hurt you none," Ed adds, sounding scared, as well he should. Still taking my time, I step within a foot of Ed and place the barrel of the gun between his eyebrows. His eyes get real big, and he wants to turn and run but I stop him with a faint shake of my head. To my left, John stands frozen in wonder and horror.

"You are both liars," I say in a cold voice. "You were not only going to rape me, you were going to kill me. Now I am going to kill you because you deserve to die. But you should be grateful I'm using a gun. A few nights ago I would have used my teeth and nails, and you would have died much slower." I pause. "Say goodbye to John, Ed."

Ed is consumed with murderer's remorse. "Please!" he says, his voice cracking. "I have a wife and kid back home. If I die, who will take care of them?"

"I've got two kids back home," John says passionately.

But I am unmoved. Being human has not made me more gullible.

Yet, I usually do not kill when I have the upper hand. I do not kill for pleasure. But I know these two will harm others in the future, and therefore it is better that they die now.

"It is better for your children not to grow up having to imitate trash like you," I say.

Ed's face is awash with tears. "No!" he cries.

"Yes," I say, and shoot him in the head. He falls hard.

I turn the gun on John, who slowly backs away, shaking his head.

"Have mercy," he pleads. "I don't want to die."

"Then you should never have been born," I reply.

I shoot him twice in the face. In the eyes.

Yet that is all I do. The ancient thirst is gone.

I leave their bodies for the crabs.

THREE

*I*t is only on the way back that the shock of what has just happened overwhelms me. Ordinarily, killing a couple of jerks would occupy my mind for less than ten seconds. But now it is as if I feel the trauma in every cell. My reaction is entirely human. As I stumble off the beach and back onto Ocean Ave., I shake visibly. I scarcely notice that I'm still carrying the gun in my right hand. Chiding myself, I hide it under my sweatshirt. If I was in my right mind I would throw it in the ocean in case I'm stopped and searched. But I'm reluctant to part with the gun. I feel so vulnerable; it is like a safety blanket to me.

There is a coffee shop open three blocks from the sea. Staggering inside, I take a booth in the corner and order a cup of black coffee. It is only when the steaming beverage arrives, and I wrap my trembling hands around the mug, that I notice the faint mist of blood splattered on the front of my gray sweat-shirt. It must be on my face as well, and I reach up and brush at my skin, coming away with red-stained palms. What a fool I am, I think, to be out like this in public. I am on the verge of leaving when someone walks in the coffee shop, heads straight to my table, and sits down across from me.

It is Ray Riley. The love of my life.

He is supposed to be dead.

He nods slightly as he settles across from me, and I am struck by the fact that he is dressed exactly as when he ignited the gasoline truck outside the warehouse filled with Eddie Fender's evil vampires and blew himself to pieces. When he sacrificed his life to save mine. He wears a pair of black pants, a short-sleeved white silk shirt, Nike running shoes. His brown eyes are warm as always, his handsome face serious even though he wears a gentle smile. Yes, it is Ray. It is a miracle, and the sight of him stirs so much emotion inside me that I feel almost nothing. I am in shock, pure and simple. I can only stare with damp eyes and wonder if I am losing my mind.

"I know this is a surprise for you," he says softly.

I nod. Yes. A surprise.

"I know you thought I was dead," he continues. "And I think I was dead, for a time. When the truck exploded, I saw a bright flash of light. Then everything went black and I felt as if I were floating in the sky. But I couldn't see anything, know anything, even though I was not in pain. I don't know how long this continued. Eventually I became aware of my body again, but it was as if I was at a great distance from it. The strange thing was, I could feel only parts of it: a portion of my head, one throbbing hand, a burning sensation in my stomach. That was all at first. But slowly, more parts woke up, and I finally began to realize someone was trying to revive me by feeding me blood." He pauses. "Do you understand?"

I nod again. I am a statue. "Eddie," I whisper.

A spasm of pain crosses Ray's face. "Yes. Eddie collected what was left of me, and took me away to some dark cold place. There he fed me his blood, Yaksha's blood. And I began to come back to life. But Eddie vanished before the process was complete, and I was left only half alive." He pauses again. "I assume you destroyed him?"

I nod again. "Yes."

He reaches across the table and takes my hands. His skin is warm, and it quiets the trembles that continue deep inside me. He continues his impossible tale, and I listen because I can do nothing more.

"Still, I continued to gain strength without Eddie's help. In a day—maybe it was two—I was able to move about. I was in a deserted warehouse, tied with rope. I had no trouble breaking out, and when I did I read about all the strange goings on in Las Vegas, and I knew you must be there." He stops. "It was me who was at the door."

I nod for a fourth time. No wonder the voice sounded familiar. "Why didn't you identify yourself?" I ask.

"I knew you wouldn't believe me until you saw me."

"That's true."

He squeezes my hands. "It's me, Sita. I've come back for you. It's Ray. Why can't you at least smile?"

I try to smile but I just end up shaking my head. "I don't know. You were gone. I knew you were gone. I had no hope." My eyes burn with tears. "And I don't know if I'm not just imagining this."

"You were never one to imagine things."

"But I'm no longer the one you knew." I withdraw my hands from his and clasp them together, trying to hold myself together. "I'm human now. The vampire is dead."

He is not surprised. "You let go of my hands too quickly, Sita. If you examine them, you will notice a change in me as well."

"What do you mean?" I gasp.

"I watched you at that house. I watched you enter it, and I watched you leave it. I knew you were not the same, and I wondered what had happened in there. I explored the house, and found the basement: the copper sheets, the crystals, the magnets, the vial of human blood." He pauses. "I performed the same experiment on myself. I am no longer a vampire either."

The shocks keep piling one on top of the other. I cannot cope. "How did you know what to do?" I whisper.

He shrugs. "What was there to know? The equipment was all set up. I just had to lie down and allow the vibration of the human blood to wash over my aura as the reflected sun shone through the vial of blood." He glances out the window. There is a kind of light in the east. "I did it this afternoon. Now the sunrise will no longer hurt me."

The tears in my eyes travel over my cheeks. My mind travels with them as my disbelief washes away. Swallowing thickly, I finally feel as if my body returns to my control. In a burst I realize I am not imagining anything. Ray is not dead! My love is alive! Now I can live my life! Leaning across the table, I kiss his lips. Then I brush his hair and kiss that as well. And I am happy, more happy than I can remember being in thousands of years.

"It is you," I whisper. "God, how can it be you?"

He laughs. "You have Eddie to thank."

I sit back down in my seat and feel my warm human heart pounding in my chest. My anxiety, my fear, my confusion—all these things have now transformed into a solitary glow of wonder. For a while now I have cursed Krishna for what he has done to me, and now I can only bow inside in gratitude. For I have no doubt Krishna has brought Ray back to me, not that monster Eddie Fender.

"Let's not even speak his name," I say. "I cut off his head and burned his remains. He is gone—he will never return." I pause. "I'm sorry."

He frowns. "What have you to be sorry for?"

"Assuming you were dead." I shrug. "Joel told me you were blown to pieces."

Ray sighs and looks down at his own hands. "He wasn't far wrong." He glances up. "I didn't see Joel at the house?"

My lower lips trembles. "He's dead."

"I'm sorry."

"We both have to stop saying that." I smile a sad smile. "I made him a vampire as well, trying to save him. But it just killed him in the end."

"Who created the equipment that transformed us back into human beings?"

"Arturo—old friend, from the Middle Ages. I was in love with him. He was an alchemist, the greatest who ever lived. He experimented with my blood and changed himself into a hybrid of a vampire and a human. That's how he was able to survive all these years." I lower my voice. "He died with Joel. He had to die."

Ray nods. One didn't have to explain every detail to him in order for him to understand. He knew Arturo must have still been after my blood; that he was dangerous. Ray understood that I could kill those I loved, as I had almost killed him. Ray reaches for my hand again.

"You have blood on you," he says. "Surely you're not still thirsty?"

"No, it's not like you think." I speak in a whisper. "Two

men attacked me at the beach. I had to kill them."

"How?"

"I shot them in the head."

Now it is Ray's turn to be shocked. "We have to get out of here, away from here. Besides the government, you'll have the police after you too." He glances toward the door of the coffee shop. "I know you have Seymour with you."

I understand what he wants to say. "I have told him he has to go home."

"He won't want to leave you. You'll have to leave him."

"I have been thinking about that. I just don't know how to explain it to him."

Ray is sympathetic, but a curious note enters his voice. For a moment he sounds like I used to as the pragmatist.

"Don't explain it to him," he says. "Just leave him, and don't tell him where you're going."

"That seems harsh."

"No. You of all people know that to keep him with you will be harsh. You'll expose him to danger for no reason." He softens his tone. "You know I speak from experience."

"You're right. He's asleep at the hotel right now. I suppose I can sneak in, grab my things, and be away before he wakes up." But inside I know I will at least leave him a note. "Where are we going?"

It is Ray's turn to lean over and kiss me. "Sita, we can go anywhere we want. We can do anything we want." He whispers in my ear. "We can even get married and start a family if you want."

I have to laugh, and cry as well. My happiness lingers like the warmth of the sun after a perfect summer day. It is the winter outside, the darkness, that seems the illusion.

"I would like a daughter," I whisper, holding him close.

FOUR

Two months later we are in Whittier, a suburb of Los Angeles, where the late President Nixon attended college. The city is largely middle class, completely nondescript, a perfect place, in Ray's opinion, to disappear. Certainly I have never been to Whittier before, nor harbored any secret desires to go there. We rent a plain three-bedroom house not far from a boring mall. Ray picked it out. There is a large backyard and an olive tree in the front yard. We buy a second-hand car and purchase our groceries at a Vons down the street. I have lived five thousand years to do all these things.

Yet my happiness has not faded with the passage of the eight weeks. Sleeping beside Ray, walking with him in the morning, sitting beside him in a movie—these simple acts mean more to me than all the earth-shattering deeds I have accomplished since I was conceived beneath Yaksha's bloody bite. It is all because I am human, I know, and in love. How young love makes me feel. How lovely are all humans. Shopping at the mall, in the grocery store, I often find myself stopping to stare at people. For too long I admired them, despised them, and envied them, and now I am one of them. The hard walls of my universe have collapsed. Now I see the sun rise and feel the space beyond it, not just the emptiness. The pain in my heart, caused by the burning stake, has finally healed. The void in my chest has been filled.

Especially when I discover that I am pregnant.

It happens the early morning of the full moon, two months after the nuclear bomb detonated in the desert beneath a previous full moon. A fifteen-dollar early pregnancy kit tells me the good news. I shake the blue test tube in the bathroom and Ray comes running when I let out a loud cry. What is the matter, he wants to know? I am shaking—there must be something wrong. I don't even get a chance to show him my blue urine because I accidentally spill it all over him. He gets the picture and laughs with me, and at me.

I am at the bookstore later the same day, browsing through the baby books, when I meet Paula Ramirez. A pretty young woman of twenty-five, she has long black hair as shiny as her smooth complexion and a belly larger than her enchanting brown eyes. Obviously she is expecting, much sooner than I am. I smile at her as she juggles six different baby books in one arm, while reaching for another with her free hand.

"You know," I say. "Women were having kids long before there were books. It's a natural process." I put my own book back on the shelf. "Anyway, I don't think any of these authors know what the hell they're talking about."

She nods at my remark. "Are you pregnant?"

"Yes. And so are you, unless I'm blind." I offer my hand, and because I like her, without even knowing her, I tell her one of my more real names. Even as a human, I often trust my intuition. "I'm Alisa."

She shakes my hand. "Paula. How far along are you?"

"I don't know. I haven't even been to the doctor. It can't be more than two months, though, unless God is the father."

For some reason, Paula loses her smile. "Do you live around here?"

"Yes. Close enough to walk to the mall. How about you?"

"I'm on Grove," Paula says. "You know where that is?"

"Just around the block from us."

Paula hesitates. "Forgive me for asking, but are you married?"

It is a curious question, but I'm not offended. "No. But I live with my boyfriend. Are you married?"

Sorrow touches her face. "No." She pats her big belly. "I have to take care of this one alone." She adds, "I work at St. Andrews. It's just down the block from where you live."

"I have seen the crucifix. What do you do at St. Andrews?"

"I am supposed to be an assistant to the Mother Superior but I end up doing whatever's necessary. That includes scrubbing the bathroom floors, if no one's gotten to them. The church and the high school operate on a tight budget." She adds, almost by way of apology, "But I take frequent breaks. I pray a lot."

For some reason this girl interests me. She has special qualities—a gentleness of manner, a kindness in her voice. She is not a big girl but she seems to take up a lot of space. What I mean is there is a presence about her. Yet she acts anything but powerful, and that I also like.

"What do you pray for?" I ask.

Paula smiles shyly and lowers her head. "I shouldn't say."

I pat her on the back. "That's all right, you don't have to tell me. Who knows? Prayers could be like wishes. Maybe they lose their magic if you talk about them."

Paula studies me. "Where are you from, Alisa?"

"Up north. Why?"

"I could swear I've seen you before."

Her remark touches me deeply. Because in that exact moment, I feel the same way. There is something familiar in her eyes, in the soft light of their dark depths. They remind me of, well, the past, and I still have much of that, even if I grow older with each day.

Yet I intend to brush her comment aside, as I brush aside thoughts of my own mortality that come in the middle of the night, when Ray is asleep beside me, and sleep is hard to find. My insomnia is the only obvious curse of my transformation. I must still be used to hunting in the middle of the night. Prowling the streets in a black leather miniskirt. Death with a sexy smile and an endless thirst. Now, instead, I get up from bed and have a glass of warm milk and say my prayers—to Krishna, of course, whom I believe was God. I still remember him best during the darkest hours.

Krishna was once asked what was the most miraculous thing in all of creation, and he replied, "That a man should wake each morning and believe deep in his heart that he will live forever, even though he knows that he is doomed to die." Despite my many human weaknesses, a part of me still feels as if I will never die. And that part has never felt so alive as when I stare at Paula, a simple pregnant young woman that I have met by chance in a mall bookstore.

"I just have one of those faces," I reply.

We have lunch, and I get to know Paula better, and I let her know a few censored facts about myself. By the time our food is finished, we are fast friends, and this I see as a positive step on my road to becoming truly human. We exchange numbers and promise to stay in touch, and I know we will. I like Paula—really; it is almost as if I have a crush on her, though I have had few female lovers during my fifty centuries, and certainly Ray now takes care of all my sexual needs. It is just that as I say goodbye to her, I am already thinking of the next time we will meet, and how nice it will be.

Paula is the rarest of human beings. Someone with intelligence and humility. It has been my observation that the more intelligent a man or woman is, the more dishonest he or she is. Modern psychologists, I know, would not agree with me, but they are often dishonest themselves. Psychology has never impressed me as a science. Who has ever really defined the mind, much less the heart? Paula has a quick mind that has not destroyed her innocence. As we part for the first time, she insists on paying for our meal even when it is clear she has little money. But I let her pay since it seems to mean a lot to her.

FIVE

*A*nd so, for a week, life went on, sweetly, smoothly, with a new friend, a reborn lover, and a baby growing inside me. A daughter, I am sure, even though I pray to God to make it an absolute certainty. Yet fifty centuries cannot be forgotten. History cannot be rewritten. I live in the suburbs and abide by my country's laws. I have a new library card and am thinking of buying a little dog. Yet I have murdered thousands, tens of thousands, brutally and without mercy. That is a bloody fact, and perhaps there is such a thing as karma, of sin and judgment. I wonder if I am being judged when I begin to have trouble with the baby.

It is not normal trouble.

It is the worst kind. The supernatural kind.

The baby is growing much faster than she should. As I said to Paula, I can only be two months pregnant, and yet, one week after I meet Paula, I wake with something kicking in my abdomen. After hurrying to the bathroom and turning on the light—for I cannot see very well in the dark anymore—I am astounded to see that my stomach bulges through my nightgown. In the space of hours, even, the baby has developed through an entire trimester. This does not please me.

"Ray," I say. "Ray!"

He comes running, and takes forever to see what the problem is. Finally he puts his hand on my belly. "This is not normal?"

"Are you nuts?" I brush his hand aside. "She can't be human."

"We're human," he says.

"Are we?" I ask the empty bathtub.

He puts a hand on my shoulder. "This accelerated growth doesn't have to be a bad thing."

I am having trouble breathing. I had put so much hope in the past being past. But there is no future, not really. It is only a phantom of what we want to deny, a dream in a time that will never actually be.

"Anything abnormal is bad," I say. "Especially when you have to answer yes to the question on the medical form: Have you ever been a vampire?"

"The child cannot be a vampire," Ray says simply. "Vampires cannot reproduce this way."

"You mean they haven't done so in the past," I say. "When

has a vampire ever turned human again? This is new terrain."
I lean over and spit in the sink. My spit is bloody—I bit my
lower lip the instant the light went on. "It's an omen," I say.

Ray rubs my back. "Maybe you should see a doctor. You
were going to start looking for one anyway."

I chuckle bitterly. "I cannot see a doctor. We're in hiding,
remember? Doctors report local monsters to the authorities.
Young women who have babies in three months." The baby
kicks again. I stare in the mirror at my bulge. "If it even takes
that long."

My words prove prophetic. Over the next four days the
baby grows at an insane pace, a month of development for
each twenty-four-hour period. During this time I am forced
to eat and drink constantly, but seldom do I have to use the
restroom. Red meat, in particular, I crave. I have three ham-
burgers for breakfast and in the evening four New York steaks,
washed down with quarts of Evian. Still, I burn with hunger,
with thirst, and with fear. What would an ultrasound show? A
horned harlot grinning back at the sound waves?

During this time, I avoid Paula and the world. Ray is my
only companion. He holds my hand and says little. What is
there to say? Time will tell all.

Five days after waking in the middle of the night to see
my swollen belly, I awake again in the early morning hours
in horrible pain with cramps in my abdomen. Just before Ray
wakes, I remember when I had my first child, five thousand

years earlier. My dear Lalita—she who plays. That birth had been painless, ecstatic even. I had intended to name this child by the same name. But as another spasm grips me, seemingly threatening to rip me in two, I don't know if such a gentle title will be appropriate. I sit up gasping for air.

"Oh God," I whisper.

Ray stirs beside me. His voice is calm. "Is it time?"

"It's time."

"Do you want to go to the hospital?"

We have discussed this, but never come to a decision. I can withstand tremendous physical pain, and of course I have delivered babies many times and know human anatomy inside out. Yet this pain is a thing of demons. It transcends any form of torment I have ever experienced. Literally, I feel as if I am being ripped apart, consumed from the inside. What is my child doing to me? I bury my face in my hands.

"It feels like it's eating my womb," I moan.

Ray is on his feet. "We have to get help. We have to risk the hospital."

"No." I grab his hand as he reaches for the car keys. "I won't make it. It's coming too fast."

He kneels at my side. "But I don't know what to do."

I fight for air. "It doesn't matter. It's all being done."

"Should I call for Paula?" Ray approves of my relationship with Paula, although, for some strange reason, he has avoided meeting her. How I long for her company right then, her soothing smile. Yet I know she is the last person who should see me like this. I shake my head and feel the sweat pour off my face.

"No," I say. "This would terrify her. We have to face this alone."

"Should I boil some water?"

For some reason his remark amuses me. "Yes, yes. Boil some water. We can put the baby in it when she comes out." I snort when I see his stunned expression. "That's a joke, Ray."

Yet he stares at me strangely. He speaks to me as if he is speaking to a third person in the room. "Sometimes I feel I came back just for this baby. I don't want anything to happen to her."

Another spasm grips me, and I double up and ignore his serious tone. The agony angers me. "If anything is going to happen to anyone," I whisper, "it will happen to me."

"Sita?"

"Get the goddamn water."

My daughter is born fifteen minutes later, and she puts a nice rip in me as she comes into the world. My blood is everywhere, even in my hair, and I know I am in danger of hemorrhaging to death. It is only now I let Ray call for an ambulance. But before he gets on the phone, he puts my bloody child on my chest. He has already cut the umbilical cord with a sterilized knife from the kitchen drawer. Cuddling my daughter as I lie on the verge of blacking out, I stare into her dark blue eyes and she stares back at me. She does not cry nor make any other sound. For the moment I am just relieved she is breathing.

Yet there is an alertness in her eyes that disturbs me. She looks at me as if she can see me, and all the books say a child of five minutes cannot even focus. Not only that, she stares at me as if she knows me, and the funny thing is, I do likewise. I do know her, and she is not the soul of my gentle and joyful Lalita returned to me from the ancient past. She is someone else, someone, I feel, they may have constructed temples to long ago, when mankind was closer to the gods in heaven and the forgotten creatures beneath the earth. I shiver as I look at her, yet I hold her tight. Her name just springs from my cracked and bleeding lips—I do not bring it forth consciously. The name is a mantra, a prayer, and also a name for that which cannot be named.

"Kalika," I call her. Kali Ma.

Not she who plays. She who destroys.

Still, I love her more than can be said.

SIX

Kalika is two weeks old, really a year in size and ability, when she refuses to take my milk. For the last fourteen days I have enjoyed feeding her, although I have not relished the speed at which she grows. Each morning when I wake to her sounds, I find a different and older daughter. This morning she pushes me away as I try to hold her to my breast. She is strong and actually bruises my skin as she refuses what I have to offer. Ray sits across from me and tries to comfort me in my despair.

"Maybe she's not feeling well," he says.

I stare out the window as Kalika squirms on my lap. "Maybe she wants something else to drink," I say.

"She's not a vampire."

"You don't know."

"But sunlight doesn't bother her."

It is true, I have tested my daughter under the bright sun. She just stares at it as she stares at everything else. Indeed, the glare does not seem to annoy her young eyes, a fact that does nothing to comfort me.

"No one knows what she is," I say.

"Well, what are we going to do? We have to feed her."

Maybe Kalika understands the question. Already she has begun to speak, simple words as many twelve-month-old children do. But it is probable she understands more than she says, certainly more about herself than either of her parents is willing to admit. While I am gazing out the window at the sky, she leans over and bites my left nipple. She has teeth now and she bites so hard that she draws blood. The pain, for me, is sharp, but the flow, for her, is steady. And the blood seems to satisfy her.

I look at Ray and want to cry.

Another day has gone by and Kalika is in her bedroom screaming. She is hungry but my breasts are too sore—too drained actually—to give her another feeding. Ray paces in front of me as I lie on the living room couch and stare out the big window. My thoughts are often of the sky, and of Krishna. I wonder where God is at times like this, if he is not browsing in the horror section of the cosmic library searching for another chapter to slip in my life story.

I am exhausted—I have yet to regain my strength from

the delivery. I'm a smashed doll who's been sewn together by an emotionless doctor, an aching mother whose daughter disembowels Barbies in search of something to eat. Kalika lets out another loud cry and Ray shakes his head in disgust.

"What are we going to do?" he asks.

"You asked me that five minutes ago."

"Well, we've got to do something. A child's got to eat."

"I offered her a steak, a raw steak even, and she didn't want it. I offered her the blood from the steak and she didn't want it. She just wants my blood and if I give her any more I will die." I cough weakly. "But considering the circumstance that might not be bad."

Ray stops pacing and stares down at me. "Maybe she doesn't just crave *your* blood."

I speak in a flat voice. "I have thought of that. I would have to be stupid not to have thought of that." I pause. "Do you want to give her some of your blood?"

Ray kneels on the floor beside me. He takes my hand and gives it an affectionate squeeze. But there is a look in his eyes, one I have never seen before. Of course having a child like Kalika in the house would give the Pope a new look. Ray speaks in a low conspiratorial voice and there is no affection in his words.

"Let us say she is not a human being," he admits. "I suppose that is obvious by now. Let's even go so far as to say she's some sort of vampire, although not a vampire in the traditional sense. Her indifference to the sun makes that seem certain. Now, all of this is not necessarily a bad thing if we can teach her right from wrong as she matures. She doesn't have to be a monster."

"What's your point?"

"Isn't it obvious? She's still our daughter. We still love her, and we have to give her what she needs to survive, at least until she can fend for herself." He pauses. "We have to get her fresh blood."

I smile without pleasure. "You mean we have to get her fresh victims."

"We just need blood, for now. We don't have to kill anyone to get it."

"Fine. Go down to the hospital and buy some. Take one of my credit cards. They're in my purse on the kitchen table."

Ray drew back. "I'm serious, Sita."

I chuckle bitterly. "So am I. I have experience in these matters, in case you've forgotten. The only blood she will take will be warm blood from a human being."

"I thought you sometimes survived on animal blood."

"I offered her the blood of a cat I caught and killed in the backyard and she didn't want it."

"You didn't tell me."

"Killing a cat wasn't something I felt like bragging about."

A peculiar note enters his voice, to match the strange look in his eyes. "You used to kill people all the time."

I brush off his hand and sit up. "Is that what you want me to do? Murder people for her?"

"No. No one has to die. You told me that the day you made me a vampire."

My temper flares. "The day I made you a vampire I had an arsenal of supernatural powers at my command. I could lure dozens of people into my lair, and let them go with little more than a headache. To get Kalika fresh blood, I will have to kill, and that I refuse to do now."

"Now that you're human?"

"Yes. Now that I'm human. And don't remind me of those two I wasted the night you returned. That was an act of self-defense."

"This is an act of self-preservation," Ray says.

I speak impatiently. "How am I supposed to get someone to donate blood for Kalika's breakfast? Where do you find people like that? Not in Whittier."

"Where did you go to find victims before? To bars? You went to them to lure men back to your place."

"I never took them back to my place."

Ray hesitates. "But we need someone, maybe a couple of someones we can take blood from regularly."

I snicker. "Yeah, right. And when we let them go we just tell them to please not mention what has been going on here. Just chalk the bloodletting off to a unique experience." I fume. "Whoever we bring here, we'll have to kill in the end. I won't do that."

"Then you'll let your daughter die?"

I glare at Ray, searching for the loving young man I once knew. "What's happened to you? You should be on the other side of this argument. Before the blast, you would have been. Where did you go when you died? Huh? You never told me. Was it hell? Did the devil teach you a few new tricks?"

He is offended. "I'm just trying to save our daughter. I wish you'd drop your self-righteous, pompous attitude and face the facts—Kalika needs blood or she will die. We have to get her blood."

"Fine, go out and get a young woman victim. You're handsome and you've got style. It shouldn't take you long."

He stops. "I don't know how to pick up people. I've never done it before."

I have to laugh. "You sure picked me up easily enough."

Kalika screams again.

Ray loses his dark expression and looks pained. "Please," he says. "She's all we've got. You're the only one who can save her."

Fed up with arguing, I stand and grab my black leather coat, the one I used to wear for hunting. Heading for the door, I say over my shoulder, "We used to have a lot, Ray. Remember that next time you order me to go out and kill."

SEVEN

I drive around for an hour before ending up at a local park. There are a couple of basketball courts, a baseball diamond, a circular pond with white ducks in it, and a wide field where children fly long-tailed kites. Sitting between the pond and the basketball courts, I try to think how I can fix my miserable life in one brilliant stroke.

For the last twenty-four hours I have considered taking Kalika to Arturo's secret laboratory, where the paraphernalia that completed my transformation is located: the crucifix-shaped magnets, the long copper sheets, the colored crystals. Yet the attempt, I know, to make Kalika into a human, would be a desperate act at best. One of the few times Arturo experimented on a boy—dear Ralphe—the results were disastrous. Ralphe was transformed into a flesh-eating ghoul, and I had to break his neck with my own hands to stop him from killing.

No, I realize, I cannot experiment on Kalika, not until every other alternative has been explored.

Which means I need human blood. Now.

A young man on the basketball court glances over at me. I may not be a vampire anymore, but I know I'm cute. This guy is maybe nineteen, with blond hair and a strong build, an easy six-two. His size is important to me. The more pounds he has, the more blood he can stand to lose. Yet the more difficult he will be to contain. But my daughter is screaming at home. I heard her screams as I drove away in the car, echoing in my ears like the cries of a thousand past victims.

I catch this young man's eye and smile.

He flashes me a grin. He is interested, doomed.

When his game finishes, he strolls over to say hi.

"Hi," I say in response, nodding to the court, to his companions. I sit with my profile to them—I don't want them to get a good look at me. "You know, you're pretty good. You have a great jump shot."

"Thanks. I still enjoy these pick-up games."

"You used to play in high school?"

"Yeah. Just got out last year. How about you?"

I laugh softly. "I was too short to play basketball."

He blushes. "I mean, did you just graduate?"

"Not long ago." I pause, let my eyes slide over him. "What's your name?"

"Eric Hawkins. What's yours?"

I stand and offer him my hand. "Cynthia Rhodes. Do you come here often?"

"I usually play at Centinela. This park—I haven't been here in ages."

That's good, I think. "What brings you here today?"

He shrugs. "Nothing in particular. I was just out driving around."

That's also good. The other guys he's playing with—they're not close friends.

"I was just doing the same," I say.

He glances at the ground, fidgets shyly. "Hey, would you like to go have a Coke or something?"

"Sure. I'm not doing anything."

We go to a coffee shop, and I order coffee. I have become a big coffee drinker since becoming human. It does wonders for my insomnia. Eric has a hamburger and french fries. I am happy he eats heartily. He will need his strength. Yet as he talks about himself, I begin to feel sad. He seems like such a nice boy.

"I'm taking a year off from college, but I'll be in school next year," he says. "I just got accepted to SC. I'm going to major in pre-med. My old man's a doctor and he's encouraged me to follow in his footsteps since the day I learned to talk."

"Why didn't you go straight to college?"

"I wanted to travel a little, work a little. I spent the summer in Europe. Spent a month in the Greek islands alone. You ever been there?"

I nod as I sip my coffee. "Yes. Did you visit Delos?"

"The island with all the ruins?"

"Yes. It's supposed to be the most sacred island in the Aegean Sea. Apollo was born there." I lower my voice. "At least, that's what the stories say."

"Yeah, I was there. When were you there?"

"A few years back." I pause and catch his eye, and hate myself for the blatant manipulation. "I'm glad I went to the park today."

He smiles shyly and stares down at his hamburger. "Yeah. When I saw you sitting there all by yourself—I don't know—I just felt like I had to talk to you." He adds, "I don't usually go around hitting on girls."

"I know, Eric."

We chat a while longer and he finishes his food, and then glances at his watch. "Boy, I better get going. My dad's expecting me at his office. I help out there Tuesday and Thursday afternoons."

I feel a moment of panic. I cannot imagine returning to Kalika's screams empty-handed. Reaching across the table, I touch his hand. "Could you do me a quick favor?"

"Sure. What is it?"

"It's kind of embarrassing to explain. You see, I have this ex-boyfriend who is sort of stalking me. He's not violent or anything like that, but if he sees me return home he immediately jumps out of his car and runs over and starts hassling me." I pause. "Could you follow me home in your car? Just to make sure I get in okay." I add, "I don't live far from here."

"You don't live with your parents?"

"No. Both my parents are dead. I live alone."

Eric is troubled. "Sure, I can come. But I won't be able to stay."

"I understand. If you can just walk me to my door."

Eric is agreeable, although his reluctance remains. As a human, I'm not the actress I used to be. He likes me, but he is slightly suspicious of me. I have to wonder exactly what I'm going to do with him once he's in my house.

To my immense bad luck, Paula is standing on my front porch as I drive up and park. Waving to her, I quickly run back to Eric's car, which is in the middle of the block. I ask if he can wait a minute, but he's anxious to get to his father's office.

"He loses his temper if I'm even ten minutes late," he explains.

"I'm grateful you followed me this far," I say. "But I'm still worried my ex is around. He could even be in the house."

Eric nods to Paula, who waits patiently for me. "Who is she?"

I snort, and feel another layer of guilt. "She's just this pregnant girl who stops by from time to time looking for money. I have to get rid of her, or she'll stay all afternoon." I touch his arm. "Please stay. Give me two minutes."

Eric hesitates. "Okay."

Paula flashes me a warm smile as I hurry toward her. "What are you doing here?" I ask.

"I was worried about you. I haven't heard from you in so long." Paula studies me, and I know how perceptive she is. "Have you been sick? You look pale."

"I've had a bad flu. Look, I can't talk right now. That guy in the car—he's my boyfriend's brother, and he's in deep trouble that I can't go into right now. He needs my help."

Paula is hesitant. "Fine, I can go. I was just out for a walk." She glances at Eric. "Are you sure you're all right?"

"Yeah, no problem." I gesture to her swollen belly. "It won't be long now."

Paula is radiant. "No. Another three weeks is all."

"That's great." I nod to my door. "Did you knock? Did you talk to Ray?"

"I knocked but no one answered."

"Oh." That's strange. Ray is almost always at home. He would have to be at home, with Kalika and all. I can't imagine him taking her out. But perhaps our daughter is the reason he didn't answer. I cannot hear either of them inside. I add, "I'll talk to you soon, Paula. I promise, we'll have lunch."

Paula is gracious as she carefully moves down the steps. "You take care. I'll be thinking of you."

"Thanks. Say a prayer for me."

"I always do, Alisa."

Paula leaves, and I gesture for Eric to join me on the front porch. He parks in my driveway and approaches reluctantly. He has antennae of his own. I am definitely giving off bad vibes. His car will have to be moved quickly, I think, before it makes an impression on my neighbors. I fumble for my keys, like I'm nervous. And I am nervous—I can't imagine hurting him. For that matter, he might end up hurting me.

"Sometimes my ex comes in a back window," I say as I put the key in the lock.

"You should lock your windows," Eric mutters.

"Can I get you something to drink?" I ask as we step inside. A quick look around shows neither Ray nor Kalika. Maybe he did go out with her. Eric stays near the door.

"I really should be going," he says,

"At least have a lemonade. I made some fresh this morning." I move toward the kitchen. "I really appreciate you doing this for me."

Eric feels trapped. "I'll have a small glass," he says without enthusiasm.

In fact, I did make lemonade that morning, from concentrate. Pouring a couple of glasses, I hurry back to the living room. My resentment toward Ray continues to grow. For seducing Eric to come into the house, it is good Ray is out of sight. Yet I could use Ray to knock Eric unconscious. I mean, I am a hundred-and-ten pound blond chick who just had a baby. Eric accepts his drink and I toast him with our glasses. Eric drinks without relish.

"It's good," he mumbles.

"Thanks. We have lemon trees in our backyard."

"They give fruit this time of year?"

I smile. "No, but they do in the summer."

Eric finishes half his drink and sets the glass down on the coffee table. "Well, my dad's waiting. Let's talk another time. It was nice to meet you."

I jump slightly, and speak in a hushed tone. "Did you hear that?"

Eric is puzzled. "What?"

I point down the hall. "I think he's here."

Eric frowns. "I don't hear anything."

I am a picture of fear. "Would you check? Just to be sure."

"Cynthia, really. I don't think anyone's there."

I swallow heavily. "Please? It's terrible when he sneaks up on me like this. I can't get rid of him by myself."

Eric eyes the hallway. "You're sure he's not violent? Why does he break into your house?"

"He's never violent. He's just a pest. I hope I'm imagining the whole thing."

Eric starts up the hallway. I follow close behind him, silently. Even as a human, I can move like a cat. As he reaches for the last bedroom door on the left, I lash out with my right foot, striking behind his right knee. There is a mushy tearing sound—the spot is especially vulnerable. Letting out a painful cry, Eric topples to his knees. Before he can recover, I slash out with my left hand and catch him in the left temple, which is the thinnest part of the skull. The blow stuns him but does not knock him out. Disgusted, I strike again, at the opposite temple, hitting as hard as I can, the side of my hand throbbing from the effort. Still on his knees, he sways precariously. Yet he refuses to go down. Quite the contrary, he grasps at the near wall, trying to pull himself up. He is a fighter and it breaks my heart not to let him go. But I'm committed now. Backing up a step, I jump in the air and kick him in the back of the head with the heel of my left boot. That does the trick. Eric falls forward like a sack of flour. Blood drips off the back of his head, staining the carpet. Just what we need.

"I'm sorry," I whisper as I kneel by his side, checking the pulse at the side of his neck to make sure I haven't killed him. His face against the floor, Eric breathes heavily but his pulse is strong.

Suddenly I am aware of someone at my back.

"Good job," Ray says.

I turn on him angrily. "Yeah, it's good I was able to handle him all by myself. Where have you been?"

He shrugs. "I was in the other room."

"Where's Kalika?"

He nods to the door Eric was about to open. "In there. I told her to remain silent."

"And she listened to you?"

Ray speaks seriously. "She always listens to me."

"Lucky you." I nod to Eric. "Where are we going to put him?"

"In the spare room. We'll tie him up and gag him, and take only as much blood as our daughter needs."

"That might be more than he can give," I say, stroking Eric's hair.

"We'll have to worry about that later." Ray pauses. "How should we withdraw the blood?"

"We need needles, syringes, tourniquets, tubing, flasks. I have them at my house in Beverly Hills." I stand, wiping Eric's blood from my hands. "I'll go now."

Ray stops me. "That house might be watched, you said."

I don't like being stopped. "I'll have to risk it. I'm not breaking into a drugstore to get this stuff."

"I want you to help me tie him up before you leave."

"Can't you tie him up? The sooner I leave, the sooner I can get back." I glance at the bedroom door. My daughter hasn't made a peep. "Kalika must be starving by now."

"It won't take us long if we work together. Then I can go with you to the other house."

"No," I say. "I'm going alone."

Ray hesitates. "Fine. But I think it's better this guy sees only one of us."

"Why?"

"Isn't it obvious? If he can identify me, it doubles our chances of being caught."

I stare at Ray. "You really have changed."

He shrugs. "Maybe it was Eddie's blood."

"Maybe." I hold his eye. "All right, I'll deal with him, like I deal with everything else. As long as we both understand that we're not pushing Eric beyond his limit. This boy is not going to die."

Ray nods his head, but his eyes do not seem to agree.

EIGHT

Before entering my Beverly Hills house, I search the street and the surrounding houses for signs of anyone watching. The FBI's methods are not unfamiliar to me. The house appears unwatched. Once inside, I gather the supplies I need to turn Eric into a serious anemic. But before leaving I stop to call Seymour. I haven't spoken to him since I said good night in the hotel by the beach. Even the note I left said little.

Sorry, Seymour. Got to go. You know this is for the best. Love, Sita.

"Hello?" he says.

"It's me."

He takes a long time to answer. His voice comes out harsh. "What do you want?"

I speak with sincerity. "Just to hear your voice, Seymour. I miss you."

"Yeah, right."

"I do. I really do."

"Where are you?"

"I can't tell you."

"I have to go."

"No! Wait! You know why I can't tell you."

"No, I don't know why. I thought you were my friend. Friends don't leave each other in the middle of the night." He lowers his voice and there is pain in it. "Why did you leave?"

I hesitate. I didn't plan to tell him.

"Ray's come back."

Seymour is astounded. "That's impossible."

"It's true. We're living together." I add, "We've got a daughter."

"Sita, what kind of fool do you think I am? You haven't had time to have a daughter."

My voice cracks. "I know that. But this one came rather fast."

He hears that I'm serious. "Tell me everything that's happened since I last saw you."

So I tell him because I need someone to talk to. As always he listens patiently, closely, and I have to wonder what insights he will provide when I'm finished. He's so smart—he always has something interesting to say about my numerous predicaments. Yet the next words out of his mouth shock me.

"Why do you assume this guy is Ray?" he asks when I finish.

I have to laugh, although I almost choke on it. "What kind of question is that? Of course it's Ray. I know it's Ray. Who else could it be?"

"I don't know who else it could be. But how do you know it's Ray? Remember, he died."

"Because he looks like Ray. He acts like Ray. He knows everything Ray knew. He can't be an impostor."

Seymour speaks calmly. "Let's take each of your statements. He looks like Ray you say. Okay, I grant you that because you've seen him and I haven't. But you say he acts like Ray? I don't think so. The Ray you describe isn't the Ray I remember."

"He's been through a lot. In a sense, he died during the blast. It was only Eddie's blood that brought him back to life."

"That worries me right there. Eddie was the incarnation of evil. What would his blood do to someone's psyche? Even the psyche of another vampire?"

I close my eyes and sigh. "I've worried about that myself. But please believe me, he can't be an impostor. Dozens of times we've discussed things only Ray and I knew."

"But you do accept you're dealing with a guy that has his priorities twisted?"

"Am I? I've asked myself that question many times. When you get right down to it, I would do anything to save Kalika. Ray's her father. Is he so different from me?"

"I don't know. There's something in your story—something I can't put my finger on. I think Ray's dangerous, and I'd keep an eye on him. But let's leave that for a moment. Let's talk about Kalika. How can she be a vampire and not be sensitive to the sun?"

"I wasn't that sensitive," I say.

"Because you'd been a vampire for over five thousand years. And still the sun did bother you; it sapped your strength. You say it doesn't affect her at all?"

"Not as far as I can tell. She plays out in it."

"Does she make any effort to move into the shade?"

"No. She likes the sun as much as the moon."

"Yet she wants human blood," Seymour mutters, thinking aloud. "Hmm. Is she exceptionally strong?"

"Yes. Pretty strong. She must be a vampire."

Seymour considers. "What does she look like?"

"A lot like me, except her features are darker."

"You mean she has brown hair, brown eyes?"

"Her hair is brown, but her eyes are a dark blue." I add painfully, "She's very pretty. You'd like her."

"Not if she wants to drink my blood. Sita, let's be frank with each other. You're not superhuman anymore. You're not going to be able to go around abducting people without getting caught. As far as I can tell, you were lucky with this Eric guy. And how are you going to let him go when you're through with him? He'll go straight to the police."

I bite my lower lip and taste the blood. The flavor gives me no strength.

"I know," I say.

"If you know then you've got to stop now."

There are tears pooled in my eyes but I won't shed them. Not tonight. "I can't, Seymour. Ray's right about one thing. I can't let her die."

Seymour speaks gently. "You know what I'm going to ask next."

I nod weakly. "Yes. Does the world need a monster like her? All I can say is, I'm hoping she turns out all right. For godsakes, she was just born. She hasn't had a chance to show what she's like."

"But by the time she does, it might be too late. You might not be able to stop her." He adds carefully, "But you can stop her now."

I'm aghast. "I can't murder my own daughter!"

"You can stop feeding her. Think what those feedings will cost you and your victims. You'll need a dozen Erics to keep her satisfied if she's growing at the rate you say. In fact, she'll be getting her own Erics soon enough. I know this is painful for you to face, but you should probably end it now."

I shake my head vigorously. "I can't do that."

Seymour is sympathetic. "But then I can't help you." He adds, "Unless you tell me where you are."

"It won't help for you to see her. You'll just fall in love with her. When she's not hungry, she's really very lovely."

"I was thinking I'd like to speak to this new and improved Ray."

"I don't think that's a good idea. Not now."

Seymour speaks with feeling. "You've trusted me in the past, Sita. Trust me now. You're too close to this. You can't see what's real. You need me."

"It's too dangerous, Seymour. If something happened to you, I'd never forgive myself. Stay where you are, I'll call you again. And I'll think about what you've said."

"Thinking won't stop her from growing into what she really is."

"I suppose we'll see what that is soon enough."

We exchange goodbyes. As I leave the house, I think of Eddie Fender's blood circulating in my lover's body. And I wonder what blood pumps through Kalika's veins. What it is capable of doing.

NINE

At home, Eric has regained consciousness. His feet and hands are firmly bound, and there is duct tape over his mouth, but he has somehow managed to squirm his way so that he is sitting upright in the far corner of the spare bedroom. His eyes are wide with fear as I approach him with a syringe. It is hard to blame him. As I kneel by his side, I start to stroke his head but he trembles under my fingers so I stop.

"I'm sorry," I say. "This isn't easy for me either. I wish I could explain the whole situation to you but I can't. But I can promise you that you're not going to die. I swear this to you, Eric, and I keep my word. At the same time, I'm going to have to keep you here for a few days. I'm not exactly sure how long. And while you're here—please don't freak out over this—I'm going to have to occasionally take some of your blood."

The last sentence does not go over well. Eric's eyes get so round I'm afraid they're going to burst from his skull. He shakes his head violently from side to side and tries to wiggle away. But I pull him back.

"Shh," I say. "It's not going to be as bad as it sounds. I have clean needles, and am better trained than most doctors. You can lose a little blood and it won't damage you in the slightest."

He works his mouth vigorously. His meaning is clear.

"If I remove your gag," I say, "will you promise not to scream? If you do scream, I'll have to shut you up quickly, and I don't want to have to hurt you any more than I have to."

Eric nods rapidly.

"Okay. But you mustn't raise your voice." I tear off the tape. Ouch.

Eric gasps for air. "Who are you?" he moans pitifully.

"Well, that's an interesting question. I am not Cynthia Rhodes if that's what you're asking, but I suppose you know that already." I pause. "I'm just a stranger in the park."

"What do you want with me?"

"I told you. Your blood. A little of your blood."

"But what do you want my blood for?" he cries.

"That's a long story." I pat him on the shoulder. "Just trust me that I really need it, and that in the end you're going to be okay."

He is breathing heavily. He stares down at his leg and looks so pitiful it breaks my heart. "You broke my knee. It hurts. I need a doctor."

"I'm sorry. You can see a doctor later, in a few days. But until then you'll have to stay here. You'll have to eat here, and sleep here, and go to the bathroom here. Now you see that bathroom over there? I will let you use it from time to time if you just cooperate with me. In fact, if you're real good, I won't have to keep you tied up at all. You'll be able to walk around this room, even read and listen to music. But I warn you, I'm going to board up all the windows as soon as I take care of other business. And if you do try to escape, well, let's just say that wouldn't be a good idea."

He is a little slow. "Would you kill me?"

I nod gravely. "I would kill you slowly, Eric, by draining away all your blood. It's not a pleasant way to die. So don't mess with me." I fluff up his hair. "Now stick out your arm and don't move."

He tries to back up. "No!"

"Don't raise your voice."

"No!"

I ram the heel of my palm into his nose, which stuns him. While he tries to refocus his eyes, I replace the duct tape and grab his arm. I have the tourniquet on in seconds. His veins are big and bulging. Before he can pull away, I have a needle in his vein and blood flowing into a sterile tube. I lean over and whisper in his ear.

"Don't fight me," I say. "If you force me to hit you again, it won't be in the face, but in a much more sensitive spot." I tug on his earlobe. "Understand?"

He stares at the tube as his blood drips into it. He nods.

"Good boy." I kiss his cheek. "Just think of all this as a nightmare that will soon be over."

Kalika is waiting in the living room with Ray when I bring out the blood in a flask. She has a book on her lap. I assume it is one of the picture books that I have recently bought for her, but I am mistaken. Sitting beside her on the floor, I see she has been paging through an anatomy textbook that was in the house when we rented it. I don't ask if she knows what it is. I'm afraid that she might. Her dark blue eyes brighten when she sees the blood. Her little hands shoot out.

"Hungry," she says.

"Is that all you took?" Rays asks. "She's been waiting all day."

"The less I take the more often I can take it," I say, handing Kalika the flask. I am curious if she will notice the difference between my blood and Eric's. Actually, I wonder if she will drink it at all. But that doubt is soon dispelled. She wolves it down in a few gulps. The flask is thrust back into my hands.

"Hungry," Kalika says.

"I told you," Ray says. "You have to give her at least a pint."

I stare at Kalika, who stares back at me, and a curious

sensation sweeps over me. There is a coldness in my daughter's eyes, but also a great expansive feeling. Few people in the West, who know anything of Vedic deities, understand the meaning of Kali or Kalika. To most she is simply a dark, bloodthirsty goddess. Yet that meaning is superficial, and I certainly would not have named my daughter after a monster with no redeeming virtues.

Actually, Kali *is* black, but this is because she represents space, the abyss, that which is before the creation, and that which will exist after. Her necklace of skulls symbolizes how she cares for souls after life, not just through one incarnation. Even the funeral pyre she sits on is representative of the many sins she burns to ash, when she is pleased. Kali is a destroyer, true, but she also destroys evil. Many of India's greatest saints worshipped her as the supreme being.

And they say she is easy to please—if one is careful.

Staring at my daughter, I am reminded of Krishna.

Yet Krishna had love as well as infinity.

Kalika has never been an affectionate child.

There is a bloodstain on her right cheek.

"Hungry, Mommy," she says softly.

Sighing, I take the flask and trudge back into the spare bedroom. Eric is upset to see me again so soon. Now this won't hurt a bit. I have to hit him again to get him to sit still, and I hate myself for the cruelty. I hate Krishna as well, for forcing me into this situation. But I know it is useless to hate God. It is like screaming at the night sky. The stars have no ears, and besides, they are too far away to hear. They just keep on shining, I must keep on living until death reaches my front door, or my own daughter comes for my blood in the dead of night. I have no doubt that, in a few days, she will be capable of killing me.

TEN

*A*fter boarding up Eric's room and ditching his car a safe distance away, I go for another drive, this one entirely aimless. It is dark now and the time of day suits my mood. Kalika thrust back her second empty eight-ounce glass of blood with the same numbing words: *Hungry, Mommy.* I shudder to think what her appetite will demand tomorrow. Will I have to collect a whole team of basketball players? Maybe I should drive down to the Forum and wait for the Lakers to start practice. They have some big boys who know how to shoot a ball.

But should they bleed for my daughter?

Should Eric?

Seymour has scored with many of his points, as always.

Midnight finds me at the beach where I buried Yaksha's body, or rather, where I sunk it. There was little of Yaksha

left when I sent him to a watery grave, with his full bless-
ings. Eddie Fender had done his usual number on my creator:
stabbed him, torn him, dissected him, drained him. Good
old Eddie, never one to take a joke well. But Yaksha hadn't
minded the horrific treatment. Indeed, in the end, the most
feared of all earth's ancient demons had found peace of mind
through faith in Krishna. Staring at the dark waves, I think
of how the passage of the many years does not necessarily
bring devotion, how my own suffering has more often than
not brought cynicism.

I have to wonder if that is why I keep suffering.

"What am I missing?" I ask the ocean. "Why do I have to
go on like this?"

Yet now it is more important than ever that I continue.
I am a mother; I have a responsibility to feed my daughter;
but it is very possible my daughter is capable of destroying all
mankind. No one knows, except perhaps Krishna, what weird
alchemy of blood she possesses. Bowing my head in the direction of Yaksha's grave, I turn and leave the beach.

Another hour finds me at Paula's school, inside St. Andrews
church. It's peculiar how many churches don't have posted
hours, how their doors are always open. The light of the candles, as I step inside, fill me with warm feelings. Despite my
obsession with Krishna, my respect for Jesus has never faded,
even during the Middle Ages when the Catholic Church tried
to burn me at the stake for witchcraft. Me, a witch? I'm a god-

damn vampire. I almost told them that, but then, the Church was never one to enjoy a joke.

St. Andrews is comfortably stuffy. The smoke from the candles and incense fills my nostrils as I take a seat in the third pew and stare at the stained-glass windows, dark and sinister without the sun to give them color. A statue of Mother Mary stands nearby, dozens of glowing red dishes flickering at her feet. I have never lit a candle for the Madonna in the last two thousand years, but I have a strong urge to do so now. But I won't pray to her, I won't ask for her help. Her own son was crucified, so I don't think she is the best person to run to with my problems. Yet I feel close to her, and that is reason enough to show her respect. Plus I like candles. I like fire of all kinds.

I have just lit my candles when I hear steps off to my right.

"Alisa?"

I smile as I turn. "Paula. What are you doing here at this hour? Praying?"

She is happy to see me. As best as she can with her swollen belly, she gives me a hug. "No, I was working on the school's books. I couldn't sleep tonight. I only stopped in here because I saw a car parked out front. I thought it might be yours. Why are you here?"

I gesture to Mother Mary. "I'm making my confession."

"You need a priest for that."

I shake my head. "I don't think there's a priest anywhere who would be able to sit through a list of my sins."

"Nonsense. They hear all kinds of stuff. None of us is that unique. I think it all sounds the same to them after a while."

"For once I have to disagree with you. My confession would set a record for the most difficult penance assigned." I pause as a wave of nostalgia sweeps over me. "Actually, I knew a Catholic priest once. He used to listen to my confessions. I think that's what drove him mad."

Paula wonders if I am kidding. "What was his name?"

"Arturo. He was Italian. I met him in Florence, a long time ago. But that is another story. I'm happy to see you. How are you feeling?"

Paula beams. "Wonderful. If I didn't have such trouble sleeping, I wouldn't even know I was pregnant."

"Not to mention the basketball in your belly. Well, that's great, I'm happy for you." I glance at the main crucifix and lower my voice. "Very happy."

Paula touches my arm. "Something's the matter?"

I nod grimly, still staring at Jesus, wondering how it felt to hang on the cross with so much power available to him, but unable to show it. In that instant I feel a great kinship with Jesus. Seldom in five thousand years was I allowed to demonstrate my full power, and then, when I did, people died.

Also, I think of how Krishna was killed, cut down in the forest by a hunter's arrow, mistaken for a beast and shot in the heel, the only portion of his divine body that was vulnerable to physical attack. So the legend of Achilles was born, not in

Greece, but in the deep forests of central India. It is impossible for me to look at Jesus and not think of Krishna. Honestly, all the religious dogma aside, I believe they were one and the same. So universal that they were everybody, and nobody at the same time. Like Kali, Mother Kalika.

Who is my daughter? What is she?

"Something is the matter," I say to Paula.

"What is it? Maybe I can help."

"No. Thanks, but no. No one can help me." I gesture to the empty pews. "Could I remain here a while? I have to think, to meditate. I think that will clear my mind, and then I will know what to do."

Paula kisses me on the cheek. "Stay as long as you want. I will lock the doors as I leave, but they will still open from the inside. You'll be safe in here."

I smile feebly. "Thank you. You are a true friend. Sometime, when things are less hectic, we must talk."

Paula stares deep into my eyes. "I look forward to that talk."

When she is gone, I curl up in one of the pews and close my eyes. I meditate best when I am unconscious, when I allow God to do most of the talking. Even though I am in a Catholic church, I pray Krishna will visit me in my dreams.

ELEVEN

*T*he scene is the same as it has always been. It can be no other way for it is constructed in eternity. It is only here that dialogue with the Almighty can take place.

I stand on a vast grassy plain with many gently sloping hills surrounding me. It is night, yet the sky is bright. A hundred blue stars blaze overhead. The air is warm and fragrant. In the distance a stream of people move slowly toward a large spaceship. The ship is violet; bright rays of light stab into the sky from it. I know that I am supposed to be on this ship. Yet, before I go to it, I have something to discuss with Lord Krishna.

He stands beside me on the plain, his gold flute in his right hand, a red lotus flower in his left. His dress, like mine, is simple—a long blue gown that reaches to the ground. But he wears a jewel around his neck—the brilliant Kaustubha gem, in which the destiny of every soul can be seen. He does not look at me but at the vast ship, and the stars beyond. He waits for me to speak, to answer him, but for some reason I can't remember what he last said. I only know that I am a special case. Because I do now know how to respond, I say what is most on my mind.

"When will I see you again, my Lord?"

He gestures to the wide plain, the stars overhead. "All this creation is an ocean, turbulent on the surface, silent in the depths. But like an ocean, the creatures in it are always searching for meaning in the creation, the ultimate element." He smiles to himself at the irony. "The fish searches for water in the ocean. He has heard so much about it. But he never finds it, and that is because he searches too hard." He pauses. "I am everywhere in the creation. There is nowhere that I am not. Why do you speak to me of separation?"

"Because, my Lord, I fear I will forget you when I enter into the creation."

He shrugs, he has no worries. "That is to be expected. You learn by forgetting what you once knew. Then, when you remember, it is that much sweeter."

"When will you come to earth?"

"When I am least expected."

"Will I see you, my Lord?"

"Yes, twice. At the beginning of Kali Yuga and then at the end of the age."

"Will I recognize you?"

"Not at first, not with the mind. But inside you will know me."

"How will I know you?"

He looks at me then, and his eyes are a wonder, windows into the cosmos. Time loses all meaning. It is as if the whole universe turns while I stare at him. I see thousands of people, millions of stars, so much life striving for small joys, so many illusions ending in shattering bitterness. Yet in the end it all turns to red, then to black, as the blood of the people runs cold and the fires of Kali burn the galaxies to ash. Still, none of this disturbs the eternal Lord for he never blinks, even though the sheer magnitude of the vision forces me to turn away trembling. He has stolen my very breath.

"Sri Krishna," I pray, overwhelmed, "take my soul now. Don't send me out. I surrender everything to you. I can't bear to forget you even for a moment."

He smiles. "I will tell you a story. This same story will be told by a simple man named Jesus, in the middle of Kali Yuga. Few people will recognize this Jesus with their minds, but some will know him inside." Krishna pauses before he begins.

"There is a man named Homa, who is a good person but not a perfect soul. He is a friend of Jesus and one day Jesus asks him to go to the village to buy some food for a large meal Jesus wants to give for some elders of the nearby village. Jesus says to the man, 'Take these ten coins and buy twelve loafs of bread, five jugs of wine, four fish, and one bag of a grain. Load it all on my donkey, and when you are done bring it here. I will be waiting for you.'

"At this Homa is confused, as well as excited with greed. He can see Jesus does not understand the value of the coins because he knows he can get all the things Jesus has requested for only five coins. Yet Homa also knows Jesus will need twice as much as he has asked for in order to feed all the people who are expected. Still, Homa does not plan on spending all ten coins. He says to himself, 'I will buy what I have been told to buy, and I will pocket the rest of the coins.'

"So Homa takes the donkey to town, and sets about purchasing the food. At the bakery he buys twelve loafs of bread, but as he places them on the donkey, when he is not looking, they change to twenty-four loafs. Next, Homa gets the five jugs of wine and the four fish. But like before, when he is not looking, the five jugs turns to ten, and the four fish turn to eight. Finally, Homa obtains the bag of grain, but then, on the way back, he sees that he actually has two bags, and that everything else has doubled as well. He is astounded and feels to see if the five coins are still in his pocket.

"Jesus is waiting for him when he arrives and greets him with a kind smile. The smile of Jesus is a wonderful thing. Mankind's history will portray Jesus as filled with sorrow, but the love and joy that flow toward Homa when Jesus looks at him is all-consuming. Still, Homa is worried about seeing

Jesus, even though Jesus has only kind words for him.

"Jesus says, 'Welcome back, Homa, you have brought everything we need for a great feast. Thank you.'

"But in shame Homa lowers his head and takes the five coins and places them at Jesus' feet. 'Don't thank me, Master, for I thought to cheat you. I knew you needed more than you asked for, but I was going to keep these extra coins for myself. It is only by some strange magic that all this food is here. I bought only half this.' At that he kisses Jesus' feet. 'I am unworthy to be called your friend, or even your servant.'

"But Jesus lifts him up, and says, 'No, Homa, you have done well because you have done my bidding. That is all you have to do. I ask nothing more of anyone.'"

Krishna pauses and stares up at the sky. "Did you enjoy this story?"

"Yes, my Lord. But I do not know if I understand it, or how it relates to me."

"This man, Homa, he is like every man. He is good-hearted but he has his flaws. Yet he is perfect in the eyes of Jesus because he has done what Jesus asks. You see, Sita, God does not expect you to give him all that you have. He understands the ways of the world, that it requires effort to deal with them. God only asks that you grant him half of what you possess, and then God will make up the other half. That is why the food multiplied. That is the miracle of this tale." Krishna pauses. "This story will be a part of the Gospel of Jesus, but too soon it will be removed from the holy book by those who want the peasant class to give everything to the Church, who do not understand the compassion of Jesus for those who struggle in the world." Krishna pauses again and smiles at me, that bewitching smile that steals even the hearts of the gods. "You don't need to surrender *everything* to me. Keep your head and I will take your heart. You will need your head to deal with Kali Yuga, particularly the end of the age."

"What will happen at the end, my Lord?"

Krishna laughs and raises his flute to his lips. "You will not enjoy the tale if you know the end of the tale. Enough questions, Sita, now listen to my song. It dispels all illusions, all suffering. When you feel lost, remember it, remember me, and you see the things you desire most are the very things that bring you the greatest sorrow. My song is eternal, it can be heard at all times in all places."

"But—"

"Listen, Sita. Listen in silence."

Krishna starts to play. But as he does, a sudden wind comes up on the plain and the notes of his melody are drowned out. The dust rises and I am blinded, and I can't see Krishna anymore. The light of the stars fades and everything turns black.

Yet in this blackness an even darker shadow fills the sky, and I know I see Kali, who is without color and who destroys all at the end of time. Sinners as well as saints, devils as well as angels, humans as well as vampires. And I know it is Kali who will eventually destroy me.

TWELVE

Over the next three days Kalika grows to the approximate age of five, while Eric ages ten years. During this time she reads greedily and masters English, as well as many subtleties of conversation and social convention. I have tested her—her IQ appears off the charts. Her beauty flourishes as well. Her long dark hair is like a shawl of black silk, her face a fine sculpture of hidden mysteries. Even her voice is magic, filled with haunting rhythms. When she speaks, it is hard not to listen, to agree with her, to forget everything else. But it is seldom Kalika does speak, and what runs through her mind—besides her hunger for blood—I have no idea.

It is in the middle of night when my daughter wakes me in my bed. She does this by gently stroking my hair. I am forced to wake to confusion.

"I can't wait," she says. "I need more."

I shake my head. "He can't take it. You're going to have to wait till later in the day. I have to get you another."

Kalika is gently persistent. "I can do it if you don't want to. I know how."

I frown. "Have you been watching me?" Naturally, I have not let Eric see where his blood is going. Somehow I doubt it would lift his spirits.

"Yes," Kalika says. "I watch you."

I sit up. "Has he seen you?"

"No." She pauses and glances at Ray, who continues to sleep. "He hasn't seen either of us."

"You are not listening to me. This boy can give no more blood. Already his heartbeat is erratic. In a few hours, when it is light, I will go out and find another supply. Until then you will have to be patient."

Kalika stares at me with her dark blue eyes. Perhaps it is my imagination, but I catch a glimmer of red in their depths. She smiles slightly, showing her front teeth.

"I have been patient, Mother." That is her new name for me. "I will just take a little of his blood, and then we can go for another supply. We can go in a few minutes."

I snort. "You're not going with me. You're a little girl."

Kalika is unmoved. "I will come with you. You will need me."

I pause. "Do you know that for sure?"

"Yes."

"I don't believe you."

Kalika loses her smile. "I won't lie to you, Mother, if you don't lie to me."

"Don't give me orders. You are to do what I say at all times. Is that clear?"

She nods. "As long as you don't lie to me." She adds, as if it were related, "How is Paula doing?"

Her question confuses me. Kalika has never met Paula. How would I explain that I have given birth to a child and that she has grown to five years of age, all in a month? Of course, I have talked about Paula with Ray. Perhaps Kalika was listening.

"Why do you ask?" I say.

Kalika glances at Ray. "I am curious about her. She means a lot to you."

"She's my friend. She's doing fine. One day you will meet her."

"Do you promise?"

I hesitate. "We'll see." I throw off the covers and put my feet on the floor. "We can go out now, if you insist. But we're not disturbing Eric anymore."

Kalika puts a hand on my leg. It is still a small hand but I have to wonder if I would be able to stand if she didn't want me to. I doubt it, and do not try to brush her fingers away.

It is a terrible thing to be afraid of one's own daughter.

"I will take only a little of his blood," she repeats.

"How much?"

"Eight ounces."

"That is not a little, not for him. He is weak, don't you care?"

Kalika is thoughtful. When she gets that way, she stares at the ground. I have no idea what she looks for. Her eyes close halfway, and her breathing seems to halt. The overall effect is disturbing. Finally she looks up.

"I care," she says. "But not in the way you mean."

I am curious. She is still an enigma to me. "What do you mean?"

She shakes her head. "I cannot explain, Mother."

Kalika leaves me to get dressed. Knocking lightly on Eric's door, I step in his room. I have not been able to untie him as I had hoped. As his strength has failed, his behavior has become more desperate. He thinks only of escape, or of his own impending death. I wish I could release him. An unhappy bundle of nerves stuffed in a stale corner, he twitches as I step into the room.

"No," he moans. "I can't."

I kneel by his side. "I need just a little. Less than last time."

He weeps. "Why?"

"You know I can't tell you why. But it will be over soon, Eric, I promise. I'm going out right now to—to get someone else."

He shakes his head sadly as he stares up at the ceiling. "I'm not stupid. You're never going to let me go. You're going to keep me here till I die."

"No."

He speaks with passion. "Yes. You're evil. You're a vampire. You have to kill me to keep your evil ways secret."

His words hurt. "I'm not a vampire. I don't take this blood for myself."

He is not listening. He continues to sob but grows more animated. "You're some monster from another planet. You're going to rip me open and eat my guts. You're going to have a glass of wine and have my guts all over your face, dripping on your clothes, on the floor . . ." He raises his voice. "You're going to eat me alive!"

"Shh."

"You're an alien monster!"

"Eric!"

"Help! The monster's got me! The aliens are coming!"

I am forced to strike him hard in the face to shut him up. My reflexes are still excellent, my martial art skills sharp. I believe I break his nose. Yet he continues to moan softly as I tighten the tourniquet. After I have drained away eight ounces—I know Kalika will count them—he dozes, probably out of sheer loss of blood. I kiss the top of his head before I leave the room.

"You will go home, Eric," I whisper. "I am not a monster."

While Kalika has her breakfast, I dress in my bedroom, in black leather pants, a tight leather coat. Ray sits up in bed. I do not need to turn to feel his eyes on me.

"Are you going out?" he asks.

"Yes. You know why."

"Yes. You've waited too long anyway."

"It's not an enjoyable task, you know, finding people to kill."

"Eric's still alive."

"Barely."

"Find someone you don't like. A criminal, a rapist—you used to specialize in them if I remember correctly."

I turn on him. "I may not be able to handle a criminal or rapist nowadays, or does that concern you, my love?"

He shrugs. "Take your pistol. It has a silencer on it. Just get someone you're not going to go to pieces over every time you have to take blood."

I speak with thinly disguised bitterness. "You didn't answer my question, my love. But I suppose that is answer enough. You know I enjoy this little family we have here. A gorgeous daughter who is a medical and historical first, and a supposedly loving boyfriend who has forgotten what the words *friend* and *love* mean. I mean, you've got to admit, five thousand years of intense experience has really helped me create the perfect domestic environment. Wouldn't you agree?"

He is unimpressed by my outburst. "You create what you want. You always have. If you don't like it, you can always leave."

I snort. "Leave you with Kalika! She would starve in a day."

"I doubt that Kalika will need either of us soon. She's not a normal child, you know." He adds, "Not like Paula's child will be."

I stop. "Why did you say that?"

He ignores me. "When is her baby due exactly? Soon?"

I frown. Why were they both dropping remarks about Paula? "She's not having a baby anymore," I say carefully. "She lost it."

He waves his hand. "Yeah, right, she got kicked by a donkey."

A donkey, I think. "Yeah, that is right." I turn away. "Seymour was right about you."

Ray is instantly alert. "You spoke to him. When did you speak to him?"

I reach for my black boots. "None of your business."

"What did he say about me?"

I glare at him. "He said that Eddie Fender's blood has warped your mind. He told me not to trust you, which was probably good advice."

Ray relaxes. "Good old Seymour. Did you invite him down for a pleasant evening of food and conversation?"

I have my boots on and stalk out the door. "He is not interested in our problems," I lie. "He has better things to do with his time."

But Ray's final remark makes me pause outside the door.

"I hope you didn't tell him about Kalika. I really hope you didn't."

I glance over my shoulder. "Of course not. He would never have believed me if I had."

Ray just nods and smiles.

THIRTEEN

Kalika drives with me to a club in Hollywood. It is one in the morning but the place is still hopping. What I'm supposed to do with my daughter, I'm not sure. It is she who suggests she hide under a blanket in the backseat until I bring out whoever it is who is to be our next barrel of blood. As she crawls under the blanket, she peers up at me with her serious dark blue eyes.

"You'll be warm enough?" I ask.

"I am never cold," she says.

"If you want, you can sleep. Just don't make any noise when I return to the car. I'll take care of everything." I glance at the crowded parking lot. "But I won't be able to knock him out here."

"Take him to a secluded place," Kalika says. "I will help you."

"I told you, I don't want your help."

Kalika does the unexpected then. She reaches up and kisses me on the lips. "Be careful, Mother. You are not who you used to be."

Her kiss warms me, her words give me a chill. "You know what I used to be?"

"Yes. He told me."

"Ray?"

"Yes."

"How come you never call him Father?"

"You call him Ray. I call him Ray."

"But he calls me Sita."

"Do you want me to call you Sita?"

"No, it doesn't matter." I pause. "Do you like Ray?"

She shrugs. "How I feel—I can't explain to you at this time."

"Why not?"

"You are not ready to hear."

"When will I be ready to hear?"

"Soon."

"You know this?"

She pulls the blanket over her head. "I know many things, Mother."

The music is loud as I enter the club, the strobe lights flashing, unnatural thunder and psychedelic solar flares to match the scrambled brains of the alcohol-saturated clientele. I am, of course, a superb dancer, even without my vampire strength. Without looking around, I leap onto the dance floor and wait for my daughter's next meal to come to me. Guilt makes me less discriminating. Let destiny decide who is to suffer, I will not.

A man about thirty, with an expensive sports coat and a thin black mustache, joins me within a few minutes. His speech is educated; he could be an Ivy League graduate, a young lawyer with something profitable on the side. His watch is a Rolex, his single gold earring studded with a carat diamond. He is not handsome but his face is likable. He speaks smoothly.

"Mind if I butt in?" he asks.

I smile, whirling, my hair in my eyes. "There's no one to butt out."

He chuckles. "Hey, you're a real dancer."

"You're not bad yourself. What's your name?"

"Billy. You?"

"Cynthia. But you can call me Cindy."

He grins, he's having a good time. "I'll call you whatever you want."

After twenty minutes on the floor, he buys me a couple of drinks. We catch our breath over them at the bar. I was right, he's a lawyer but he insists he's an honest one.

"I don't represent shmucks and I don't fudge my billing hours," he says proudly, sipping his Bloody Mary, my drink of choice when I am on the prowl. I am already on my second. The alcohol soothes my nerves, although I don't suppose it sharpens my reflexes. At my waist, above my butt and beneath my leather jacket, I carry my pistol and silencer. But I know I won't need it on Billy. He will go the way of Eric, to endless misery. Guilt hangs over my head but I keep it away with a stiff umbrella of denial.

"What firm are you with?" I ask.

"Gibson and Pratch. They're in Century City. I live in the valley. The traffic's hell coming over the San Diego Freeway in the morning. What do you do?"

"I'm a music teacher," I say.

"Cool. What instrument do you play?"

"Piano, some violin."

"Wow, that's incredible. I have an expensive piano that was left to me by my rich uncle. I've always meant to take lessons, but never got around to it." He pauses and then has a brilliant idea. God inspires it. I know what it is; he hasn't been able to take his eyes off my body. "Hey, will you play me something on my piano?"

I laugh and look around. "Did you bring it with you?"

"No, at my place. It doesn't take long to get there at this time of night."

I hesitate. "Like you say, Billy, it's late. I have to get up in the morning."

"Nah! You're a teacher. You call your students and tell them when you want to see them. Really, we can go in my car. I've got a brand-new Jag."

I'm impressed. "I love Jags." I glance uneasily at my watch, playing the role to the hilt. "Okay, but I'm going to have to follow you there. That way I can head straight back to my place after your song."

Billy is pleased as he sets down his drink. "I'll drive slowly. I won't lose you."

Kalika is asleep when I return to the car. Her soft rhythmic breathing follows me as I steam onto the freeway and chase Billy's Jag into the valley. He has lied to me—he drives like a maniac.

My plan is simple. I will knock him out the second we get inside, then load him into my trunk. He looks like he's been drinking all night, an easy mark. He won't even know what hit him.

Kalika is still asleep when we reach Billy's place.

I leave my gun in the glove compartment.

Billy's house is modest, considering his new car. The driveway is cracked, the landscaping neglected. He lives in a cul-de-sac. His car disappears into the automatic garage as I park in the street. A moment later he is on the front porch, waving to me. Making sure Kalika is resting comfortably, I get out and walk toward Billy, my boots clicking on the asphalt and concrete. Billy thinks he's in for a night of sex and more sex. His grin as he greets me belongs to a sixteen-year-old. I'm not surprised when he kisses me the moment we're inside with the door closed. His mouth is sweet with the taste of alcohol, his groping hands moist with the thrill of seduction. He presses me against the wall and I have to turn my head to catch my breath.

"Hold on a second, Billy," I protest. "You haven't even shown me the house. And where's your piano?"

He stares at me with a gleam in his eye. "I don't have a piano."

"What do you mean. You said your uncle . . ."

"I don't have an uncle," he interrupts.

Right then I smell it. The odor is faint, probably something most young women would miss, but I have had extensive experience with this smell. I don't need supernatural nostrils to identify it. Somewhere in Billy's house, perhaps buried beneath his bed, perhaps cemented into his bathroom floor, is one or more dead bodies. My best estimate as I look deeper into his manic eyes is that it is more than one. I curse myself for being such a fool, for being caught off guard. Certainly as a vampire I would have heard his lies a mile away.

Careful, I let none of my insights show on my face.

"That's all right, Billy," I say. "I don't know how to play piano anyway."

He is dizzy with pleasure. "You lied to me?"

"We lied to each other."

There is a single metal click. The sound is very specific, the snap of a switchblade. His right arm begins to slash upward. He is close to me, though, perhaps too close. Giving him a nudge in the chest, I yank my right knee up as hard as I can, catching him clean in the groin. But Billy must have balls of steel. My blow stuns him but he doesn't double up in agony. His switchblade continues its terrifying course toward my throat. Only by twisting to the side at the last second do I manage to avoid having my jugular severed. But even though I momentarily break free, the blade catches the tip of my left shoulder and slices through my leather jacket. The knife is incredibly sharp; it opens a four-inch gash in my tender flesh. Blood spurts from my body as I stagger into the center of the living room.

How I long for my pistol right then.

Billy limps toward me, holding his bloody knife in his right hand, his bruised balls in his left. He grins again but he is no longer a happy-go-lucky serial killer.

"You are a spunky little bitch," he says.

I grab a vase of flowers and cock it back in my right hand. "Stop! I'll scream if you don't."

He laughs. "My nearest neighbors are all old and hard of hearing. This house is completely soundproof. Scream all you want, Cindy."

"My name's not Cindy. Yours isn't Billy."

He is surprised. "Who are you then?"

"Why should I tell you?"

"Because I want to know before you die."

I harden my voice. "I am Sita, of the ancient past. I am older than I look and I have dealt with scum like you before.

It is you who will die this night, and I don't care what your name is."

He charges, and he moves fast for a nonvampire. The vase, of course, I throw at him merely to upset his balance. But he seems to know that ahead of time; he ducks and prepares for my real blow. I am already in the air, however, lashing out with my right foot, the heel of my boot, aiming for the sensitive spot on his jaw that professional boxers covet. One hard punch will put him out cold.

Unfortunately my human muscles fail me once again. I am short on the reach. As a result my devastating kick barely contacts his jaw. The blow backs him up, cuts him even, but it by no means puts him down. Wiping at his face, he has hatred in his eyes.

"Where did you learn this stuff?" he demands.

"Through a correspondance course," I snap as I begin to circle. Now I have lost the element of surprise. He watches my feet as he stalks me with his knife. Someone has trained him as well, I see. He does not lunge carelessly, but plots his strikes. One such swipe of his knife slashes open the back of my right hand. The pain is electric, burning, my blood is everywhere. Still, I maintain my balanced stance, circling, searching for an opening. He is skilled at defense; however, he never stops moving his arms. I know I can't let him catch my leg. He would probably saw off my foot, and make me watch.

Then he makes a mistake. Going for my eyes, he subtly

telegraphs his intention. My initial reaction is simple—I duck. Then I leap up just after the knife swishes over my head and sweep his lower legs with my left foot. The move is kung fu, very old and effective. Billy, or whoever the hell he is, topples to the floor. I am on him in an instant. When he tries to rise, I kick him in the face, then again in the chest. He smashes into his coffee table and his knife bounces on the blood-stained carpet and I kick it away. Lying on his back, breathing hard, he stares at me in amazement. Standing over him, I feel the old satisfaction of triumph. I step on his left wrist and pin his arm to the floor.

"I actually can play the piano," I say. "If you had an instrument here, I would play Mozart's *Requiem* for the dead after I stuff you in a closet."

He still has a weird gleam in his eye. "Is your name really Sita?"

"Yes."

"How old are you? You're older than you look, huh?"

"Yes. How old are you and how do you want to die?"

He grins. "I'm not going to die."

"No?"

"No." And with that, before I can react, he pulls out a snub-nose silver revolver and points it at my head. "Not tonight, Sita."

Once again I am furious at myself, for not taking him out immediately when he was helpless. I know what my problem is. I am used to playing with my victims, a luxury I can no longer afford now that I am mortal. There is no way I can dodge the bullet he can send hurtling into my brain. It is his game now. Taking my foot off his wrist, I back up a couple of steps. He gets up slowly and guards me carefully. He is not one to repeat a mistake, as the odor in his house testifies.

"How many girls have you cut up here?" I ask.

"Twelve. The youngest was five." He grins. "You're going to be lucky number thirteen."

"Thirteen is traditionally an unlucky number," I remind him.

He gestures with his gun. "On your knees. Keep your hands on top of your head. No sudden moves."

I do as he says. Like I have a lot of choice. The blood from my hand wound drips into my hair and over my face. Like those of a full-fledged vampire, my tears are once again dark red. My situation is clearly desperate, and I cannot think of a clear course of action. He ties my wrists behind my back with a nylon cord. Although I can work my way out of any knot, even with my current strength, he complicates my dilemma by redoing the knots several times over. When he is finished he crouches in front of me and takes out his switchblade. He plays with my hair with the tip of the blade, with my eyes even, letting the silver razor brush the surface of the whites. I won't be surprised if he gouges one of my eyes out and eats it.

"You're so beautiful," he says.

"Thank you."

"All my girls have been beautiful. I don't *carve* them unless they are."

I have to restrain myself from spitting in his face. "Why do you *carve* them?"

"To give them more dimension. I enjoy it."

"Obviously."

He leans close, his breath on my face, his knife now inside my right nostril. "You know, I never met a girl like you. Not only can you fight, you are totally fearless."

I smile sweetly. "Yeah, I could be your partner. Why don't you untie me and we can talk about it?"

He laughs. "See! That's exactly what I mean. You make jokes in the face of death." He slides the knife a little farther up my nose and loses his smile. A typical serial killer, moody as hell. "But some of your jokes aren't that funny. Some of them annoy me. I don't like to be annoyed."

I swallow thickly. "I can understand that."

He pokes the inside of my nose and a narrow line of blood pours over my mouth and down my throat. His eyes are inches from mine, his mouth almost close enough to lick my blood. I am afraid he will do that next, and not like the taste. It hurts to have a switchblade up my right nostril. Still, I cannot think of a way out of my situation. Yet I find I am more concerned about Kalika, asleep in the car, than I am about myself. Truly I am a good mother. It was only my love for my daughter that brought me into this evil place. Krishna will understand.

I feel I will be seeing him soon.

"You know what I don't like about you?" he asks. "It's your cockiness. I had a cocky girlfriend in high school once. Her name was Sally and she was so sure of herself." He pauses. "Until she lost her nose and her lips. A girl with only half a face is never a smart mouth."

I wisely keep my mouth shut.

There is a knock at the front door.

Billy pulls the knife higher, still inside my nose, forcing my head back. "Don't make a sound," he whispers. "There is dying all at once and there is dying piece by piece. Believe me, I can take a week to kill you if you try to get their attention."

My eyelashes flash up and down. Yes, I understand and agree.

I know who is at the door. The person knocks again.

Billy is sweating. Clearly he fears some noise has escaped his soundproof spider's lair and that a neighbor has called the police. All he can do is wait and worry. But he is not kept in suspense long. The door slowly opens and a beautiful five-year-old girl with stunning dark hair and large black-blue eyes pokes her head inside.

"Mother," Kalika says. "Are you okay?"

Billy is astounded and immensely relieved. He lowers his switchblade. "Is that your daughter?" he asks.

"Yes."

"What is she doing here?"

"She came with me. She was sleeping in the car."

"Well, I'll be goddamned. I didn't know you had a daughter."

"There are a few things about me you don't know." I glance at Kalika, wondering what I should do: be a good mother, warn her to get away, or remain silent and try to get out of this hell hole alive. Honestly, I don't know how quick Kalika is, exactly how strong she is. But a vampire her size and her age could take Billy. I speak carefully, "I am not okay, darling."

"I told you," she replies.

Billy withdraws his knife and stands in front of me. He is bleeding as well, and he has plenty of my blood on him. He holds his messy knife in his right hand and he has his shiny revolver tucked in his belt. Plus the light in his eyes is radioactive. He looks as trustworthy as Jack the Ripper on a PCP high. Yet he gestures to Kalika to come closer, as if he were Santa Claus anxious to hear her wish list.

"Come here, darling," he says in a sweet voice.

And she comes, slowly, observing every blessed detail: the composition of the floor, how Billy stands, the height of the ceiling, the arrangement of the furniture—moving precisely the way an experienced vampire would move while closing in for the kill. Her arms hang loose by her sides, her legs slightly apart, well-balanced, and she is up on her toes so that she can move either way fast. Billy senses there is something odd about her. When she is ten feet from him, he drops his smile. For my part, I watch in wonder and terror. Only then do I realize the full extent of my love for my daughter. I would rather die a dozen times over than have anything happen to her.

"What's your name, sweetie?" Billy asks when she stops directly in front of him. His voice is uneasy, perhaps as a result of the power of her stare, which is now locked on his face. Kalika tilts her head slightly to one side, ignoring me for the moment.

"Kalika," she says.

He frowns. "What kind of name is that, child?"

"It's a Vedic name. It's who I am."

"What does it mean?" he asks.

"It has many meanings. Most of them are secret." She finally gestures to me. "You've hurt my mother. She's bleeding."

Billy gives an exaggerated sigh. "I know that, Kalika, and I'm sorry. But it was your mother who hurt me first. I only hurt her back to defend myself."

Kalika doesn't blink. "You are lying. You are not a good man. But your blood is good. I will drink it in a moment." She pauses. "You can put your knife and your gun down now. You will not need them."

Billy is having a night of amazement. His face breaks into a wolfish grin and he looks down at me. "What kind of nonsense have you been teaching this child, Sita?"

I shrug. "She watches too much TV."

Billy snorts. "God, I can't believe this family." He takes a step toward my daughter, his knife still in his right hand. "Come here, girl. I'm putting you in the other room. I have business with your mother that can't wait. But I'll let you out in a little while, if you behave yourself." Billy holds out his free hand. "Come, give me your hand."

Kalika innocently reaches up and takes his hand. She even allows his fingers to close around her tiny digits. But then, in a move too swift for human eyes to properly follow, she grabs his other hand, twists his wrist at an impossible angle, and rams the knife into his stomach. Literally the blade is sunk up to the hilt. An expression of surprise and grief swallows Billy's face as he stares down at what she has done to him. Slowly, as if in a dream, he lets go of the knife. It is obvious his right wrist is broken. Blood gushes over his pants and Kalika stares at it with her first sign of pleasure.

"I am hungry," she says.

Billy gasps for air but finally he is getting the idea that he is in mortal danger, that he might be, in fact, already screwed. Summoning his failing strength, he makes a swipe for Kalika's head. But she is not standing where she was an instant before, and he misses. She is her mother's daughter. Twice she kicks with her right foot, with her shiny black shoes that I bought for her at the mall, and the cartilage in both his joints explodes. Falling to his shattered knees, he lets out a pitiful scream,

"How can you do this to me?" he cries.

Kalika steps over and grabs him by his hair and pulls his head back, exposing his throat. The calm on her face is eerie even for me to see.

"If you understood the full meaning of my name," she says, "you would have no need to ask."

Billy dies piece by piece, drop by drop.

Kalika satisfies herself before she releases me.

Even I, Sita the Damned, cannot bear to watch.

FOURTEEN

The following week Kalika attains full maturity, approximately twenty years of age, about the same age I was when I was changed into a vampire. At this point her growth seems to halt. I am not surprised. It is a fact that a human being is at his or her greatest strength, mentally and physically, just out of his or her teens. Certainly Kalika is very powerful, but how powerful I'm not sure. Except for the incident with Billy, she never demonstrates her abilities in front of me. One thing is sure, though—she no longer needs me to bring her lunch. Now she leaves the house for long stretches of time—on foot and at night. When she returns, I don't ask where she's been or who she's been with. I don't want to know.

Of course that's a lie. I scrutinize the papers each day for reports of unexplained murders. Yet I find none, and it makes me wonder.

The police have yet to find Billy—what is left of him. I know it is only a matter of time. I hope they will uncover his victims as well.

My hand and shoulder are still bandaged. I did not allow myself the luxury of a doctor and hospital, but I did manage to sew myself up fairly well. Still, I know I will be scarred for life.

The change in my daughter's eating habits means that I no longer need to keep Eric locked in the spare bedroom. Unfortunately, I can't figure out a way to let him go and keep him from running straight to the police. Simply moving to another city, or even another state, is not a solution. Well, it would probably help, but I don't want to move, not until Paula has her baby. Kalika and Ray don't want to move either. They have stated their opinion many times.

So I keep Eric locked up, but have stopped taking his blood. It had been my hope that this would cheer him up, and he'd be able to gain back his strength. But Eric is now deep in the throes of depression and won't eat a bite.

"Come on, Eric," I say as I offer him a hamburger and fries. "This is a McDonald's Big Mac and their golden delicious french fries, large size. I've even brought you a vanilla shake." I touch his head as he refuses to even look at me. He has lost over thirty pounds since meeting me, and his skin is a pasty yellow. There are black circles under his eyes, from his grief, and from the times I hit him. His nose is still broken;

he has trouble breathing, especially tied up as he is. I add gently, "You've got to eat something. You're just wasting away in here."

"Then why don't you let me go like you promised?" he asks quietly. "I'm sick—you know I'm really sick."

"I am going to let you go. Just as soon as I figure out the logistics of the release. You understand I have to worry about you talking to the police. I have to be long gone from this place before you are freed."

"I won't talk to the police. I just want to go home."

"I know you do. It won't be long now." I push the hamburger his way. "Have a bite, just for me, and I'll have some of your fries. We can pretend we're in that coffee shop you took me to on our first date."

That is probably not the best thing to say. He begins to sob again. "I thought you were a nice girl. I just wanted to talk to you. I didn't know you would hurt me and take all my blood."

"But I stopped taking your blood. Things are looking up. Soon you'll see your mom and dad. And they'll be so excited to see you. Just think of that, Eric, and try to keep a positive attitude. Imagine what an incredible homecoming you're going to have. You'll be interviewed by every TV station in the country. You can even make your story more exciting than it really was. You can say how a whole horde of vampires tortured you night and day and used your blood for satanic rituals. The media will love that—they're really into the devil. You'll be a celebrity, a hero, and after that you'll probably get lots of dates. The girls will come to you. Heroes are sexy. You won't have to go looking for girls in the park."

My pep talk is wasted on him. He stares at me with blood-shot eyes and sniffles. "Even if you wanted to let me go, she'd never let you."

I pause. "Who's she?"

"The one you've been giving my blood to."

"I don't know what you're talking about."

"I've seen her. You serve her and you don't know it, but I know she's not human. I've seen her *eyes,* the red fire deep inside. She drinks human blood and she's evil." He nods like a man who's been granted a vision by God and won't be convinced otherwise. "After she kills me and eats my guts, she's going to kill you and eat your brains."

Well, I don't know what to say to that.

Placing the hamburger in his lap, I leave the room.

Ray is sitting in the living room. Kalika is in the backyard, sitting in the full lotus and meditating with her eyes closed in the bright sun, wearing a one-piece black bathing suit. She sits on a white towel in the center of the lawn and doesn't move a fraction of an inch, or even seem to breathe. This is a new habit of hers, but I am afraid to ask what she mediates on. Perhaps her own name, or the secret forms of it. They are reputed to be powerful mantras.

Ray looks up at me. "Is he eating?"

"No."

"What are we going to do with him?"

I sit on the couch across from Ray. "I don't know. Let him go."

"We can't let him go. Not now."

"Then we'll let him go later," I say.

Ray shakes his head. "I think that's a bad idea. It will require us to cover our tracks. He'll just give the authorities information we don't want them to have. Think about it a minute before you dismiss it. You said yourself that the government might still be searching for you. What are they going to think when they hear the story of a young man who was held captive by a beautiful blond woman who systematically drained his blood? They'll put two and two together, and they'll start a manhunt for you unlike anything that's been seen in this country. Remember, they still want that vampire blood."

I speak in a flat voice. "What is it you want me to think about?"

Ray hesitates. "Just getting rid of the problem."

"You mean kill Eric and bury him in the backyard?"

"I don't think we should bury him there. But, yes, I don't see how we can let him go and expect to remain free ourselves."

I smile as I stare at him. It is one of those smiles a salesperson gives to a customer. "You know, something just occured to me."

"What?"

"I don't know who you are. Oh, you look like Ray. You talk like him and you even have his memories. But I honestly don't know who you are."

"Sita, be serious. You have to face reality."

"That's exactly what I'm doing. The Ray I met and loved would never talk about killing an innocent young man. No matter what the consequences to himself. The idea would never even enter his mind. And one more thing, I've been watching our daughter the last few days and I swear she doesn't look a bit like you. You don't share a single feature. How can that be?"

Ray snorts. "You're the one who should be able to answer that question. You're the one who got pregnant."

"I wish I could answer it. I believe if I could, many other questions would be answered as well."

"Such as?"

I lose my smile. "I don't know how much I should tell you. I don't trust you, and I'm not going to kill Eric. We'll leave here before it comes to that. I don't care if he does set the government on my tail."

"You will not leave here until Paula has her baby."

"Paula's baby is not the topic of this conversation. Also, I notice you're not responding to my accusations. You're not even trying to defend yourself."

"They're so ridiculous. What can I say?" He glances down the hall. "Eric has to die, and the sooner the better."

"Have you shared this with Kalika?"

"Yes."

"Does she agree with you?"

Ray is evasive. "She didn't say one way or the other."

"She never says much." I straighten up and point a finger at Ray. "But let's make one thing perfectly clear. If you so much as harm a single hair on Eric's head, you'll regret it."

Ray is amused. "You're not a vampire anymore. You have nothing to back up your threats.

I'm not given a chance to respond. By chance, if anything is chance, a police car pulls into our driveway at that moment. The two officers are almost to the door when I remember that I have not replaced Eric's gag. I've been letting him be without it for the last few days. He knows the penalty for crying out.

Yet if he hears the police in the house, what will he do?

Ray runs into the back room, not into Eric's. I answer the door. A blond-haired cop and a dark-haired one. The handsome black one holds a picture of Eric in his hand. Wonderful.

"Hello," he says. "I'm Officer Williams and this is my partner, Officer Kent. We're canvassing the neighborhood for information concerning the whereabouts of this young man. His name is Eric Hawkins. He vanished close to three weeks ago." He pauses. "May we come in?"

"Sure." I open the door wider. As they step inside, I ask, "Was this guy from around here? Excuse me, please, have a seat."

Kent and Williams settle themselves on my couch. Williams does the talking. He is the leader of the two—his eyes are everywhere, searching for clues. Well-muscled Kent sits content like a comfortable jock after a hard game. I plop down across from them.

"Actually. Eric lives some distance from here," Williams says. "But we have a report from one of your neighbors that a guy who fit his description was seen entering your house. Also, this same neighbor believes she saw Eric's car parked out in front of your house on the day he disappeared."

"So you're not just canvassing the neighborhood. You've come here specifically to see me?" I gesture to Eric's picture. "I've never seen this guy in my life."

Williams is grave. "We also have a description from two guys that Eric was playing basketball with on the day he disappeared. They say he left Scott Park in the company of a young woman who matches your description."

I raise my hand, palm out. "Hold on! You do not have *my* description. I don't even know where Scott Park is. What exactly did these guys say?"

Williams consults notes jotted on a piece of folded paper. "That he left the park in the company of a beautiful blond girl approximately eighteen to twenty-one. Her hair was long, like yours."

I'm not impressed. "There are literally tens of thousands of cute blond girls with long hair in Southern California."

"That is true, ma'am," Williams says. "You're just a lead we're checking out." He pauses. "Did you have a guest with a blue Honda Civic park in your driveway three weeks ago?"

"I can't remember. Lots of friends drop by. They have all kinds of cars."

"Do you have a friend who looks like Eric?" Williams asks. "Someone your neighbor might have mistakenly identified as Eric."

I shrug. "I have a couple of friends who resemble him superficially."

Williams glances in the backyard. Kalika was no longer there. "Would you mind if we looked around?" he asks.

"Do you have a search warrant?"

Williams is cagey. "We just stopped by to ask a few questions."

"Then I certainly do mind. Look, I live here with my boyfriend and a girlfriend. We're not kidnappers, and I resent your implying that we are."

Kent speaks for the first time. 'Then why won't you let us look around?"

"That's my choice."

"What happened to your hand?" Kent asks, pointing to the bandage that covers Billy's second good swing at me.

"I cut it on a broken glass," I say.

"Hello?" Kalika says softly as she enters the living room from the direction of the hall, a towel tied around her waist over her bathing suit. "Is there a problem?"

"No," I say quickly. "These men were just leaving."

Williams stands and holds out the picture of Eric for Kalika to see. "Have you ever seen this young man?"

Kalika studies the photograph. Then looks my way with a cool smile. "Yes."

That's my daughter. She would talk about Billy next.

"Where did you see him?" Williams demands, casting me a hard look.

Kalika is thoughtful. "I can show you the place. It's not far from here. Would you like to take me there?"

I clear my throat. "That's not necessary."

"I don't mind," Kalika says. "It's not a problem."

I lower my head. Arguing with her in front of these men will not help.

"Don't be gone long," I say.

Kalika leaves with the officers. She doesn't even bother to change out of her suit. The men don't seem to mind. Kalika is more stunning than her mother, and they can't take their eyes off her. I pray they don't take their eyes off her, and that they don't have families. It is them I am worried about now.

Paula calls ten minutes after Kalika leaves.

She's in labor. I'll be there in two minutes, I promise.

Running out the door, Ray stops me. "Call us when the baby's been born."

I step past him. I haven't told him who was on the phone

but I suppose it shows on my face. "I'll think about it."

He speaks to my back as I go down the steps. "Remember, you promised Kalika you would let her see the baby. Don't forget."

I ignore him, or wish I could.

FIFTEEN

*P*aula is having contractions in my car when I decide we are not going to the local hospital where her doctor is waiting. I turn left and head for the freeway. Paula is in pain, and in shock when I floor it.

"What are you doing?" she cries.

"I don't like your hospital," I say. "It's ill equipped. I'm taking you to a much nicer one. Don't worry, I have money, I'll pay."

"But they're expecting me! I called before I left!"

"It doesn't matter. This hospital is only thirty minutes away." It is actually over forty minutes away. "You'll like it, we can get you a room with a view of the mountains."

"But I'm not going on vacation! I'm going to have a baby! I don't need a room with a view!"

"It's always nice to have a view," I reply, patting her leg. "Don't worry, Paula, I know what I'm doing."

This baby—I don't know what's special about it. I don't know why Ray and Kalika are obsessed with it. But I do know they are the last people on earth who are going to see it.

The hospital I take her to, the famous Cedars-Sinai, is surprised to see us. But the staff jumps to attention when I wave cash and gold credit cards in their faces. What a terrible thing it is that the quality of emergency care is often determined by money. Holding Paula's hand, I help her fill out the paperwork and then we are both ushered into a delivery room. The baby appears to be coming fast. A nurse asks me to put on a gown and a mask. She is nice, and lets me stay with Paula without asking questions.

Paula is now drenched in sweat and in the throes of *real* pain, which I have often been intimate with. An anesthesiologist appears and wants to give her Demerol to take the edge off the contractions, maybe an epidural to partially numb her lower body. But Paula shakes her head.

"I don't need anything," she says. "I have my friend with me."

The anesthesiologist doesn't approve, but I am touched by the remark. I have become so human. Even sentimental nonsense has meaning to me. Paula's hand is sweaty in mine but I have seldom felt a softer touch.

"I am with you," I say. "I will stay with you."

The baby fakes us all out. It is eight hours later, at night, when the child finally makes an appearance—a handsome male of seven pounds, five ounces, with more hair than most babies, and large blue eyes that I assume will fade to brown over the next few months. I am the first to hold the baby—other than the delivering physician—and I whisper in his ear the ancient mystical symbol that is supposed to remind the child of its true essence or soul.

"Vak," I say over and over again. It is practically the first sound the infant hears because he did not come out screaming, and the doctor and the others fell strangely silent at the moment of his birth. Indeed, it was almost as if time stood still for a moment.

Vak is a name for Saraswati, the Goddess of speech, the Mother above the head who brings the white light to saints and prophets. The baby smiles at me as I say Vak. Already, I think, I am in love with him. Wiping him gently off and handing him to Paula, I wonder who his father is.

"Is he all right?" she asks, exhausted from the effort but nevertheless blissful.

"Yes, he's perfect," I say, and laugh softly, feeling something peculiar in my words, an intuition, perhaps, of things to come and a life to be lived. "What are you going to call him?" I ask.

Paula cuddles her child near her face and the baby reaches

out and touches her eyes. "I don't know," she says. "I have to think about it."

"Didn't you think about a name before?" a nurse asks.

Paula appears puzzled. "No. Never."

Death is a part of life. Calling home to see how Kalika has fared with the two police, I know the grave and the nursery sit on opposite sides of the same wall. That they are connected by a dark closet, where skeletons are hidden, and where the past is sometimes able to haunt the present. All who are born die, Krishna said. All who die will be reborn. Neither is supposed to be a cause for grief. Yet even I, with all my vast experience extending over fifty centuries, am not prepared for what is to happen next.

Kalika answers the phone. It is ten at night.

"Hello, Mother," she says.

"You knew it was me?"

"Yes."

"How are you? Did you just get home?"

"No. I have been home awhile. Where are you?"

I hesitate. "Ray must have told you."

"Yes. You're at the hospital?"

"Yes. How did you get on with the police?"

"Fine."

I have trouble asking the next question. "Are they all right?"

"You don't have to worry about them, Mother."

I momentarily close my eyes. "Did you kill them?"

Kalika is cool. "It is not your concern. The baby has been born. I want to see it."

How does she know the baby has been born? "No," I say. "Paula's still in labor. You can't see the baby now."

Kalika is a long time in responding. "What hospital are you at?"

"The local one. Let me speak to Ray a moment."

"Ray is not here. What is the name of this hospital?"

"But he seldom goes out. Are you sure he's not there?"

"He's not here. I'm telling you the truth, Mother. You will tell me the truth. What is the name of the hospital where you're at?"

Even as a human, I do not like to be pushed around. "All right, I will tell you. If you tell me why it is so important to you to see this baby?"

"You wouldn't understand."

"I gave birth to you. I am older than you know. I understand more than you think. Try me."

"It is not your concern."

"Fine. Then it is also not my concern to tell you where the child is. Let me speak to Ray."

Kalika speaks softly but there is tension in her words. "He's not here, I told you. I don't lie, Mother." She pauses. "But Eric is here."

I hear my heart pound. "What do you mean?"

"He's sitting on the couch beside me. He's still tied up

but he's not gagged. Would you like to speak to him?"

I feel as if I stand on melting ice in a freezing river that flows into a black sea. A mist rises before me and the next moments are played out in shadow. There is no way I can second-guess Kalika because all of her actions—when judged by humans or vampires alike—are inexplicable. Perhaps it was a mistake to snap at her.

"Put him on," I say.

There is a moment of fumbling. It sounds as if my daughter has momentarily covered the phone with her hand. Then the line is clear. Eric does not sound well.

"Hello?"

"Eric, it's me. Are you all right?"

He is breathing heavily, scared. "I don't know. She . . . This person says you have to tell her something or something bad will happen to me."

"Put her back on the line. Do it now!"

Another confused moment passes. But Eric remains on the line. "She doesn't want to talk to you. She says you have to tell me which hospital you're in. She says if you lie she will know it, and then something *really* bad will happen to me." Eric chokes with fear. "Could you tell her the name of the hospital? Please? This girl— She's so strong. She picked me up with one hand and carried me out here."

"Eric," I say, "try to convince her that I need to talk to her directly."

I hear Eric speaking to Kalika. But Eric is forced to stay on the line. I imagine his arms and legs still bound, Kalika holding the phone up to his ear. The tears in his eyes—I can see them in my mind, and I hear the many vows I swore to him.

"But I can promise you you're not going to die. I swear this to you, Eric, and I keep my word."

"You have to help me!" he cries. "She has long nails, and she says she's going to open the veins in my neck unless you tell her what hospital it is. Ouch! She's touching me!"

"Tell her the hospital is called St. Judes!"

"It's St. Judes!" he screams. Another soul-shattering pause. "She says you're lying! Oh God! Her nails!"

Sweat pours off my head. My heart is a jackhammer vibrating.

"Kalika!" I yell into the phone. "Talk to me!"

"She keeps shaking her head!" Eric weeps. "She's scratching my neck! Jesus help me!"

I fight to stay calm, and lose the fight. "Eric, shove the phone in her face!"

"Oh God, I'm bleeding! She's cut my neck! The blood is gushing out! Help me!"

"Eric, tell her I'll tell her the name of the hospital! Tell her!"

He begins to choke. "This can't be happening to me! I can't die! I don't want to die!"

Those are the last intelligible words he speaks. The rest—it goes on another two minutes—is slobbering sounds and pitiful weeping. It trails off into strangled gasps, then I must assume his heart has stopped beating. I sag against the wall of the hospital next to the place where the phone is attached. People stare at me from down the hall but I ignore them. Kalika lets me enjoy the silence. Another minute goes by before she returns to the phone.

"Then he should never have been born," she says calmly. "Is that what you wanted to tell him, Mother? Your famous quote."

I am in shock. "You," I whisper.

"I want to see the baby, Mother," she repeats.

"No."

"What is the name of the hospital? Where is it located?"

"I would never tell you!" I cry. "You're a monster!"

It is as if she smiles. I hear her unspoken mirth, somehow. Yet her voice remains flat. "And what are you? What did Krishna say to you about vampires in Kali Yuga?"

I can only assume Ray explained my dialogue with Krishna to Kalika. It doesn't matter—I am not in the mood for philosophical discussions. There is an aching void inside me that I had always believed a daughter would fill. Well, the irony is bitter, for the real Kali has always been described as the abyss, and now the void inside me feels as if it stretches forever. Eric's death screams continue to reverberate inside my skull.

"I am human now," I whisper. "I don't kill unless I have to."

"The same with me. This baby—you don't understand how I feel about it."

"How *you* feel about it? You have no feelings, Daughter."

"I will not argue. I will not repeat my questions. Answer now or you will regret it."

"I will never answer to you again."

Kalika doesn't hesitate. "There is someone else here I want you to speak with. He also sits on the couch beside me. But I have gagged him. Just a moment and I will remove his gag."

Oh no, I cringe. My demon child.

Seymour comes on the line. He strains to sound upbeat.

"Sita. What's happening?"

My voice is filled with agony. "What are you doing there?"

"Your daughter called me six hours ago. She said she needed to speak to me. I think Ray gave her my number. You remember Ray and I used to be friends when we were both normal high school kids? I caught the first plane down. Your daughter met me at the airport." He hesitates and probably glances at Eric's body. "She seemed really friendly at first."

"I told you not to come. I told you it was dangerous."

"Yeah, but I was worried about you."

"I understand. Is Ray there?"

"I haven't seen him." Seymour coughs and I hear his fear. There is talking in the background. "Your daughter says you're to tell me the name of the hospital where you are."

"Or something bad will happen to you?"

"She didn't say that exactly, but I think it would be safe to bet that will be the case." He pauses. "She seems to know when you're lying."

"She knows an awful lot." Yet Kalika is unable to "tune into" where I am. I find that curious, what with her incredible psychic abilities. "Tell her I want to talk to her."

I catch snatches of more mumbled conversation. Seymour remains on the line. "She says you are to tell me the name and location of the hospital." Seymour stops, and a note of desperation enters his voice. "What she did to Eric—you'd have to have been here. She made the old you look like a Girl Scout."

"I can imagine." I think frantically. "Tell her I'll make her a counter proposal. I'll bring the child to her in exactly twenty-four hours. At the end of the Santa Monica Pier at ten tomorrow night. Tell her if she so much as scratches you, she'll never see this baby, if she searches the entire globe."

Seymour relays my offer. Kalika appears to listen patiently. Then the phone is covered and I imagine my daughter is talking to Seymour. A minute goes by. Finally Seymour returns.

"She wants to know why you need twenty-four hours?"

"Because the baby has to remain in an incubator for a day. Tell her that's normal hospital procedure."

Seymour repeats what I say. He doesn't cover the phone this time but I still can't hear Kalika speak—her voice is too soft. I tire of this game. But there is a reason why my daughter doesn't let me talk to her directly at critical times. It heightens my helplessness, and her strategy says a lot about how her mind works. She is a master manipulator. I have as much hope for the two missing police officers as I do for Eric. Seymour finally relays her latest message.

"She says you are lying about the incubator but she doesn't care," he says. "As long as you bring the baby, she will wait to meet you."

"She has to bring you as well," I say. "Alive."

Seymour acts cheerful. "I made that a condition of the bargain."

"Does she know where the Santa Monica Pier is?"

"We both know where it is, in Santa Monica."

I try to sound optimistic. "Hang loose, Seymour. I'll get you out of this mess somehow."

He pauses. "Do what you have to, Sita."

Kalika must have taken the phone from him. It goes dead.

SIXTEEN

Midnight has arrived, the witching hour. I stand in a clean hallway and stare through the glass at the newborn babies in their incubators. There are six—they all look so innocent, especially Paula's. A pediatric nurse busies herself with the infants, checking their temperatures and heartbeats, drawing blood. She sees me peering through the glass, and I must look like a sight because she comes to the door and asks if I'm all right. I shuffle over to her.

"Yeah, I was just wanting to hold my friend's baby again. Before I leave the hospital." I add, "I'm not sure when I'll be able to come back."

The nurse is sweet. "I saw you earlier with the mother. Put on a gown and mask and you can hold him. I'll get you the stuff. Which one is he?"

"Number seven."

"He doesn't have a name?"

"Not yet."

Soon I am dressed appropriately and I am led into the newborns. I watch as the nurse draws blood from Paula's baby and places the vial in a plastic rack, with the other vials. *Ramirez* is all she writes on the white label. The nurse hands me number seven to hold.

"He's so beautiful," she says.

"Yeah. He takes after his mother."

It is good to hold the baby after the shock I have been through. Somehow the nearness of the child soothes me. I stare into his lovely blue eyes and laugh when he seems to smile at me. He is full of life; he kicks the whole time, tries to reach up and touch me with his tiny hands. It is almost as if I am his mother, I treasure him so.

"Why couldn't this have been my child?" I whisper.

Of course I had prayed for a daughter.

Ten minutes later, when the nurse is prepared to leave, she says I can take the baby to Paula's room if I want. The nurse has her back to me as she speaks.

"I'll do that," I say.

"I'll come check the child again in an hour," she says, working with the last baby on her rotation. I turn toward the door.

"I'll tell Paula," I say.

Then I stop and stare at the vials of blood. Warm red

blood—it has been the center of my life for five thousand years. Perhaps that is why I halt. I want to be near it, to smell it, to enjoy its dark color. Yet a part of me has doubts. There is *something* about this blood in particular—number seven's—that draws me. It is almost as if the red liquid hypnotizes me. Hardly thinking, I remove the vial from its plastic rack and slip it into my pocket. The nurse doesn't look over.

I take the baby to Paula.

She is sitting up and praying when I enter, a rosary in her hands. Standing silently at the door, I watch her for a full minute. There is something about how she focuses as she prays. She projects an intensity and at the same time an ease that baffles me. She hardly speaks above a whisper but it is as if her words fill the room. "Our Father, who art in heaven . . ."

"Hello," I say finally. "I brought you a present."

Paula is pleased. But she only smiles as I hand her the child. The boy is wise—he immediately searches for and finds her right nipple. I sit by Paula's bed in the dim room. The window is open, we are high up. The city lights spread out beneath us like a haze of jewels and dust. Seymour never leaves my thoughts, nor does Eric. I have twenty-two hours left to do the impossible.

"How do you feel?" I ask.

"Wonderful. I'm hardly sore at all. Isn't he adorable?"

"If he was any more adorable we would do nothing else but stand around and admire him."

"Thank you for staying with me."

"Are you still mad that I brought you here?"

Paula is puzzled. "I like this hospital, but why did you bring me here?"

I lean forward. "I'd like to answer that question honestly because I lied to you before, and I think you know it. I'll tell you in a few minutes. But before I do, may I ask about this child's father?"

Paula appears troubled. "Why do you ask?"

"Because of your precise reaction right now. The day I met you, you reacted in the same way when I asked about the father." I pause. "I really would like to hear how you got pregnant."

Paula tries to brush me off. "Oh, I think it was in the usual way."

"Was it?"

Paula studies me. Even though she is feeding her baby, her gaze is shrewd. It is ironic that she pays me precisely the same compliment.

"You're perceptive, Alisa," she says. "I noticed that the day we met. You miss nothing. Have you always been this way?"

"For a long time."

Paula sighs and looks out the window at the city lights. "This is called the City of Angels. It would take an angel to believe what I have to say next. The priest at St. Andrews didn't believe me. I told him my whole story one day, in confession. He ordered me to do ten Hail Marys." She adds, "That's a huge penance."

"It must be a great story."

Paula shakes her head. "It's a confusing story. I hardly know where to begin."

"At the beginning. That's always easiest."

Paula continues to stare out the window, while her child suckles her breast. "I grew up in an orphanage—I told you that—and was alone most of my life, even when I was surrounded by people. I purposely lived in my own world because my whole environment seemed harsh to me. But I wasn't what you would call unhappy. I often experienced moments of unusual joy and happiness. I could see a flower or a butterfly, or even just a tree, and become joyful. Sometimes the joy would become so strong I would swoon. A few times I lost track of where I was, what I was doing. When that happened I was taken to the doctor by the woman who ran my orphanage. They did all kinds of tests and I was given a grim diagnosis."

"Epilepsy," I say.

Paula is surprised. "How did you know?"

I shrug. "Saint Paul and Joan of Arc have since been diagnosed as epileptic because they had visions and heard voices. It's the current fad diagnosis for mystics—past and present. I'm sorry, please continue."

"I didn't know that. I just knew that at the moments I was most alive, I had trouble maintaining normal consciousness. But when I swooned it wasn't like I passed out. The opposite— I felt as if I was transported to a vast realm of beauty and light.

Only it was all inside me. I couldn't share it with anyone. These experiences went on throughout my childhood and teens. They invoked in me a sense of . . . This is hard to explain."

"When you swooned you felt close to God," I say.

"Yes, exactly. I felt a sacred presence. And I found, as I got older, that if I prayed for long periods the trances would come over me. But I didn't pray for them to happen. I prayed because I wanted to pray. I wanted to think of God, nothing else. It was the only thing that completely satisfied me." She paused. "Does that sound silly?"

"No. I often think of God. Go on."

"It gets bizarre now. You have to forgive me ahead of time." She pauses. "I love the desert. I love to drive deep into it all by myself. Especially Joshua National Park—I love those tall trees. They stand out there in the middle of nowhere like guards, their arms up, so patient. I feel like they're protecting the rest of us somehow. Anyway I was out there nine months ago, by myself, near sunset. I was sitting on a bluff watching the sun go down and it was incredibly beautiful—the colors, the clouds shot through with red and orange and purple. It looked like a rainbow made out of sand and sun. The air was so silent I thought I could hear an ant walking. I had been there all day and as soon as it was dark I was going to head back to town. But as the sun vanished beneath the horizon I lost track of time, as I had done often before."

"But this time was different?" I ask.

"Yes. It was as if I just blinked and then it became pitch-black. The sky was filled with a million stars. They were so bright! I could have been in outer space. I can't exaggerate this—they were so bright they weren't normal. It was almost as if I had been transported to another world, inside a huge star cluster, and was looking up at its nighttime sky."

"You were completely awake all this time?"

"Yes. I was happy but I hadn't lost awareness of my surroundings. I could still see the Joshua trees."

"But you had lost awareness of a big chunk of time?"

"It was more like the time lost me. Anyway, something else started to happen. While I marveled over the stars, the blue one directly above me began to glow extremely bright. It was as if it were moving closer to the earth, toward me, and I felt afraid. It got so bright I was blinded. I had to close my eyes. But I could still feel it coming. I could feel its heat. It was roasting me alive!"

"Were you in pain?"

Paula struggled for words. "I was overwhelmed, is a better way to put it. A high-pitched sound started to vibrate the area. Remember, I had my eyes closed but I could still see the light and knew that it was growing more intense. The rays of the star pierced my eyelids. The sound pierced my ears. I wanted to scream—maybe I was screaming. But I don't think I was in actual physical pain. It was more as if I were being transformed."

"Transformed? Into what?"

"I don't know. That's just the impression I had at the time. That somehow this light and heat and sound were changing me."

"What happened next?"

"I blacked out."

"That's it?"

"There's more. The next thing I knew it was morning and I was lying on the bluff with the sun shining in my eyes. My whole body ached and I was incredibly thirsty. Also, my exposed skin was slightly red, as if I had been burned." She stopped.

"What is it?"

"You won't believe this."

"I'll believe anything if I believe what you just told me. Tell me."

Paula glanced at me. "Do you believe me?"

"Yes. But tell me what you wanted to say."

"The Joshua trees around me—they were all taller."

"Are you sure?"

"Quite sure. Some were twice the size they had been the evening before."

"Interesting. Could you take me to this spot someday?"

"Sure. But I haven't been back to it since."

"Why not?" I ask, although I know why.

Paula takes a deep breath and looks down at her son. "Because six weeks after this happened I learned I was pregnant." She chuckled to herself. "Pretty weird, huh?"

"Only if you weren't having sex with someone at the time."

"I wasn't."

"Are you a virgin?" I ask.

"No. But I didn't have a boyfriend at that time. Not even around that time. You must think I'm mad."

"I don't know," I say. "A few times in my life aliens have swooped down and tried to get me to go to bed with them."

"I didn't see a flying saucer," Paula says quickly.

"I was joking. I know you didn't." I am thoughtful. "Did you have any other unusual symptoms after this incident? Besides being pregnant?"

Paula considers. "I've had colorful dreams for the past few months. They're strong—they wake me up."

"What are they about?"

"I can never remember them clearly. But there are always stars in them. Beautiful blue stars, like the ones I saw out in the desert."

I think of the dreams I've had of Krishna.

"What do you think this all means?" I ask.

She is shy. "I haven't the faintest idea."

"You must have a theory?" I ask.

"No. None."

"Do you think you were raped while you lay unconscious in the desert?"

Paula considers. "That would be the logical explanation. But even though I was sore when I woke up, I wasn't sore down there."

"But is it possible you were raped?"

"Yes. I was out cold. Anything could have happened to me during that time."

"Were your clothes disturbed in any way?"

"They were— They felt different on me."

"What do you mean?"

Paula hesitates. "My belt felt tighter."

"Like it had been removed, and then put back on, only a notch tighter?"

Paula lowers her head. "Yes. But I honestly don't think I was raped."

"Do you think you had an epileptic attack?"

"No. I don't think I have epilepsy. I don't believe that diagnosis anymore."

"But you believe Joshua trees stand guard over us? Like angels?"

She smiles. "Yeah. I am a born believer."

Her smile is so kind, so gentle. It reminds me of Radha's, Krishna's friend. I make my decision right then. Leaning forward and speaking seriously, I make Paula jump by the change in my tone.

"I have some bad news for you, Paula. I want you to brace yourself and I want you to listen to me with as open a mind as I have listened to you. Can you do this?"

"Sure. What's wrong?"

"There are two people I know who—for reasons I do not fully understand yet—want your baby."

Paula is stunned. "What do they want it for?"

"I don't know. But I do know that one of these people—the young woman—is a killer." My eyes burn and I have trouble keeping my voice steady. "She killed a friend of mine two hours ago."

"Alisa! This can't be true. Who is this woman?"

I shake my head. "She is someone so powerful, so brilliant, so cruel—that there is no point in going to the police and explaining what happened."

"But you have to go to the police. If a murder has been committed, they must be told."

"The police cannot stop her. I cannot stop her. She wants your baby. She is looking for him now and when she comes here for him you won't be able to stop her." I pause. "You are my friend, Paula. We haven't known each other long but I believe friendship is not based on time. I think you know I'm your friend and that I would do anything for you."

Paula nods. "I know that."

"Then you must do something for me now. You must leave this hospital tonight, with your son. I have money, lots of money I can give you. You must go to a place far from here, and not even tell *me* where it is."

I am talking too fast for Paula. "Is this the reason you took me to this hospital?"

"Yes. They thought you were going to the local one. But they know you've given birth to a baby somewhere in this city. They're clever—they'll check all the hospitals in the city to see where you're registered. Eventually they'll locate you."

"You spoke of a young woman. Who is the other person?"

I am stricken with grief. "My boyfriend."

"Ray?"

"Yes. But he's not the Ray I once knew." I lower my head. "I can't talk about him now. It is the girl who's the danger— she's only twenty. Her name is Kalika. Please believe me when I tell you there is literally no one who can stop her when she sets her mind on something."

"But how can she be so powerful?" Paula protests.

I stare at her. "She was just born that way. You see, she wasn't born under normal circumstances. Like your son, there's a mystery surrounding her birth, her conception even."

"Tell me about it."

"I can't. You wouldn't believe me if I did."

"But I would. You believed me."

"Only because I have gone through strange times in my life. But Kalika transcends anything I've ever encountered. Her psyche *burns* through all obstacles. She could be on her way here now. I swear to you, if she gets here before you get away, your child will die."

Paula doesn't protest. She is strangely silent. "I was warned," she says.

It is my turn to be stunned. "Who warned you?"

"It came in a dream."

"But you said you didn't remember any of your dreams."

"I remember this one. I was standing on a wide field and this old man with white hair and a crooked grin walked up to me and said something that didn't make sense. Until right now."

"What was it?" I ask.

"He said, 'Herod was an evil king who didn't get what he wanted. But he knew where the danger lay.' Then the old man paused and asked me, 'Do you know where the danger lies, Paula?'" She stops and looks once more at her child, we both look at him. "It was an odd dream."

"Yes." My heart is heavy with anxiety. "Will you leave?"

Paula nods. "Yes. I trust you. But why can't I tell you where I'm going?"

"This girl, this Kalika—I fear she could rip the information from my mind."

Paula cringes. "But I must have a way to get hold of you."

"I will give you a special number. You call it a month from now and leave your name and number. But don't tell me where you are. Wait until you talk to me—until you are certain it is me—to tell me that. That is very important."

Paula is worried for me. "Are you in danger?"

I lean back and momentarily close my eyes. My greatest task is still before me and I am exhausted. If only I had my old powers. *If*—the most annoying word in the English language.

But what if I was powerful again?

Powerful as a vampire?

Seymour would not have to die, nor would I.

But my daughter would die. Perhaps.

"Don't worry, I have a protector," I tell Paula. "This wonderful man I once met—he promised to protect me if I did what he said. And he was someone capable of keeping his promises."

Of course I don't tell her that I have disobeyed Krishna many times.

SEVENTEEN

*A*rturo's alchemy of transformation works by having the substance of what one wishes to become vibrate at a high level in one's aura. To become human, I took Seymour's blood and placed it—above my head—in a clear vial the sun shone through while I lay on a copper plate surrounded by specially arranged magnets and crystals. Only Arturo knew how to use these tools fully. The New Age is still centuries behind his knowledge. The proponents of New Age mysticism hold quartz crystals or amethysts and relax some, but Arturo could use these minerals to attain enlightenment, or even immortality. His only weakness was that he strove for immortality with a vampire for a girlfriend. He was a priest and erroneously thought I could give him the equivalent of the blood of Jesus. His blasphemy was his sin, and his eventual ruin. He tried to use me, betrayed me. But he is dead now and I mourn him.

To become a vampire again, I need a source of vampire blood.

I lied to Seymour, naturally. There is one possible source—Yaksha. Yet I have sunk Yaksha's body in the sea and will never be able to locate it, not without the powers of a vampire. Still, there is one other possible source of his blood, besides that in his body. Eddie Fender kept Yaksha captive in an ice-cream truck for several weeks, kept him cold and weak. It was from this very ice-cream truck that I eventually rescued Yaksha, who had no legs and hardly any lower torso. He bled in that truck and his blood must still be there, frozen and preserved.

But that truck was parked on the street in the vicinity of a warehouse I burned down to kill Eddie and his crew of vampires. That was approximately two months ago. The chances that the truck will still be there are slim. The police will almost certainly have confiscated it, towed it off to some forsaken lot. Yet I hurry to the dirty street in the poor part of town on the off chance that I can uncover a bloody Popsicle. Desperate people do desperate things.

And the ice truck is still there. Wow.

A homeless man with white hair and a grimy face sits in his rags near the driver's door. He has a shopping cart loaded with aluminum cans and blankets that look as if they were woven during the Depression. He is thin and bent but he looks up at me with bright eyes as I approach. He sits on the curb, nursing a small carton of milk. I immediately reach for my money. It is his lucky night. I will give him a hundred and tell him to hit the road. But something in his voice gives me reason to pause. His greeting is peculiar.

"You look very nice tonight," he says. "But I know you're in a hurry."

I stand above him and glance around. There is no one visible, but it is the middle of the night and this ghetto is a wonderful place to get raped or killed. Last time I was here I had to rough up a couple of cops. They thought I was a hooker, and one of them wanted to arrest me. I study the homeless man.

"How do you know I'm in a hurry?" I ask.

He grins and his smile is much brighter than I would have anticipated. Bright like his eyes even though he is covered in dirt.

"I know a few things," he says. "You want this truck I suppose. I've been guarding it for you."

I laugh softly. "I appreciate that. I have a horrible craving for an ice-cream bar right now."

He nods. "The refrigerator unit still works. I've kept it serviced."

I'm impressed. "You're handy with tools?"

"I have fixed a thing or two in my day." He offers me his hand. "Please help me up. My bones are old and sore, and I have been waiting here for you for such a long time."

I help him—I don't mind a little dirt. "How long have you been here?"

He brushes himself off, but ends up making a worse mess of his torn clothes. He blinks at my question as if I have confused him, although he does not smell of alcohol. He finishes his carton of milk and sets the empty container in his shopping cart.

"I don't rightly know," he says finally. "I think I've been here since you were last here."

I pause, feeling an odd sensation coursing through my body. But I dismiss it. I have too much on my mind to waste precious minutes with an old man in the middle of the night.

"I haven't been here in a couple of months," I say, reaching in my pocket. "Look, can I give you . . ."

"Then I must have been here that long," he interrupts. "I knew you'd come back."

I stop with my hand wrapped around a few twenties. "I don't know what you're talking about," I say quietly.

He grins a crooked grin. "I don't need your money." He turns and shuffles up the street. "You do what you have to do. No one can blame you for not trying hard."

I stare at him as he fades into the night.

Such a strange old guy. He left his shopping cart behind.

I wonder what his name was.

The rear compartment of the truck is locked, but I break it with a loose brick. Actually, I could have sworn that I broke the lock the last time I entered it. The interior is ice cold as I squeeze inside, a flashlight in my hand.

Just inside the door is a puddle of frozen blood.

I slip a nail under it and pull up the whole red wafer at once. Shining my flashlight through the frosted glass, I feel a surge of tremendous power. I hold in my hands immortality, and I feel as if Krishna saved this blood just so I'd find it. Back in my own car, I break the ice into small pieces and let them melt in a stainless-steel thermos.

Now I must return to Las Vegas. If it were not the middle of the night, I would fly, but driving it will have to be—at least four hours of pushing the speed limit. Also, I have to worry that Arturo's house is being watched by government agents. From reading the papers, I know the dust has not settled from the nuclear explosion in the desert. They must think I am dead, but will not assume that I am. There is an important difference.

The rays of the sun will power my transformation. What is crucial is that I have most of the day to complete the transformation back to becoming a vampire, if it is possible. There is a chance I will end up like Ralphe, a bloodthirsty ghoul. But I have no choice except to risk the alchemist's ancient experiment. To give up my hard-sought humanity will be bitter, yet I have to admit a part of me craves my old power. It will be nice to confront my daughter one on one and not tremble in my shoes.

Yet I intend to tremble, especially if I am a vampire.

She will not know until too late who it is she faces.

EIGHTEEN

The drive to Las Vegas is more pleasant than I anticipated. There is something about roaring along a
dark empty road that relaxes me. Keeping an eye
out for police, I set the cruise control at an even eighty. It seems
only a short while before the horizon begins to glow with the
polluted lake of colored neon that is the gambling capital of
the world. I will roll the red dice today, I think, and pray for
a successful combination of DNA. The eastern sky is already
warm with light. The sun will rise soon.

I park a block down the street from Arturo's house and scan
the area for FBI agents, cops, or army personnel. But the place
appears quiet, forgotten in the fallout of the incinerated army
base. Slipping over Arturo's back fence, I am through an open
window and into the house in less than a minute. An eight-
and-a-half-by-eleven photograph stands in a cheap frame on the

kitchen table—Arturo and me, taken one night while we were out on the Strip together. When I believed he was a down-on-his-luck government employee and he thought I was a sucker. The picture gives me reason to pause. I pick it up and study Arturo's features. They remind me so much of someone I know.

"You are Kalika's father," I whisper, stunned.

Everything makes sense in an instant. Vampires are sterile, with one another, with human partners. But Arturo was neither a vampire nor a human. He was a hybrid, forged in the Middle Ages, a combination of the two, and I slept with him in a Las Vegas hotel room just before he betrayed me to the government. I was pregnant from before the transformation. In other words, I was still a vampire when Kalika was conceived. Yet she is partially human, and that no doubt explains her lack of sensitivity to the sun. She is the result of a queer toss of the genetic dice, and perhaps that's what it took for a soul of her dark origin to incarnate on earth.

And I assumed Ray was her father.

I'm aware of him at my back even before he speaks.

"I'm surprised you didn't guess earlier," he says.

I turn, still holding the photograph. Ray remains hidden in the shadows, appropriately enough. It is not just Kalika's birth that I suddenly understand. But my new insights, which are not entirely clear to me yet, are ill-defined ghosts that refuse to enter the living body of logical reason. Despair and denial engulf me. I feel as if I stand in a steaming graveyard with a tombstone at my back. The death date of the corpse is carved in the future, the name scribbled in blood that will never dry. I know the truth but refuse to look at it.

And there is a mirror on this tombstone.

Covered with a faint film of black dust.

"You could have told me," I say.

"I could only tell you what you wanted to hear."

The weakness of grief spreads through my limbs. Ray has become a travesty to me, someone I cannot bear to look at, yet I don't want him to go away. He is all I have left. The graveyard in my mind is littered with hidden mines. I fear that if I move or speak to him, one might explode and toss a skeleton in my lap.

"How did you get here?" I ask.

"You brought me here."

"Does Kalika know I'm here?"

"I don't think so. But she might."

"You didn't tell her?"

"No."

Putting down the photograph, I take a moment to collect myself. My imagined graveyard falls away beneath me as the tombstone collapses. Yet I am forced to remain standing in this house where Arturo once lived.

"Can I ask you a question?" I say finally.

He remains in the shadows. "Don't ask anything you don't want answered."

"But I do want answers."

He shakes his head. "Few really want the complete truth. It doesn't matter if you're a vampire or a human. The truth is overrated, and too often painful." He adds, "Let it be, Sita."

There is emotion in my voice. "I need to know just one thing."

"No," he warns me. "Don't do this to yourself."

"Just one little thing. I understand how you found me in Las Vegas. You explained that and it made sense to me, but you never explained how you picked up my trail again in Los Angeles. While I was driving here, you should have been in the basement in this house, changing back into a human."

"It was dark that night," he says.

His answer confuses me. "It's dark every night."

"It would have been dark in the basement."

The confusion passes. "You need the sun to power the alchemy."

"Yes."

"You must still be a vampire?"

"No."

"You must have followed us to L.A.?"

"No."

"Who are you? What did Eddie's blood do to you?"

"Nothing. Eddie's blood never touched me."

"But you said—"

"I lied," he interrupts. "You asked me to lie to you. You do not want the truth. You swear to yourself that you do but you swear at the altar of false gods. Let it be, Sita. We can leave this place together. It can be as it once was between us, if you will just let it. It is all up to you."

"You are not ready to hear."

"When will I be ready to hear?"

"Soon."

"You know this?"

"I know many things, Mother."

"Why is it all up to me?" I ask. "You're as responsible for what happened to us as I am."

"No."

"Stop saying no! Stop saying yes! Explain yourself!"

He is a long time answering. "What do you want me to say?"

I place my hands on the sides of my head. "Just tell me who you are. Why you are not like the old Ray. How you found me in the coffee shop." I feel so weak. "Why you knocked at my door."

"When did I knock at your door?"

"Here." I point. "You knocked at that door right there. You said it was you."

"When did I knock at your door?" he repeats.

Of course I have not answered his question. He is asking about time, and I am talking about place. I have to force my next words into the air where they can be heard and understood.

"You appeared right after I changed into a human," I say.

"Yes."

"You're saying that's a remarkable coincidence."

"I am saying you should stop now."

I nod to myself, speak to myself. "You are saying the two events are related; the transformation and your reappearance. That you only reentered my life because I had become human."

"Close."

I pause. "What am I missing?"

"Everything."

"But you just said I was close!"

"When you roll the dice, close does not count. You either win or you lose."

"What did I lose when you returned?"

"*What* is not important. *Why* is all that matters."

"*Now listen to my song. It dispels all illusions . . . When you feel lost remember me, and you will see that the things you desire most are the very things that bring you the greatest sorrow.*"

"I have always desired two things," I say, remembering the Lord's words. "For five thousand years I have desired them. They were the two things that were taken from me the night Yaksha came for me and made me a vampire. The night he stole my daughter and husband. I never saw either of them again."

Ray is sympathetic. "I know."

I hang my head and it is now me who stands in shadows.

"But when you came into my life I felt as if Rama had been returned to me. And when I became human and thought I was pregnant with your baby, I felt as if Krishna had returned Lalita to me." There is a tear on my face, maybe two, and I have to stop and take a deep breath. "But it didn't work that way. The things I craved so long were my greatest illusions. And they have brought me the greatest sorrow."

"Yes."

I lift my head and stare at him.

"They are not real," I say.

"Yes."

"As a vampire, I could see through my illusions, and that kept me going all these years, but as a human I couldn't see what was real and what wasn't. I was too weak."

"You create what you want. You always have. If you don't like it, you can always leave."

He speaks with gentle passion. "Don't say it, Sita."

But I have to. I feel as if I can see through him. Now I understand why he never went out. Why he never met my friends or spoke to anyone besides Kalika and me. Why I had to do everything with my own hands. Between us, they were the only pair of hands we had.

"You're not real," I say.

He steps out of the shadows. His face is so beautiful.

"It doesn't matter, Sita. We can pretend it doesn't matter. I don't want to leave you."

My body is a chalice of misery. "But you're dead," I moan.

He comes close enough to touch me. "It doesn't matter."

No tears fall from my face. Dry sobs rack my body. They are worse than moist tears, worse because they are the evidence of evaporated grief, and I have only these to show to this silhouette of a boyfriend who stands before me now. This lover who can only love me as I deem myself worthy. No wonder he turned against me when I turned against him. He is a mirror on the tombstone. The film of black dust clears, and I see in the mirror that I have slowly been burying myself since I first came up the stairs of this house and heard the knock at the front door.

Who is it? Your darling. Open the door.

"I can't keep this door open," I whisper.

He touches my lower lip. "Sita."

I turn my head away from his hand. "No. You must go back."

"To where?"

"To where you came from."

"That is the abyss. There is nothing there. I am not there."

A note of quiet hysteria enters my voice. "You're not here. You're worse than a ghost. No one can see you! How can I possibly love you?"

He grabs my hand. "But you feel me. You know I'm here."

I fight to shake free of his hand but I just end up gripping it tighter. Yet I do not press it to my heart, as I used to. His hand is cold.

"No," I say. "I know you're not here."

He lightly kisses my finger. "Do you feel that?"

"No."

"You lie."

"You are the lie! You don't exist! How can I make you cease to exist!"

My words wound him, finally—they seem to tear the very fabric of his existence. For a moment his face shimmers, then goes out of focus. Yet he draws in a sudden breath and his warm brown eyes lock on to my eyes. He is not merely a mirror, but a hologram from a dimension where there are more choices than time and space. He is the ultimate *maya*, the complete illusion. The perfect love dressed in my own grief. No wonder when I met him in the coffee shop he was wearing the clothes he died in. He is nothing but a memory shouted back down the tunnel all mortals pass through when they leave this world. Yes, Ray is dead but I have let him become my own death as well.

He seems to read my thoughts.

His hope fades. He answers my last question.

"I died a vampire," he says. "You must kill me the way you would kill a vampire." He grabs a knife from the nearby table and presses it into my hand. "My heart beats only for you."

He wants me to cut his heart out. I try to push him away,

but he holds me close. I can feel his breath on my face, like the brush of a winter wind. Yet now, here at the end, his eyes burn with a strange red light, the same light I have occasionally glimpsed in my daughter's eyes. He nods again as he reads my mind.

"If I return to the abyss," he says, "I'll see Kali there." He squeezes the handle of the knife into my palm. "Do it quick. You're right, the love is gone. I do want to die."

"I should never have been born," I whisper, addressing his last remark.

He manages a faint smile "Goodbye, Sita."

I stab him in the heart. I cut his flesh and his bones, and the blood gushes over my hands, onto my clothes, and over the floor. The black blood of the abyss, the empty space of Kali. But I scream as I kill him, scream to God for mercy, and the knife mysteriously falls from my hand and bounces on the dry floor. The blood evaporates.

His heart no longer beats and I'm no longer bloody.

He is gone, my ancient love is gone.

Out the window, the sun rises.

Taking Yaksha's blood, I pour it into the vial that once held Seymour's blood, the clear vial that I place above the copper and the crystals, between the cross-shaped magnets and the shiny mirror that reflects the rays of the sun directly into Arturo's hidden basement. I recline on the copper and the alchemy begins to work its dark magic on my trembling body.

I have to wonder exactly *what* I will be when the sun finally sets and the process is complete. On impulse I have added to the vial a few drops of blood from Paula's child. The blood of the infant that Kalika covets above all else.

I can only hope it does me good.

NINETEEN

Eight o'clock that evening I sit in the living room of Mr. and Mrs. Hawkins, in the very house Eric longed to return to until his throat was cut. Eric's parents are younger than I would have guessed. Mr. Hawkins can be no more than forty-two and I doubt his wife has reached forty. They must have married young and had Eric when they were barely out of their teens. He is stern faced, but it is a practiced expression, one he wears for his patients. But I see his intelligence and natural curiosity beneath it. She is plump and kindly, fussing with her hands as she constantly thinks of her son. She wears her heart on her face, her eyes are red from constant crying. Their address was in the phone book.

I just knocked at their door and told them I have information concerning their missing son. They invited me in because I am young and pretty and look as if I could harm no one.

They sit across from me and wait for me to speak. There is no easy way to say it.

"Your son is dead," I say. "He was murdered last night, I thought you would want to know rather than to be left wondering. Before I leave here, I'll give you the address where his body can be found. He's in a house not far from here." I pause. "I'm truly sorry to have to bring you this information. It must be a great shock to both of you."

Mrs. Hawkins bursts into gasping sobs and buries her face in her hands. Mr. Hawkins's nostrils flare with anger. "How do you know this?" he demands.

"As you look at me you must see that I match the description of the young woman who picked up Eric in the park. I am, in fact, that person. But I am not the one who killed your son. On the contrary, I fought hard to save him. I'm very sorry I failed. Eric was a sweet boy. I liked him quite a lot."

They are in turmoil, which is inevitable. "This can't be true," Mr. Hawkins stammers.

"It is true. You will verify that for yourself when you go to the house. But I would rather you sent the police ahead of you. Eric died from a serious throat wound." I add reluctantly, "Just before I came here I tried to clean up, but there is still a lot of blood."

Mrs. Hawkins continues to sob. Mr. Hawkins leans forward in his chair, his skin flushed with blood, his face quivering with fury. "Who are you?" he asks.

"My name is not important. It's true I kidnapped your son but I meant him no harm. I do understand that you won't believe me. That you must hate me. If the situation were reversed I would probably hate you. But I can give you nothing to identify me with, and after I leave here, you will never see me again. The police will never find me."

Mr. Hawkins snorts. "You're not leaving this house, young lady. I'm calling the police as soon as I'm through with you."

"You should call the police. I've written down the address you need on a piece of paper." I take the scrap and hand it to him. He frowns as he glances at the slip. I continue, "I can give you directions to the house, but I must warn you two police officers who were there yesterday were also killed. Or rather, I must assume they were killed because they went off with the same person who killed your son and they didn't come back."

I add this last remark because I'm puzzled that no one has been to the house searching for them. When I stopped by half an hour earlier, looking for Kalika and Seymour, I could find no sign that the place had been examined by the authorities. Especially since Eric was still lying on the couch in all his gore. It was not pleasant trying to clean him up. He looked as if he had died in agony, which, of course, he had.

"You are talking a bunch of trash," Mr. Hawkins snaps.

"I am telling you the truth," I reply simply.

Mrs. Hawkins finally comes up for air. "Why did this person kill my boy?"

"To try to force me to reveal the whereabouts of a newborn baby. The person who murdered your son is obsessed with this child. She would do anything to get to him. But I refused to give her the information she needed, so Eric was killed." I pause. "None of these facts are important to you. None of them will make any sense to you. But I do want you to know that when I leave this house, I am going to meet with this young woman, and I am going to do everything in my power to stop her. I know you'll want revenge for what has happened to your son, or at the very least justice. I will try to give you both tonight, and keep this person from murdering again." I stand suddenly. "Now I have to go."

"You're not going anywhere!" Mr. Hawkins shouts as he tries to rise. But before his bottom can leave the chair, I effortlessly hold him down with one hand. My strength startles him.

"Please," I say gently. "You can't keep me here. It's not possible. And you won't be able to follow me. Just know that your son was brave and that forces beyond our control conspired to end his life before it should have ended. Try to understand his death as an act of God's will. I try to see it that way."

I leave them then quickly. They hardly have a chance to react, and later they will both wonder if my visit was a dream. But I know they will go straight to the house after they call the police. I know they will see their dead son before anyone else does. They loved him, and they should be the ones to close his eyes.

My car is around the block. Soon I am in it and driving for the ocean. There is an appointment I have with destiny and my daughter. I don't know which I trust less.

TWENTY

The transformation has worked and I am indeed a vampire again. Yet I am different, in a variety of ways, from what I was before. It was largely Yaksha's blood that filtered the sun's rays into my aura, and no doubt that is the main reason for the great increase in my strength. If I could jump fifty feet in the air before, I can leap a hundred now. If I could hear a leaf break and fall a mile away, now I can hear an ant crawl from its hole at twice that distance. My sense of smell is a wonder; the night air is an encyclopedia of fragrant information to me. And my eyes are like lasers. Not only can I see much farther than before, I feel the fire in my gaze, and I seriously doubt if even Kalika can withstand the power of it.

Yet these refinements are not confined to strength and power. There is something else that has entered my life, something that I have never known before. I don't even have a word for it. I just feel—lucky, as if good fortune will smile on me. A white star seems to shine over my head, or maybe it is blue. I have to wonder if this is the effect of what I added to Yaksha's blood.

I am confident as I race toward the pier.

Santa Monica Beach, by the pier, is deserted as I drive up. I find that fact curious; it is, after all, only ten in the evening. The night is cold, true, but I have to wonder if there is another force at work. It is almost as if a psychic cloud hangs over the area, a fog of *maya* wrapped in astral matter. I clearly sense the force and my confidence wavers. For only my daughter could create it, and it is like nothing I have ever seen before. It seems to suck up life itself, which is why people have shunned the place. As I park my car down the block from the pier, I see not a soul. They may all be in their homes, trying to explain to their children that nightmares are not real. I myself feel as if I'm moving through a dream. My newly regained powers are physically exhilarating, but my dread of confronting Kalika is a heavy burden.

I see them, the two of them, at the end of the pier.

Seymour is looking out to sea. Kalika is nearby, in a long white dress, feeding the birds crumbs of bread. I am a half mile distant yet I see their every feature. Seymour pretends to be enjoying the view but he keeps glancing at Kalika. The muscles in his neck are tight; he is scared. Yet he appears unhurt and I am grateful for that.

Kalika is a mystery. There is an almost full moon, which shines through her long black hair like silver dust blowing on a black wind. As she feeds the birds, she is fully focused on them as if nothing else has greater meaning to her. This is a quality I have noticed in Kalika before. When she is doing something, nothing else occupies her mind. No doubt when she opened Eric's throat she was with him a hundred percent. It is a sobering thought given the fact that she has a hostage beside her. Kali and her string of skulls. Will my daughter have three fresh ones to add to her necklace before the night is over?

I think of Paula, who caught a cab from the hospital. Running out into the night with twenty thousand dollars in cash and a beautiful baby boy wrapped in a hospital receiving blanket. All because a new friend told her she was in danger. Then again, she had her dreams to warn her. Odd how the old man she described in her dream looked like the guy who was guarding the ice-cream truck.

"You look very nice tonight. But I know you're in a hurry."

Who was that guy?

It is a mystery that will have to be solved another time.

I make no effort to hide my approach. I know it would be useless to do so. Nevertheless I move as a human moves. My steps are tentative, my breathing tight. The muscles of my face are pinched with anxiety and my shoulders are slumped forward in defeat. Yet my performance goes unheeded as Kalika continues to feed the birds and doesn't glance up until I am practically on top of them. I pause twenty feet short of the end of the pier. By this time Seymour is looking at me with a mixture of hope and terror. He cannot help but notice I don't have the child with me. The sight of Eric's spurting arteries must have dug deep into his brain. He has little of his usual confidence, although he struggles to make up for it. He forces a smile.

"I'm glad you're not late," he says, and gestures to the moon, which was full the previous night, when Paula's child was born. "Lovely evening, isn't it?"

"I am here," I say to Kalika. "Let him go."

She stares at me now, a handful of pigeons still pecking at the crumbs beside her sandaled feet. Her long white dress—I have never seen it before—is beautiful on her flawless figure, the silky material moving in the moonlit breeze, hugging her mature curves. The birds scatter as she brushes her hands and slowly rises.

"I did not think you would bring the child," she says calmly.

"But I came myself. Release Seymour."

"Why should I?"

"Because I am your mother and I'm requesting this. That should be reason enough."

"It's not."

"He's young. He should not be brought into our affairs."

At that Kalika smiles faintly. "I am young as well, Mother.

I should be forgiven any indiscretions I might have committed during my short life."

"Do you need my forgiveness?"

"I suppose not." There is one bird that continues to eat at her feet. Kalika bends back down, plucks it into her hands, and straightens. She strokes the pigeon's feathers and whispers something in its ear. Then she speaks to me. "You should know by now that it's not a good idea to lie to me."

"You force me to lie to you," I say. "Your complaint is absurd."

"Still, it's your habit. You have lied through the ages. You see nothing wrong in it."

"I would have told a million lies to have saved that boy's life." I add, "But you must know I hate to lie to those I love."

Kalika continues to stroke the bird. "Do you love me, Mother?"

"Yes."

She nods in approval. "The truth. Do you love Seymour?"

"Yes."

"Would you be upset if I ripped off his head?"

"I hope this is not a trick question," Seymour mutters.

"You must not hurt him," I say. "He's my friend, and he's done nothing to you. Let him go now and we can talk about the child."

Kalika is once again the master manipulator. She holds up the pigeon. "What about this bird? Should I let it go? Just let it fly away and complete this particular birth? You should know, *Old One,* that it doesn't matter if I do or if I don't. Whenever the bird dies, the bird will simply be reborn. It is the same with humans. If you kill one, it will in time be reincarnated in another body. Perhaps Eric and Billy will both be reborn in better conditions. Eric was not in the best shape when he died." She pauses and coos in the bird's ear again. "What do you think, Mother?"

There is something disturbing in her question, in her examples, besides the obvious. Maybe she is honestly trying to tell me something about her inner state, who she is, what she really is. It is said many times in the Vedas that whenever a demon dies in Krishna's hands, that demon gains instant liberation. But there are fewer books written about Kali's incarnation, her many exploits; and I am not yet ready to accept that my daughter is in fact the real Kali. Of course, I could ask her directly but the mere thought of doing so fills me with apprehension. Many things do: the way she holds the bird close to her mouth; her quick glances at Seymour; the steadiness of her gaze as she studies me, missing nothing. It is impossible to gauge what she will do next, and when she will do it. I try as best I can to answer her, trying to think what Krishna would say to her. Really, I am no saint; I cannot preach morality without sounding like a hypocrite.

"There is a meaning behind each life," I say. "A purpose. It doesn't matter if humans or birds live thousands of lives before they return to God. Each life is valued. Each time you take one, you incur bad karma."

"That is not so." She brushes the bird against the side of her face. "Karma does not touch me. Karma is for humans, and vampires."

She reproaches me, I realize, for being exactly what I tried not to be. "These last few centuries I have seldom killed without strong reason," I say.

"Eric and Billy died for a reason," she says.

"For what reason did Eric die?"

"To inspire you."

I am disgusted. "Do I look inspired?"

"Yes," she says. "But you did not answer my earlier question, about Seymour's head." She takes a dangerous step toward him. Seymour jumps and I don't blame him. But I catch his eye; I don't want him to make any more sudden moves. Kalika continues, "Would you be upset if I ripped it off?"

I have a choice to make and I must make it quickly. Before she can move any closer to Seymour, I can attack. If I leap forward, I can kick her in the nose and send her nasal cartilage into her brain and kill her. Seymour wouldn't even see my blow. Kalika would simply be dead. But I am still twenty feet from my daughter, not an ideal distance. She could react in time and deflect my blow. Then, before I could recover, Seymour would die.

I decided to wait. To be patient.

I wonder if my patience is grounded in my attachment to Kalika.

She is my daughter. How can I kill her?

"Yes," I say. "You know I would be upset."

Kalika squeezes the pigeon gently. "Would you be upset if I ripped this bird's head off?"

I am annoyed. "Why do you ask these silly questions?"

"To hear your answers."

"This sounds like a trick question," Seymour warns.

I hesitate. He's right. "If there is no reason to kill it, I would say you should leave it alone."

"Answer my question," she says.

"I would not be upset if you killed the bird."

Kalika rips the bird's head off. The tearing bone and tissue make a faint nauseating sound. Blood splashes over the front of my daughter's pretty white dress. Seymour almost faints. Casually, while still watching me, Kalika throws the remains of the bird over her shoulder and into the dark water below. It is only then I catch a glimmer of red light deep inside her pupils. The fire at the end of time, the Vedas call it. The smoky shadow of the final twilight. Kalika knows I see it for she smiles at me.

"You look upset, Mother," she says.

"You are cruel," I say. "Cruelness without rational thought is not far from insanity."

"I told you, I have my reasons." She wipes the blood on the

left side of her face. "Tell me where Paula Ramirez's child is."

I glance at Seymour. "I can't," I say.

"Damn," he whispers, and he's not being funny.

"Why do you assume I am going to harm this child?" she asks.

"Because of your previous erratic behavior," I reply.

"If I had not killed Billy, you would not be here tonight. If I had not killed Eric, you would also not be here tonight."

"I didn't need Eric's death to survive the last twenty-four hours."

Kalika teases without inflection. "Really?"

She may be hinting at the fact that I am now a vampire, that I would never have gone through with the transformation without the motivation Eric's horrible murder gave me. She would be right on that point, if it is what she is hinting at. But I continue to hope she thinks I'm helpless. I feel I must attack soon, favorable position or not. The bird's death has not increased my faith in her nonviolent nature. She waits for me to respond.

"I cannot trust you around Paula's baby," I say, taking a step closer. "Surely you must understand that." When she doesn't answer right away, I ask, "What did you do to the police?"

"I fulfilled their karma."

"That's no answer."

Kalika moves closer to Seymour, standing now five feet from his left side. He can't even look at her. Only at me, the creature who saved him from AIDS, who inspires his stories, his savior and his muse. His eyes beg me for a miracle.

"What if I promise you that I will not hurt the child," Kalika says. "Will you take me to him?"

"No. I can't."

She acts mildly surprised. But there is no real emotion in her voice or on her face. Human expressions are merely tools to her. I doubt she feels anything at all, while eating or reading, walking or killing.

"No?" Kalika says. "Have I ever lied to you before?" She moves her arms as if stretching them. Blood drips from her sharp fingernails. In a microsecond, I know, she can reach out and grab Seymour and then it will all be over. She adds, "I am your daughter, but I do not have your habit of lying."

"Kalika," I plead. "Be reasonable. You refuse to tell me why you want to see this child. I can only conclude that you intend to harm it." I pause. "Is that not true?"

"Your question is meaningless to me."

I take another step forward. She is now only twelve feet away, but I want to be closer still "What is so special about this child?" I ask. "You can at least tell me that."

"No."

"Why not?"

She is subtly amused. "It's forbidden."

"Oh, and killing innocent people isn't? Forbidden by whom?"

"You wouldn't understand." She pauses. "Where's Ray?"

I freeze in midstep. "He's gone."

She seems to understand. "He was forbidden." She glances at Seymour, smiles at him actually as a pretty girl might while flirting. But the words that come out of her mouth next are far from nice. They sound like a warning. She says, "Certain things, once broken, are better left unfixed."

The decision is made for me. Something in her tone tells me she is going to reach for Seymour and that his head will go over the railing as the bird's did—and with the same emotional impact on Kalika. I attack.

My reclaimed vampiric body is no stranger to me. I have not needed time to readapt to it. Indeed it feels almost more natural than it used to. But I definitely decide to stick with an old technique of killing—the nose into the brain thrust. It is straightforward and effective. My only trouble—as I tense my muscles to respond—is that I still love her.

Kalika begins to reach out with her right arm.

I leap up and forward. My lift off the ground is effortless. If I were taped and the video later slowed down for viewing, the human eye would assume that gravity had no effect on me. Of course this is not true—I cannot fly. Only strength is responsible for the illusion. I whip toward Kalika, my right foot the hammer of Thor. I cock it back—it will soon be over.

But somewhere in the air I hesitate. Just slightly.

Probably it makes no difference, but I will never know.

The red flames smolder deep in Kalika's eyes.

My divine hammer is forged of crude iron ore. My daughter grabs my foot before it can reach her face. Real time returns, and I begin a slow horizontal fall, helpless as she grips my foot tighter. Seymour cries in horror and my own cry is one of excruciating pain. She has twisted my ankle almost to the breaking point. I hit the asphalt with the flat of my back and the back of my skull. Kalika towers over me, still holding onto my boot. Her expression is surprisingly gentle.

"Does it hurt?" she asks.

I grimace. "Yes."

Kalika breaks my ankle. I hear the bones snap like kindling wood in a fire, and a wave of red agony slams up my leg and into my brain. As I writhe on the ground, she takes a step back and patiently watches me, never far from Seymour's side. She knows vampires. The pain is intense but it doesn't take long before I begin to heal. The effect of Yaksha's blood on my system no doubt speeds up the process. In two minutes I am able to stand and put weight on the ankle. But I will not be kicking her again in the next few minutes, and she knows it.

Kalika grabs Seymour by the left arm.

His mouth goes wide in shock.

"I will not ask you again what I want to know," she says.

I try to stand straight. Insolence enters my tone. "You know what bugs me most about you? You always hide behind a human shield. I'm here and you're there. Why don't we just settle this between us? That is, if you've got the guts, girl."

Kalika seems to approve of my challenge. She smiles and this particular smile seems genuine. But I'm not sure if it is good to push her into too happy a mood for she suddenly reaches over, picks Seymour up with one hand by grabbing his shirt, and throws him over the side of the pier. The move is so unexpected that I stand stunned for a second. I hurry to the railing in time to see Seymour strike the water. She threw him hard and high—he takes a long time to return to the surface. He coughs as he does so and flays about in the dark but he seems to be all right. I hope he is not like Joel who couldn't swim.

"Seymour!" I call.

He responds with something unintelligible, but sounds okay.

Kalika stands beside me. "He has a sense of humor," she says.

"Thank you for sparing him." The pier is long and the water is cold. I hope he is able to make it to shore. I add, "Thanks for giving him a chance."

"Gratitude means nothing to me," she says.

I am curious. "What does have meaning to you?"

"The essence of all things. The essence does not judge. It is not impressed by actions, nor does it reward inaction." She shrugs. "It just is, as I am."

"I can't tell you where the baby is. I deliberately told Paula not to tell me where she was going. They could be in Canada by now or in Mexico."

Kalika is not disturbed by my revelations. "I know there is

something you are not telling me. It relates to future contact with the child. You told Paula one other thing besides what you just said. What was it?"

"There was nothing else."

"You are lying," she says.

"So I lie? What are you going to do about it? I'm not going to tell you anything. And if you kill me you still won't get the information you want." I pause. "But I can't believe that even you would kill your own mother."

She reaches out and touches my long blond hair with her bloody hand. "You are beautiful, Sita. You have lived through an entire age. You have outsmarted men and women of all nationalities, in all countries and times. You even tricked your creator into releasing you from his vow to Krishna."

"I did not trick Yaksha. I saved him."

She continues to play with my hair. "As you say, Mother. You have faith in what you know and what you remember. But my memory is older, far older, and death or the threat of death is not the only means of persuasion I have at my disposal." She tugs lightly on my hair. "You must know by now that I am not simply a vampire."

"What are you then?"

She takes my chin in her hand. "Look into my eyes and you will see."

"No. Wait!"

"Look, Mother." She twists my head around and catches

my eyes. There is no question of my looking away. It is not an option. The blue-black of her eyes have the pull of a black hole, the grip of the primordial seed that gave birth to the universe. The power that emanates from them is cosmic. They shine with colors the spectrum has forgotten. Yet they are such beautiful eyes, really, those of an innocent girl, and I fall in love with them all over again. From far away I hear my daughter's voice, and it is the voice of thunder echoing and also the mere whisper of a baby falling asleep in my lap in the middle of the night. "Behold your child," she says.

I look; I must look.

There are planets, stars, galaxies, and they are seemingly endless. Yet beyond them all, beyond the backbone of the sky, as the Vedas say, is the funeral pyre. There sits Mother Kali with her Lord Kala, who destroys time itself. As each of the planets slowly dies and each sun gradually expands into a red dwarf, the flames that signal the end of creation begin to burn. They lick the frozen asteroids and melt the lost comets. And there in that absolute space Kali collects the ash of the dead creation and the skulls of forgotten souls. She saves them for another time, when the worlds will breathe again, and people will once again look up at the sky and wonder what lies beyond the stars. But none of these people will know that it was Kali who remembered them when they were ash. None of them will know who buried them when there was no one left to cover their graves. Even if they did remember, none of them would worship the great Kali because they would be too afraid of her.

I feel afraid as I remember her.

As she asks me to remember.

There is another voice in the sky.

I think it is my own. The shock breaks the vision.

I stumble back from my daughter. "You are Kali!" I gasp.

She just looks at me. "You have told me the phone number Paula will call in one month." She turns away. "That's all I wanted to know."

It is hard to throw off the power of the vision.

"Wait. Please? Kalika!"

She glances over her shoulder. "Yes, Mother?"

"Who was the child?"

"Do you really need to know?"

"Yes."

"The knowledge will cost you."

"I need to know!" I cry.

In response Kalika steps to the end of the pier. There she kneels and pulls a board free. It is an old board, long and narrow, but as she works it in her powerful fingers it begins to resemble something I know all too well from more superstitious eras. Too late I realize she has fashioned a stake. She raises the tiny spear over her head and lets fly with it.

The stake goes into the water.

Into Seymour's back. He cries out and sinks.

"No!" I scream.

Kalika stares at me a moment. "I told you it would cost you." She turns away. "I don't lie, Mother."

My ankle is not fully recovered but I am still a strong vampire. Leaping over the side of the pier, I hit the cold salt water not far from where Seymour flounders two feet below the surface. Pulling him up for air, I hear him gasp in pain. My eyes see as well in the dark as in the daylight. The stake has pierced his lower spine. The tip protrudes from where his belly button should be. His blood flows like water from a broken faucet.

"This hurts," he says.

"Seymour," I cry as I struggle to keep him afloat, "you have to stay with me. If I can get you to shore, I can save you."

He reaches for the stake and moans in pain. "Pull it out."

"No. You'll bleed to death in seconds. I can take it out only when we reach the beach. You must hold on to me so that I can swim as fast as possible. Listen to me, Seymour!"

But he is already going into shock. "Help me, Sita," he chokes.

"No!" I slap him. "Stay with me. I'll get you to shore." Then, wrapping my right arm around him, I begin to swim as fast as I can with one free arm and two boot-clad feet. But speed in the water is not Seymour's friend. As I kick toward the beach, the pressure of the passing water on the stake makes him swoon in agony. The rushing water also increases his loss of blood. Yet I feel I have no choice but to hurry.

"Stop, Sita," he gasps as he starts to faint. "I can't stand it."

"You can stand it. This time you're the hero in my story. You can write it all down later. This pain will not last and you will laugh about it in a few days. Because tonight you're going to get what you've always wanted. You're going to become a vampire."

He is interested, although he is clearly dying. The beach is still two hundred yards away. "Really?" he mumbles. "A real vampire?"

"Yes! You'll be able to stay out all night and party and you won't ever get old and ugly. We'll travel the world and we'll have more fun than you can imagine. Seymour?"

"Party," he says faintly, his face sagging into the water. Having to hold his mouth up slows me down even more but I keep kicking. I imagine an observer on the pier would think a power boat were about to ram the beach. The sand is only a hundred yards away now.

"Hang in there," I tell him.

Finally, when we are in five feet of water, I am able to put my feet down. I carry him to the beach and carefully lay him on his right side. There is no one around to help us. His blood continues to gush out around the edges of the wooden stake, at the front as well as at the back. He is the color of refined flour. He hardly breathes, and though I yell in his ear I have to wonder if he is not already beyond hearing. Already beyond even the power of my blood. The situation is worse than it was with Ray and Joel. Neither of them had an object implanted in them. Even vampire flesh cannot heal around such an object, and yet I fear I cannot simply pull it out. I feel his life will spill out with it and be lost on the cold sand.

"Seymour!" I cry. "Come back to me!"

A minute later, when all seems lost, when he isn't even breathing, my prayer is mysteriously answered. He opens his eyes and looks up at me. He even grins his old Seymour grin, which usually makes me want to laugh and hit him at the same time. Yet this time I choke back the tears. The chill on his flesh, I know, is from the touch of the Grim Reaper. Death stands between us and it will not step aside even for a vampire.

"Seymour," I say, "how are you?"

"Fine. The pain has stopped."

"Good."

"But I feel cold." A tremor shakes his body. Dark blood spills over his lips. "Is this normal?"

"Yes. It is perfectly normal." He does not feel the stake now, or even recognize how grave his condition is. He thinks I gave him my blood while he was unconscious. He tries to squeeze my hand but he is too weak. Somehow he manages to keep talking.

"Will I live forever now?" he asks.

"Yes." I bury my face in his. "Forever and ever."

His eyes close. "I will love you that long, Sita."

"Me, too," I whisper. "Me, too."

We speak no more, Seymour and I.

He dies a minute later, in my arms.

EPILOGUE

His body I take to a place high in the mountains where I often walked when I lived in Los Angeles. On a bluff, with a view of the desert on one side and the city on the other, I build a funeral pyre from wood I am able to gather in the immediate area. Seymour rests comfortably on top of my construction. At the beach I had removed the bloody stake and thrown it away. He is able to lie on his back and I fold his hands over his big heart.

"You," I say. "You were the best."

There is a wooden match in my right hand, but somehow I am unable to light it. His face looks so peaceful I can't stop staring at him. But I realize the day is moving on, and that the wind will soon pick up. The flames should finish their work before then. Seymour always loved the woods, and wouldn't have wanted them harmed by a raging forest fire. He loved so many things, and I was happy to be one of them.

I strike the match on the bark of a tree.

It burns bright red, and I can't help but think of Kali.

Many things pass through my mind right then.

Many question and so few answers.

Yet I let the flame burn down to my fingertips.

There is pain, a little smoke. The match dies.

And from my pocket I withdraw the vial of blood.

Number seven. *Ramirez.* I look up.

"What is the cost, Kalika?" I ask the sky.

After opening the vial, I pour half the blood over Seymour's wound, and the other half down his throat. Then I close my eyes and walk away and stand silently behind a tall tree for five minutes. Some mysteries are best left unexplained. My hope refuses to be crushed. I have found love and lost love, but perhaps what I have finally rediscovered is my faith in love. I stand and pray— not for bliss or miracles—I simply pray and that is enough.

Finally I walk back to the funeral pyre.

Seymour is sitting up on the wood and looking at me. His fatal wound has healed.

"How did we get here?" he asks.

Of course I have to laugh. "It's a long story," I say.

But I wonder how to finish the story for him.

I still wonder who the child is.

More, I wonder who he *was*.

EVIL THIRST

For my sister Ann, who is a vampire

ONE

I am a vampire. For centuries I believed I was the last vampire on Earth, that I was the most powerful creature in existence. That belief gave me great self-confidence. I feared nothing because nothing could harm me. Then one remarkable day, my supposedly dead creator, Yaksha, came for me, and I discovered I was not omnipotent. A short time later another vampire appeared, one Eddie Fender. He had Yaksha's strength, and once again I was almost destroyed. Yet I survived both Yaksha and Eddie, only to give birth to a daughter of unfathomable power and incomprehensible persuasion—Kalika, Kali Ma, the Dark Mother, the Supreme Goddess of Destruction. Yes, I believe my only child to be a divine incarnation, an *avatar,* as some would describe her. In a devastating vision she showed me her infinite greatness. The only problem is that my daughter seems to have been born without a conscience.

Actually, I do have three other small problems.

I don't know where Kalika is.

I know I must destroy her.

And I love her.

I don't know which of these dilemmas is worst, but together they make a very dangerous combination. There is another child who has recently been born to rival my daughter. I don't know the child's first name, but he is the son of my friend, Paula Ramirez. The power of this child is still a mystery to me. I only know that a tiny vial of his blood was able to bring my closest friend, Seymour Dorsten, back from the dead. I don't know where Paula and her son are either. I don't know if they're with Kalika. If they are, I do know they are both probably dead. Above all else, my daughter wants this child.

But why? I don't know.

I am beset with problems.

They seem never to stop.

I stand outside the Unity Church in Santa Monica, Seymour Dorsten by my side. Three months have passed since we were last in Santa Monica, on the pier. On that day Kalika first chose to spare Seymour's life, but then threw a stake into his spine while he thrashed in the ocean water below us. She said she did so to make a point.

"Do you really need to know?"

"Yes."

"The knowledge will cost you."

The question I had asked was who Paula's child was. Kill-ing Seymour was her answer to the question, a very curious answer. Had Kalika not killed Seymour, I never would have thought to use the child's blood on a dead person. I never would have known just how special the child was. Yet Seymour does not remember any of this. The shock of being impaled has dimmed his memory of that night's events. He remembers being thrown off the pier and into the water—that's it. Of course he is still pressuring me to make him a vampire. He thinks then we will have great sex, or at least *some* sex. I don't sleep with him because I am afraid it would destroy our deli-cate balance of love and insults.

For the tenth time Seymour wants to know why I have dragged him to a New Age lecture. It is entitled: The Birth of Christ—an Egyptian Prophecy Fulfilled. The speaker is to be a Dr. Donald Seter, founder of the New Age group the Suzama Society. I want to attend Dr. Seter's talk because of two incred-ible facts he has publicly announced. On a radio talk show he stated that Christ has been reborn—his birth took place on the exact day Paula's child was born. Of course he makes no mention of Paula and does not know to whom the child was born. The second fact is his claim that he has in his possession an ancient Egyptian scripture that supposedly gives details of this rebirth.

I would immediately discount the latter claim if the date had not been so personally coincidental, and if I had not happened to have known the original Suzama when I was in Egypt almost five thousand years ago. At one point Suzama was my teacher, and I know for a fact she was clairvoyant.

Yet I have never heard of the Suzama scripture before.

I wonder where Dr. Seter obtained it, and how accurate it is.

But these things I can't explain to Seymour without telling him that he was brought back to life by the blood of a three-hour-old Hispanic infant. I feel there is a reason for his memory block, and I hesitate to tamper with it. Besides, I am afraid he might not believe me if I told him the truth. Who would? It is difficult to contemplate God and His Son and immaculate conceptions without feeling like a potential fanatic. Especially since Paula was not—in her own words—a virgin.

"We could be at a movie," Seymour says. "We could be having dinner. Besides, this whole Christian thing bores me. They have been waiting two thousand years for him to show up. If he was coming back, he would be here already."

"Krishna promised to return," I say. "He said he would not be recognized."

"He won't be bringing his flute?"

"I think he will return in humble surroundings."

Seymour studies the poster outside the church announcing the lecture. "You *are* history. What can you learn from this joker?"

I have to let something slip or Seymour won't attend. Actually, I'm not sure why I've brought him, but I suppose I know that at some point I'll have to open my heart to him and ask his advice. I always have in the past. I want him at the lecture so that he'll have all the facts when I need his advice.

Yet I hesitate before speaking. Every time I bring him deeper into my life, I bring him closer to danger. Still, I remind myself, it is his decision to stay with me, even after he has seen what my daughter can do. He at least knows that I am searching for her, even if he doesn't realize I am also desperately seeking Paula and her child. Yet Paula hasn't called the number I gave her to call. She should have tried to contact me two months ago, a month after I said good-bye to her. It worries me that Kalika may have gotten to her first. I am at Dr. Seter's lecture in the hope that he can give me some clue as to where they might be. It is unlikely, I know.

"Dr. Seter says he has a copy of a scripture Suzama wrote," I tell Seymour. "She was a real person, a revered priestess of the Church of Isis, a high adept in ancient Egypt." I pause. "I knew her, I studied with her."

Seymour is impressed. "What did she teach you?"

"How to bring the white light above my head into my heart."

"What?"

"She taught primarily esoteric forms of meditation. She had many gifts." I grab his arm and drag him toward the church door. "I will tell you more about her later."

On the way in there is a registration table and a donation

basket. I throw a few dollars in the latter. A young man in a dark blue suit and a red tie stands near the door greeting people. Actually, there are a number of people similarly out-fitted—young, handsome people, males and females, wearing navy blue clothes and shiny faces. They are Dr. Seter's followers, I realize, but I hesitate to make the judgment that the man has formed a cult. Not all New Age groups, or Christian groups for that matter, signify sects. Besides, I don't care if he has formed a cult or not. I just care if he knows what he's talking about.

The young man greeting people pauses to say hello to me.

"Welcome," he says. "May I ask how you heard about our lecture?"

"On the radio," I say. "Yesterday night. I heard Dr. Seter's interview."

"KEXT?" he asks.

"That was the one," I say. "Have you known the doctor long?"

"I should say." The young man smiles and offers his hand. "James Seter—I work for my father. Have since I can remember." He pauses. "And your name?"

"I'm Alisa. This is Seymour."

"Hi," Seymour says, shaking James's hand when I'm through with it. But James Seter only has eyes for me.

"Have you read Dr. Seter's book?" he asks me.

"No," I say. "I was hoping to obtain a copy here."

"They will be on sale after the lecture," James says. "Fascinating reading, if I do say so myself."

"What allowed your father to predict so accurately the birth of Christ?" I ask.

"The Suzama scripture. It contains very detailed knowledge about the next coming of the messiah. It predicted Christ's coming the first time very accurately."

I smile. "And you believe all this?"

He nods. "Suzama had a great gift. Studying her words, I have never found her to make a mistake."

"It sounds like a remarkable document," I say. "Why haven't modern archaeologists, linguists, and theologians had a chance to study it?"

James hesitates. "My father will address all these questions in the lecture. Better to ask him. His knowledge of the scripture is extremely comprehensive."

"Just one last question," I say. "Has he brought the original scripture with him tonight?"

"I'm afraid not. It's a priceless artifact. We cannot risk it at a public lecture."

I detect no deceit in his words, and I have a sharp ear for it. Also, there is an ease in his manner, a naturalness. He does not act like a fanatic. His dark eyes continue to study me, though. I think he likes me. He is remarkably handsome, and cannot be more than twenty-two years old.

After muttering my thanks and taking Seymour's hand, I

step into the church and search for a seat. The place is crowded but we manage to squeeze in near the front. The audience is remarkably diverse, made up of old and young, tramps and professionals. I am disappointed I will not have a chance to study the scripture. I am certain I would know if it were authentic. Suzama had a fine hand for hieroglyphs. I remember her work well.

Dr. Seter enters five minutes later.

He is a small man with white hair and an unassuming manner. As he walks toward the podium, I estimate his age at seventy, although he appears less than sixty. It is his vitality and bright gray eyes that make him seem younger than he really is. He wears a medium-priced gray suit and expensive black shoes. He is not so handsome as his son, though. Indeed, I suspect he is not the biological father, that James is adopted. There is a scholarly air to Dr. Seter that I find interesting. The lines on and the planes across his face show intelligence and extensive education. I see all this in one penetrating vampiric glance.

James Seter comes forward to introduce his father. He lists a number of academic achievements. Dr. Seter has Ph.D.s in both theology and archaeology, from Harvard and Stanford respectively. He is the author of numerous published papers and three books. For the last decade, James says, his father has been studying the Suzama scripture and bringing the knowledge contained in it to the world. James does not mention where his father obtained the scripture, probably to leave his father something of interest to discuss. The introduction is brief, and soon Dr. Seter is at the podium. His voice is pleasant, although somewhat reedy. He starts by welcoming us and thanking us for coming. Then he pauses and flashes a warm but shy smile.

"It is quite a claim for one to make," he says, "that one knows that the messiah is in the world. That he has been born on such and such a day in such and such a country. Had I attended this lecture as an observer ten years ago, I don't think I would have sat through the introduction. For as my son James has pointed out, I come from a fairly rigorous academic background. Until ten years ago, I never thought of the second coming or even, quite frankly, much of Christ himself. This may come as a surprise, since I hold a doctorate in theology. But the truth of the matter is my studies of religion were purely academic. I was an agnostic. I neither believed nor disbelieved the world's religions, yet I found them fascinating.

"Now this is where I may lose half of you. In fact, when I first began to lecture on the Suzama scripture, it was normal for a quarter of my audience to get up and leave at this point—my introduction to the scripture. Since those days I have managed to decrease that number by initially asking all of you to please set aside your doubts for the next few minutes to listen to what I have to say. You can form your judgments later. There is plenty of time, believe me."

Dr. Seter paused to sip from the glass of water on the podium. Then he cleared his throat and continued.

"The Suzama scripture comes from the culture of ancient Egypt. Carbon dating and an analysis of its hieroglyphic style place it back approximately five thousand years, in what is commonly called pre-dynastic Egypt. I did not find the scripture in Egypt, but in a country in Western Europe that I cannot reveal at this time. The reason for this secrecy may be obvious to some, and despicable to others." He pauses. "I took the Suzama scripture back with me to America to study, without the permission of the country where I found it. In that sense I am guilty of stealing, but I make no apologies. Furthermore, as long as I refuse to name the country from which I took it, I cannot be legally prosecuted for the act. But with my background, I felt I was best equipped to study the scripture.

"Now many of you may feel that is the height of egotism on my part. By keeping the original scripture to myself I immediately bring into question its authenticity. What reputable scientist would do such a thing? If you had told me ten years ago that I would be guilty of this behavior, I would have said it would not be possible. I would have said that every ancient artifact belongs to the world. Nothing should be hidden away and kept secret. That is a basic scientific credo. And yet I have hidden this document. Why?

"Because I believe the Suzama scripture contains information that could be dangerous if publicly revealed. Dangerous to whom, you might ask? To the Christ himself, as an infant, and to the public as a whole. For Suzama, a powerful clairvoyant of her time, has set down information that might allow one to find the Christ before his time. Also, the scripture contains information on powerful forms of meditation that are, in my estimate, dangerous for the inexperienced.

"Who am I to decide what knowledge is too dangerous for mankind to receive? I can only say in my defense that I have experimented personally with many of Suzama's instructions, and almost lost my life in the process. From my point of view, it would be the ultimate in irresponsibility to throw all of the Suzama material out there.

"Then why should you believe anything I have to say? Why should you even believe there was a Suzama? Well, you don't have to believe me. I don't ask that you do. But as a measure of proof I have turned over numerous slides of the original scripture to eminent archeologists. Because I have not allowed them access to the original artifact, they are unwilling to state unequivocally that the Suzama scripture is authentic. But many of them are willing to certify that as far as they can tell it is the real thing. A list of these experts is recorded in my book.

"What does this long dead woman have to say about the birth and rebirth of the Christ? For one thing Suzama states that Christ has not come just once, but at least four times in our history: as Lord Krishna of India, two hundred years before Suzama's birth, as Adi Shankara of India, five hundred years before Christ's birth, and finally as Christ himself. The Suzama scripture predicts each of these births, and says that the soul of all these great prophets and masters was identical. Furthermore the text predicts that this same infinite soul took birth in a human body recently, in the last three months. The exact date is given, in fact, as last March fifteenth, and the child was destined to be born here, in California."

A loud stir went through the audience. Dr. Seter pauses to have another drink of water. He deserves one, I thought, after the mouthful he had just said. Clearing his throat once more, he continues.

"What proof do I have that Suzama knew what she was talking about? If I accept her scripture as authentic, a product of ancient Egypt, then I am forced to accept that she has had a pretty good track record so far. But beyond that is the inner validation the material has given me. Following her prescribed instructions, I have been given an intuitive insight into the hidden meaning behind certain of her verses. Now I see many eyebrows rise with that statement. Are her instructions and her predictions presented in an obscure form? So obscure a form that their meaning is open to interpretation?

"The answer to both these questions is yes and no. Suzama is often specific when it comes to dates. She says when Shankara and Christ were to be born. But as far as esoteric practices are concerned she can be very subtle. A study of her text requires a study of one's own mind, and it is this last point more than any that has stopped me from letting the whole of the scripture become public. Scientists demand that knowledge be objective, empirical, when the very nature of this type of study, the search for the soul, for the God, is in my mind almost entirely a subjective exploration."

Dr. Seter pauses and scans the room. "I never like to lecture too long without taking questions. I will take some now."

Many hands shoot up. Dr. Seter chooses a middle-aged man not far from where we are seated. The man stands to speak.

"How did you manage to find this religious text in the first place?" he asks. "What led you to it?"

Dr. Seter does not hesitate. "A dream. I simply dreamed where it was and I went and dug in a certain spot and found it."

The man is stunned. "You're not serious?"

Dr. Seter holds up his hand as a murmur goes through the crowd. "Believe me I would like to give another answer. Unfortunately another answer would not be true. This is how I found the scripture. There was no research involved, no tedious digs lasting decades. I found it as soon as I started looking for it."

The man continues to stand. "So you believe God directed you to it?"

"I believe somebody directed me to it. I don't know if it was God himself. Actually, Suzama never speaks of Christ or Shankara as God. She calls them masters, or perfected beings. And she believes we are all evolving to the same heightened state of perfection." Dr. Seter pauses. "It was an especially vivid dream, unlike any I had ever had before. It would have had to be for me to act on it, I assure you." A pause. "Next question."

He chooses a young woman at the back. Even before she speaks, it is clear she has a chip on her shoulder.

"What if I were to say that you made this all up? That the Suzama scripture is a complete fraud?"

"I would say that's not a question." Dr. Seter pauses. "Do you have a question?"

The young woman fumes. "There was only one Christ. How can you dare to compare him to these heathens?"

Dr. Seter smiles. "It is questions like this that reaffirm my decision not to make public everything I know about the Christ's birth in our time. Each of the others I spoke of was a great spiritual leader in his time. Had you been born in India, even today, you might follow their teachings. It is largely because you were born in this country that you are a Christian." He pauses. "Don't you agree?"

The young woman is uncomfortable but remains defiant. "I hardly think so. You twist the teachings of Christ, comparing them to these others."

"Frankly, I think I compliment all of them by comparing each to the other. But that is beside the point. I never asked you to believe that the Suzama scripture is accurate. I am merely saying that I believe it is, based on my research and personal experience. If you believe it is a fraud, fine. But the text warns that those who profess to worship the Christ will be the first to dismiss him when he returns."

I approve of the manner in which Dr. Seter deals with

the young woman's insolent attitude. I have never appreci-
ated religious dogma. It seems to me only a more insidious
form of racial prejudice. Yet I am not sure if I agree with Dr.
Seter when he says the three spiritual leaders were one and
the same being. Having known Krishna personally, I have
trouble reconciling many of Christ's teachings with Krishna's,
although I suspect the early disciples of Christ distorted
what their master said. At the same time I am familiar with
Shankara's work, particularly his commentary on the Brahma
Sutras, which I have studied over the centuries. I agree with
the Eastern claim that Shankara was the greatest intellect who
ever lived. Yet his style of teaching was very different from
either Krishna's or Christ's. For one thing, he never claimed
to be anyone special, either the son of God or God himself.
Yet he worked many recorded miracles.

Nevertheless I find the doctor's words fascinating. I raise
my hand and catch his eye, using a fraction of the great power
I have in my eyes to rivet a person's attention. He immediately
picks me. I also stand as I ask my question.

"You say Suzama gives exact dates as to the births of these
various avatars," I say. "Yet the solar calendar was not used
in ancient Egypt until two thousand B.C. Suzama surely must
have used a lunar calendar when presenting her dates. How did
you translate one to the other?"

"No translation was necessary. The dates are not expressed
in terms of a lunar calendar but a solar one."

I am disappointed in his answer. "But you realize as an archaeologist how unlikely that is. It almost certainly means the scripture you have found is either from a much later period, or that it is fake."

Dr. Seter is not dissuaded. "As an archaeologist I was *surprised* she predicted the birth of these masters in terms of a solar calendar and not a lunar one. Yet if we accept as true her profound intuition, then we must also accept that she would understand that in the future her lunar calendar would not be used. Actually, at least to my mind, the fact that she did not use a lunar calendar supports her claims."

"Did she mention any other avatars besides the three you mentioned?" I ask.

Dr. Seter hesitates. "Yes. But she says they are of a different line."

"Does she mention Isis for example?"

Dr. Seter is taken aback. "I did not discuss that in any of my books. But, yes, it is true, Suzama was a high priestess of a group that worshipped Isis." He pauses. "May I ask why you ask that question?"

"We can talk about it another time," I say and quickly sit down. Seymour leans over and speaks in my ear.

"You're drawing attention to yourself," he warns.

"Only enough to make him want to meet me afterward," I reply.

"Do you think he's telling the truth?"

"He is definitely *convinced* he is telling the truth. There is not a shred of deceit in him." I pause. "But that is not the same as saying he is right. Far from it."

There followed dozens of questions.

"How did Suzama describe California?"

Answer: "At the other end of the great continent across the ocean, where the sun always shines."

"What kind of family was Christ reborn into?"

Answer: "A poor broken family."

"What nationality will the Christ be?"

Answer: "Brown skinned."

A lot of people didn't like that answer. Of course it would have made me chuckle, except Paula's baby had brown skin, like his mother.

Toward the end there was one question that disturbed me, or rather, Dr. Seter's answer did. He was asked if the reborn Christ was in any danger, as an infant. Dr. Seter hesitated long before responding. Clearly the Suzama text contained a warning of some kind.

"Yes," he says finally. "Suzama states that the forces of darkness will bend even the will of the righteous to try to find the child and destroy him. She further states that it is the duty of the old and powerful to help locate the child and protect him."

My hand is up in an instant.

"Does Suzama describe the form these forces of darkness will take?" I ask.

He pauses. "No. Not really."

It is the first lie he has told all night. Curious.

The old and powerful?

Who on the planet is older and more powerful than I am?

TWO

It is my desire to have coffee with Dr. Donald Seter this very night, and to increase my chances of success I send Seymour away. He's only too happy to try to catch a late movie in Westwood. Seymour, I feel, may hold me back because I plan to reach the esteemed doctor through the son, James Seter. Picking up a copy of Dr. Seter's book, *The Secret of Suzama,* on the back table for a mere twenty bucks, I stroll over to where bright-faced James is saying good-bye to people. He stands near the exit and thanks people for coming. Such a nice young man, with a firm handshake, no less. He lights up when he sees me.

"Alisa," he says. "Your questions were very interesting."

"You remember my name. I am flattered." I pause. "I am perhaps a little older than I look, and a little more educated. I have made a thorough study of ancient Egypt, and would enjoy chatting with you and your father about the Suzama scripture."

He doesn't take me seriously. "I'm sure that would be fun and informative, but my father has to catch a plane for San Francisco tomorrow morning early."

I catch his eye, put an ounce of heat behind my words. "Maybe you could talk to him about me. He expressed an interest in my knowledge of Suzama's connection to Isis."

James blinks a few times. He must have a strong will; he does not immediately jump at my suggestion.

"I could talk to him. But as you can see he is not as young as he once was. I worry about tiring him unnecessarily."

I do not want to push James too hard. There is always the possibility I might damage him in some way. Since my rebirth as a vampire, I have found the power in my eyes particularly biting. I use it in small doses. But I do not want Dr. Seter to just walk away. I decide to let a portion of my ancient knowledge drop, but in the form of a lie. Making a drama of it, I pull James Seter aside and speak in hushed tones,

"Your Suzama scripture is not the only one in existence," I say. "I have another one, but I think it is different. I would be happy to trade information with your father."

James pauses a moment to take this all in. "You can't be serious?"

I speak evenly. "But I am. If your father will meet with me, I would be happy to talk to him about it." I pause. "He will know within a minute whether I have discovered something authentic."

"He will want to question you before spending time with you."

I shake my head. "I will not talk here about what I have found. But please assure your father that I'm not a crackpot."

"Where do you want to meet?"

"There's a coffee shop three blocks from the ocean near Ocean Avenue and the freeway. I can meet you there in, say, half an hour."

That is the coffee shop where my beloved Ray came back to me, where he in fact returned to life. He appeared just after I shot two men to death after they'd tried to rape me. I was covered with a fine spray of blood at the time, a fitting ornament for dark delusions. I have not been back to the coffee shop since, but for some perverse reason I want to go there tonight. Maybe another phantom will appear to spice up my life. Yet I hope not. The pain of the last one is still an open wound for me. Just the thought of Ray fills me with sorrow. James is studying me.

"When you came here tonight," he says, "you acted like you had no knowledge of Suzama. Why?"

I reach out and straighten his tie. "If you knew what I know, James, you would make a point of appearing ignorant." I pause. "Tell your father to come. I will be waiting."

A half hour later I sit in the coffee shop across from Dr. Seter and his son. They have come alone, which is good. Actually it is good that they have come at all, but I suspect son dragged father along. The doctor doesn't look at me as if he expects to receive any divine revelation from me. But he does seem to be enjoying the apple pie and ice cream I've ordered for him. When you're a cute five-thousand-year-old blond, you can get away with murder.

"James tells me you're a student of archaeology," Dr. Seter says as he forks up a heaping piece of pie. He has taken off the tie he wore to his lecture but otherwise he is dressed the same. His manner is relaxed, a scholar enjoying himself after giving a lecture he has obviously given a thousand times before. Briefly I wonder about his motivation for publicizing the Suzama scripture. I don't think he can be making much money from doing so. The cost of his book is nominal and he doesn't teach any high-priced seminar. He seems like a nice man with no hidden agenda.

"I am a student of Suzama," I say seriously. "I was not boasting when I said I possess a manuscript of hers."

Dr. Seter is amused, "Where did you find this manuscript?"

"Where did you find yours?" I ask.

"I have explained why I am reluctant to reveal that information."

"I have the same reluctance for the same reasons," I say.

He returns to his pie. He thinks I am a nice girl with nothing to say.

"Then I guess we'll just have to enjoy the food," he says politely.

I open his book to a photograph of a portion of the Suzama scripture. I point to the hieratic writing on the ancient papyrus.

"There are probably only two dozen people on Earth who can read this at a glance," I say. "You are one of them, I am another. This line says, 'The secret of the Goddess is in the sixteenth digit of the moon. Not the moon in the sky, but the moon in the high center. It is here the ambrosia of bliss is milked by the sincere seeker. It is only there the knowledge of the soul is revealed.'" I pause. "Is my translation accurate?"

Dr. Seter almost drops his fork. "How did you know that? I don't translate that line in the text."

"I told you, I am a student of Suzama."

James interrupts. "How do we know someone else didn't translate the line for you?"

"Because I can give you information that must be in the portion of your scripture that you keep hidden, as it is in mine. For example, I know of the four-word mantra Suzama used to invoke the white light from above the head, where the moon digit is really located. I know how the first word relates to the heart, the second to the throat, the third to the head. I know how the breath is synchronized with the mantra and that on the fourth word the divine white light of Isis is brought down into the human body."

Dr. Seter stares at me, stunned. "What is the four-word mantra?"

I speak seriously. "You know from your scripture that it is only to be revealed in private, at the time of initiation. I will not say it here. But you must realize by now that I know a great deal about Suzama's secret meditation practices. Therefore, it should be easy for you to believe that I must have access to another scripture belonging to her." I pause. "Am I correct?"

Dr. Seter studies me. "You know something, that's for sure. Frankly, I would be very curious to see your scripture."

"You have to show me yours first," I say. "I will be able to tell if it is authentic."

"How?" James interrupts.

I smile for him. "I will compare it to mine."

"Do you believe your scripture is identical to mine?" Dr. Seter asks.

"No. Yours speaks of a danger to the new master. Mine does not address that point." I add, "You lied when you said your scripture did not specify what the danger is."

Dr. Seter sits back. "How do you know that?"

"It doesn't matter. It's true." I pause. "Tell me how the danger is described?"

"I'm afraid that's not possible," James says. "Only inner members of our group are given such information."

"Ah," I say. "This inner group you have organized, what's its purpose? To protect the child once it is found?" By their reaction I see I have scored a bulls-eye. "Isn't that rather presumptuous of you? To think the messiah needs your protection?"

Dr. Seter is having trouble keeping up with me. Still, I have his full attention. "What if the scripture itself says he will need protection?" he asks.

"Does it?" I ask.

Dr. Seter hesitates. "Yes."

He is telling the truth, or at least the truth he knows.

"Father," James interrupts. "Should we be talking about these things in front of a stranger whom we have just met?"

Dr. Seter shrugs. "Isn't it obvious she knows as much about Suzama as we do?"

"But I don't," I say again. "I know different things about her. I am working with different source material. But back to your group, and how they will be used to protect the child. How exactly is that going to work?"

"Surely you can understand that we can't divulge the inner workings of our group," Dr. Seter says. "Not the way the government is scrutinizing every spiritual group in the country, searching for the next crazy cult. Please, let's try to keep this on an academic level. I would like to see your material, you would like to see mine. Fine, how can we work a place and a date to exchange information?"

"I told you," I say. "You have to show me yours first. If I am convinced it is authentic, I will show you what I have."

Dr. Seter is suspicious. "Why not have a simultaneous exchange?"

I smile warmly. "I will not harm your material. I'm sure when you show it to me there will be a dozen of your well-dressed boys and girls gathered around." I pause. "I suspect you travel with it. Why don't you show it to me tonight? I will not have to study it long to reach a conclusion."

Dr. Seter and James exchange a long look. "What could it hurt?" the doctor says finally, testing the waters.

James is unsure. He continues to study me. "How do we know you don't work for the FBI?"

I throw my head back and laugh. "Where will you find a FBI agent who can read hieroglyphics?"

"But you are curious about the purpose of our group?" James persists. "These are the kinds of questions the government might ask."

I catch James's eye and let my power out in a measured dose. "I am not from the government. I represent no one other than myself. My interest in the Suzama material is motivated only by the highest and best desires." I pause and catch the eye of the doctor as well. "Let me see it. You will have no regrets."

Dr. Seter touches his son's arm as he nods in answer to my request. "We don't exactly travel with it, but it's not far from here." He pauses. "It's out in Palm Springs."

"Palm Springs," I mutter. What a coincidence. One passes through Palm Springs on the way to Joshua Tree National

Monument, where Paula supposedly conceived her child. I have been meaning to go out there for some time.

"James can show you the scripture tomorrow morning," Dr. Seter says, checking his watch. "It's too late to see it tonight."

I stand. "But I'm a night girl. And I would like you to be there, Dr. Seter, when I examine it. If you please? Let's go now."

He is taken aback by my boldness and gazes up at me. "May I ask how old you are, Alisa?"

I smile. "You must know that Suzama was not very old when she wrote your scripture."

Dr. Seter shakes his head. "I didn't know that. How old was she?"

"I take that back. I'm not sure how old she was when she wrote it. I only know she died before her twentieth birthday."

I don't add, like me.

Some, of course, consider vampires the walking dead.

THREE

*B*efore heading for Palm Springs, I leave Seymour a message on the answering machine in our new home in Pacific Palisades. We stay in regular contact. It's a promise we keep to each other. I have left him before in the middle of the night without explanation and have promised never to do it again. Also, my daughter, Kalika, still walks the streets, and it is impossible to tell when she will come for us again. Seymour and I, we cover each other's backs. But I feel in my heart it will not be long before I see Kalika again. A part of me senses that she has yet to find the child, but is searching constantly for him. I have to wonder if my intuition about her is attached to the psychic thread that connects all mothers to their children.

Dr. Seter and James drive ahead of me on the long road to Palm Springs. They have an old white Volvo, I a brand-new red Porsche. James is behind the wheel. I keep only fifty feet behind, just off to their right in the fast lane. They would be surprised to know that I can hear them as they speak. Yet it is only when we have been on the road an hour that they finally begin to talk. Before then Dr. Seter had been slipping in and out of sleep.

James: "Why are we doing this?"

Dr. Seter: "Do you think we should just ignore her?"

James: "Not at all. I'm as curious about her as you. Remember it was I who insisted upon the meeting. But I think we should investigate her background before letting her see the scripture."

Dr. Seter: "What harm can she do to it? She will not be able to translate a fraction of the hieroglyphics without hours of time. I don't care how well versed she is in the field." A pause. "She must be older than she looks. It takes years to learn to read the way she did."

James: "I'm sure she's older than she looks. Notice she didn't actually tell you her age?"

Dr. Seter: "What are you saying? That she has mastered Suzama's practices and managed to reverse her age?"

James: "It's possible. She knew enough about the high initiation."

Dr. Seter: "That's what startled me about her, too. There are few people in our group who know about that." A pause. "She must be telling the truth. She must have another text."

James: "I agree. But she's evasive. I don't trust her. I want full security when we show her the papyrus."

Dr. Seter: "Of course. You've called ahead? They know we're coming?"

James: "Yes. The whole group will be there."

Dr. Seter: "Really? Why? We don't need all of them there. The others should be on their way to San Francisco."

James: "I told you, I don't trust this girl." A pause. "But I have another reason."

Dr. Seter: "What?"

James: "I wonder if Alisa has direct knowledge about the child."

Dr. Seter: "Now you're speculating."

James: "I'm not so sure. She seemed particularly concerned about the child being harmed." A pause. "Maybe I say that backward. I wonder if she already knows about the Dark Mother."

I almost drive off the road. They are talking about Kalika.

My daughter? Did Suzama brand her as evil five thousand years ago?

Dr. Seter: "I didn't get that impression."

James: "Can I say something really off the wall?"

Dr. Seter: "It's a long drive. We may as well discuss every possibility."

James: "What if this Alisa is working for the Black Mother?"

Dr. Seter laughs: "She hardly seems the type, do you think?"

James: "Consider. She looks like a twenty-year-old, but she appears to have the education of someone who has studied for thirty years. Also, her manner is curious. Notice the way she catches your eye, and then says things you have trouble resisting."

Dr. Seter laughs some more: "I never noticed that. I think you are the one who is having trouble resisting her."

James: "I don't know. I just hope we're not leading her to the child by letting her study the scripture."

Dr. Seter: "But there's nothing in the scripture that points to where the child is at this time, except perhaps still in California."

James: "To us maybe. But she may find clues in the text we have missed." A pause. "I pray to God we're not doing anything to endanger the child further. From the descriptions I have read of the Dark Mother, I wouldn't want anyone, friend or foe, to run into her. I think that kind of evil lives to kill."

Dr. Seter: "But you know, son, we have spent the last ten years preparing to meet her." A pause. "It's inevitable, if we're to believe half of what we've read."

James: "Do you really think we're the ones chosen to defend the child?"

Dr. Seter: "I wouldn't have bought so many automatic weapons unless I did." A sigh. "I'm more worried that Alisa may be from the government than that she represents the Dark Mother."

James: "Then why show her anything?"

Dr. Seter: "As I said, it can cause no harm. She will not have time to translate the portions of the scripture we don't want her to translate. And she will find nothing in our center the government would be excited about."

James: "I hope you're right." A pause. "She is incredibly beautiful."

Dr. Seter: "I noticed."

I find their private conversation fascinating.

The center they have referred to is a large house in an area clearly zoned for both business and residential properties. There are many cars parked along the street as we pull up. Like Dr. Seter, I am surprised that James has directed the whole group here, especially when they have a lecture the following night in San Francisco. Yet James's intuitions about me are shockingly accurate. He wonders if the Dark Mother has sent me. How would he feel if he knew I am the Dark Mother's mother? I would have a hard time convincing him I'm on his side, not hers.

Yet the one thing I have learned by eavesdropping is that the Suzama Society is there to protect the child, not harm it. Still, the reference to automatic weapons disturbs me. It is true that they might come in handy should Kalika show up, but I know guns in the hands of true believers seldom get pointed in the right direction at the right time.

What is the source of James's excellent intuition? Perhaps it is a result of following Suzama's meditation practices. I found his reference to reversed aging intriguing. Is James older than he looks? I remember Suzama's often saying that aging is a product of lower consciousness, and immortality the gift of highest consciousness.

Dr. Seter and James welcome me warmly as I climb from my car.

"Did you have a pleasant drive?" Seter asks.

"I listened to loud music the whole way," I say, gesturing to all the cars. "Is there another lecture here tonight?"

Dr. Seter glances at James. "Many in our group have returned here to collect supplies for the remainder of my tour," the doctor explains. "I have to fly to the East Coast after my San Francisco lecture." He gestures to the house. "Please come in. Would you like some coffee?"

"Thank you, no. I am wide awake."

"That's right," James says, moving up behind us. "You're a night person."

Inside there are two dozen navy blue suits, half and half, pants and skirts, male and female, all young and attractive. I don't get the uniform thing, especially around Dr. Seter, who seems so laid back. Perhaps it is James's idea, although he seems far from a fanatic. The group studies me as I step into the huge house. The place is orderly, the furniture traditional, every corner clean and dust free. There is a faint odor of fried chicken in the air, mashed potatoes, and broccoli. They are not vegetarians, even though Suzama was.

Staring at the innocent faces, I wonder if they practice using their automatic weapons deep in the desert when no one is around. Simply to own an automatic weapon is to invite a felony charge, jail time. Dr. Seter must be convinced the enemy is at hand to go to such extremes. Of course, who am I to judge? He has not fed the enemy another person's blood in the middle of the night just to get her to stop crying. My dear daughter—my how fast she grew and how strong. She can kick my ass in a fight. That, I know from experience.

The memory of Eric Hawkins, Kalika's personal snack bar, is never far.

"Oh God, I'm bleeding! She's cut my neck! The blood is gushing out! Help me!"

But I could not help him. I was only able to use him.

A young woman about my apparent age steps forward to shake my hand. "My name is Lisa," she says. "You're Alisa?"

"Yes."

"We hear you can read hieroglyphics?"

"Hieroglyphics and comic books have always been favorites of mine," I say. There is a murmur of laughter. "Where are you from, Lisa?"

"North Dakota. I met Dr. Seter there last year—"

"Lisa is our accountant," Dr. Seter interrupts. "I call her boss."

The group laughs. They obviously love the man.

I am led down into a basement. Few homes in Southern California have basements, and this one is special, to say the least. As James closes the door behind us, I notice that it has a rubber seal all around it. Almost immediately I notice a change in the air pressure, and I understand why. They are worried about dust and dampness and the effect they would have on the scripture. The air in the basement is carefully filtered.

Six of the group have followed me into the basement, including James and Dr. Seter. A young man named Charles steps to a vault at the far end of the basement. In the center of the room is a large white table with brilliant overhead lights and a double ocular over-size microscope at one end. There are also a couple of magnifying glasses and loupes sitting handily by. Charles spins the steel knob on the vault, dialing the combination. His body is between me and the knob but I listen closely and in a moment I know the combination, R48, L32, R16, L17, R12, L10.

The vault pops open. Charles lifts out a pale yellow sheet of papyrus wrapped in acid-free tissue paper and carries it to the table to set down under the bright lights. The scripture is a foot across, two feet long. A rush of excitement makes my heart pound. Even through the covering tissue paper, I smell ancient Egypt!

I recognize the hieratic writing.

It is tiny, carefully crafted.

It is definitely in Suzama's cursive.

Dr. Seter gestures for me to examine it closer after he lifts off the tissue paper.

As I bend over the table, he has no idea I am about to read it much faster than he would read a large-print book. Yet James stands close beside me, his eyes on mine.

I begin to read.

I am Suzama and my words are true. The past and the future are the same to my illumined vision. You who read these words are warned not to doubt what is recorded lest you fall into error and lose your way on the path. I am Suzama and I speak for the truth.

The lord of creation is both inside and outside creation. He is like the sap in the flower, the space in an empty room. He is always present but unseen. His joy shines like the sun in the sky, his will swims like a fish beneath the ocean. He cannot be known by the mind or even the heart. Only the inner silence recognizes him.

He is both male and female and he is neither. To speak of him as one or the other is only a manner of speaking. In order to protect the righteous and destroy the wicked, he takes birth again and again throughout the ages.

His most recent birth was as Sri Krishna in the land of the Pandu brothers. Then and there he slew demons and granted realization to the worthy. His life lasted 135 years, from 3675 to 3810. He will be remembered as the divine personality.

His next birth will be as Adi Shankara in the land of the Vedas. Then and there he will make available the knowledge of the Brahman, the highest reality. His life will last 32 years, from 6111 to 6143. He will be well remembered as the divine teacher.

His subsequent birth will be as Jesus of Nazareth in the land of Abraham. Then and there he will embody and teach perfect love and compassion. His life will last 108 years, from 7608 to 7716. He will be well remembered as the divine savior.

The scripture ends there. I look over at Dr. Seter.

"Where's the rest of it?" I ask.

"You do not need all of it to judge its authenticity," Dr. Seter says.

"That doesn't answer my question," I say.

"The rest of it is in the vault," James interrupts, close to my right side. "But we decided it wouldn't be a good idea to bring it all out tonight."

On the road, I was briefly separated from them by a distance of two hundred feet. At that point they had their radio on and their windows up. Even I, with my supernatural hearing, could not hear what they were saying. They must have made this decision at that time. Naturally, I am disappointed not to see it all. Yet I am thrilled by what I have read. Already I am convinced the scripture is authentic. The papyrus even feels as if it is five thousand years old. I stroke it gently, making James jump.

"Don't do that," he says.

I withdraw my hand. "I know how to handle such things. I did not harm it in any way." I pause and look at the doctor. "It is my belief that this scripture is authentic."

Dr. Seter is taken back. "You can tell that by such a brief study?"

"Yes. This portion matches what I have. I take back what I said earlier. They're almost identical." I pause. "It would help us if I could see the rest."

Dr. Seter is apologetic. "Alisa, surely you understand what an act of good faith it was for us to show you what we have shown you. Now it's only right, before we reveal any more, that you show us at least a portion of what you have discovered." He pauses and smiles. "I think that is fair. Don't you?"

"Very fair. May I have a day or two to deliver the material to you?"

"Certainly," Dr. Seter says. "James will not be accompanying me east. You can bring what you wish to show us here and he will have a look at it."

"Fine," I say. "But you must look at it yourself, Dr. Seter."

"But I have told you about my commitments on the East Coast."

"What I have to show you will make those commitments seem unimportant."

Dr. Seter is troubled. "I am not willing to cancel any of my lectures until I have more proof."

"I will give you such proof before you leave for the East. Where will you be staying in San Francisco?"

"At the Hilton by the airport," James says. "You can leave a message there. We'll return your call promptly."

I offer Dr. Seter my hand. "I look forward to meeting you again soon."

The doctor is surprised at my sudden departure. "But you've said hardly anything about what we've shown you."

I keep my tone light. "It's what you haven't shown me that I would have a lot to say about."

James touches my arm. "I'll walk you out, Alisa, if you'd like."

I smile. "I would like that very much."

Outside James is a study in politeness.

"I hope you can understand our caution," he says. "We just met you tonight. While we're all impressed with your understanding of the Suzama material, we still have to take things one step at a time."

"No problem," I say as I open my car door. "I doubt that I would have been nearly as open as you and your father have been."

James smiles. "Actually, Alisa, you haven't been very open." He pauses. "You can at least tell us where you found your material."

"In India."

He frowns. "Are you serious? Where?"

"In Sri Nagar."

He nods. "I know where that is. In the Himalayas. What were you doing there?"

"I had a few dreams of my own." I pause. "How old are you, James?"

"Twenty-eight."

"You look much younger. I am twenty-five, for your information."

"You look much younger," he says. "Do you practice anything Suzama taught?"

I smile. "A personal question. I don't know if I want to answer that."

"Come on," he insists.

"I'll tell you what, I'll make a deal with you. Tell me what you practice and I'll tell you what I practice."

He gives a sheepish grin. "You're a clever young woman, Alisa. I don't know if it's smart to share too many secrets with you."

Before I climb into my car I place my palm on his chest. I catch his dark eyes once more, and for the first time I notice how deep they are, how beautiful. There is more to him than meets even my penetrating eyes. A soothing warmth sweeps over me, for him, as well as for his father. Beneath my soft hand his warm heart beats faster. He may not trust me, but I know he likes me, maybe even wants me.

It is strange how I suddenly want him. Since Ray, I have not really desired any man. Even with Joel and Arturo, it was more my love for them that bound me to them. Yet, out of the blue, James has me all hot and bothered. Seymour would be incredibly jealous.

"Secrets are what make us all interesting," I say, and give him a light peck on the cheek. "Have fun in San Francisco. I will call you."

He grabs my arm.

"There is something unusual about you, Alisa," he says in a gentle voice. "I'm going to figure out what it is."

I laugh. "And tell the whole world?"

He smiles, but when he speaks there is a seriousness in his voice. "I have a feeling few in the world would believe me."

FOUR

The time is well after one, but I do not drive straight home. Being a vampire, I find one in the morning not unpleasant. Also, since my rebirth as a vampire, I have found I need little rest, an hour's nap here and there. Even when the sun is high in the daylight sky, my powers are hardly affected. Once again I attribute this to the fact that I used primarily Yaksha's blood to bring about my transformation.

And a few drops of Paula's child's blood.

I, like Seymour, have the influence of it in my life.

I drive to Joshua Tree National Monument, and when I arrive the moon is high in the sky. The park is large, and I have no idea where Paula sat when the brilliant blue light came out of the sky and blessed her. Only that she sat on a bluff watching the sunset. After the blue light left and the sun rose the next morning, the surrounding Joshua trees were larger.

"*The Joshua trees around me—they were all taller.*"

"*Are you sure?*"

"*Pretty sure. Some were twice the size they had been the evening before.*"

I park in a spot that catches my eye and get out and walk across the desert. The moonlight, as it pours over me, seems to seep into the crown of my head, and I am reminded of the time in the desert outside Las Vegas when I escaped a nuclear explosion by filling my body with moonlight and floating high into the sky. As I prowl the sandy terrain among the Joshua trees that stand like sentinels from another age, I feel my step lighten. It is almost as if I can bob off the ground, and that possibility fills me with excitement. To fly up with the stars and escape the prison of my problems. My bare arms begin to glow with a milky white radiance. I can almost see through them.

Then I see the place. My recognition of it is immediate. I do not even have to take note of the tall surrounding trees to confirm my belief. I simply know it is the spot. A feeling of tranquillity, of sanctity even, radiates from the place. It draws me forward. Clearly something momentous occurred here. In a minute I am standing atop the bluff where I am convinced Paula conceived her child. I lift my arms to the stars. "Suzama!" I call. "Show me what you saw!" There is no answer, at least no obvious one. Yet I am suddenly overcome by a wave of fatigue, and I sit down to close my eyes and meditate with the rhythm of the breath and the secret mantra. Soon white light is pouring, not from above, but from a place inside me, and I am lost in memories of nights of wonder and terror at the feet of a tender clairvoyant, who saw not only the birth of God, but the death as well. There was, of course, a reason Suzama died so young, and perhaps I was a part of that reason.

When I arrived in Egypt, it was fifty years after the death of Lord Krishna, fifty years into the dark age, what was to become known as Kali Yuga. Following the trail of adventurous merchants, who traveled the Far East thousands of years before Marco Polo was born, I arrived in an Egypt that to my eyes was infinite in splendor and riches. Truthfully, it overwhelmed me, although I was also relieved to be out of India, where Yaksha was in the midst of a bloody rampage to destroy every living vampire, as part of a vow he had made to Krishna.

The bright sun was hard on a young vampire like me. Riding into the enchanted city on the back of a camel, I had to keep my head covered with many layers of cloth. The sun burned into my brain, sapping every ounce of my strength. Yet the sight of the Great Pyramid, four times larger than the present-day pyramid that bears the same name, filled me with wonder. Covered with shiny white ivory and capped with glistening gold, it stole my breath away. All I could think as the bright rays heated my already boiling blood was to escape into its dark interior, rest, and try to forget the many trials of my journey. I thought it more than a coincidence that one of the first people I met when I entered the magical city was Suzama herself.

She was far from a high priestess that day. Only sixteen, with long dark hair and eyes as bright as they were kind, she wore a slave's simple garment. I saw her bending over the bank of the Nile to collect water in a large clay jar. On my exhausted camel, moving slowly toward her, I thought she seemed to stiffen. She glanced over her shoulder at me, almost as if she felt me approach. Later she was to tell me that she'd already had many visions of my coming. As our eyes met, my heart beat faster. I could remember no dream I'd had about her, but I knew her face was one I would never forget awake or asleep.

Suzama was not merely beautiful, although she would have been considered attractive in any age or place. Her allure came from the marks that austerity and pain had stamped on her young beauty, marks that made her enchanting, not repulsive. It was as if she had witnessed a thousand lives of suffering and come to a realization that transcended mortal acceptance. She was both saintly and sensual. Her lips so generous, she had only to smile to make you feel kissed. I loved her when I saw her, and until then I had never loved anyone on sight, except for Krishna himself.

She offered me a drink from her jug.

"I am called Suzama," she said. "Who are you?"

"Sita," I answered, giving her my real name. I drank the water hungrily, and splashed some on my dusty face. The Nile was cool and sweet in those days. I don't know what has become of it now. "I am new here."

But Suzama shook her head. "You have always been here." Then she touched her heart and I saw tears in her eyes. "I know you, Sita. You have great power."

This was my first sign of her power. Suzama knew things from inside herself, not from outside. Indeed, later, I came to believe the entire world was a dream to her. Yet paradoxically it could still cause her intense pain. Her deepest feelings were enigmatic, dispassionately unattached, but at the same time passionately involved. When she took my hand and led me in the direction of her family, I felt I had been touched by an angel. Yet I did not know that for the next three and a half years, I would hardly ever leave her sight. Her mystical mission had not yet begun, but soon it would hit like a bolt of lightning. And I would be her thunder.

FIVE

The next morning I have been only seconds in my expensive and exquisitely furnished tri-level home in Pacific Palisades when the phone rings. Upstairs I hear Seymour snoring peacefully, yet the call makes me anxious. Our number is unlisted. Who would know to call? And so early in the morning?

I pick up the phone and hold it close.

"Hello?"

There is a pause. Then the soft voice, the gentle inflections. "It is I," she says.

The blood freezes in my veins. "Kalika."

"Yes, Mother, you remember me. That is good. How have you been?"

"Fine. How are you?"

"Wonderful. Busy."

"You haven't found him yet," I say. "You're not going to find him."

Kalika could be smiling. "You are wrong. I haven't found him but I am going to find him. You are going to help me."

"I hardly think so."

"You think too much. Your thoughts blind you. I told you I'm not going to harm the child. I'm your daughter. You should believe me. I believe you even when I hear you lying to me."

"Where are you?" I ask.

"Not far. I'm high up. I have a view. You would enjoy it."

"How did you get this number?"

"It wasn't difficult." A pause. "I saw you last night at that boring meeting. I saw you talking to those people."

If possible, my blood grows colder. Just by meeting and talking to people, I put them suddenly in danger. It does not seem fair that I should love someone who causes me such grief. Yes, I am chilled by Kalika's call, and grateful for it as well. How hopeless mothers are.

"Those people are no concern of yours," I say harshly.

"I think the doctor is a nice man. But I see you like the son. Handsome devil, isn't he?" A pause. "Is it appropriate for a daughter to comment on the company her mother keeps?"

"No."

She laughs softly. "Nothing is as it seems. Black can appear white when the light is blinding. But white loses all luster at the faintest sign of darkness. Why trust them when you can trust me?"

"Because you are a coldblooded murderer."

"Oh. We all have our faults. When did you become so judgmental?"

My tone is bitter. "You know when."

"I suppose. How is Seymour?"

"He's dead."

"That was his corpse at the lecture last night?"

I sigh. "He's fine, no thanks to you."

"See. I can be merciful. I am a mother as well, you know."

"You called Paula. You faked my voice, and even so she did not call you back."

"That is true," Kalika says. "But Suzama would know how to set up a meeting with Paula. She might have spelled that out in her book. You knew her, didn't you?"

I hesitate. "Yes."

"And you still think fondly of her. But to this day you do not know what destroyed her."

"She was destroyed in the big earthquake, along with the Setians. Her death is no mystery to me."

"But who were those Setians? You stared them straight in the eye and did not recognize them."

"I knew they were evil, in the end."

She mocks me. "But too late to save Suzama."

"Why do you talk about them? Or are you just up to your

old tricks? The master manipulator trying to confuse the issue. If you want to come for me, fine. Come now, I tire of your games. You don't scare me."

Kalika is a long time answering. While I wait for her next words, I listen closely and hear in the background, not far from where Kalika is, the splash of water. My daughter must be near an open window, standing on a balcony perhaps. There is definitely a swimming pool in her vicinity. It is far below her I believe. There are many people in it, children playing with a ball, laughing and shouting, and more serious athletes swimming serious laps. I hear the latter turn in the water as they finish each lap and push off the walls. I count the strokes, and there are many of them. It is a large pool. There are not many such large pools in the Los Angeles area. I should be able to get a list of them.

Kalika finally speaks.

"I do not want to harm you, Mother. I am here for the child. But if you stand in my way, I cannot promise you that you or your darling Seymour will survive." She adds, "That is not a threat, merely an observation."

"Thank you. I feel much better. Why did you call?"

"To hear your voice. For some reason your voice carries special meaning to me."

"I don't believe that," I say.

"It is true."

"And the other reason for your call?"

"If I tell you that it will spoil all the fun." A pause. "Is there anything I can do for you, Mother?"

"Leave Dr. Seter and his people alone. Leave the child alone."

Kalika hesitates. "I'm afraid I can't do that. Is there anything else you want?"

I slump against the wall, exhausted. "You know, Kalika, the night you were born was hard for me. The delivery was agonizing and I lost a lot of blood. I almost died, and even when I held you in my arms and looked into your eyes I was scared. Even then I knew you were not normal, not even by vampire standards. But despite all that a part of me was happy, happier than I had ever been in my life. I didn't realize this until later. I had wanted a daughter and now I had one. God gave you to me, I thought, and I thanked him for you." I have to take a breath. "Do you understand what I am saying?"

"Yes."

"You are what you are. Your nature is to kill, and I understand that because I'm a killer as well. But over the centuries I have learned to control that instinct. Now I only kill when it is necessary. You can learn to do the same." I pause. "That is what I ask of you. Only that."

She considers. When she speaks next, her voice is particularly soft. It is almost as if she is speaking inside my brain. And I find her words strangely moving.

"I can do that for you, Mother. But my list of who can live

and who must die is vastly different from yours. The phantom, Ray, was one of your illusions, one of your *mayas*. Your desire to have your child Lalita reborn is still a maya for you. You refuse to let it go. That is why you were given me as your daughter—one of the reasons. But anyone who sees through the veil of maya cannot fathom the divine will. The veil is stained and the absolute is without flaw. One cannot reveal the other. In the same way, I am your own daughter but you cannot fathom me."

I have to shake myself to resist her subtle spell.

My memory reminds me that she is using me.

"Was torturing Eric to death part of God's will?" I ask.

She speaks matter-of-factly. "I did what I did to Eric to inspire you to tell me the location of the child." A pause. "Besides, he was not well. He was going to die anyway. His next birth will be more auspicious."

I snort. "Of course he was not well! You had been drinking his blood night and day! He died in horrible pain, in your hands!"

"So he did, and he stained my dress." She laughs again. "Goodbye, Mother. Don't think about what I have told you. It will only confuse you more. Just have faith in your darling daughter. It is the only thing now that can save you from suffering much greater pain."

Kalika hangs up the phone.

SIX

As Seymour comes down for his breakfast, I am sitting at the kitchen table. I have made him bacon and eggs and toast, his favorite high-cholesterol meal. He has on a brown robe and is fresh from a warm shower. He smiles at me as I pour his hand-squeezed orange juice from the other side of the table.

"One day you're going to make somebody a great wife," he says.

"Thank you. One day you're going to make a girl have a nervous breakdown."

"You worry about me too much. I just went to the movies. God knows where you were." He picks up his fork and tests his eggs. "Did you get me the morning paper? You know I can't enjoy my food unless I'm fully informed on current events," he jokes.

I speak seriously. "I am your morning paper."

He butters his toast. "What's the matter? Did Suzama predict that I am the next messiah?"

"The scripture is authentic."

"You saw it?"

"A piece of it. Suzama wrote it."

He puts down his butter knife. "But how come you never saw her working on it?"

"I was with her most of the time, but not every second. She could have written it on any number of days."

"But she didn't talk to you about it? And you were her best friend?"

"She never talked about it to me. But Suzama kept her own counsel. I doubt if she spoke to anyone about the scripture. But she left it in a place where it could be found—at a time she wished it to be found."

Seymour considers. "How did you talk Dr. Seter into letting you see it?"

There is an edge to his question.

"Are you asking if I slept with his son?"

"I noticed you were talking to him after you told me to get lost."

"I didn't tell you to get lost. I told you to go have fun." I pause. "I convinced both son and father that I have a similar scripture. They want to see it soon."

"Great. We can make one up this afternoon. We can

make papyrus and age it in the sun, then you can give me a lesson in drawing hieroglyphics." He pauses. "It wasn't a very inventive lie."

"It served its purpose." I frown. "I will have to give them something substantial to make them let me see the remainder of the scripture."

"Why don't you just give them me to use as a human sacrifice?"

"Stop that. They are not such a bad bunch." Then I have to smile. "But they are busy practicing with automatic weapons in the desert."

"They sound like a nice all-American cult."

"No, I don't think they're that, but they really do have guns. I heard the Seters talk about them when they didn't think I was listening." I pause. "But those guns might come in handy."

"Why?"

"Kalika called."

This shocks him. "When?"

"A half hour ago."

"Did she call here?"

"Yes."

He has lost his appetite for his breakfast and sits, staring out the window, his face pale. In the distance is the blue Pacific. Only he and I know how red the water can run when it is diluted with blood. Yet I remind myself that Seymour doesn't remember exactly what Kalika did to him. The time has come, I know, to tell him. Many things.

"How did she get our number?" he mutters.

"Who knows? She gets what she wants."

"If she has our number she has our address. She could be on her way here now."

I shake my head. "If she just wanted to kill us, I don't think she would have called first."

"Why did she call then?"

"She said she wanted to hear my voice."

"Like Hitler used to call home to talk to mom?" he asks.

"She hasn't found the child. She wants me to help her find him."

"But you don't know where the kid is."

"She knows that. Still, she seems to feel I can lead her to Paula and the baby."

Seymour is puzzled. I can see the question coming.

"You must have some idea what is so special about this child?"

I pour myself a glass of orange juice. I have drunk blood only three times since my rebirth as a vampire, and none of my snacks were any the worse for wear in the morning. I suspect, toward the end of his life, that Yaksha did not need blood at all to survive. Still, it tasted good to me, the warm red elixir, better than the orange juice I now sip.

"This child could be the one spoken of in the Suzama scriptures," I say softly.

Seymour stares at me. "You've got to be kidding?"

"No."

He is annoyed. "That's ridiculous. All right, I believe in vampires. I believe in you. I even believe in your bad-tempered daughter. But I don't believe that Jesus was just born in a hospital in Los Angeles. I'm sorry but I can't. It's too weird."

"Do you remember what happened to you after Kalika threw you off the pier?"

He hesitates. "Yeah. The water was freezing and I got hypothermia and passed out and you came to my rescue."

"Where did you regain consciousness?"

"Up in the mountains. The next morning."

"You were unconscious for a long time, don't you think?"

"So? What does this have to do with this kid?"

I speak carefully. "Seymour, you did not simply pass out in the cold water. Kalika did not let you go so easily. She threw something at you, a sharp stake. It was shaped like a spear." I pause. "She threw it so hard it stabbed through your spine and out through your stomach."

Seymour stands. "That's not true."

"It is true. I jumped off the pier and helped you to shore, as I told you. But you were on the beach less than a minute when you finally lost consciousness."

He is agitated. "Then how did the wound disappear? You told me you didn't give me any of your vampire blood."

"At the time I intended to give you my blood. But I was afraid to pull out the stake. I thought it would kill you." I shrug. "So I left it in."

He is breathing hard. "You're not answering my questions."

I stand and step to his side and put a hand on his shoulder.

"You lost too much blood. Even I couldn't save you." I pause. "You died that night on that beach."

He forces a smile. "Yeah, right. I'm Lazarus, back from the dead."

"There was a vial of the child's blood. I stole it from the nurse who was caring for the baby at the hospital. I had that vial with me when I took you up to the mountains."

"Why did you take me up there? You never explained that."

"To cremate your body. You must remember that when you woke up you were lying on a huge pile of wood." I squeeze his shoulder. "Seymour."

He jumps back and trembles. "That's not possible. You're making this story up. I couldn't have been dead. When you're dead you're dead. God damn it, Sita, don't lie to me this way. You're scaring me and I don't like it."

I am patient. "Just before I lit the wood, a strange feeling swept over me. I was looking down at you and I was holding this burning lighter and I couldn't stop staring at your face and thinking how you shouldn't be dead. Then I remembered the vial of blood, and I took it out of my pocket and poured some over your wounds and some down your throat. Then I walked away and stood behind a tree and prayed to God that everything would be all right." I move to his side again and put my arm over his shoulder. Both our eyes are damp. "And you were all right, Seymour. It was a miracle. You were sitting there and everything was perfectly all right." I kiss the side of his face and whisper in his ear. "I wouldn't lie to you about this, you know. I don't lie to those I love."

He is still shaking. "But I don't remember any of this."

"Maybe that is part of the miracle. Maybe it is for the best."

He looks at me with a sad little boy's face. "She really killed me?"

"Yes."

"And that baby's blood brought me back?"

"Yes."

He is awed as well as shocked. "That must mean . . ." He can't finish.

"Yes." I bury my face against his chest and dry my eyes on his robe. "I can't let my daughter get to him or to Paula. I just can't. I have to stop her and the only way I can do that is to kill her."

Seymour strokes my hair. Now he comforts me. We make a fine pair.

"Can she be killed?" he asks.

I raise my head. "I think so. Even Yaksha could be killed."

"But she is more powerful than Yaksha. You said so yourself."

I turn away and look at the ocean out the window.

"She must drink blood to survive," I say. "She has needs that only mortal flesh can fulfill. A portion of her must be mortal. She must be vulnerable."

"To the fire of automatic weapons?" He is recovering from the shock. His inner strength never ceases to amaze me. But he is a believer now, even if he won't admit it. Perhaps Lazarus argued that he had never been dead. For God's sake, Jesus, it was just a bad cold. Yeah, well, why do you smell so bad, Laz?

I continue to stand with my back to Seymour.

"I have thought of enlisting their aid," I say. "But to do so I would have to tell them an awful lot, maybe even what I am. I might have to give them a demonstration."

"You don't want to do that. They'd kill you after they killed Kalika, just to be on the safe side." Seymour considers. "Kalika is described in their scripture?"

"That's a perceptive question. Yes. But they haven't let me read that portion of the scripture. I only know of their knowledge of Kalika because I eavesdropped on their conversation."

"Did they call her Kalika?"

"The Dark Mother. It is the same difference." I grimace. "They have a horrible opinion of her."

"No doubt. Especially if Suzama was as accurate as you say." Seymour scratches his head. "You can't tell them that you're a vampire and knew Suzama personally. You would have to drink some blood in front of them to get them to listen to you after that, and then they would go running for their guns. But if you're able to describe Kalika in clear enough terms, they might believe you enough to check her out. How many of them are there?"

"Two dozen, which is a small army if they have the guns I think they do."

"You can give them some of your high-tech weapons."

"I've thought of that as well," I say.

"The only problem is that you don't know where your daughter is."

"That may not be true." I explain how Kalika spoke of her wonderful view, and the large pool below her. Yet this tip only seems to disturb Seymour.

"She mentioned the view," he says. "She went to the trouble to stand out on a balcony when she spoke to you. She knows all about your phenomenal hearing. And she probably knows how few places fit the description of her current residence. Does this add up to something in your mind?"

"A trap, of course. She might be lying in wait for us."

"She might be lying in wait for the entire Suzama Society. If she was watching you last night, she might suspect you will turn to them for help."

"I don't know if she takes them seriously. She called last night's lecture boring." I pause. "Plus she promised she wouldn't kill unless it was necessary."

"Oh, that's a relief. I feel a whole lot better now. The Mother of Darkness promises her vampire mother she's not going to get rough unless she gets pushed around. If I understand you correctly, the Suzama Society thinks it is their destiny to kill Kalika. Well, your daughter's not going to stand around and let them fill her full of lead."

I shake my head. "Kalika is many things, but I don't think she would have said such a thing to me unless it was true."

"By that reasoning you should believe she has no intention of harming the child."

"No. Obviously she intends to kill the child. She has killed to try to get to him. She is not some star-struck devotee who wants to gaze upon him in wonder. But her promise to me was something else. In fact, she asked if there was anything she could do for me."

"Still, the Suzama gang will have to hit her hard and quick if they're to survive."

"Agreed. But should we go to them for help? Should we risk their lives? Do we have the right?"

He shrugs. "It's their decision."

"Don't be so flip. No matter what you or I tell them, they won't understand how deadly Kalika is until they come face to face with her."

"I meant what I said. Their decision would not be flip. This is something these people believe in. They have dedicated their lives to it. Also, if all this is true, look at what's at stake? If this baby is the Big Guy then the world needs him. Kalika must be stopped, and I have to say no price is too high to stop her."

I nod sadly. "You said something similar when she was just a baby."

"Yes. And you wanted to give her a chance to see who she turned out to be." He pats me on the shoulder. "I'm sorry I have to put it that way. I just think we have to get a hold of all the firepower we can. Let's try to track down Kalika today. If we find her, and we live, then we'll go talk to Dr. Seter. He'll listen. It's just a question of how far you have to go to persuade him."

"Is there anything I can do for you, Mother?"

There is pain in my voice as I speak next.

"This child is special, there can be no question about that. But to me, Kalika, even if she is evil, is special as well." My head hangs heavy. "I don't know whether to pray for success or failure."

SEVEN

A local realtor informs me that there are only a dozen places in Los Angeles that fit my description of a tall apartment building with a large pool. The one with the largest pool is in Century City, at Century City Park East. Seymour and I decide to go there first. The place is exclusive, with two towers that rise twenty stories into the sky. There is valet parking, a gym, and a tennis court beside the wonderful pool. I let the valet take the car, but I don't immediately head for the woman at the reception area.

"I appreciate what you said about this being a trap," I say to Seymour, who insisted on coming so that he could serve as lookout. "But the chances are she doesn't know we're here. I don't want to walk in and request her by name."

"Chances are she's working under a different name. Did you bring a picture of her?"

"Yes. I have several of her taken when she was fully grown. But I don't want to tip our hand. If we quiz the woman at the desk, and show her Kalika's picture, she may tell Kalika someone was looking for her. These people are trained to do that. I would rather check out the underground garage first. If Kalika has a car, it will probably be new and I should be able to smell her on it."

"She could be out," Seymour says.

"It is a possibility. But I want to do this first."

So we head underground. We're dressed properly, like rich sophisticates, so no one pays any attention to us. On the second garage level a new white Mercedes catches my eye. From where I am standing, forty feet away, I don't smell my daughter. Yet there is something about the car that draws my attention. I wonder if the vehicle is emitting *vibrations*. Certainly my daughter has a very powerful aura.

A moment later we have our hands on the car.

"If this is hers," Seymour says, "she has good taste."

"I need to smell the interior," I say.

Seymour points to a tiny flashing red light inside. "Don't set off the alarm."

"I see it," I mutter as I flex my palms over the driver's side window. Very slowly I begin to push the window down. A crack appears and I let go and stick my nose close to it. There is a faint musky odor, which, according to the Vedas, is Kali's smell. But I don't need my knowledge of the Vedas to remember what my own daughter smells like. The odor fills me with nostalgia for her, but I don't know why. Ray and my darling daughter never allowed us to have a normal family life. He was a ghost and she was a demon. I glance at Seymour. "This belongs to her."

He is not as happy as he was a moment ago. He may not remember the stake through his back, but he was there when Kalika opened Eric's throat. I carefully push the window back up and wipe away the faint impressions my palms have made on the glass.

"We'd better get out of here," he says.

I study the number at the front of the parking spot. "Eighteen twenty-one. It must be her suite number. We need to stake out this building."

"Not down here," he says quickly.

"No. We'll cross the street to the high-rise office building and find an empty office that has a view of the valet parking area. When she leaves, I'll break into her condo and search it."

He swallows. "Do we have to do that?"

"You don't have to do anything. I'll do it."

"But then you'll think I'm a coward."

"I know you're a coward," I lie.

He is insulted. "Is that why you won't sleep with me?"

"No. It's because you're still a nerd. Let's get across street."

Back outside we cross Olympic Boulevard and enter one

of the triangular towers that overlooks the condo towers. This commercial building has forty floors, twice what the condo towers have. A glance at the office listings in the main lobby tells me that 3450 and 3670 and 3810 and 2520 are empty. I steer Seymour toward the elevator. We are alone as we rise up to the thirty-sixth floor.

"Maybe she never goes out," he says. "We could wait all day for her to leave."

"You're free to go to a movie if you like."

"That's not fair. You're a vampire. You don't have to fear her the way I do."

"You will recall that last time I tried to attack her on the Santa Monica Pier, she grabbed my foot before I could touch her and snapped my ankle." I shake my head. "She can kill me as easily as she can kill you, if she chooses."

"But you do think a bullet in the head or in the heart will stop her?"

"Who really knows?"

Suite 3670 appears empty. I listen at the door for a moment before breaking the lock, stepping inside, and closing the door behind us. Suite 3670 directly overlooks the condo towers. We have a clear view of the valet area. If Kalika comes down and asks for her car, or simply gets it herself, we will know. Briefly I scan the portion of the eighteenth floor that faces us. It is possible I can see 1821, but I can't tell without examining the interior of the building or seeing a floor plan. Yet all of the condos on that floor have closed vertical blinds, so even if I was staring directly at her place, it would do me little good.

Seymour and I sit down on the floor and take up the watch. Actually, it is only my eyes that are of any use. This high up, Seymour wouldn't recognize his own mother if she came out of the building across the street.

An hour goes by. Seymour gets hungry and goes for a sandwich. While he is gone I see a beautiful young woman with long dark hair come out of the condo tower. She hands the parking valet a dollar after he brings up her shiny white Mercedes. I am staring at the Dark Mother, the scourge of Suzama's prophecies, my own daughter.

"Kalika," I whisper to the glass. "What do you want?"

She climbs into her car and drives away. I am out the door in a flash. I run into Seymour on his way back with a sandwich for me. One look at my face and he is a mass of nerves. I raise my hand.

"I want you to stay here," I say. "I'm going into her condo, and you'll just get in my way."

"But you'll need a lookout," he protests.

"No."

"But I can't stay behind and let you take all the risks."

I decide not to be too quick to crush his brave initiative. Also, I am not in the mood to argue.

"All right," I say. "But if she rips your head off don't blame me."

He throws the sandwich in the garbage and we grab an elevator.

This time, at the condo tower, I have to speak to the receptionist, but I purposely keep the conversation short and silent. Catching her eye through the glass, I press her with my fiery will and mouth the words: *"Open the door."*

A moment later the door swings open.

Suite 1821 is naturally on the eighteenth floor. I do not want to break the lock because I still hope Kalika will know nothing of my visit. With a couple of pins I have brought for just this purpose, I quickly pick the lock. The door creaks open. Seymour stands behind me, the color of a hospital bed sheet.

"It's more fun to write about this stuff than do it," he says.

"Shh," I say as we step inside and close the door. "Stand on the front balcony and keep a lookout for her white Mercedes."

"What are you going to do?"

"Look for evidence of her state of mind."

Kalika owns, or rents, a two-bedroom corner condo. She has twin balconies and glorious views of the city. The place is elegant, the plush carpeting new, the white paint fresh. Her furnishings are few but tasteful. She seems to prefer traditional to modern, but nothing she has is old-fashioned. There are no magazines in the living room or dining area, yet she has a rather large TV, and I wonder how many channels she subscribes to and what her favorite programs are.

While Seymour stands outside on the balcony, I step into her office, the first bedroom on the right. She has a desk, a computer, a fax machine. Her drawers are unlocked and I rifle through them. Not entirely surprisingly, I find several maps. Most of them are of California, blow-ups of Big Sur, Mount Shasta, and Lake Tahoe. She has travel books on these areas also. There is also a guidebook on Sedona, which is located in Arizona. In another drawer are more books on these same places, but these are not typical travel guides. They contain personal accounts of the spots. I scan the books—I can read over thirty thousand words a minute with total comprehension. Quite a few of the stories describe how powerful the *vibrations* are in each place. I am fascinated because Kalika appears to be doing a lot of research on spots that have been New Age retreats for the last couple of decades.

"Do you like these places?" I whisper to myself. "Or do you think the child will be drawn to them?"

I move into my daughter's bedroom. Her queen-size bed is neatly made, covered with a hand-made quilt from China. In the corner, on top of a chest of drawers, a white silk cloth has been spread, almost as if a small altar has been set up. There are only a few books and a small Shiva Lingam set beside a brass incense holder in which a stick of musk incense has recently been burned.

The lingam is a polished gray phallic-shaped stone with three red marks on it. The shape and the markings are natural to the stone, I know. When I was a child, still a mortal, five thousand years ago, our tiny village had a Shiva Lingam. The rocks are supposed to contain the energy of Lord Shiva himself, Mahakala, who is the spouse of Mother Kali and the supposed destroyer of time at the end of all ages. Geologists describe lingams as the offspring of meteor crashes. In either case, they are highly magnetic. Brushing my hand over the stone, I feel its charge.

Kalika has three books beside the lingam: the *Bhagavad-Gita,* the *Upanishads,* the *Mahanirvana Tantra.* The Gita is the gospel according to Krishna, the *Upanishads* are collected stories of divine knowledge from ancient rishis, and the *Mahanirvana Tantra* describes Kali in her different avatars, and details her various modes of worship and innovation. All this reading material is entirely spiritual in nature. But try as I might, I cannot understand what that means. If I should be relieved or frightened. It is an old and regrettable truth that more people have been killed in the name of God than anything else.

I am picking up her copy of the *Gita* when Seymour bursts breathlessly into the room. "Her car just drove up," he says. "She wasn't gone long."

I replace the book in its exact spot. "It will take her a minute to get up here. Come, we have time."

Back out in the hallway, however, standing in front of the elevators, I begin to have doubts. As Seymour starts to push the down button, I stop him.

"Even in the garage basement," I say, "she might note the elevator going up to the eighteenth floor. She is shrewd—she might consider that more than coincidence." I pause. "Let's take the stairs."

"I just want to get out of here," Seymour says with emotion.

Halfway down the stairs I stop Seymour. Straining my ears to listen far below, I hear someone climbing up the stairs. The person is in no hurry and it could be anybody. But I don't like the fact that this person stands in our path, and that I can't see who it is—each floor is partitioned off. Seymour watches me anxiously.

"What is it?"

"Someone's coming up the stairs."

"Is it she?" he gasps.

"I can't tell." I pause. "I think it is a woman. This person has a light step."

"Oh God."

"Shh. She is far below still. Let's grab the elevator."

In the elevator, Seymour starts to push the button for the lobby, but I stop him for the second time and push the button for the second garage level. Seymour throws a fit.

"Why did you do that?" he asks.

"It is the last thing she'll expect us to do, if she thinks we know where her car is parked."

"But for all we know she's still in her car."

"Relax, Seymour. I know what I'm doing."

I hope. When the elevator *whooshes* open, I am tensed for an attack. But none comes. We appear to be alone in the underground garage. Signaling for Seymour to remain where he is, I step lightly into the garage and stretch my sensitive senses to their limits. There is no sign of Kalika. I signal to Seymour to join me.

"Let's just get our car and get out of here," I whisper in his ear.

He nods vigorously. "I am not cut out for this crap."

EIGHT

I call Dr. Seter in San Francisco but end up speaking to James, who acts happy to hear my voice. Perhaps it is not an act, but he does want to know if I am ready to show them my scripture. I tell him I have something even more important to show him. After making an appointment to see him and his father at the Hilton, after the lecture, I book a flight for San Francisco. As the plane lifts off the ground, Seymour nods to the manila envelope in my hand.

"What's that?" he asks.

"Newspaper clippings. Proof."

"I won't ask."

"You'll see soon enough."

We do not attend the lecture because I have a slight fear that Kalika will be there. We are waiting in the lounge area of the Hilton when Dr. Seter returns to the hotel. The elderly doctor looks fatigued from his travels and lecture, but James is as bright faced as ever. I introduce Seymour as an old friend and they take seats across from us. Dr. Seter orders a scotch and James a Coke. Seymour munches on the pretzels and sips cranberry juice.

I have nothing to eat or drink, not even a few drops of blood. I fear there may soon be enough blood flying to satisfy my most perverse thirsts. I wonder if Kalika still kills her victims, how many she hunts a night.

Dr. Seter studies me with tired eyes. For the first time I listen to his heart beat in his chest. He has clogged arteries, cardiac arrhythmia. He must know—I sense he is experiencing a tightness in his chest even now. Yet he smiles warmly before he begins to speak. He is a charming man.

"James tells me you have something exciting to show us," he says.

I stare at both of them for a moment.

"I know where the Dark Mother is," I say. "I need your help to kill her."

This gets their attention. Dr. Seter takes a moment to catch his breath. James glances at him anxiously, but I don't know if his anxiety is concern for his father's health or concern for the confrontation. Finally the doctor manages to speak.

"How do you know about the Dark Mother?" he asks. "You said your scripture did not speak of a particular danger to the child."

"It speaks of her in general terms," I say. "And I know this young woman." I open the manila envelope I have brought with me. "I have chronicled her behavior. But perhaps you have as well. She's been in the papers lately."

First I give them clips from the *Los Angeles Times* of the series of brutal murders that were committed last December. Crazy Eddie Fender and his gang of nasty vampires were responsible for these crimes, but the murders are of such a bizarre nature—heads torn off, bodies drained of their blood—that I feel they strengthen my case. Next I show them clippings of the major shoot-out the police had with a gang of terrorists in downtown L.A.: three helicopters downed and dozens of police killed by a tiny but invincible force. Of course, I was responsible for those deaths. The police and FBI had the bad judgment to chase after me and Joel for our vampire blood.

I show them clippings of the Nevada nuclear explosion, and finally give them articles on Eric Hawkins, who was kidnapped from the park while playing basketball with friends. He was not found until weeks later, his throat scissored open by what appeared to be sharp fingernails. Yes, the words of the city coroner have made it all the way into the article, and they are surprisingly accurate. Naturally, it is only this last death Kalika was responsible for but now is not the time to reveal that. Dr. Seter and his son study the clippings for several minutes and then the doctor frowns at me.

"I don't see what this has to do with the Dark Mother," he says.

His voice is without conviction. I suspect that either he or James has been collecting similar clippings. The possibility strengthens my position and I decide to hold nothing back. I lean forward slightly as I speak and my tone is deadly serious.

"The Dark Mother is vampiric in nature," I say. "The original serial murders in L.A. all bear a vampiric stamp. This is when the Dark Mother moved into the Los Angeles area. Notice the dates of the murders, how they cease right after the terrorist shoot-out with the police. Yet these terrorists have never been found, never been identified. The media says it's because they escaped, but the real reason is that these terrorists never existed. In fact, the only one the police ever spoke about definitively was a young woman who was able to move extremely fast."

"We have read about her," James says, glancing at his father.

"Then there is the nuclear explosion in the Nevada desert," I continue. "Once again the media and the government drew a connection to terrorists, but here, too, they failed to identify the terrorists. Because there weren't any. For a brief time the Dark Mother was a prisoner of the military camp where the explosion occurred. But even with all their guns, all their tanks and soldiers, they couldn't contain her and she broke free and destroyed them. She went underground after that, yet she didn't leave the Los Angeles area. Note the description of Eric Hawkins's supposed kidnapper and compare it to the descriptions the police gave of the young woman who helped mess up downtown L.A. You will see they match. That's because all these events originate with one young woman who is not really a human being at all." I pause. "I know her name. I know where she lives. She may know I know this, I'm not sure. She won't remain where she is long. If you want to destroy her, you'll have to strike at her tonight. And don't look so shocked. I know you've prepared for a long time to do exactly this."

Dr. Seter is so taken aback by my words he can't speak. James takes up his role. "How do you know these things?" he asks. "You didn't read about them in an ancient scripture."

"I had a friend in the FBI who leaked parts of this information to me. He came to me originally because his agency was researching the Suzama material. This friend is now deceased— he died in the Nevada explosion. But before he died he gave me enough clues to locate and speak to the Dark Mother."

They both almost fall off their chairs. "You have seen her?" Dr. Seter exclaims.

"I have, too," Seymour says on cue. "We both spoke to her at the end of the Santa Monica Pier three months ago. She almost killed us both, but in the end decided to let us go."

"Why would she let you go if you're a danger to her?" Dr. Seter asks.

"She obviously doesn't think we are a danger to her," I say.

"Or else she thinks we may eventually lead her to the child. That's why she agreed to meet us, to quiz us about the Suzama material."

"We still need to see your scripture," Dr. Seter says.

"You can't," I say. "She destroyed it this afternoon. Furthermore, she might be on the verge of destroying your copy, along with the rest of you." I pause. "She was at your lecture last night."

James's voice is harsh. "Why didn't you tell us?"

"I didn't know," I say honestly. "I only found out today when she called me at home to tell me."

"Why would she call you?" Dr. Seter asks.

"I told you. I think she stays in touch because we—Seymour and I—might possibly lead her to the child. Plus you do not know her the way we do. To you she is just a name. To us she is a witch, who calls to taunt us, to let us know we live in her shadow."

Dr. Seter regards me critically. "What is her name? Do you know?"

"If I tell you, will you believe me?" I ask.

"Not necessarily," Dr. Seter says. "But I will at least give more credence to your wild story."

"Her name is Kalika, Kali Ma. This dark age of Kali Yuga is named after her."

Clearly Kalika is mentioned in Suzama's scripture. Their suddenly shocked expressions confirm this fact. Yet the information fills me with dismay. Is there no hope for my daughter? I know I am here to solicit aid in killing her but a part of me still longs to discover that I have made a terrible mistake, that all the horrors Kalika has committed since she drew her first breath are nothing more than misunderstandings. But it is not to be and I know it. Either my daughter dies or we do, and then also the child who can save the whole world. Dr. Seter is again having trouble catching his breath.

"Can this be true?" he whispers to himself.

"It is true," Seymour says. "I have seen with my own eyes what she can do. She is stronger than two dozen men combined, as fast as lightning. She is already stalking your group. You don't have much time."

James stares at Seymour. "How do you know Alisa?"

Seymour shrugs. "We're old friends."

James turns to me. "Neither of you has ever given us a last name. We have no way to check your background. We still don't know if you're with the government or not."

"The names we have given you are false," I say. "So what is the point in giving you a false last name? Surely you can understand our reasons for secrecy. We can talk all night and into the next morning. There is only one way of convincing you that we have found the Dark Mother, and that is to bring you to her. But when you do meet her, you have to be ready to kill her or else to be killed by her. It is that simple. You lose nothing by trusting me enough to check her out. Once again, that is if you have all your forces standing at full readiness."

Dr. Seter scoffs. "We don't have any forces."

"You are a poor liar, doctor," I say. "The FBI knows about your training exercises and your automatic weapons. They didn't interfere with you because there were agents, like my friend, who knew about the Suzama material and understood what you were preparing for. But those agents are dead now. Kalika killed them. As a result your group is threatened from all sides, politically and spiritually. You might even think I'm a threat, that I've been sent here by the Black Mother to lure you into a trap. Actually, there may be a particle of truth in that. I am not working for her, but if you do choose to confront her you may be wiped out. Seymour is not exaggerating her strength. But at least if you hit first you stand a chance. If you go after her you must hold back nothing. Yet you must first explain to your people what the real nature of the risk is. Tell them that several dozen police and marines couldn't stop her."

Dr. Seter is shaking his head. "This is all happening too fast. We can't do anything tonight. It's out of the question."

I don't want to push him, to fry his brain, or even to confuse his mind. I want the decision to be his because I suspect I am not exaggerating when I say many of his people may die. So I assuage my conscience. Yet I cannot let him stall. I feel he is close to agreeing with me. I have told him much that only he would know is true. It doesn't matter to me that I have lied to him a lot as well.

"You knew when the time came there would be no time

for hesitation," I say gently. "She is down in Los Angeles, right now, in a condo with a wonderful view of the city. We were in her place this afternoon."

"She told you where she lives?" James asks.

"No. She made a mistake when she called me. That is all I can say. Seymour and I were then able to figure out where she lives."

"You traced her call?" James persists.

"In a manner of speaking," I say. "Dr. Seter, this is all real. I know you have been talking about it so long that it has lost some of its reality to you. But you only have to come with me tonight and bring your group, and you will see a five-thousand-year-old prophecy fulfilled before your very eyes."

He looks at me. "You are not a normal young woman, Alisa. There is something in your face, in your voice, in your eyes. James mentioned it last night and now I see it." He pauses. "How do we know you're not the Dark Mother?"

I smile sadly. "Some nights I feel as if I am. And even if I were, then that's all the more reason to heed my warning." Reaching over, I touch his knees. "Trust the inner senses that Suzama's material has given you. Trust what they are telling you right now." I pause. "Your whole life has led up to this moment."

Dr. Seter flashes a faint smile. "Somehow I can't imagine you are evil." He turns to James. "I need to talk to my son, alone, for a few minutes, if you please."

I stand and point to the entrance. "We will wait over there. We will give you all the privacy and time you need to decide."

Of course the moment we leave I stand still and listen to every word they say. It is a short but intense conversation.

James: "She knew the name of the Dark Mother! No one in our group except us knows that!"

Dr. Seter: "She knows many things I would have thought impossible. But that doesn't mean we can trust her."

James: "But you heard her argument. It's the same argument I've been giving you for the last few months. Those incidents we read about were all caused by a single deadly force. Only she has put the pieces together much better than we did. I'm telling you, Father, I believe her. I say we throw everything we've got behind her."

Dr. Seter: "But just last night you were worried she was working for the Dark Mother."

James: "She is not behaving like someone who is trying to harm us. Right now she gave us a ton of information she didn't have to. Information that could be used against the Dark Mother."

Dr. Seter: "Only if it's true."

James: "It is true! Look, she only asks us to trust her so far. We will know within seconds of meeting this person if she is the Dark Mother. But she is right, we must be prepared for a major attack. It is the only way to protect our people."

Dr. Seter: "But what if she's lying to us? If she's working

for the government and is trying to trap our group while it is engaged in illegal activities? Think about it, Jim, we're going to be storming a residence of some kind. If it is a government trap, we'll look like just another evil and confused cult in the eyes of the public."

James: "We'll have her with us when we make our attack. If she's lied to us, she'll pay the price."

Dr. Seter: "That's just talk. You wouldn't hurt her."

James: "I don't think I'll have to hurt her. I think our enemy will be so evil our hatred will be turned totally on her." A pause. "Let's do it. If we don't, Father, we will regret it for the rest of our lives. That's what my inner feelings tell me."

Dr. Seter is a long time answering. But finally he gives his okay.

NINE

The attack has yet to begin but already I realize something is very strange. I had initially gone to Dr. Seter and James because I knew I was physically and emotionally ill-equipped to kill Kalika. She is too strong for me, and I can't imagine hurting her. All I wanted to do was send in twenty people with guns, close my eyes, and be told it was all over. Your daughter is dead, the world is safe for democracy again. Yet the Suzama Society seems to be much more than twenty people with guns. It should reassure me that they are better prepared than I imagined, yet it does not, and I puzzle over this.

I stand in Suite 3670, in the commercial building across the street from Kalika's condo tower. Olympic Boulevard lies between us and my daughter, but at this time of night—three in the morning—it is rare that a car drives by. Beside me are

Dr. Seter, Seymour, James, and two sharpshooters with laser-assisted rifles. They have cut away a circular panel in the glass and now are focusing their weapons on Kalika's windows, which are visible, barely—for we are eighteen stories above her. All of Kalika's windows are covered with vertical blinds, however. We have better views of her two balconies and the large pool far below. Of course, we have a clear view of the roof of the tower. It is at this spot that I stare as my doubts continue to grow.

Dr. Seter and his son have not assembled a group of spiritual fanatics and trained them how to aim and fire automatic weapons. Instead they have managed to construct the equivalent of a highly trained commando unit. I am staggered by the way they go about surrounding Kalika, who, by the way, is definitely at home. Their attack is much more coordinated than the attack the LAPD and the FBI sprang to capture me and Joel.

There are two units: Alpha Top and Alpha Bottom. The former has somehow managed to make it onto the roof of the building with ropes and pulleys. Alpha Bottom is already on Kalika's floor. The security guards are apparently unconscious, if we are to believe the radio reports that are constantly streaming in. We're all tied together with short wave. Both Alpha Top and Alpha Bottom have ten members each, male and female, all dressed in black. They have night goggles, gas grenades, even grenade launchers. Where they bought all this stuff, I have no idea.

I watch as the last of the Alpha Top team assembles on the roof.

"How do they plan on getting down to Kalika's balcony?" I ask James, pointing at the people on the roof. James is also dressed in black, a radio in his hand. His face shines with excitement. Apparently he likes playing soldier. The whole situation strikes me as odd, and yet I am the one who instigated it—I think.

"The same way they got on the roof," he says. "We will lower six of them onto the balconies before we attack, three onto each balcony. We won't attack until everyone is in position. Why?"

"She will hear them on the balcony," I say.

James peers through a pair of binoculars hung around his neck. "We have pretty much determined that she is asleep."

"I wouldn't count on that," Seymour mutters.

"We must give her a chance to cooperate," Dr. Seter says for perhaps the tenth time. Although the doctor is supposed to be the boss, it is clear to me the attack units are taking orders only from James.

"She'll be given every chance she deserves," James says. He clicks on his radio. "Alpha Bottom, this is Control. Are you still holding by the eighteenth floor elevators? Over."

"Control, this is Alpha Bottom. We are near the elevators. Over."

"Alpha Bottom, this is Control. Alpha Top will be swinging

onto the balconies momentarily. Do not move toward Suite Eighteen Twenty-one until you are ordered. Over."

"Control, this is Alpha Bottom. Understood. Out."

James studies the top group through his binoculars. Then he clicks his radio back on. "Alpha Top, this is Control. Any signs that Kalika is in the living room or kitchen area? Over."

"Control, this is Alpha Top. We have detected no activity in the living room or kitchen area. Over."

"Alpha Top, are your ropes in place? Over."

"Control, we are ready to swing down. Over."

"Alpha Top, this is Control. You may start down. But hold on the balconies until you hear from me. Over."

"Control, understood. Alpha Top out."

"You guys seem to know what you're doing," I say.

James smiles. "You sound disappointed."

I give a wan smile. "I always have a thing for the underdog." More than a thing. Watching them all converge on Kalika, I feel sick to my stomach. I have to keep telling myself that Kalika is totally unpredictable, that they have to be careful. Dr. Seter puts a hand on my arm.

"We have trained for this day for a long time," he says. "But we will not shoot first, I promise you that. She will be given every chance to surrender."

I shake my head. "She will never surrender."

In teams of three, dropping off from two points on the roof, the Alpha Top people begin to slide down toward the balconies. They land in seconds; I watch as they unclip the ropes from their belts. Each carries a weapon, has a radio in an ear, and night goggles. The guy in charge of Alpha Top comes back on the line, speaking in hushed whispers.

"Control, we are in position. Over."

"He shouldn't be talking," I say. "She'll hear him. In fact, they should be ready for her to attack. Now. Tell them to get their weapons drawn. She could come at them any second."

James ignores me. He talks into his radio.

"Alpha Top, this is Control. You will go on my command. Stand ready. Over."

Separated by a corner of the building, neither group of three can see the other group. This is a major weakness in the plan. They should know to the split second what every one of them is doing. Their radios are not fast enough. James continues to bark instructions.

"Alpha Bottom, this is Control. Move toward Suite Eighteen Twenty-one. Alpha Top is in position on the balconies. Over."

"Control, this is Alpha Bottom. Understood. Over."

The ten people on the Alpha Bottom team will crowd one another as they move along the hallway. I point this out to James and suggest he hold back half of them by the elevators. He brushes aside my comment.

"They know what they're doing," he says. "They won't accidentally shoot each other."

"You don't understand how fast she can move," I say. "The more room they have, the more chance they have of getting off a clean shot."

"I want Alpha Bottom to knock at the door first," Dr. Seter says. "She has to be told that she is surrounded and that escape is impossible."

"She doesn't think in terms of impossibilities," Seymour mutters. "I think it will be a mistake to knock."

James checks with me. "Do you agree?"

I think of Kalika riddled with bullets while she lies in bed.

"I agree." I turn to Dr. Seter. "There is no point in talking to her. Honestly."

Dr. Seter trembles. "But this could be coldblooded murder."

"I say we listen to Alisa," James says. Before anyone can protest he clicks on his radio. "Alpha Top and Alpha Bottom, this is Control. We will move on the count of five. One . . . two . . . three . . ."

He does not reach five.

There is loud screaming.

We hear it over the radio and through the air.

We look down to see that the balcony farthest from us is empty—of Suzama people, that is. Kalika, alone, is out there, her hair hanging down the back of her white robe. Below her, three individuals in black float down toward the large swimming pool. Float is perhaps too kind a word. They are falling to their deaths, and they know it. The few feet of pool water are not going to absorb their falls. Their horrified screams rend the air and I scream at myself for believing that Kalika would just lie down and die.

The three hit the water, landing on top of each other, crashing through to the bottom. Their limbs and skulls explode on contact. The pool is well lit. Within seconds a red wave expands across the blue water. The screams cease. I turn to James.

"Call off the attack!" I yell. "Get your people out of there! She may let them go if they pull back now!"

James stares down in horror as blood fills the pool.

"This is incredible," he mumbles.

I grab him. "I was wrong! She can't be stopped this way! Tell them to back off!"

He looks at me and frowns. "No. We have only started to fight." He touches his two sharpshooters on the shoulders, the two that crouch below us. "Open fire."

Their bullets begin to ricochet off the balcony. Kalika moves inside.

"Alpha Top!" James shouts into his radio. "She is coming."

No, she has come. Before James can finish speaking, Kalika attacks those on the second balcony. Only my eyes are fast enough to see exactly what she does. The person closest to the balcony door is a woman with long red hair. Kalika grabs her and twists her head all the way around. Catching the dead woman's weapon as it falls, Kalika then shoots the other two in the face. One, a handsome guy with no top skull, falls over the balcony and lands on the sidewalk seventeen floors below. The third one, a short dark guy, simply sits down and dies. Before our sharpshooters can readjust their aim to the nearer balcony, Kalika has retreated inside. And now she has an automatic weapon with her. James struggles to turn his radio back on.

"Alpha Bottom!" he yells. "You must attack!"

"What has happened to Alpha Top?" the guy wants to know.

"Those on the balcony have been taken out!" James says and forgets all the "Alpha" this and "over" that. There is no time for such formalities. "She is still inside! Get her!"

"Tell them she has a gun!" I say.

"She has a gun!" James yells. "Alpha Top, you must get down to the balconies! Alpha Bottom is going in!"

The four still on the roof are peering over the edges. They see that the pool is full of bodies and so is one of the balconies. Why, there is even a body down on the sidewalk. They don't want to go anywhere. I wish they would go back the way they came. I know they are in extreme danger just by being on the roof.

"We have to stop!" Dr. Seter cries to his son, his face ashen. "Alisa is right! Don't send any more people."

The radio is screaming.

Now Alpha Bottom is dying.

They have kicked in her door, violated her space. There are gunshots, sounds of tearing flesh, splattering blood, breaking bones. And over it all I hear Kalika laughing. She is unstoppable and knows it. It is only then I realize that from the very beginning this has been a trap. Seymour was right. Kalika let me hear enough to figure out where she lived. She knew I would try to get help, and since she obviously doesn't like the Suzama group, so much the better that they should come to her to die. I hear one woman begging for mercy and then it sounds as if she is smashed against a wall. James trembles with the radio in his hand.

"Alpha Top!" he shouts. "Help your partners!"

The four still on the roof look at one another and shake their heads. They would be better off getting down from the roof, yet they must think they are safe up there because they hardly move while the screaming continues. But when it stops, and the firing stops, I finally grab the radio from James's hands.

"Alpha Top," I say calmly. "She knows you're up there. Try to go back down the way you came up. Don't wait for her to come to you. Please, listen to me. Swing down to the nineteenth floor and get in the elevator. There's still time."

But what time there is they squander. A precious minute elapses while they seem to argue among themselves. At the end of that time, Kalika, her white robe now soaked red, peeks over the edge of the roof. They see her, and those left of Alpha Top are too scared even to level their weapons. As Kalika climbs up onto the roof, they slowly back into the corner farthest from her. Even the sharpshooters at our knees stare in awe. James slaps one on the head.

"Shoot her!" he shouts. "She's an easy target!"

But my daughter makes nothing easy. As a bullet sparks at her feet, she leaps forward and grabs one of the men and holds him as a shield in front of her. The other three continue to stand immobilized by fear. But now Kalika is looking our way. The sharpshooters cease firing. James throws a tantrum.

"Don't stop!" he screams. "Kill her!"

"But she's holding Charles," one protests.

"Oh God, this can't be happening," Dr. Seter moans.

James shoves the guy aside. "Give me that gun!"

But I stop James. "Let me," I say quietly.

He glares at me. "What do you know about sniper rifles?"

"She knows a lot," Seymour says.

James continues to glare at me, but finally lets me take the gun.

"Just don't miss," he says bitterly.

Kneeling behind the stationary rifle, I peer into the telescopic sight. Kalika is standing relatively motionless, but she still has the guy held neatly in front of her. Only her face is visible behind the guy's right shoulder. The laser guide is helpful, even for someone like me who can hit a dime-size object at two miles if I have the right gun. For a moment I am able to plant the red dot precisely in the center of Kalika's forehead. My finger sweats over the trigger. I merely have to pull it and put a bullet in her brain and the night can still be considered a success, at least as far as the world is concerned.

But then I catch sight of her eyes, and I hesitate. She seems to be looking directly at me. Who am I fooling? Of course she knows who tracks her. The fact seems to amuse her because she smiles ever so faintly. Her lips move to form a soundless word, yet I hear it, hear it inside.

"Mother."

I momentarily lose my concentration. In that time Kalika moves swiftly and with deadly purpose, vanishing from the field of view of my laser scope. Pulling back from the weapon, I watch her throw her human shield off the side of the roof. She tosses her victim straight at the pool—perhaps it amuses her to see the big red splash the screaming people make—and a moment later there is that much more blood to clean out of the filter.

In quick succession she grabs two of the three who are left. These she kills by smashing their skulls together. They are unrecognizable as she lets them fall onto the rooftop, their brains hanging over their collars. Then her attention turns to the final member of the Suzama Society, and I recognize her. Lisa, the accountant from North Dakota, whom I met last night. So great is Lisa's fear that she backs away from my daughter, right off the side of the roof. Kalika does not let her fall, but grabs her at the last instant. James yells at me.

"Why don't you shoot!" he says.

I set the gun down. "No. I can't kill Lisa."

"Lisa is as good as dead!" James cries. "Shoot!"

But Kalika has already disappeared with her prey, a spider crawling back into her web with a kicking insect in tow. The roof is now empty except for two virtually headless bodies.

I stand and look at all of them. "Stay here. I am going to speak to her."

Dr. Seter grabs my arm. "You can't go over there, child. It's a bloodbath."

I gently remove his hand. "I am responsible for this." I turn to Seymour. "I have to go."

Seymour is devastated by my decision. "There's no point."

"That is probably the understatement of the year," I agree.

TEN

The moment I am out the door I switch into hyper-mode. Using the stairs instead of waiting for the elevator, I reach the condo in less than one min-ute. In the distance I hear the cry of a dozen sirens. Yet the police are not really late to respond. Since the beginning of the attack less than seven minutes have elapsed. Kalika was definitely not sleeping.

Standing outside the building is a tide of moaning souls in pajamas and robes. Somebody should at least turn off the pool lights, I think. The floating bodies create a particularly grue-some sight. A few of the people, all men in their forties, have guns in their hands. They are arguing with one another as I dash inside the building.

I take the stairs to the eighteenth floor. Between the

sixteenth and seventeenth floors I find two brutally slain bodies, their heads literally torn from their bodies.

"Would you be upset if I ripped this bird's head off?"

"Why do you ask these silly questions?"

"To hear your answers."

The sight of these poor people upsets me greatly, but it makes me pause to ask myself the question: what am I doing? Am I trying to save Lisa in order to bandage my shattered conscience for the other deaths I have caused? Not that Lisa is not worth my effort, but I know she is as James said, as good as dead. And if I die with her who will be left to stop Kalika?

But these questions, like most, are academic.

I hear cries above me. Lisa, in the claws of a jackal.

Picking up an automatic rifle, I continue up the stairs.

Kalika is waiting for me in the center of her living room. I have to walk over a glut of slashed bodies to get to her. The place is not as neat as it was that afternoon when Seymour and I investigated. There is hardly a square foot of wall or ceiling or floor that is not splattered red. Apparently my daughter let them come as far as they wanted into her home before she welcomed them as only she knows how.

Yet Lisa is still alive. In Kalika's arms.

I level my gun at the two of them.

"It's a coward who hides behind another," I say to my daughter.

Kalika smiles. Her face, her arms, even her hair are drenched in blood, and she has never looked happier. Tightening her hold on Lisa, she lifts the young woman a foot off the floor. For her part, Lisa is half in shock, with at least one foot in the grave. Yet she continues to struggle against my daughter, all the while making feeble whimpering sounds. The fight in her is instinctive. I believe Kalika has already shattered her mind.

"We did this once before," she says. "But you were not carrying a weapon that night."

"I am not going to put the gun down," I say.

Kalika chuckles. "Then I should kill her now?"

"No." I take a step forward. "Let her go. Show your mercy."

"Drop the gun. Show your courage."

"You will just kill us both."

"Perhaps," Kalika agrees.

"You set me up. You wanted me to bring them here. Why?"

"I would think the answer to that question is obvious."

"The police will be here in minutes," I say.

"The police do not concern me." She raises a sharp nail to Lisa's throat. "I cannot let you shoot me, Mother. I have a mission yet to perform."

"What is it?"

"To protect the righteous and to destroy the wicked."

I sneer. "Tonight is a fine example of that mission of yours."

"Thank you." Kalika presses her nail into Lisa's neck. A drop of blood appears and traces a line down the young woman's throat. Lisa, even though in shock, suddenly gasps and struggles harder. But Kalika's hold is stronger than steel. She speaks casually. "You remember this part, don't you, Mother?"

I begin to panic. I cannot let this girl die. She is almost a stranger to me, true, but she is all that Dr. Seter has left. If I can save her, I think, I can save the doctor. I know his heart will give out soon after this night. You will see prophecies fulfilled. Yeah, right. The Satanic Prophecies. How could I make him such promises? Kalika is right about one thing. I lie to suit my needs. It is an old habit of mine.

"You promised me this morning that you would not kill unless it was necessary," I say.

Kalika digs her nail in a little deeper. The red line on Lisa's throat thickens. Soon the blood will gush. Lisa's eyes are as round as overripe strawberries. Her breathing sounds labored. Or is that her heart I hear, skipping inside her trembling chest? Lisa is almost gone but still her expression begs for me to save her.

"This is becoming necessary," Kalika says. "Put down the gun."

"I can't."

"I will open her throat. She will go the way Eric did. You know how much that upset you."

Now I shake. "But this young woman is innocent."

"She came to kill me. Innocence is hardly the word I would apply to her."

"I brought her here. I am to blame. Please, Kalika, for the love of God, let her go."

Kalika pauses. "For the love of God? How can you say that to me after you have gazed into my eyes? Don't you know I do everything for the love of God?"

With that Kalika scratches her sharp nail all the way across Lisa's throat, opening two of the young woman's major arteries. The blood shoots out as if fired from a hose under tremendous pressure. But I am hardly given a chance to react, to fire through Lisa's body now that it has ceased to be a viable living shield. My daughter is swifter than Eddie Fender was. Lisa gags on pieces of throat as Kalika throws her at me. The blow is enough to knock me over and send my weapon flying. The back of my skull strikes a wall as Lisa slowly slips from me and everything is a blur to me for a moment. There is blood on the back of my own head. I reach up to feel the extent of my injury when I see a figure out of the corner of my eye. It is my daughter holding my gun. She speaks in a kind voice.

"Are you in pain?" she asks.

The room continues to spin. Lisa's body weighs heavily on my lower legs.

"Go to hell," I mumble.

"I am beyond heaven and hell." She reaches out and grabs my arm. "You have friends in the other building. Save me time and tell me what suite they're in."

Finally my eyes begin to refocus. I stare at her.

"You've got to be kidding," I say.

She smiles. "Just thought I would ask. Do you know how to swim?"

"Yes."

"Do you know how to fly?"

Sounds like a trick question to me.

I don't answer it but it doesn't matter.

Tossing aside the gun, Kalika grabs me by the chest and with one hand drags me outside and onto the balcony where she dealt with the first three members of Alpha Top. Far below the bodies continue to float in the red-stained pool. The police have finally arrived. Numerous black and white units are jammed into the valet parking area, their search beams pointed at us. I would wave but I'm afraid they might shoot me. Kalika sighs in wonder as she sweeps the city night with her dark eyes.

"I told you the view was stunning," she says.

"I am pleased that my only daughter should be so successful that she is able to afford such a nice place," I say sweetly.

Kalika leans over and kisses me on the cheek. Her lips are soft and gentle. She speaks in my ear and there is a trace of concern in her voice.

"Can you survive such a fall? Tell me the truth."

"I honestly don't know."

She pulls back slightly and strokes my hair. "Krishna loves you."

I am having trouble breathing. Her grip is cruel.

"It is good somebody does," I gasp.

"Did I ever tell you that I love you?"

"No. Not that I can remember."

"Oh." A deadly pause. "I must have forgotten."

"Kalika—"

I am not given a chance to finish the sentence.

My own daughter throws me over the side of the balcony.

The moon is out, it is true, and it is very bright. But there is no time to allow its gentle rays to pour into the crown of my head and fill my body to float me safely away as it did when the nuclear bomb threatened to kill me. At the moment I could be a mortal. Certainly I fall as fast as one. Kalika has thrown me toward the pool. As the bloody mess rushes toward me, I can only pray that I land in the deep end.

When I hit, my arms and legs are spread as far as they will go. I reason that this will give me more of a chance to break my fall. But I know even before I strike the water that something else will break when I strike the bottom of the pool.

The shock is crushing. There is a flash of red followed by an agony so searing I lose consciousness. But the oblivion is cruel; it does not last. When I awake my face is pressed into the floor of the pool. Indeed I have cracked the plaster, and half the bones in my body. My nose seems to have been obliterated, my face is a pancake of gross tissue. Inside my torn mouth I feel a lump of crumbled teeth. My chest feels as if ribs poke through my lungs and my shirt, pouring more blood into the pool.

Honestly, I don't think I can live through this.

Especially under nine feet of water.

The dead float above me, their expressionless faces inviting me to join them. The water seems to swim with nightmarish creatures. One of my black boots floats by. My sock, covered in red, is still inside. My spinal cord is possessed by a pain demon. He has brought sharp tools. I throw up in the water and blood and teeth come out and form a ghastly cloud over my head. I start to lose consciousness again, and I know if I do, I will never wake up. Yet my eyes refuse to remain open. They are broken as well. Closing them, I sink into a deeper level of darkness.

Krishna. Let me have one more chance. That is all I ask.

To stop her. To save the child.

My heart keeps beating. The agony keeps throbbing.

Time goes by but pain counts it at a different speed. This time is what is called hard time by all those who have suffered. And hard times bring hard truths. My brains may be leaking from my ears, but I finally understand that Kalika cannot be defeated by guns and bullets. Twenty people, maybe more, had to die to make me understand that.

But I will never understand how she can be so cruel.

"But anyone who sees through the veil of maya cannot fathom the divine will. The veil is stained and the absolute is without

flaw. One cannot reveal the other. In the same way, I am your own daughter but you cannot fathom me."

No matter how many die, I will not understand.

From far away, I feel feverish activity. It comes, I realize, from deep inside me, in my muscles, beneath my veins, and all around my joints. My supernatural body is trying to knit itself back together. Beneath my shirt, I feel my sternum grow back together into one piece. Next there are pops in my legs and ankles. The bones are resetting themselves at a frantic pace. My jaw flexes involuntarily and I feel new teeth pressing up from beneath my mangled gums. Finally I am able to open my eyes, and I give myself a gentle push toward the surface. The beat of my heart has turned to a shriek. If I do not draw in a breath soon, especially with all the repair work going on, my chest will explode.

The night air tastes good. Never better.

On the surface, I am forced to float on my back for a minute before I am strong enough to make my way to the side. There is a crowd gathered, and some of the people in it are cops. I hear screams as I begin to pull myself out of the pool, but a brave cop rushes to my side with a clean blanket. He is fat with a bushy mustache. He carefully wraps the blanket around me.

"You're going to be okay," he says. "Just lie here on the deck. Don't try to move. You may have broken bones."

I wipe at the blood on my face. I know I don't have much time.

"You have friends in the other building."

"No, I'm fine," I say. "Don't worry about me."

I try to stand but he tries to stop me.

"But you were thrown off that balcony," he protests. "It's a miracle you're still alive."

I finish wiping my face and hair with his blanket and hand it back to him all bloody. "You're a kind man," I say. "But I have to get out of here."

I move too fast for him to stop me—yet I am far from healed. Even as I dash across Olympic Boulevard, I feel the tissue inside my body struggling to recover. If I meet Kalika in the next minute I will be at a serious disadvantage. Not that it will make much difference. But it is fear that hurries me along, or maybe it is foolish hope. Hope that she might have let some of them survive.

In the office building, the elevator takes me to the thirty-sixth floor. The stairs are too much for me in my condition. When I stagger out of the elevator, the first thing I see is blood. For a moment all hope in me dies. The door to Suite 3670 has been pulverized. Yet there is a sound, soft words, faint moans. I hurry forward and peer inside.

Seymour and Dr. Seter huddle in one corner. My old friend appears to be taking care of the doctor, who's having trouble catching his breath. Twenty feet away from them, in the center of the room, the two sharpshooters lie in an ugly heap. It looks as if she kicked each of them so hard in the chest that she ruptured their hearts—an old Sita move. Yet Seymour and Dr. Seter appear unharmed. I almost weep I am so relieved.

It is only then I notice that James is missing.

"Where is he?" I demand.

They jump and look over. I am still covered with blood.

Dr. Seter gasps. "We thought you were dead."

I stride toward them and look down. "Where is James? Did she take him?"

Seymour stands and shakes his head. "He went after you, right after you left. We haven't seen him since." He hugs me; there are tears on his face. "Thank God you're alive. We saw her throw you off the balcony. I thought it was all over."

I comfort him, but also catch his eye. "That was someone else you saw. Not me." I turn back to the doctor. "You have a heart condition. Will you be all right? Should I call for an ambulance?"

"I'll be fine." He reaches up. "Just help me up."

I do so. "What happened?" I ask.

Seymour gestures weakly. "The door exploded and she walked in. The guys tried to shoot her, but she didn't give them a chance. Then she pinned Dr. Seter to the wall and demanded he tell her where the scripture was."

Dr. Seter looks crushed. "And I told her everything. I tried to resist but I couldn't." He stops and he is close to crying. "Do you think she got James?"

"No." The voice comes from the door. James steps into the room. He surveys the dead sharpshooters and a shudder goes through his body. "I am unharmed," he says.

I step to his side. "Did you see her leave?"

"Yes. She stole a cop car and drove away in it."

"Did you see anything else?"

I am asking if he saw me hit the pool and survive.

He stares at me. "No. I mean, what do you mean? It's a holocaust over there."

"Nothing. I am sorry about tonight," I say. "I know the words sound stupid but I must say them. At least now you can see why she must be stopped." Placing my hand over his heart, as I had the previous night, I am surprised at how evenly it is beating. He got rattled during Kalika's attack but has quickly regained his cool. I add, "You have to show me the remainder of your scripture. If it is still there."

ELEVEN

Kalika was thorough. The Suzama Society has only two members now. The news shocks me. Surely, I say to James as he drives us toward Palm Springs, there have to be some personnel at the center who weren't involved in the attack.

"No," he replies. He adds with a bitter laugh, "We're all true believers. We believed your story, and went after the Dark Mother with everything we had." The morning sun is bright in his face but James appears close to despair as he thinks about the previous night. "We don't even have a secretary at the center now."

I reach over and rub his shoulders. "It wasn't your fault. If anyone is to blame, it is I. I knew what she could do."

"But you did warn us. You warned me. If I had listened to your suggestions, maybe fewer would have been killed."

"No. It wouldn't have made any difference. She was determined to kill them all."

He frowns. "Why did she spare my father and your friend?"

"That puzzles me," I say honestly. "The only thing I can think is that she must believe that either your father or Seymour, working with us, will eventually find the child."

He is concerned. "Do you think she's following us now?"

I have been checking to see if we are being shadowed.

"Not at this very moment, no," I say.

"Do you think my father and your friend will be safe at your house?"

He is not asking about a threat from Kalika. We are all fugitives from the law now, from the government. I have no doubt my description has been relayed to those higher-ups who knew I was at the military base in Nevada. My face has shown up at too many public slaughters lately. There is an excellent chance, I think, that the police or the FBI will be waiting for us at the Suzama Center in Palm Springs. When the bodies are all identified, they will make the natural link. That's why I have insisted we go to the center immediately. I have yet to decide if I will kill to see the scripture.

"For the time being," I say. "Your father can rest there, and Seymour will take good care of him." I pause. "You worry about him, don't you?"

He nods. "His heart is lousy."

"Are you adopted?"

My question surprises him. "Yes. I was adopted late. I was sixteen when my parents were killed in a car accident. At the time Dr. Seter and my father were colleagues at Stanford. He started out watching me so I started calling him Dad, at first only as a joke. But now I feel closer to him than I did to my real father. A short time after I moved in with him he found the scripture and then we shared a mission together as well as a house."

"Where did he find it?"

He hesitates. "Israel. In Jerusalem."

"That's not Western Europe."

"It's better if he's not specific. Where did you find yours? Tell me the truth this time."

"In Jerusalem."

He nods. "And Kalika destroyed it yesterday?"

"She took it. I don't know if she destroyed it."

"So she lets you live as well."

"I suppose," I say, feeling sad. My own daughter tried to kill me. And there had been a time not so long ago when I was willing to risk losing the world to save her. Now I see I have lost my bet, even though I am still angling for another chance to win back what has been lost. I wonder if Krishna heard my prayer while I lay on the bottom of the pool, if he let me live for a reason. I wonder if Paula's child is Krishna.

From the outside the center appears to be undisturbed, but

once we are in the basement it is clear that someone has been in the vault. Sheets of the scripture lie spread on the table in the center of the room. James grabs them frantically and studies them. The color drains from his face.

"She was here," he says. "Some papyrus sheets are missing. Others are torn in pieces."

His conclusion seems logical, yet I can find no trace of her smell in the basement, and that puzzles me.

"Are you sure there are no other members of the Suzama Society alive?" I ask.

"There are just me and my dad," he says.

I stop him. "Go upstairs and keep watch. Let me try to read what is here."

"But less than half of it is here."

I realize his whole adult life has been built around the document. Giving him a comforting pat on the back, I shoo him away. Finally I am alone with a piece of the puzzle I have never held before. But I have to wonder about what is missing.

The first piece I read deals specifically with the child.

Of all the previous avatars, he who is born at the end of that time's millennium will manifest the greatest divinity to the world. He will have the playfulness of Sri Krishna, the wisdom of Adi Shankara, and the compassion of Jesus of

Nazareth. He will be these divine beings, but
something more, something that humanity has
never seen before.

He will be born in a city associated with lost
angels, but it will be dark angels who force him
and his mother to flee to the mirror in the sky,
where shoes move without feet and the emerald
circle is seen in the morning light. There the dark
forces will once again converge on him, but a
powerful angel will rescue him only to lose him
again. Then the place of sanctity will be defiled
by red stars, and only the innocent will see the
blue light of heaven. Faith is stronger than stone.
The rest is a mystery.

The war between the Setians and the Old Ones
never ends. I am Suzama of the Old Order.
Even as these words are recorded, the mother
of an angel burns under Setian stars. Her
pain is my pain. I wait for the enemy, for the
splinter in the earth element, and for my own
death. This splinter will become a crack, and
civilization will end as we know it. But all ends
are temporary and all life is born from death. I
am Suzama and I fear neither this end nor the
loss of my own life. For this ancient war is for

the purpose of dark angels and blue angels
alike. Both are divine in my illumined vision,and
all color is erased in the infinite abyss.

There is another piece of papyrus, torn in two.
It is much thinner than the others.
It speaks of Kalika.

She is the Dark Mother, all consuming and not
to be trusted. She brings the light of the red
stars, and a wave of red death flows from her
fingertips. She is the scourge of the child, not its
protector as she claims to be. Her name is Kali
Ma, and it is her name that matches the dark
age. All who know her will fear her.

"Suzama," I whisper, shaking. "You don't know how you curse your old friend."

But does it matter what she says about my daughter? Wasn't tonight proof enough of my daughter's demonic nature? She laughed as she killed, and no doubt drank the blood of many of those who slumped to their deaths. Suzama can tell me nothing new about my own child.

But what about the holy child? Where is this mirror in the

sky, where shoes move without feet and the emerald circle is seen in the morning light? It is difficult to imagine Suzama being any more ambiguous. I almost curse her. The last thing I need now is more riddles, and all the stuff about dark angels and mistaken angels confuses me. Even worse are Suzama's references to the Setians. They were destroyed when Suzama was destroyed, in the great earthquake of ancient Egypt. Why does she go on about the war? That war is over as far as I am concerned.

"I will wait here for you. I will be here when you return."

But there was no one there when I returned.

Suzama's last prediction to me was wrong.

I call to James and he returns to the basement quickly.

"There are people outside on the street pointing at the center," he says. "I think the police will be here any minute."

"We will go then. Gather up what is left of the scripture and take it to your father."

"Aren't you going with me?" he asks.

"No. I need some time alone to think. Do you have an extra car?"

He grimaces. "We have plenty of extra cars now. You can take any one you want. Should I go to your house?"

"Yes. I will join you there shortly. Go out the back way so you won't be stopped."

He is dying to ask the question.

"Did you find out anything useful?" he asks.

I give a wan smile. "Only time will tell."

TWELVE

On the spot where Paula's child was conceived, on the sandy bluff in Joshua Tree National Monument, I lie in the shade of a tall Joshua tree and stare up at the sky. It strikes me as a small miracle how the sky has not changed in five thousand years. Why, I could be lying on my back in ancient Egypt, beside the Nile, and there would be no difference in the sky.

But it is not easy for me to remember.

Suzama took me in, into her home, her heart. She shared a small shack with her parents. It is ironic that the greatest seer of all time should be born to a blind mother and a blind father. Neither of them ever knew what I looked like, yet they treated me with great kindness. They even tolerated the strange hours I kept. For in those days I needed to drink blood almost every night to quench my thirst. It was still difficult for me to feed myself and keep my victim alive. I lacked the control that was to come with age. Yet many people naturally died in those days during the night, especially the old, and I tried to confine my feeding to them so as to raise fewer suspicions.

When I returned home from one nightly sojourn, I found Suzama awake. At that time I had been in Egypt a month. There was pain in Suzama's large soulful eyes. She sat outside beneath a blanket of stars. I sat beside her.

"What's the matter?" I asked.

She would not look at me. "I followed you tonight."

I drew in a sharp breath. "What did you see?"

"What you do to people." She had tears. "Why do you do it?"

I took a while to answer her. "I have to do it to survive."

It was true. She of almost perfect clairvoyance could not see what her friend really was. When she had first met me, she had only suspected.

She was horrified. "Why?"

"Because I am not a human being. I am a vampire."

Even in those days they had a word for creatures like me. Suzama understood what I meant. Yet she did not flee from me, but instead held my hand.

"Tell me how it happened," she said.

I told her the entire story of my life, which even though it had just begun, seemed awfully long to me. Suzama heard of Yaksha and Rama and Lalita and Krishna. I told her every word Krishna had said to me, of the vow he had placed me under to make no more vampires, and of the vow he had made Yaksha take to destroy all vampires. Suzama listened as if in a dream. When I was finished she whispered aloud.

"I have seen this Krishna in many visions," she said.

"Tell me what you see?"

She spoke in a distant voice. "He has the whole universe in his eyes. The sun we see in the sky is only one of many. All these stars—more than can be counted—shine inside the crown of his head." She paused. "You must be a very special kind of monster to receive his grace."

I was able to relax.

Suzama was telling me she was still my friend.

It was shortly after that night that she began to heal others.

The cures started innocently enough. Suzama was fond of collecting herbs. Even as a child she had had a knack for knowing which ones to prescribe for which illnesses. It was normal for a handful of ailing people to stop by each day for medical advice. Sometimes Suzama would have the sick person stay. She would have the person lie on his or her back and take long, slow deep breaths while she held her left hand above the forehead and her right hand over the heart. Invariably the person felt better afterward, or at least they said they did.

Then came a crippled man. He had not walked since a

massive stone had fallen across his hips five years earlier. He had no feeling from the waist down. At first she prescribed some herbs and was about to send him away when the man begged her to bless him. Reluctantly, as if she knew this act would forever change the course of her life, Suzama put him down on the floor and had him take deep breaths. Her hands shook as she held them over the man, and there was sweat on her face. I couldn't take my eyes off her. A milky white radiance had begun to shine above her head. Even when the man's lower legs began to twitch, I couldn't stop staring at her angelic face. For the uncountable stars were shining through her now.

The man was able to walk home.

After that there was always a line outside Suzama's house. She continued to perform many healings, although only a few matched her healing of the crippled man. For many seriously ill people she was unable to do anything. It is their karma to be ill, she would say. They had the word karma in that part of the world at that time, and they understood its meaning.

More than healing, Suzama preferred to foretell the future and to teach meditation. A series of special meditation techniques had come to her in visions and each of them was related to the worship of the Goddess Isis, the White Goddess, who shone in each soul above the head. Suzama taught mantra and breathing techniques, and sometimes she mixed the two together. I was her first student, as well as her last. While doing the practices she showed me, I began to experience peace of mind. She was my guru as well as my friend, and I always felt deeply indebted to her.

A time came when Suzama's exploits reached the ears of the rulers of the land. The king at that time was named Namok, and his queen was Delar. Namok was forty years older than his wife, and their beliefs, so the rumors said, were contrary to each other. Namok was firmly behind the powerful priest caste at the time, the fabled Setians, who supposedly gained divine insight from the ancient past, as well as from beings in the sky. The Setians worshipped a number of angry-looking deities, all of which were reptilian. I was curious, at the time, why Isis was supposed to be married to Osiris, who was Set's brother. The deities couldn't have been more different. The Setians did not approve of Isis worship, and went out of their way to destroy it. That is why Suzama always conducted her initiations in secret.

But the secret was out as far as Suzama's foretelling abilities were concerned. She was summoned to the Great Pyramid, and as her closest friend, I was allowed to come with her. In fact, Suzama refused to go without me. By this time she knew of my great physical power and felt safer with me by her side.

It seemed that Queen Delar had had a dream the Setian priests and priestesses were unable to decipher, at least to the queen's satisfaction. Delar wanted Suzama to try. Together, we were ushered into the royal meeting room. Its opulence was breathtaking. Never again would Egypt have such wealth, not even in the supposed golden ages of latter years. The very floor we walked on was made of gold.

Both king and queen were present, old and shrewd Namok on his high throne, with his tall and muscular spiritual adviser, Ory, at his right shoulder. Delar sat beside him on her own throne, with her young but hard face. It was Delar who bid us come closer and I couldn't help noticing out of the corner of my eye how Ory watched me. It was as if he had seen me before, or at least had had my features described to him. I wondered if his army of secret police, the dread Setian initiates, who had eyes like snakes, had taken note of my nocturnal ways. Ory wore a special dagger in his silver belt with which, it was reported, he cut out enemies' eyes before eating them. At that time the soul was thought to reside in the eyes.

Delar cleared her royal throat and spoke.

"You are Suzama. Your reputation precedes you. But who is this other person you have brought with you?"

Suzama bowed. "This is Sita, my queen. She is an Aryan— which is why her skin is fairer than ours. She is my friend and confidante. I ask your permission that she be allowed to remain by my side while I complete your reading."

Delar was curious about me. "Are you from India, Sita? I have heard stories of that land."

I also bowed. "Yes, my queen. I am far from home, yet I am happy to be a guest in your great land."

"What brought you to our land?" Ory asked. "Were you fleeing from danger?"

"No, my lord. It is only a love of adventure that brought me here."

Ory paused and whispered something in Namok's ear. The king frowned and nodded. But Ory smiled as he asked his next question and I couldn't help noticing how flat his eyes were. His hand never moved far from his dagger.

"It seems improper that a woman of your age should have traveled so far alone," he said. "Who were your companions along the road, Sita?"

"Merchants, my lord. They know the road to India well."

"Then you are also a merchant," Ory persisted.

"No," I said. "I have no special title."

"But you live in the house of slaves," Ory said. "Suzama is a slave. You, too, must be a slave."

I held his eye and there was strength in my gaze.

"No one owns me, my lord," I said.

My answer seemed to amuse Ory. He didn't reply but the power in my eyes did not seem to affect him. Perhaps he had goaded me on purpose, I thought.

Delar cleared her throat once more. "Come closer, Suzama and Sita. I will tell you my dream. If you are able to decipher it, your reward will be great."

Suzama bowed. "I will try, my queen. But tell me first—did you have this dream at the last full moon?"

Delar was impressed. "I did indeed. How did you know?"

"I was not sure. But dreams that come at that time are particularly auspicious. Please tell me your dream, my queen."

"I was standing on a wide field in tall grass with lush rolling hills all around. It was night, but the sky was bright with more stars than we normally see on the clearest of nights. Many of these stars were deep blue. In the distance was a group of people who were walking into a ship that gave off a brilliant violet light. I was supposed to be on that ship, I knew, but before I could leave I had to talk to a beautifully dressed man. He stood nearby with a gold flute in his hand. He had bewitching dark eyes, was dressed in a blue robe, and had long dark hair. Around his neck was an exquisite jewel—it shone with many colored lights and hypnotized me. As I stared into it, he asked me, 'What is it you wish to know?' And I said, 'Tell me the law of life.' I don't know why I asked this question, but he said, 'This is the eternal law of life.' And he pointed his finger at me."

Delar paused. "That was the entire dream. It was incredibly vivid. When I woke from it I was filled with great wonder, but also great confusion. It seemed I was given a great secret but I don't understand what it is. Can you help me?"

"A moment please, my queen," Suzama said. Then she turned to me and spoke in whispers. "You have had dreams like this?"

My eyes widened. "Yes. How did you know?"

Suzama merely smiled. "Who is the man?"

"Lord Krishna. There is no doubt."

"And why did he point at her?"

"I don't know. Krishna often taught with riddles. He was mischievous."

"He was careful," Suzama said to me before turning back to the queen. "Delar, the answer to your dream is very simple."

Both the king and the queen sat up in anticipation. Even Priest Ory seemed to lean forward. He was no doubt one of those who had failed to decipher the dream properly.

"The blue stars signify the blue light of divinity," Suzama said. "You stood on a spiritual world in the spiritual sky. The man beside you was the Lord himself, come to give you instructions before you were born into this world. You asked the question you did because you wanted to know what law of life you should follow as queen of this land. You wanted to know what was fair, a means by which you could decide how to pass judgment on those you knew you would rule." Suzama paused. "He gave you the means when he pointed his finger at you."

Delar frowned. "I don't understand."

"Point your finger at me, my queen," Suzama said.

The queen did so. Suzama smiled.

"When you point your finger at someone, anyone, it is often a moment of judgment. We point our fingers when we want to scold someone, point out what they have done wrong.

But each time we point, we simultaneously point three other fingers back at ourselves."

The queen looked down at her hand and gasped. "You are right. But what does that mean?"

"It means you must be very careful in your judgments," Suzama said. "Each time you decide fairly about someone, you gain three times the merit. But each time you make a poor judgment, you incur three times the debt. That is the law of life, whether you are a queen or a priest or a slave. When we do something good, it comes back to us threefold. When we harm someone, we harm ourselves three times as much." Suzama paused. "The Lord was telling you to be kind and good, my queen."

Queen Delar was impressed.

King Namok was unsure.

The high priest Ory was annoyed.

The main players in the drama were set.

The dice had been thrown.

It was only a question of how they would land.

And who would be left alive to collect the promised reward.

THIRTEEN

Back in Los Angeles the same day, I do not drive straight to my home in Pacific Palisades, but I do call to see if everyone is safe. Seymour says there is no sign of either the cops or Kalika. It sounds as if he has been enjoying Dr. Seter's company, but I don't think joy is a word I could attach to his relationship with James. I promise Seymour I will be home soon.

At five in the evening I am once more in the living room of Mrs. Hawkins, in the very house Eric longed to return to before his throat was cut open by my daughter. Hot-tempered Mr. Hawkins is fortunately not at home with Mrs. Hawkins. As before, she is plump and kindly, always fussing with her hands. Curiously, since I am associated with the kidnapping and death of her son, she does not appear unduly afraid of me. Indeed, she promptly invites me in when I come to the door.

But perhaps she believed me the last time I visited, when I told her I did everything I could to save Eric.

"Would you like something to drink?" she asks as she takes a seat across from me.

"No, thank you." I pause. "You don't seem surprised to see me again."

Her face twitches with the painful memory of her dead son. Truly it is not the tragedies that destroy us, but the memories of them. Clearly not a minute goes by when she does not think about Eric.

"I thought I would see you again," she says.

"Why?"

"You just flew in that night, and then flew back out like a bird. My husband and I have talked about that a lot since you were here." She flashes a sad smile. "I think we convinced ourselves you weren't a devil, but an angel."

"I'm sorry I'm not an angel. I'm sorry I wasn't able to save your son."

She stops fussing with her hands for a moment. "You really tried, didn't you?"

"Yes." I lower my head. "I tried everything I knew."

She nods quietly. "That's what I told my husband. He didn't believe you at first, but maybe he does now." A pause. "Are you sure I can't get you something? I just baked some chocolate-chip cookies. Eric used to love them."

I look up and smile. "Sure. I would love a cookie."

She stands. "I have milk as well. You can't enjoy a cookie without milk."

"Ain't that the truth." I have to sit in the pain of the house while she busies herself in the kitchen. Since my rebirth I have noticed I sense the *feelings* of a place much more acutely. The chair where I sit feels as if it has been used to electrocute people. It is Mr. Hawkins's seat, I realize. He wanted to keep me from leaving the last time I came to visit. He wanted to call the cops.

Yet I also smell something as I wait for Mrs. Hawkins to return.

The foul odor of illness. A human would never detect it, but I do.

Mrs. Hawkins bustles in with a plate of cookies and a glass of milk.

"You must have more than one," she says, setting the plate before me. "Really, Eric and my husband used to finish a whole plate of these in a single afternoon. But with Eric gone and my— Well, Ted just doesn't seem as hungry as he used to be."

I pick up a cookie. "I'll have at least two."

She sits back down across from me. "You never told us your name last time, dear. Don't worry, I won't tell it to the police. I would just like to know what to call you."

"It's Alisa."

"Where are you from, Alisa?"

"Lots of places." I sip the milk. It is cold, good. The

questions need to be asked but I find myself postponing them.

"I'm taking the year off from college, but I'll be in school next year. I just got accepted to SC. I'm going to major in pre-med."

"How do they taste?" she asks.

"Very good." But I end up putting the cookie down, half eaten. "Mrs. Hawkins, may I ask you a delicate question? It concerns Eric."

She hesitates. "What is the question?"

"Your son wanted to be a doctor. He said he wanted to follow in your husband's footsteps. Now I've met your husband, and he seemed like an intense and driven man. That is not a criticism but an observation. Eric was not so driven, yet I imagine some of that intensity must have rubbed off on him."

"That's true," she admits carefully.

"You see, this is hard for me. I don't want to walk on your pain, and I apologize if I am. But I was just wondering why, if Eric was so keen to be a doctor, he was taking a year off from college? I mean, I know a break from studying is not so unusual," I pause, "but was there a special reason for his extended vacation?"

She stares blankly for a moment. "Yes."

"May I know the reason?"

A tear runs down her cheek. "Eric had cancer. Lymphoma. It had spread through most of his body. It had gone into remission three times but it always came back." She swallows thickly.

"The doctors said he had less than three months to live."

"I see." I am stunned. Eric had told me he wasn't well. Kalika had told me the same thing. Indeed, she had implied that was one of the reasons she killed him. So that he would have a better birth in his next life.

"I'm your daughter. You should believe me. I believe you even when I hear you lying to me."

Perhaps Kalika had told me the truth.

Mrs. Hawkins sobs quietly.

"There were a couple of police officers who came to the door the day Eric died," I say carefully. "They were looking for him, but the person I told you about—the one who killed your son—she convinced them to go off with her. And I never saw those men again. I assumed this woman killed them as well. But I never saw an article in the paper about them, and you know what big news any police killing is. I was just wondering, in your conversation with the police about your son, after his body was found, did they make any mention of the fact that they had lost two men?"

Mrs. Hawkins wipes at her face. "No."

I speak out loud, but mainly to myself. "It seems they would have, don't you think? If the disappearance was tied up with the same case as your son's death?"

"I would think so. Maybe the police are all right."

I pick up the cookie again, thinking.

"How did you get on with the policemen?"

"Fine."

"Are they fine?"

"You don't have to worry about them, Mother."

"They might be all right," I say.

Maybe I am worrying about all the wrong things.

FOURTEEN

The night I turned myself back into a vampire, I went searching for an ounce of Yaksha's blood to serve as an auroic catalyst. The only place to look, I thought, was the ice-cream truck where Eddie Fender had kept Yaksha's tortured body in cold storage. There I found the blood I needed, frozen beneath a box of Popsicles. But before I scraped it from the floor of the refrigerated compartment, I had a highly unusual conversation with an elderly homeless man with thinning white hair and a grimy face. He was obviously down on his luck. But when I strode up to say hello, he reacted as if he was expecting me.

"You look very nice tonight. But I know you're in a hurry."

"How do you know I'm in a hurry?"

"I know a few things. You want this truck I suppose. I've been guarding it for you."

"How long have you been here?"

"I don't rightly know. I think I've been here since you were last here."

The ice-cream truck should not have been there. The police should have hauled it away a couple of months earlier. Yet not only was the truck parked where it had been when it held Yaksha, the refrigerator unit was still working, and the homeless man implied he had kept it working for me. That was crucial, because if the blood had melted and rotted, it would have been of no use to me. I wouldn't have been able to turn back into a vampire. I would have possessed no special abilities with which to protect the child.

Now the big question was . . .

Did the homeless man know that?

He obviously knew something.

The bigger question was *how* he knew.

With the sun setting and with no better place to go, I return to the street where I met the man. There, to my utter astonishment, I find him sitting near the spot where the ice-cream truck had been parked. It is gone but the man has not changed. In fact, he is drinking a carton of milk as he was the last time we met. He looks up as I approach and his eyes sparkle in the dull yellow light of the street lamps. He doesn't rise, though. He is an old man and getting up is hard on his knees. I remember I had to help him up the last time. He flashes me a warm smile.

"Why if it isn't you again," he says. "I thought you might come back."

"Have you been waiting for me?" I ask.

"Sure. I don't mind waiting around. Don't have a lot to do these days, you know."

I crouch by his side. "What do you do when you're not waiting for me?"

He is shy. "Oh, I just move around, pick up an odd job here and there, help out where I can."

I smile. "Well, you sure helped me last time."

He is pleased. "That's good. But you're a bright girl. You know how to help yourself." He stops. "Hey, would you like to play a game of cards?"

I raise an eyebrow. "Poker?"

He brushes his hand. "No. That's too hard a game for an old fella like me. You have to think too much. How about a game of twenty-one? I'll be the house. I'll play by house rules. I'll hit on every sixteen and give you a tip every now and then if you need it. As long as you promise to tip me if you win in the end. How does that sound? You know how to play twenty-one?"

I sit cross-legged in front of him. "I am a born gambler. Do you have cards?"

He reaches in his old coat pocket and pulls out a pack. "Do I have cards? These are fresh from a high roller's blackjack table in Las Vegas. Mind if I shuffle? Those are house rules, you know. Dealer has to shuffle."

"You shuffle. What are we betting?"

He takes a sip of his milk as he opens the pack. "It doesn't matter." Then he laughs and the sound is like music to my ears because it has been so long since I have heard the sound of pure joy. "An old bum like me—I have nothing to lose!"

I laugh with him. "What's your name, old bum?"

He pauses and catches my eye. "Now just one moment. You're the youngster here. You've never told me your name."

I offer my hand. "I'm Sita."

He shakes my hand. "Mike."

"Where are you from, Mike?"

He lets go of my hand and shuffles the cards. He is a pro with them; he obviously can shuffle both sides of the deck with as few as five fingers. Yet a trace of sorrow enters his voice. The tone is not painful, more bittersweet.

"Lots of places, Sita," he says. "You know how it is when you get as old as I am, one place blurs into another. But I try to keep moving, try to keep my hand in. Where are you from?"

"India."

He is impressed. "By golly, that's far away! You must have had plenty of adventures between here and India."

"Too many adventures, Mike. But are you going to stop talking and start dealing? I'm getting anxious to beat you at what I know is your favorite game."

He acts offended, although he is still smiling.

"Hold on just one second," he says. "We haven't decided what we're wagering. What have you got?"

"Money."

He nods. "Money is good. How much you got?"

I reach in my back pocket. "Three hundred dollars in cash."

He whistles. "My sweet lord! You carry your bankroll on you. Now I know that ain't smart, no sir."

I flip open my wad of twenties. Got them from an ATM down the street.

"I don't mind betting this. What are you betting?"

My question seems to catch him off guard. He asks with a trace of suspicion, "What do you want?"

"Oh. Just a few friendly hints, what you offered. Can you give me some of those? When I win I mean?"

He speaks with mock confidentiality. "You don't need them when you win, girl. You need them when you lose." He begins to deal the cards. "Sure, I'll help you out. Just don't you get too rough on old Mike."

I throw a twenty down. "I'll try to behave myself."

He deals me a fifteen, bust hand. He is looking strong, showing a ten. He peeks at his hole card and grins. By the rules, I know I should hit. But I hate chasing a strong hand with so little room to maneuver. He waits for me to make a decision, a sly grin on his old lips.

"Going to risk it?" he asks, teasing me.

"Sure." I scratch the ground between us. "Hit me."

I get a seven. Twenty-two. Bust. I'm twenty down.

He deals another hand. I get eleven, and he shows a six, the weakest card he can show. By most house rules I am allowed to double down at this point. But I ask if it is okay to be sure. He nods, pleased to hit me again. I don't know what he'll do if he gets in my debt. I lay another twenty beside my turned-over cards and he deals me a card.

"A nine," I mutter. "Twenty. I'm sitting pretty."

"You are pretty, Sita," he says as he flips over his cards, showing a five, a total of eleven. He draws and gets a ten, twenty-one, beating me by one again. My forty belongs to him.

"Damn," I mutter.

I lose the next six hands. Every decision I make is wrong, yet I am playing by the book. The published rules say I should win about half the hands. Yet I don't think he is cheating me, even though he seems to take great pleasure in taking my money. He already has two hundred bucks, two-thirds of my bankroll. If I don't win soon I'll have to walk.

On the ninth hand he deals me a natural. Blackjack.

He is showing only a seven. I have finally won.

He offers me a twenty. The amount I bet.

"You want it?" he asks, and there is a gleam in his eye.

"You were going to give me a tip," I say.

"But you won. Fate favored you, Sita, you didn't have to do anything. When a winning hand is coming around, it's going to come no matter what." He gathers the cards together. He is down to the bottom of the deck; he has to shuffle again. He comments on the fact, as an aside. "You know if this was a casino and I had myself a shoe, I could deal as many as six decks without shuffling. What do you think of that?"

I go completely numb.

But it will be dark angels that force him and his mother to flee to the mirror in the sky, where shoes move without feet and the emerald circle is seen in the morning light.

Lake Tahoe, I remember suddenly, was called "the mirror in the sky" by the original Indians who lived in the area, because they had to hike up the mountain to reach it, and then, it was such a large, clear lake, it looked to them like a perfect mirror reflecting the sky. Also, there is a small but gorgeous cove in the lake called Emerald Bay. Finally, there are casinos nearby that have special shoes for playing twenty-one. As we are playing twenty-one right now, only without one of those shoes that moves without feet.

Kalika had a book on Lake Tahoe.

Mike stares at me. "Want to play another hand?"

I slowly shake my head. "It's not necessary, thank you."

He nods as he reads my expression. "I guess you'll be on your way now. I'm sorry to see you go."

I gaze into his bright eyes. "Are you sorry, Mike?"

He shrugs. "I know you have a job to do. I don't want to interfere with that none. It's just that I like it when you stop by, you know. It reminds me of when I was young."

"I'm older than I look. You must know that."

He gives me a wistful expression. "Well, I suppose I do. But I have to say you're still a youngster to me."

I lean forward and hug him, and feel his bony ribs, his dirty clothes, and his love. A powerful feeling sweeps over me, as if I have finally found a member of a family I never knew existed. But the hug can last only so long. He is right—I have a job to do. Letting go, I climb to my feet. The thought of leaving him is painful. I have to ask the next question even though I know he will not give me a straight answer.

"Will you be here when I return?"

He scratches his head and takes a sip from his milk carton. For a moment he appears slightly bewildered. He quickly counts the money he has won and stuffs it in his coat pocket. Then he coughs and looks up and down the street to see if anyone is listening. Finally he looks at me again.

"I'm sorry, Sita, I don't rightly know. I'm always moving around, like I said, trying to keep my hand in. But I hope I see you again." He pauses. "I like your spirit."

I lean over and kiss his forehead.

"I like your spirit, Mike. Be here for me again. Please?"

He flashes a faint smile. "I'll see what I can do."

FIFTEEN

The inevitable happened. Queen Delar became a student of Suzama's and a short time after the dream reading, Suzama privately initiated the queen in a small room in Suzama's own home. Suzama refused to do it in the Great Pyramid, saying the vibrations in there would never recover from Ory and the evil Setian initiations. Also, Suzama did not want the powerful priests to know what was happening. She asked the queen to keep quiet about her practices for the time being. Suzama knew King Namok did not have long to live.

Six months later the king did die, and Queen Delar moved more boldly than Suzama wished. The queen immediately proclaimed her spiritual path via the Isis techniques and encouraged any who wished to follow Suzama to do so. Yet the queen was wise enough not to make it a state order.

Suzama refused to teach anyone who was forced into the practice. At the same time the queen instructed a large team of laborers to build a temple to Isis not far from the Great Pyramid, which Suzama refused to enter. The queen wanted an elaborate temple but Suzama persuaded her to construct a modest building, and so Suzama had her own place in which to teach within a year of the king's death. Suzama filled it with plants and flowers and different-colored crystals brought from all over the continent.

Naturally, during this period, the Setians suffered a great setback as far as their influence was concerned. Yet the queen did not banish them from the land, because Suzama had advised her not to. I questioned my friend about not banishing them. But Suzama felt so strongly about freedom of thought that she even protected what was clearly an evil group. Yet I doubt if even Suzama knew how many assassins Ory sent to dispose of Suzama and me. Of course, none of those assassins ever returned to their leader, even when they came in groups of three and four. I seldom rested in those days and never sat with my back to a door.

But I never drank Setian blood. Just the smell of it filled me with bad feelings. The group was definitely working with subtle powers of some kind, and I began to pay more heed to their rumored contacts with an ancient reptilian race, which they achieved through a mind-meld process that used identical twins as catalysts. Even more important, I began to investigate their rumored liaisons with the direct remains of the same race, which now existed on different worlds circling other suns. I knew the Setians were getting their power from somewhere else, and I wanted to find the root of it. Yet I made little progress.

Even the Setians I killed had great strength in their eyes, a magnetic field they could generate to subdue weaker wills. Naturally, their power did not work on me, but I could see the effect on the people in the city, wherever they were allowed to speak. Suzama should have been welcomed as a great prophet and the masses should have embraced her teachings, yet her following, even when her temple was complete, was relatively small. The Setians were constantly stirring up hate and lies against her.

Fortunately, Suzama did shield the queen from Ory and his cult. Queen Delar wouldn't even meet with Ory once the king died, although I did see Ory from time to time. Even though he was always polite to me, I never failed to hear the hiss of a snake beneath his breath. Why shouldn't I recognize it? In a sense we were cousins. Yaksha, a yashini by nature, had created me. And the yashinis were well known in India as a race of mystical serpents.

Yet Ory never reminded me of Yaksha, who loved Krishna above all things. And my power to influence the wills of others was much different from the power of the Setians. For their power left their victims weak and disoriented. Many never recovered from it and this power became known by the seldom spoken name of *seedling*, because it sowed seeds of consciousness that were not one's own.

I could see that matters would eventually come to a head with the Setians, only the climax came more quickly and with a destructive force greater than I could ever have imagined. Suzama was only nineteen when I received a personal invitation from Ory. He wanted to meet me alone in the desert so that we could discuss our differences and try to put an end to our conflict. This was only six days after I had slain ten of his people who had stolen into the Temple of Isis in the middle of the night. Ory had never sent so many before and I had been lucky to kill them all. Had he sent twice the number both Suzama and I would have died. Actually, I wondered why he had not, which should have served as a warning to me.

I sent back a messenger saying I would be happy to meet him.

He planned to kill me as surely as I planned to kill him.

Before heading to the desert I met with Suzama to tell her my plans. She was in her inner chamber in the temple and in a particularly reflective mood. She was writing when I entered but put aside the papyrus so that I could not see it. Her usual warm greeting was missing. Before I could speak, she wanted to know why I was dressed for the desert.

"You are wrong to think your enemies possess any virtues," I say. "I tire of our always having to be on guard. I am meeting with Ory tonight deep in the desert. He has chosen the spot but I know it well. When the head vanishes, the body falls. It will end tonight."

But Suzama shook her head. "This is not my will. You have not asked my permission. Tonight the stars are particularly inauspicious. Cancel the meeting right now."

I sat beside her. She almost seemed to disappear in the large silk cushions. Dressed in a simple white robe, she wore a blue scarf around her neck. Woven inside it were threads of gold that outlined all the constellations in the sky, even those seen from the bottom of the world. The latter, Suzama said, she had seen in visions. I had no doubt they were correct, even though I would not listen to her when it came to Ory. It was my turn to shake my head.

"I never told you how many of his people I slew last week," I said.

"How many?"

"Ten."

She grimaced. "In here?"

"I was able to deal with most of them outside. But there will be more if I don't destroy Ory now."

"But you don't know Ory. You don't know what he is."

"Of course I do. He is a Setian."

Suzama spoke gravely. "He is a real Setian. Just as you are no longer human, he is not one of our kind. Those he sent to kill us before were mere students." She paused. "I suspect he is not from this world."

"I don't care," I say. "If he comes alone, I can deal with him. And if he doesn't, then I will know and decide what to do. But I know I must face him. It is foolish to wait."

Suzama was reflective. "Wisdom is not always logical."

"Lacking your wisdom, I can only decide based on what I see and know."

She stroked my leg, which was bare beneath my robe.

"You know, I foresaw this conversation," she said. "Nothing I say to you right now will change your mind. That is because of who you are and because of the stars above. They pretend to be your stars but they're not." She paused and spoke as if she were far away. "They are arranged as they were the night you were transformed into a vampire."

I am shocked. "Is this true?"

She nods solemnly. "The serpent walked the forest. The lizard crawls in the sand. It is the same difference." She squeezed my leg and her eyes were damp. "Tonight is a time of transformation for you. Do you understand what I'm saying?"

"Yes. Death is the biggest transformation. Ory might kill me."

"Yes. It is possible."

"You don't know for sure?"

She was a long time answering.

"No. The Divine Mother does not show me." She shook herself and came back to Earth, for a moment. She kissed the side of my face. "Words are useless tonight, even written words.

Go then, and go with light. I will wait here for you. I will be here when you return."

I hug her. "I owe you a great deal. Tonight, perhaps I can repay you."

There was a place twenty miles from the city, deep in the desert, called the Bowl of Flies. In the late spring the flies would be so thick there during the day that it would be hard to breathe without inhaling them. Yet at night they would all but vanish, and there was no reason to explain why they came at all. There was nothing for the flies to eat, unless a small animal chanced to die there. But then again, an unusual number of animals did collapse in that spot. Even a bird could seize up in midflight and fall dead into the place.

Ory wanted to meet me in the bowl.

I arrived early to see if he had assassins hidden. The area appeared empty for far around. There was no moon but I didn't need it. My eyes were not drawn to the sky as they usually were when the stars were so bright. Suzama's words continued to haunt me. She had ended our good-bye almost in midsentence. *Words are useless now.*

Ory was suddenly there, sitting on a camel.

It was strange how I hadn't heard him approach.

He got down off his animal and slowly moved toward me. I had also come on a camel but had sent my beast off. For me to run twenty miles across the desert at night was nothing.

On the way home I hoped to be carrying Ory's head. Like me, he wore a long naked sword in his belt, along with his sharp dagger. Listening closely, I could still detect no others, and I thought him a fool to meet me under such circumstances. Yet he smiled as he approached, his huge bald head shiny even in the faint starlight. It smelled as if he had oiled his skull before coming, a disgusting ointment smell.

"Sita," he said. "I thought maybe you would not come."

I mocked him. "It is not often I am granted an exclusive audience with such a renowned spiritual figure."

"Do you know whence our spiritual power comes?"

"An unhappy place. A place without love or compassion. I do not know the name of this place, but I do know I never want to go there."

He stood close, yet his hands stayed clear of his sword. He gestured to the sky. "This world is not the only one. There are many kingdoms for us to rule, and I can gain you safe passage to these other places, if you will join me. I have watched you closely these last two years, Sita, and I know you are one of us. You have power, you take what you wish. You kill as a matter of course to satisfy your hunger, to satisfy your lust for life. You move without the burden of conscience. Yet you hide behind the dress of that slave fortune teller. This I do not understand."

"I hide behind no one. Suzama is much more than a seer of the future. She sees into the hearts of men and women. She brings peace where there is pain, healing where there is sickness. The Setians do none of these things. They are interested in power for power's sake. Nothing could be more boring to me, or more offensive. You think we are kin only because I am strong. But that is the only thing we have in common, and before this night is over, even that will not be true. Because you will be buried in the sand, and I will be laughing in the city as I free it of the last of your kind."

He was amused at that. "Does your blessed Suzama permit such killings?"

"I will tell Suzama about it after I am done."

"And you think you could destroy all Setians so easily?"

I shrugged. "I have had no trouble in the past."

He came close and his smile vanished. "You are a fool. I sent mere apprentices to test your strength. In all the time you have been in the city, you have met fewer than a handful of our secret order. And you didn't even know them when you met them. We seldom come out from the depths of the Great Pyramid. Only I, Ory, the leader regularly attends to the things of this world. But I will not share this world with another, neither you nor Suzama. It is your choice. You join us now, and swear a sacred oath to me, or you will not leave this place alive."

I laughed. "You keep telling me what I don't know. I tell you that you don't know what I am." I drew my sword. "The blood that runs in my veins is not human, but I have the strength of many humans. Draw your sword and fight me, Ory. Die like a soldier rather than a coward and fake priest who puts silly spells on unsuspecting souls."

But he did not draw his sword. He lifted his arms upward.

A strange red light shimmered in his eyes.

His voice, as he spoke, boomed like thunder.

"Behold the night of Set, the will of those who came before humanity. It lives inside the stars that shine with the light of blood. Look up and see what force you think to defy."

Such was the strength in his voice, that I did glance up for a moment. To my utter astonishment the night sky had changed. Above me were fresh constellations laid over the old ones. They shone with brilliant red stars that seemed to pulse like stellar hearts feeding the burning blood of one huge ravenous cosmic being. Just the sight of them filled me with nausea. How had he managed to change the heavens? He must be a powerful sorcerer, I thought.

I drew my sword and moved toward him to cut off his head.

But there was flash of green light.

The metal of my sword flowed like liquid onto the sand.

My hand burned, the flesh literally black. The pain was so excruciating that I was forced to my knees. Ory towered over me, and behind his large skull the red stars seemed to grow even brighter. It was as if a bunch of them had clustered together and begun to move toward us. Through the mist of my agony I saw them form a circle and begin to spin. The very air seemed to catch fire around them. Ory gloated over me.

"We Setians control the elements," he said. "That was fire, in case you didn't know. Now I will show you the earth element."

He laid his big foot on my chest and kicked hard. He was many times stronger than I, I realized too late. Crashing down hard on my back, my arms spread out to my sides as if I were about to be crucified. No doubt that was the effect he was searching for. Before I could bring them back up and defend myself, the red stars over his head seemed to throb again and I heard the sand crack on both sides. For a moment it seemed alive, the very ground, liquid mud shot through with veins of brains, and I watched in horror as it reached out like a thick fist and grabbed my lower arms and covered my hands. Then the sand turned to stone and I could not move. All this seemed to happen in a moment. Ory withdrew his dagger and knelt beside me and held the tip close to my eyes.

"Now you have seen a demonstration of real power," he said.

I spat in his face. "I am not impressed."

He wiped away the spit and played the tip of the dagger over my eyelids. "You are beautiful, Sita. You could have been mine. But I see now it would have been impossible to dominate you. Above all else a Setian must control those who are beneath him."

"Kill me and be done with it. I am tired of talking to you."

He smiled softly. "You will not die easily. I know how quickly your wounds can heal, but I also know that a deep wound cannot heal around a dagger such as this, which is poisoned, and which will fit nicely somewhere in your barren womb."

He stabbed me then, low down in my abdomen, and the blade burned like ice frozen from the tears of a thousand previous victims. I knew then that the stories about him and his dagger were true. He had cut out many eyes and eaten them in front of his victims. But he wouldn't blind me now because he wanted me to see the sun when it rose, and the millions of flies that would cover my body. His poison was subtle, not designed to immediately kill, but to draw out my agony.

I noticed that the red stars were no longer in the sky.

Ory stood and climbed back onto his camel.

"The earth can move as easily in the city as it can in this place," he said. "When the sun is high in the sky, the Temple of Isis will be buried along with your precious Suzama. You may hear the destruction even from here. Just know that the flies that feed here are always hungry, and that it will not be long before you join her."

"Ory!" I called as he rode off.

He paused. "Yes Sita?"

"I will see you again someday. It is not over."

"For you it is." He laughed as he rode away.

The sun rose and the flies came. Slowly my wound bled and steadily my pain increased. It seemed as if the desert wind were fire and the sky rained darts. The sound of the many flies sucking on my blood was enough to drive me mad. The filthy insects polluted my soul as much as my wound. All I had to look forward to was the midday sun, when my friend would die. I had a feeling I would hear something.

The day wore on. Breathing became a nightmare. Existence itself was the greatest torture. How I prayed to die then, for the first time ever. How I cursed Krishna. Where was his fabled grace now? I had not disobeyed him. Only he had set me up before an unstoppable foe. There was no hope for the world, I realized. The Setians were worse than a million vampires. And they were spreading across the stars.

The sun reached its high point. It was a red sun.

The interior of my skull began to boil and I heard myself scream.

Then the noise came, waves of rolling thunder. The ground began to shake, then to dance, tearing apart at the seams. The frozen sand that bound my arms and legs cracked, and I would have been able to stand if the entire desert had not suddenly been transformed into a torrential ocean. What had Ory set in motion? The elements had gone insane. The earth believed it was water. Beyond the Bowl of Flies I heard sand dunes pitch and break like waves upon a shore.

Then it stopped and all was silent.

Pulling out the dagger, I brushed off the flies and crawled out of the bowl. When I reached the upper rim, I stared at a desert I did not recognize.

It was entirely flat.

Slowly, for me, my wound healed.

Somehow I managed to stagger back to the city. Ory's poison was still in my veins but maybe it had lost some of its potency. When the city finally came into view, I saw that Ory's day had passed, as had Suzama's. Either Ory had lost control of his precious earth element or else Suzama had seized control of it at the last moment and stuffed it down his throat. The worship of Isis and Set was over for that time.

A gash in the earth as thick as the Great Pyramid had opened up and swallowed the bulk of the city. The pyramid and all the other temples were gone. Those buildings that had not fallen into the chasm were nevertheless flattened. A handful of survivors stumbled around in the midst of this destruction but few looked as if they still possessed their wits.

I searched for Suzama but never found her.

Not long afterward I left Egypt.

SIXTEEN

We cannot get a flight to Lake Tahoe or even into Reno. San Francisco is our next best choice. The four of us, Seymour, James, Dr. Seter, and I, fly to San Francisco and rent a car in the Bay Area. Airport security has not allowed us to take weapons with us, so along the way, close to ten o'clock, I have the others wait while I break into a gun shop and steal two shotguns and several rounds of ammunition. James seems impressed when I get back to the car. He sits up front with me while Seymour talks to Dr. Seter in the backseat. The doctor is not looking good, and I wonder if he suffered a mild heart attack the previous night.

"How did you get into the store?" James asks as we race back onto the freeway and head east at high speed.

"I picked the lock," I say, doing the driving.

"Did an alarm go off?" James asks.

"Not one that I could hear." I glance over my shoulder. "Do you need to use the restroom, Dr. Seter? There's a gas station a couple of miles ahead."

His face is ghastly white but he shakes his head. "We don't have time. We have to get there before she does." He pauses. "I'm still furious at myself that I didn't allow you to see all of the scripture the first night. How were you able to decipher the clues as to the child's location so quickly?"

"I had a little help," I say.

"From whom?" James asks.

"You wouldn't believe me if I told you."

"I think everyone in this car is ready to believe anything," Seymour mutters.

"Ain't that the truth," Dr. Seter says.

Yet I hesitate to talk about Mike. "A little bird helped me."

James gently persists. "Does this bird have a name?"

I give him a look. "Not that I can remember."

We reach the mountains surrounding Lake Tahoe and I plow up the winding road that leads to the lake. The others sit, clutching the ceiling grips; I have rented a Lexus sports coupe and I push the car to its limit. Dr. Seter looks as if he will vomit over the backseat but he doesn't complain. There's too much at stake.

As we come over the rim of the mountain and see the lake, I smell Kalika. I am surprised at my own surprise because I should have expected her to be here, but in reality I didn't. Yet I still don't think she has deciphered Suzama's code before me. On the contrary, I think she is following us, using some invisible psychic tracking. I believe she still waits to see what moves we'll make next. And this is a paradox for me because I realize I might endanger the child most by trying to find it to protect it. Certainly there must have been a reason why my daughter has left so many of us alive. She didn't know where I was when I was at the hospital with the child. Yet she knew where I was when I was living in Pacific Palisades with Seymour. I have to wonder if the child has a mystical shield around him that Kalika can't pierce but maybe I can.

It may not matter.

If I can smell her, she can see us.

But I cannot have come this far just to turn away from the child. I cannot trust in my theories. I only know that if I can find Paula and her baby I can take them to some safe place. That is logical; it is something I can envision without employing the wisdom or intuition of Suzama. Starting downhill, I floor the accelerator and turn toward Emerald Bay.

We reach it twenty minutes later.

The spot is one of the most enchanting in all of nature. The bay is maybe two hundred yards across, sheltered on three sides by majestic cliffs with tall pines hugging them. The isthmus is narrow, giving the bay excellent shelter from the lake itself, which can get rough in stormy weather. There is a tiny island in the center of the water, a place for children to play and adults to relax. Even at midnight, beneath the brilliant moon, the circular bay is magical. But tonight it is silver, not emerald. Silver like the dagger Ory stabbed in me.

For some reason, I have to remind myself that that was long ago.

My abdomen cramps and I brush away a fly that has entered the car.

The odor of Kalika overpowers my other senses. Truly, since being touched by Yaksha's blood, my sense of smell has become my most potent weapon. Rolling down my window all the way, I use my nose like a needle on a compass, and it doesn't fail me. It points in only one direction, toward a small wooden house set on redwood stilts above an abandoned stone church at the floor of the cliff, not far above the water. The place is almost hidden in the trees, but I see it.

I drive faster.

I stop some distance from the house. The road we're on circles all of Lake Tahoe but at this place it is three hundred yards up the side of the mountain. Grabbing a shotgun and ignoring the others, I slip six shells into it. The remainder of the ammunition is in the box that I stuff into my pocket. Popping open the driver's door, I am almost outside when James grabs my arm.

"Where are you going?" he demands.

"Some things you can't help me with," I say.

"Alisa," Seymour says. The others only know me by that name.

"It has to be this way." I shake off James. "Stay and take care of one another. She may come this way yet"

I don't give them a chance to respond. Jumping out of the car, I run around the bend, and the moment I am out of sight I switch into hyper-mode. The tangled trees and uneven boulders don't even slow me. I reach the house in thirty seconds.

The front door has already been kicked in.

Kalika was watching which way my nose turned.

Inside I find Paula staring out a window that overlooks Emerald Bay. There is a small boat on the cold water, with an outboard motor softly churning through the night, heading away from us. Grabbing Paula from behind, I turn her around.

"Did she take the child?" I demand.

Pretty dark-haired Paula is the color of dirty snow.

"Yes," she says with a dry voice.

"Stay here." I pump my shotgun. "I will get him back."

The next moment finds me outside, running along the edge of the bay. In places this is difficult because the sides are sheer stone. When I come to such a spot I jump higher for any inch of ledge that will support my feet and keep running. Kalika's outboard motor is not very strong. I reach the isthmus seconds before her boat does. Dressed in a long white coat, the baby wrapped in a white blanket on her knees, she looks up at me as I raise my shotgun and take aim at her bow. She is only fifty yards away. Her eyes shimmer with the glow of the moon and she doesn't seem to be surprised. The baby talks softly to her, infant nonsense. He is not afraid, but fear is almost all I know as I sight along the barrel and squeeze the trigger.

The blast of the shotgun echoes across the bay.

I have blown a hole in the front of the boat.

Water gushes in. Kalika grabs the handle of the outboard and turns the boat around. For a moment her back is to me, an easy shot. Yet I don't take it. I tell myself there is a chance I might hit the child. At first Kalika seems to be headed back toward the beach below Paula's house, but then it is clear the miniature island in the center of the bay is her goal. Perhaps the water is gushing in too fast. Kalika picks up the child and hugs him to her chest even before the boat reaches the island. Then she is up and out of the sinking craft, scampering up the dirt path that leads to a small abandoned house at the top of the island. Sliding the shotgun under my black leather coat, I dive off the low cliff and into the water.

The lake temperature is bracing, even for me. But vampires never like the cold, although we can tolerate it far better than human beings can. My stroke is hampered by my clothes and gun, but I reach the island in less than a minute. Shivering on the beach in the rays of the moon, I remove the shotgun and pump another round into the chamber. There is a good chance it will still fire. If it doesn't then this will be the last moonlit night of my life.

I find Kalika sitting on a bench in the stone house at the top of the island. It is not properly a house, more an open collection of old walls. Last time I was here a guide told me people came here for tea during the Second World War. Kalika sits with the baby on her lap, playing with him, oblivious of me and my shotgun. I feel I have to say something. Of course I am not fooled. I keep my weapon held ready.

Yet maybe I am the biggest fool of all.

"It is over," I say. "Set the child down."

Kalika doesn't even look up. "The floor is cold. He might catch cold."

I shake my gun. "I am serious."

"That is your problem."

"Kalika—"

"Do you know what name Paula gave the child?" she interrupts.

"No. I didn't stop to ask her."

"I think she named him John. That's what I've been calling him." Finally she looks at me. "But you know Mike, don't you?"

I am bewildered. "Yes. Have you spoken to him?"

"No. But I know him. He's a bum." She lifts the child to her breast. Kalika has a voluptuous figure; she could probably bear many healthy children. God knows what they would be like. She strokes the baby's soft skull. "I think we have company."

"What are you talking about?"

"Your friend is coming."

"Good," I say, although I don't hear anyone approaching. "More reason for you to surrender the child." I grow impatient. "Put him down!"

"No."

"I will shoot."

"No, you won't."

"You murdered two dozen innocent people. You ripped their hearts and heads off right in front of my eyes and you think I can still care for you? Well, you're wrong." I step closer and aim the shotgun at her face. "You are not immortal. If I fire and your brains splatter the wall behind you, then you will die."

She stares at me. We are out of the moonlight. There should be no light in her dark eyes at all. Nevertheless they shine with a peculiar white glow. I had thought it was red the last time I saw them during our confrontation on the pier. But maybe the color is not hers but mine. Maybe she is just a mirror for me, Kali Ma, the eternal abyss, who destroys time itself. My mother myself. I cannot look at her with the child and not think of when she was a baby.

"The body takes birth and dies," she says. "The eternal self is unmoved."

I shake my shotgun angrily. "You will move for me, goddamn you!"

Kalika smiles. She wants to say something.

But suddenly there is a blade at my throat.

"I will take that shotgun," James says softly in my ear.

I am surprised but not terribly alarmed.

"James," I say patiently, "I am not going to shoot the child."

He presses the blade tighter and forces my head back.

"I know that, Sita," he says calmly. "I still want the gun."

I swallow. Now I am concerned.

"How do you know my name?" I ask.

He grips the shotgun and carefully lifts it from my hands.

"We have met before," he says. "You just don't remember me."

"She remembers," Kalika says, standing now, her expression unfathomable.

James points the shotgun at her while he keeps the blade at my throat. Out of the corner of my eye I get a glimpse of it. A dagger of some kind, ancient design, cold metal. James is calm and cool. He gestures with the tip of the shotgun.

"You will set the child down on the bench beside you," he says to my daughter. "If you don't I will shoot, and you know I won't miss. Either of you."

Kalika does not react.

James scrapes me lightly with the knife and my throat bleeds.

"I will kill your mother," he says. "You will have to watch her die."

A shadow crosses Kalika's face. "No," she says.

James smiles. "You know me. You know I do not bluff."

Kalika nods slightly. Really, it is as if she knows him well.

"All right," she says in a soft, perhaps beaten, voice.

"Do it!" James orders.

Kalika turns to set the child down. The baby is almost out of her hands when I see her change her mind. Maybe James sees the same thing, I don't know. But he is ready for her when she suddenly grabs the baby and bolts. Kalika moves extraordinarily fast but James is no slouch when it comes to reflexes.

He shoots her in the lower back.

Kalika staggers but manages to hold on to the child. Keeping his blade tight to my throat, he pumps the shotgun again and takes aim. It is then I ram an elbow into his side. He seems ready for that as well, because even though I have hurt him, he manages to draw the blade all the way across my throat. And he doesn't just nick me. Suddenly my life's blood is pouring over my chest and James has got Kalika in his sights again and there is absolutely nothing I can do to stop him.

James shoots Kalika in the back, behind the heart.

Kalika is covered in blood. She tries to turn, perhaps to attack, but seeing James pumping again, she puts her back to him once more. He fires a third time, hitting her right shoulder. Kalika slumps to the floor, her right arm useless now. Still she manages to hold on to the child, to shelter him from the blasts that ravage her body. As I collapse to the floor, James pumps again and points the shotgun at Kalika's head, actually touching her left temple with the black barrel. He still has the dagger in his right hand and I finally recognize it.

Ory's knife. I feel his poison once more in my system.

I even recognize Ory's voice when James speaks next.
Funny how I didn't before. Too bad, huh.

"I just want the child," James says to my daughter.

She stares up at him. "Your kind never wants just one thing."

He pulls the trigger back dangerously far.

"You missed me at the condo," he says. "That was your chance. But you will have no more chances if you do not do what I say. Nor will the child."

Kalika stares up at him a moment.

Then she hands him the baby with her left arm.

He takes the infant in his knife arm.

He turns to walk away.

Kalika tries to get up.

"No!" I gasp, choking on my own blood.

James pivots and shoots her directly in the heart. Stunned, she staggers back. He pumps again and shoots her in the exact same spot. Her chest cavity literally explodes. Her white coat and white dress are a mess of red tissue and torn threads. Reaching out a feeble left arm, trying to give it one last desperate try, she suddenly closes her eyes and falls face first on the floor. James stares down at her for a moment and then drops the shotgun and kneels beside me. The infant's face is only inches from my own but I am unable to reach out and touch him. The baby seems worried, but James looks as if he is having a good time.

"What did you tell me?" he asks. "'I will see you again someday. It is not over.'" He pauses. "Yeah, I think that was it. Well, at least you were half right."

I drown in red blood. My voice bubbles out.

"How?"

"How am I here again in a different body? That is a Setian secret, isn't it? But to tell you the truth I never left. Oh, I have transferred many times, into many forms, but that is a small trick for beings such as ourselves." He glances at motionless Kalika. "It is a pity your daughter had to destroy my entire crop of new apprentices. But there will be more from where they came."

"What?" I whisper.

He chuckles. "What am I going to do with the child now that you have led me to him? Honestly, you don't want to know. Better you go to your grave with no horrific image in your pretty head." He raises the dagger. "Where do you want me to put in the poison? It is a new and improved brand. It is guaranteed to kill even the strongest of vampires. And slowly."

"Go to hell," I gasp.

"Sita, I just came from there."

He stabs me in midback and leaves the blade in.

I am too weak to pull it out. To find it, even.

James stands and walks away with the child.

Finally, I hear the infant begin to cry.

SEVENTEEN

Red, searing pain and black despair. These two colors, these two forms of torture, are all I know for the next few minutes. It is not as if I lose sight of the room, it is just that I see it from another angle. A place of pain and judgment where my soul floats above the boiling cauldron I am sure is waiting for me on the other side. To realize I have been working all along for the enemy, that I was in fact their greatest ally, is too much for me. Death, if it would just involve oblivion, would be more than welcome. But I know there must be a special hell prepared for the one who sold the messiah to the jackal.

From far away I feel something moist and warm touch my lips.

It tastes like blood, very sweet blood, but it is such a potent elixir that I swear I have never encountered it before. Before my mind knows it, my body is hungrily licking the substance. The flow of blood that has been steadily dripping from my throat finally begins to slow. At first I think it is because my body is running out of blood, but then I realize I am healing, which should be impossible with a severed neck, a knife in my back, and Setian poison pumping in my veins. Yet after a time my vision clears and I am able to see normally.

My daughter lies beside me.

She is feeding me her own blood with her cupped palm.

For a moment I think that means she is recovering. But then I see that her horrible wounds have not healed at all. My eyes register my sorrow but she smiles even now.

"There is only enough life left for you," she says.

I push her hand away. "You mustn't. You are the only hope."

"You are." She forces more of her blood down my throat and then rolls me on my side. There is a sharp pain in my back as she pulls out Ory's dagger. I still feel the poison in my system, however, crawling through my veins and feeding on my internal organs. Kalika opens the vein on her wrist and forces me to feed, and it is as if the current of her life energy overwhelms the poison, and I feel it die inside me. A peaceful warmth steals over my physical form. Already I think the wound in my throat has closed. Yet inside I am still in torment. Even as I sit up Kalika seems to lose strength and lies back down. The massive wound to her chest is still open and I cringe because I worry I may actually see her heart beating, or slowing down. I don't know, of course. I do try to open my vein to drip my blood over her wound, but she stops me.

"It's too late," she says.

This death I cannot bear.

"No," I moan.

"You see I did not want to harm the child. I just wanted to protect him from the Setians."

"That's why you came into this world?"

"Yes." She raises her left hand and touches my hair. "And to be your daughter."

The tears on my face are so red. They will stain my skin, I think, and I will carry the burden of this loss the rest of my days, out where people can see it. I want to bury my face in her chest but I am afraid I will hurt her more. So I take the hand she touches me with and I kiss it.

"I should have listened to you," I say.

"Yes."

"You never hurt the police, did you?"

"No."

"And you knew Eric had a fatal illness?"

"Yes. His suffering would have been worse if I had not killed him."

My voice is choked. "You should have told me."

This amuses her. "You hear what you wish. You are more

human than you know. But that is your greatest strength as well. Krishna loves all humanity as his children."

"Who is the child, Kalika? Is he Krishna? Is he Christ?"

Her voice is weak, her gaze far away. "He is like me, the essence of all things. A name, a title, does not describe him. Divisions are for men. God knows only one being."

"Does the child need my help to survive?"

She is a long time answering. Her eyes are focused on the ceiling.

"You will help him. That is why you were born."

Sobs rack my body. "All this time you never lied to me."

That makes her look at me. "Once I did. When I told you I would not let you stand in my way to the child." A spasm shakes her body and I hear her heart skip as she begins to die. "I could never hurt you, Sita."

"How do I stop Ory?"

"Your age-old weapons, strength and cunning, will not do it."

"But what will?"

"Faith is stronger than stone," she whispers.

"The scripture." I am confused. "But it spoke against you."

That makes her smile. "Parts Suzama wrote. Parts Ory wrote to make it look like Suzama's writing."

"The papyrus about you was of a different texture."

"Yes. You cannot believe everything you read, even when it is supposed to be scripture." A convulsion suddenly grips her body and her back arches off the floor. My tears are a river. Five thousand years of life and death have not prepared me for this. To see my own daughter die, all because of me—how cruel the irony is. Yet Kalika, with her failing strength, pulls my hand down and kisses my fingers. "Words cannot inspire faith. Only love can destroy the maya."

"Is this just an illusion to you? Even your own death?"

She squeezes my hand and her eyes are bright.

"You are no illusion. I really am your daughter." A sigh escapes her lips and her eyes close. Inside her chest I hear her heart stop, but there is air left in her lungs, and she says in that special soft voice of hers, "I love you, Mother."

Those are her last words.

She is gone, back to the abyss from which she came.

Another death, another farewell, waits for me on the shore, on the beach beneath Paula's house. There I find Dr. Seter slumped against a stone wall, his skin the blue color of a failing cardiac patient's. Seymour and Paula are nowhere to be seen. Dr. Seter has had a major heart attack and I do not have to stretch my imagination to figure out how he got it. James returned with the child and revealed that he was not a nice and kind son, after all. As I kneel beside the doctor, he opens his eyes and gasps for air.

"You're bleeding," he says.

I am soaked with blood but I am no longer bleeding.

"I am all right." I put a hand on his chest and feel his erratic pulse. "Can I get you a doctor?" I know that will not help him, and am relieved when he shakes his head.

"I am finished," he says, and his face is so sad. "I never knew."

"I didn't either."

He is bitter. "Suzama lied to us both."

"No. Most of the scripture was true. James only created the part that dealt with Kalika." I pause. "She was my daughter."

He is amazed. "Where is she now?"

"On the island. She's dead." I sigh. "We were fools."

He weeps for my pain. "I was the fool. It was my arrogance that made me believe God was giving me visions. That I understood the mind of God." He coughs. "James put those dreams in my mind. He led me to the scripture."

I nod. "He led you to where he buried it."

"But why would he do these things? How could he do them?"

"He was never your son. He only came into your life to use you. He possesses the body of the young man we see. He is neither young nor is he human. Please do not blame yourself, Dr. Seter. I fought with this creature long ago and I did not recognize him. If anyone is to blame it is I."

He stares up at me. "Who are you, Alisa?"

"I am your friend." I hug him. "And I will get the child back."

My words seem to comfort him. He dies a minute later but there is peace written on his face. He was a good man, I know.

Paula stands behind me.

"Sita," she says gently.

I turn and look at her. Around her neck she wears a blue scarf with gold threads running through it. These threads make a wonderful design, but I am in too much of hurry to pay it much heed. Letting go of Dr. Seter, I stand and step to her side.

"I know where the enemy is taking your child," I say.

She nods. She believes me, she always has. Such faith.

"Your friend," she says.

I grab her arms. "Seymour!"

She nods her head to the side. "He is out front. He has been shot."

"Is he dead?" I ask.

She hesitates. "He is close."

I gaze at the small island in the center of Emerald Bay. I had swum back ashore. It had not been easy to leave my daughter's body.

"Find a boat," I say to Paula. "That was my daughter who took your child, but she was only trying to protect him. Her body is on the island, in the house. Please bring her back here and wrap her in a blanket until I return." I turn away. "I will take care of Seymour."

She stops me. "I will help you with your friend first."

I shake my head. "No, Paula. I have to be alone with him to help him."

There are tears in her eyes. "Your daughter gave her life to save John?"

"Yes. She gave more than any of us knew."

Seymour lies on his side in a pool of blood fifty yards up the hill from Paula's house, wedged cruelly between two large rocks. James had shot him in the stomach. One close-range blast was enough. He is unconscious and slipping away fast. The child is gone, and this time I do not have the mystery and magic of the universe in a convenient vial in my pocket. The only way I can save him is to grant his oldest wish. That I will do for him because I love him, and I know Krishna will forgive me. Indeed, if I can only find the child again, and give him a chance to grow old enough to understand me, then I can ask him to take away my vow. Leaning over, I open a vein and whisper in Seymour's ear.

"Now, old buddy, just because you're going to be a vampire doesn't mean you automatically get to sleep with me. We'll have to date first."

I give him my blood. It is all I have to give.

EIGHTEEN

The next evening, at sunset, I arrive at the bluff in the desert where the child was conceived. The tall Joshua trees stand around me like guards that would offer me help if they could. But there is no one to help me. Even my own strength and cunning cannot aid me if I am to believe my daughter and Suzama.

I have brought the dagger James stuck into me.

It is my only weapon, pitiful as it is.

Faith is stronger than stone.

James will not simply murder the child. The divine blood is as important to a demon as it is to a saint. Only the two do not make the same use of it. I know he will have to bring the child to this spot. He did not locate the Suzama Center in Palm Springs, so close to this place, by coincidence. Plus my old friend has said as much.

Then the place of sanctity will be defiled by red stars, and only the innocent will see the blue light of heaven.

Am I the innocent? At the moment I feel far from it. I know Kalika told me that my thoughts blinded me but I still cannot stop thinking how she let James get so close to the child when she clearly knew what he was and where he was. Of course it could be argued that I stopped her from fleeing, yet in the last minutes of her mysterious life she was content to quit running and sit and play with the child to let what was to be, be. James clearly used me to defeat Kalika; he could not have done it alone. Yet Kalika let herself be defeated. Was it because she wished to fulfill the ancient prophecy?

There the dark forces will once again converge on him, but a powerful angel of mistaken color will rescue him only to lose him again.

No one mistook Kalika more than her own mother.

But what am I to do now?

The rest is a mystery.

For once, I wish Suzama had hinted a little more.

What am I to have faith in? I do not miss the fact that Suzama placed faith and stone together in the same sentence, since it was Ory's control of the earth element that allowed him to defeat me the last time. All right, I have faith in the child. He seems like a cute little guy with incredible vibes and a darling smile. I love him, I really do, and I only got to hold him for a short time. But what am I supposed to do with this faith? It seems I should be able to use it somehow.

The sun slowly sets. The stars come out.

The moon has yet to rise.

I stare at the stars and pray for them to help me.

Then I realize something quite extraordinary.

The last time I went to see Suzama, she was wearing a blue scarf that had gold threads woven in it depicting the constellations in the sky, both the northern and the southern sky. Last night Paula was wearing a blue scarf as well, also woven with a pattern in gold thread. In fact, the more I think about it, the more convinced I am that the scarves are identical.

I am hardly given a chance to wonder how that could be possible.

Because something strange starts to happen.

The more I visualize those hauntingly beautiful star patterns in Suzama's scarf the brighter the stars above me grow. And what is even stranger is that this experience has already been described to me by Paula.

"The sky was filled with a million stars. They were so bright! I could have been in outer space. . . . It was almost as if I had been transported to another world, inside a huge star cluster, and was looking up at its nighttime sky."

The stars grow so bright I can feel their energy on the top of my head, streaming down into my whole body. One star in particular, a bright blue one straight overhead, seems to soar in brilliance as I look up and concentrate on it. It grows in size. It could be a blue saucer racing toward the earth. A high-pitched sound starts to vibrate through the area. Paula's words are still in my mind.

"The rays of the star pierced my eyelids. The sound pierced my ears. I wanted to scream. Maybe I was screaming. But I don't think I was in actual physical pain. It was more as if I was being transformed."

I think I am screaming too. This is how it felt when the moon would pour into the top of my head and turn me into a nice friendly ghost that could float off on the desert wind. But this vibration is thousands of times more intense. It feels as if the starlight is irradiating the nerve fibers in my spinal cord, changing them into magnetic circuits on a cosmic grid, a stellar system of communication and propulsion that has been there since the beginning of time, even though no one imagined it existed. I only have to want to plug into it to be able to use it. At the same time, I don't know if I am in physical distress. Blissful terror is a better expression for it; the entire experience is destroying everything that I thought is me, and yet there is relief in the destruction as well. But just when I think I will either explode or turn into a galactic android, it stops.

Unlike Paula I do not black out.

I am suddenly floating high above the desert.

In a glistening blue body.

It is very nice. This body, this state of being, carries none of the burdens of the physical realm. I am quite content just to float around with the stars. I can still see the desert far below, the rolling hills of sand, the edges of the shadows of the tall Joshuas shimmering under the intoxicating rays of the galaxy's stars. I realize then how crucial a role the stars play in our lives, their constant subtle influence bubbles on the edges of energy fields we are unaware we possess. Yet I do not think about it too much because I cannot be bothered thinking.

After some time I become aware that there is a highly dense bundle of red energy descending from above. Just the sight of it fills me with revulsion and I want to get out of its way. It is the opposite of what I am; it is neither love nor bliss. I desire to avoid it at all costs and I know that I merely have to will myself to be gone.

It is only then that I fully remember who I am.

The transformation had caused me momentary amnesia.

I remember why I have come to the desert. The child.

Far below me, I see James holding the baby. He is encapsulated in the same red light, but the baby glows in his arms like a tiny blue star. My awareness goes up and down, back and forth between them. As the red energy bundle comes closer I see that it is taking on substance, gaining the vague shape of a flying saucer. It seems as if from an unseen realm I am presented with a choice. I can try to enter this ship, in my blue body, and stop what is being planned by the Setians, or I can simply float away and be happy. Yet if I choose the former course, there is danger.

I can become trapped, I sense. My very soul can be chained in a place of demons.

Because if I go into the ship I will have to go into a demon.

The choice, the universe seems to say, is mine.

I think of Kalika then, of her great sacrifice.

This thought makes the choice for me.

I float into the ship.

It is a vessel of serpents. There are six of them, big ugly brutes with long tails and scaly hides, thick snouts and cold, dead eyes, all sitting around a square viewing port and each manipulating controls of some kind. But one is clearly in charge. Besides being the largest, he has the most highly charged energy field. He is like a swollen red sun from the wrong side of the galaxy. And I know he is the one I have to attack.

In a moment I am inside his body.

His mind. What a pit it is.

This is a true Setian, a genuine demon. His lusts and passions seem to spin in a vortex, yet he is highly intelligent and has worked long and hard to attain the rank he now holds. He is being sent by his superiors on this important mission to bring back the human avatar, the crowning jewel of all prizes. If he is successful, he will be given an opportunity to consume the energy of the child with his masters. His name is Croka and he lives off the emotions of hate and fear. They are food to him as humans are food to him. He can consume the holy child and be strengthened by him. On his home world, I see that black ceremonies will be performed to prepare the feast.

But Croka is not yet aware that I am in his mind.

The ship lands in the desert and the six Setians climb out into the night air. Still inside Croka I move with them. Yet I know this ship, these creatures even, are not really physical. The average human, if he or she were to pass this spot, would see nothing, yet he or she would most certainly feel a great dread. Simply to be inside Croka's mind is a torture as great as any that I have ever known. It is as bad as seeing my own daughter die. Yet I am now determined that her death will not be in vain.

James can see the Setians. He bows as they sit in a semi-circle around him. He stands respectfully, the child in his hands. Little John gazes at them in wonder, the red light cracking and sparking around his blue aura. Clearly the baby can see them, yet he does not cry out. The reptilian Setians are large; even though they are sitting, their ugly heads rise above James's. The one farthest from Croka bids James bring the child closer. It seems the monster wants to gloat over it, paw it even, and this to me is unbearable. Yet I know the creature will not really harm it. The feast is planned for later, on the Setian hell planet.

James brings the child to each beast, and each one pokes at it a bit. The child does not cry out and this seems to annoy both the visitors and James. Finally it is brought to Croka, but before he can touch it my eyes fasten on the child's eyes, and so, in effect, the Setian commander's eyes are also focused, against his will actually, on the same spot, on the profound gaze of the infant. It is only then that Croka becomes aware that I am sitting deep within his mind, and I understand that this is the moment of greatest danger. For Croka, like most advanced Setians, is a master of *seedling,* the manipulation of will, and I feel his furious will suddenly rise up against mine.

He reaches for me too late, because I already have the *kavach* of the child's gaze, the armor or protection of the avatar, and seedling loses all power in the presence of a saint. Like Ory of old, Croka carries a dagger in his silver belt, and I reach for it with Croka's own arm. Before the Setian can stop me, before James even knows what I am up to, I stab the blade in James's left eye.

Then all at once I am back in my vampiric body.

Back in the desert with only James and the child standing before me. The saucer and the Setians appear to be gone. But James is in pain, and I realize that I have already stabbed his *own* knife into his eye. Well, I think, this time I must have come out of nowhere on him. Quickly, before he can recover, I withdraw the knife and poke it in his other eye, effectively blinding him. He howls in pain and the blood that pours from his wounds is black and foul smelling.

He drops the child and puts his hands over his torn eyes.

I catch the child before he hits the ground and set him down gently.

Then I turn back to James.

"Jimmy," I say sweetly, "where do you want me to put the poison? It is a new and improved brand. Guaranteed to kill even a slimy lizard like you."

He swings at me with his right arm and misses, spinning helplessly in front of me, and I stab the knife in his spine behind his heart, just where he shot my daughter. Screaming in agony, he falls to his knees and bows his head. His flaying hands desperately strain to pull out the knife but I know just how powerful the poison is, soaked deep in the folds of the blade itself. He is already doomed.

"Sita," he gasps. "You don't understand what this moment means to this part of the galaxy. You can't interfere."

I laugh. "Are you talking about your lizard friends? They are probably still here right now. I'm sure they are, but they don't have a physical body like mine. They have to work through scummy agents like you. And right now their poor agent can't even see well enough to tie his own shoes. Oh my."

His face is a mass of black blood. Yet it is as if he is weeping.

"You can't do this," he says. "This night was planned for ages."

I kick him and he cries out again.

"Yeah?" I say. "Who planned tonight for ages? Not Suzama. Not me. I just wish there were a swarm of flies here and I had the luxury of killing you slowly. But I have other things to do right now." I grab him by his mane of messy hair and pull his head back, exposing his throat. "This, I am going to enjoy."

"Wait!" he cries. "I have not completed my mission! I will not be allowed to transfer to another body!"

I pull out the dagger impaled in his spine. "James," I say. "I honestly don't care."

"Stop!" he screams. "I don't want to die!"

Ah, there is a divine sweetness to total revenge.

God might not agree but I would argue the point.

"Then you should never have been born," I say.

His blood, when I open his neck, flows like black ink.

There is a loud hiss in my ear. The wind tugs at my hair.

A flash of red light momentarily blurs the stars.

The Setians have left, and in a hurry.

I let go of James and he falls dead on the sand.

Drawing in a deep breath of fresh air, I laugh out loud.

The child laughs with me as I carry him back to the road.

I think he likes me. Really, he is so cute.

CREATURES OF FOREVER

For Jambi, wherever she may be

ONE

I am a very powerful vampire. In the recent past several encounters have served to increase my abilities. My creator, Yaksha, allowed me to drink his blood before he perished. Yaksha, who originally made me a vampire five thousand years ago, was much stronger than I was. His final transfusion of blood heightened my strength as well as my senses, both my physical senses and supernatural ones. After that my blood was mingled, through the secret of ancient alchemy, with that of the divine child. I am not exactly sure what this child's blood did for me because I am still not sure what this child can do. Yet it did make me feel stronger, definitely more invincible. Finally, before she died, my own daughter Kalika gave me her blood in order to save me. And this last infusion has done amazing things for me. Really, I feel I have become my daughter, the irreproachable Kali avatar, and am capable of anything. The feeling is both reassuring and disturbing. With all this increase in power, I have to wonder if I have grown any wiser.

I am still up to my old tricks.

Killing for kicks, and for love.

In a sense, since vampires are considered dead by living beings, I killed my friend, Seymour Dorsten, by making him a vampire. But I only did this to prevent his certain death. I have to wonder if Lord Krishna will forgive me this—the third exception to my vow to him. I question if I am still protected by his divine grace. Actually, I wonder if Krishna has allowed me to become so powerful because he no longer intends to look after me. It would be just like him, to bestow a boon and a curse in the same act. God has a wicked sense of humor. I once met Krishna and still think about him.

At present I sit in a bar in Santa Monica with Seymour on the stool beside me. We are drinking Cokes and chatting with a young lady, but Seymour is thinking of blood and sex. I know his thoughts because, since drinking my daughter's blood, my mental radar has become incredibly sensitive. Before I could only sense emotions, now I get all the particulars. And I know that while Seymour flirts with the young lady, the guy at the end of the bar, with the swan tattoo on his left wrist and the shine on his black wing tips, is thinking of murder.

I have been watching this guy since I sat down, quietly reading his mind. He has killed twice in the last month and tonight he wants to make it number three. He prefers helpless young females, who silently scream as he slowly strangles them. But even though I try to catch his eye—smiling, winking—I am not successful and that puzzles me. I mean, I am cute and helpless looking, with my long blond hair and clear blue eyes, my tight blue jeans and my expensive black leather coat. But I intend to kill this guy, oh yes, before the night is through. He will die as slowly as his victims, and I will not feel a twinge of guilt.

"So what do you do when you're not partying?" the girl asks Seymour. She is pretty in a lazy sort of way, with short red hair that has been cut to mimic that of a popular magazine model, and nervous glossy lips that need to be moving, either talking or drinking. She is currently drunk but I do not judge her. Her name is Heidi and I know to Seymour she is the second cutest thing in the world. Since becoming a vampire, he has conquered his virginity and then some. But I haven't slept with him, and I suppose that is why I'm still a goddess in his eyes. Seymour leans close to Heidi and smiles sweetly.

"I'm a vampire," he says. "Every night is a party to me."

Heidi clasps her hands together and laughs heartily. "I love vampires," she says. "Is your sister one as well?"

"No," I interrupt. "I have a day job."

"She works undercover for the LAPD," Seymour continues. "She's really good, too. Last week she caught this thief in the act and blew off the back of his head."

Heidi frowns, her lower lip twitching. "Do you carry a gun?" she asks me.

I sip my Coke. "No. My hands are lethal weapons." I know Seymour intends to sleep with this girl, and I don't mind. But I don't want him to use his eyes to manipulate her into bed. This is a warning I have repeatedly given him, that his vampiric will cannot be used to dominate human will in order to gain sex. To me, that is just another form of rape, and so far Seymour has obeyed my rule. Also, I have forbidden him to drink from his conquests. He lacks the skill and control to stop feeding before he kills a person. For that reason, when he has to drink blood, he does so with me beside him. But unlike Ray, Seymour is not squeamish about blood. He loves being a vampire so much so that he should have been born one.

"Do you know karate?" Heidi asks me.

"She is a walking Kung Fu machine," Seymour gushes.

I stand and cast Seymour a hard look. "I am going to go talk to this guy at the end of the bar. I'll meet up with you later. Okay?"

Seymour understands that I intend to kill this guy. He is not squeamish about blood, but death still disturbs him. We have never actually killed any of his meals. He pales slightly and lifts his glass.

"Let me know what you're up to," he says.

"Good luck," Heidi exclaims as I step past.

"Thank you," I say.

The guy at the bar notices my approach and makes room for me. Sliding onto the chair beside him, I bat my long lashes and smile innocently. I am sweet, the type I hope he enjoys.

"Hello," I say.

"Good evening," he replies. He is terribly good looking, and young, twenty-two at most, with a Rolex on his wrist to cover his tattoo and a seductive smirk on his adorable face. His hair is longish, brown and curly. "What's your name?" he asks.

"Alisa," I say, not being too secretive because I know he won't live long enough to repeat it. "You?"

"Dan. What're you drinking?"

"Coke. I'm on a diet."

He snorts. "What kind of diet is that?"

I laugh softly. "An all-sugar diet. Do you come here often?"

He sips his scotch. "No. To tell you the truth, this place bugs me."

I'm already tired of making conversation. I just want to kill him and be done with it. Since inheriting Kalika's psychic abilities, I have gone out of my way to kill a few bad apples. Of course, I have no intention of making it my life's work.

"Do you want to leave?" I ask.

He acts surprised. "Who are you?" he asks, with an edge to his voice.

I catch his eyes. I have a very strong stare. Just by looking at metal, I can make it turn to liquid. I pitch my voice so there is no way he can refuse my invitation.

"Just a girl. You're looking for a girl, aren't you?"

He finishes his drink and stands. "Let's go," he barks.

Out on the street, he walks fast toward a car he never seems to find. I have to adopt a brisk pace to keep up with him. People move past us in the dark, the nameless faces of a humanity I have known forever. The summer air is warm.

"I have a car if you can't find yours," I finally offer.

He shrugs. "I just thought we'd take a walk first, get to know each other."

"Fine. What do you do for a living?"

"I'm a plumber. What do you do?"

"I'm an artist."

He is amused. "Oh, yeah? Do you paint?"

"I sculpt. Statues."

He gives a wolfish grin. "Nudes?"

"Sometimes." It's so nice to get to know each other.

Yet there's something wrong, more than the obvious. He's not at ease with me, and his discomfort goes beyond his thoughts of wanting to murder me. He fantasizes how my bright blue eyes will dim as my brain dies beneath his grip. Yet I am more than just another victim to him.

He is afraid of me.

Someone has told him something about me.

But who that someone is, I don't know. My concentration

is divided between Seymour and my situation. Yet I don't know why I should worry about Seymour. Certainly Heidi is not going to harm him. I scanned the girl's mind for a few seconds when I met her and there was nothing in there but thoughts of drink and sex. No, I tell myself, Dan is all that matters. I wonder where he's leading me, who we'll meet on the other end. He makes a sharp left into a dark alleyway. Naturally, to my eyes, everything in the alley is perfectly clear.

"Where are we going?" I ask.

"My place," he says.

"Can you walk to your place from here?"

"Yeah." He pauses and studies me out of the corner of his eye. Although he's striving to act cool, his breathing is rapid, his heart pounds. He definitely knows I am more than I seem, more dangerous than a cop with a gun. But he doesn't know I'm a vampire. There are no images in his mind of my drinking his blood. But the farther we walk, the more difficult his thoughts are to penetrate—another mystery. Yet I know he is worried what will happen with me in connection with another, how our meeting will go. This *other*, I sense, is also dangerous, in the same way he thinks I am.

The other is close. Waiting.

Are we going to meet another vampire?

There should be no other vampires, other than Seymour and myself.

I smile. "Do you live alone?"

"Yeah," he says, and his hands brush against his coat pocket. I realize he has a weapon there, and wonder why I didn't spot it before. The gun must be unusually small, I think. But when I sniff with my nose, I detect not even a trace of lead or gunpowder in the air, and I can smell a bullet from a quarter of a mile away. My questions pile one on top of the other, but I am far from ready to walk away from the encounter. There is a puzzle here—I must solve it.

"I live with my brother," I say.

"The guy back at the bar?"

"Yeah."

"He doesn't look like your brother." There is a bite to his remark. For some reason, Seymour is still very much on this guy's mind. Why?

"We had different fathers," I say, and my own hand brushes against the knife I wear in my belt beneath my black leather coat. Nowadays, I can kill a man at better than a mile with my trusty blade. Even good old Eddie Fender, a psychopath if ever there was one, would be useless against my new and improved reflexes.

Dan snorts. "I never knew my father."

That is one truth in a string of lies.

There is a warehouse at the end of the block, a shabby affair built to house dirty equipment and sweaty workers. Using a key, he opens the door and we go inside. The warehouse is chock full of shelves of metal gear, the nuts and bolts of larger pieces of machinery. There is a pronounced smell of diesel fuel. The yellow lights, coated in grime, are few and far away. The shadows seem to shift as Dan turns toward me. If he reaches for his weapon, I will put a foot in his heart. Already, I think, I should kill him. Yet I want to know why he has brought me to this place, who the other is. Even though I reach out with my mind, I sense no one else in the building. He studies me in the poor light

"Are you really an artist?" he asks. His curiosity is genuine, as is his continuing fear. He wants the other to arrive soon, so he can return to the streets.

"No," I say. "I lied."

My remark unsettles him. He thinks about his weapon— the small something in his coat pocket. He shifts uneasily.

"What are you then?" he asks.

"A vampire," I say.

He smiles, a lopsided affair. "No shit."

"Yeah. It's true." Still staring at him, I begin to move around him. He feels my eyes—I let the fire enter them, sparks of pressure. Sweat appears on his forehead and I continue. "I am a five-thousand-year-old vampire. And you are a murderer."

His upper lip twists. "What are you talking about?"

"You, Dan, your private occupation. Because I'm a vampire, I can read your mind. I know about the two girls you killed, how you strangled them and then ate a big red steak afterward. Killing makes you hungry—that's one of the reasons

you do it. That's opposite of me. I kill to satisfy my hunger."
I reach out and finger the sleeve of his shirt. "I'm thinking of
killing you."

He brushes my hand away. Yet he doesn't go for his gun.
Someone has warned him that could be fatal. "You're insane,"
he says angrily.

I laugh softly. "You don't mean that, Dan. Someone told
you I was different so you're not completely surprised by what
I say. I want to know about that someone. If you tell me now,
tell me everything you know, I might let you live." Once more
I reach out. This time I touch his left ear, but before he can
swat my hand away, I pinch it. Rather hard, I think. He is in
pain. "Talk," I say softly.

"Stop," he pleads, as I force him to bend over.

"Just a slight tug of my hand," I say, "and your ear will
separate from your head. I am very strong. So talk to me, while
you still can. Who is to meet me here?"

"I don't know." He squeals as I twist his ear. "I don't
know!"

"Tell me what you do know."

He gasps for air. "She is just someone I know. She came to
me after I killed the first girl. She said I could work for her. She
gave me money. Please, you're hurting me. Let me go!"

I shake him hard. "What is so special about her? Why
didn't you just kill her and take her money?"

Red appears on the left side of his head. His ear is coming

loose. He tries to straighten up and I force him back down.

"Her eyes," he cries. "She has strange eyes."

I pause, and then let him go. He is bleeding badly now.

"What is strange about her eyes?" I ask quietly.

He holds his hand to his ear, panting. "They're like yours," he says bitterly.

"Is she a vampire?" I ask.

He shakes his aching head. "I don't know what she is." He takes his hand away; it is soaked in blood. "Oh God."

I frown. "Does she have exceptional strength?"

The blood continues to drip from his ear onto his blue shirt. "I don't know. She never hurt me like you just did."

"When is she coming here?" I demand.

"She should be here now."

There is a sound off to my right, deeper in the warehouse. As I whirl to confront it, I also reach into Dan's coat pocket and remove his weapon. It is not something I can use to protect myself, not without study. It is a small rectangle of metal, with buttons on the side. Really, it looks like some sci-fi creation to defeat alien monsters.

Two figures move in the shadows beyond the towers of drawers. One is Heidi, the other Seymour. Heidi has one of these funny little boxes in her right hand, pressed to Seymour's neck. She stands behind him, using him as a shield. She is no longer drunk. When she speaks, her voice resonates with power and authority.

"Throw down the matrix or I will kill your friend," she says. "Do so now."

The matrix will take me several minutes to master and is of no use to me right then so I throw it down. Heidi takes a step closer, bringing Seymour with her. It is clear, from her body language, that she is stronger than my vampiric friend. The big question is, am I stronger and quicker than she is? Seymour stands relatively still, knowing the danger is real. Heidi's expression is harder to decipher. There is an emptiness to it, an almost total lack of humanity. I wonder at the transformation in her, and realize that Seymour and I have been set up. Dan fidgets on my left, anxious to be gone. His left ear continues to bleed freely. He speaks to Heidi.

"I have done everything you asked," he says.

She nods. "You may leave."

Dan turns toward the door we entered.

"Wait," I say in a simple yet powerful tone.

Dan pauses in midstride and glances over at me, sweating, bleeding, shaking. But my attention is on Heidi, or on the creature inside her. Right then she reminds me of James Seter, Ory of ancient Egypt, the Setian that possessed Dr. Seter's adopted son. Yet there is something different about her as well.

"I don't want Dan to leave," I add softly, planting the idea deep inside Dan's mind, so he has no choice but to stay. But I am not the only one in the room with subtle powers.

"Leave now," Heidi tells Dan.

His paralysis breaks. He takes another step toward the door.

I reach out and grab him, and now Dan is my shield. My fingers are around his neck and I push him toward Heidi and Seymour.

"Release Seymour or I will kill him," I say.

In response Heidi levels her matrix in our direction and pushes a button on the side of the black box. There is a flash of red light, and I let go of Dan and dive to the side, behind a tower of drawers. The weird light hits Dan and he is vaporized. Just like that, on a gust of burning air, he vanishes on the tail of a piercing scream.

Wow, I think. Heidi has a ray gun.

In a flash, I move through the building, using the equipment and machinery as camouflage. Heidi seems able to follow my movements, but not well. I estimate her powers to be equal to mine before Yaksha, the child, and Kalika restyled my nervous system. Yet her psychic control must be greater. In the bar she knew who I was, but I knew nothing about her.

I end up in a dark corner, up high, behind a bunch of boxes. For the moment, Heidi seems to have lost me. But I know if I speak to her, she will find me. Yet I am capable of projecting my voice, making it bounce off inanimate objects. Perhaps I can fool her yet. I do want to talk to her. She continues to keep Seymour close.

Heidi finally stops searching for me.

"We do not wish to destroy you," she calls out.

"Could have fooled me," I reply.

"We wish to meet with you, make you an offer," she says. "Come out where we can speak. You know this to be true. We could have killed you in the bar if your death was all we wished."

"I will come out only after you have explained who you are," I say. "And don't threaten Seymour. He is all you have to bargain with, and I think we both know it."

"We are of an ancient tradition," she says. "Our line is mingled with yours, and with that of others. We hold all powers. This world moves toward a period of transition. The harvest must be increased. We are here as caretakers, as well as masters. If you join us in our efforts, your reward will be great."

"Could you be a little more specific?" I say,

"No. You agree to join us or not. The choice is simple."

"And if I refuse?"

"You will be destroyed. You are fast and strong, but you cannot survive against our weapons."

"But I must have something you don't have," I say. "Or else you would not be interested in my assistance. What is this thing?"

"That is not to be discussed at this time."

"But I want to discuss it."

Seymour cries out in pain.

"This one is dear to you," Heidi says. "And you are wrong.

We have more to bargain with than his physical shell. At the moment I am twisting off his arm. If you do not come out of hiding, he will be destroyed."

I hear no bluff in her voice.

"Very well," I say, "But if I show myself, you must give me your word that neither Seymour or myself will be destroyed."

"I give you my word," she says flatly.

I wish I still had the matrix with me, even if I don't know how to use it. But it is still in her sight lines: I cannot get to it. All I have is my knife. Just before I step into the light, I position it on a shelf near the circular area where Heidi holds Seymour captive. I point the tip of the blade toward them, then I appear around a tower of shelves. Heidi is not surprised. She continues to press the matrix into Seymour's neck.

"Release him now," I say.

"Not yet," she says. "Not until you join us."

"Don't be foolish," I say. "I cannot join a group I know nothing about. Where are your people from?"

"Here, and elsewhere."

"Are you from another world?"

"Yes and no."

"Are you human?"

"Partly."

"How many are in your group?"

"The number cannot be measured by human or vampire standards."

"So you know I am a vampire. Who told you?"

"You did."

"No. When?"

"Long ago." Heidi shakes Seymour and I hear the bones in his spine crack. "Enough of these questions. You join us now or you will be destroyed."

"What do I have to do to join you?" I ask.

"You must swear an oath, and offer us a large portion of your blood."

"What do I get in return?"

"I have told you. Power."

"Power to do what?"

She sharpens her tone. "Enough! What is your decision?"

Since she has a weapon at my friend's throat, I feel I have no choice. "I will join you," I say. "On the condition you release Seymour."

"Agreed." She pushes Seymour forward so that he stands midway between us.

"Seymour," I say quickly. "Leave this place."

He has been hurt and frightened, but he is no coward.

"Will you be all right?" he asks. He does not want to leave.

"Yes," I say firmly. "You cannot help me by remaining. Leave."

He turns toward the door.

"No," Heidi says. Seymour stops—there is strength in her tone. "He is not to leave. He is to be your sacrifice."

"We have an agreement," I say bitterly. "He is to be let go."

"No," Heidi repeats, and there is cold evil in her voice. "I agreed only to release him. I have done so. But to join us you must sacrifice him. It is part of your initiation."

My tone is scornful. "Is this the way of your people? You splice words so thinly they become lies."

Heidi points the matrix at Seymour's back. "Your choice remains the same. You have five seconds to make it."

I imagine she is good at keeping time. Seymour's face is ashen. He believes, either way, that he is a goner. But I have not lived five thousand years to be so easily tricked. Clearly this creature knows a great deal about me, but not everything. Since the recent infusion of Kalika's blood into my system, I have the ability to move things with my mind, as well as read minds. I have no doubt my daughter could effortlessly affect objects from immense distances. This psychokinesis, however, requires great concentration on my part and I have never used it under adverse conditions. Up at Lake Tahoe, where my friend Paula lives with the divine child, I have only practiced pushing rocks and sticks from place to place.

But now I must move a knife.

Push it through Heidi's throat.

The blade is above and behind her. I can see it; she cannot. Yet I am afraid to focus completely on it, afraid Heidi will guess what I am up to. Instead I must continue to stare at Heidi, while I think of the knife, only of the knife. Rising up on its own, flying through the air, digging deep into her soft flesh, slicing open her veins, ripping to pieces her nerves. Yes, I tell myself, the knife will fly. It can fly. The very magnetism of my mind commands it to do so now. At this very moment.

"You have two seconds," Heidi says.

"You have only one," I whisper as I feel my thoughts snatch hold of the cold alloy, a special blend of metals, far more powerful than steel, an edge far sharper than that of a razor. For me, it is almost as if I hold the blade in my fingers. There is pleasure for me in this killing. But for her, there is only surprise.

The blade swishes through the air.

Heidi hears it, turns, but too late.

The knife sinks into the side of her neck and suddenly her blood is pouring onto the dirty floor. Yet I do not take this to mean my victory is complete. Heidi's will is strong; she will not die easily. Even as her left hand rises up to remove the blade, her right hand brings up the matrix and aims it at both Seymour and me. We are standing in a straight line in front of her. I anticipate this move, and already am flying toward my friend. I hit him in the knees just as a flash of red light stabs the air where he was standing. Together Seymour and I roll on the floor. But I am quickly up and kick the matrix from Heidi's hand before she can get off another shot. My knife in her neck has slowed her down some, but she almost has it out, and perhaps she is capable of healing even fatal wounds, as I can. But I will not give her the chance. Before she can totally remove the knife, I reach out and grab her head and twist it all the way around, breaking every bone in her neck. She sags lifeless in my arms, dead, but still I am not finished with her. Ripping off her head, I throw it into the far corner. Now there is no way she can recover.

"Nice," Seymour says behind me.

"Get those two weapons," I say as I drop to my knees and examine Heidi's headless corpse. "We are leaving here in a few seconds. Her partners must be nearby."

"Understood."

While Seymour goes off to collect the two ray guns, I rifle through Heidi's clothes, coming up with a wallet and a passport. These I will study later. Feeling her from neck to foot, I find nothing else on her person. Seymour is quick on his feet. Already he stands behind me with the matrixes in his hand.

"Who was she?" he asks.

"I haven't the slightest idea." I stand. "Let's get out of here."

TWO

The following morning I sit beside Paula Ramirez on the edge of Emerald Bay in the area of Lake Tahoe. The sun is brilliant in a clear cerulean sky. Inside Paula's house, Seymour sleeps, a young vampire still allergic to the sun. Now the sun doesn't affect me in the slightest, and again I must credit this to my daughter's blood. Even the burning Surya, the sun god, could not intimidate the Dark Mother, Kali. Kalika's ashes rest in a vase that sits beside me in the sand. I have brought the vase with me from the house. I don't know why. Except I still miss her so, my beautiful, mysterious daughter, killed by a Setian.

Paula holds her three-month-old son, John, and listens as I describe what happened in Los Angeles. I have driven all night to reach Paula. The infant kicks his bare feet in the cold water. He looks and sounds happy. I am happy just to see him.

He always has that effect on me. It was this child's blood that brought Seymour back from the dead. Yet I did not take John's blood—once I had saved him from the Setians—to save my daughter. I knew it was not what she wanted. But I ask myself over and over how I could not have wanted it.

Unfathomable Kalika, Kali Ma, where are you now?

I finish my tale and Paula sits quietly staring at me with her warm eyes.

"She said she saw you before," she finally says. "Do you think she was lying?"

"It was impossible for me to tell if she was telling the truth or not," I explain. "She seemed to operate under a psychic shield. It was very strong—even I could not penetrate it. Certainly I could not bend her will to mine."

"But there wouldn't be any reason for her to lie about such a detail."

"Perhaps. But still, I don't remember her."

Paula stares out over the sparkling water at the small island in the center of the bay where Kalika met her end. "You know I have begun to remember many things, Sita," she says softly.

I nod. I've suspected for a while that certain memories were returning to her, but I have waited until she felt ready to talk about them.

"Suzama?" I say.

"Yes. I remember Suzama."

I suspected this, but still the statement is stunning to me.

Paula remembers Suzama, my mentor from my time in ancient Egypt, because she is the reincarnation of Suzama. It is the only logical explanation, and I ask her to confirm the truth for me. Paula shakes her head.

"We may be the same from life to life," she says. "But we are also different. Do not expect Suzama to answer when you speak to me. Her time was long ago."

I probe deep into Paula's brown eyes and feel a rush of joy, and of sorrow. "But she is in you," I protest. "A part of me must have known that from the beginning. When I met you at the bookstore, I knew I could not leave you. You are Suzama, the great oracle. Can't you just admit it?"

She is flattered by my praise, and yet unmoved as well. "Perhaps I can't because I'm not able to see what happens next." She pauses. "Yet I knew, when you were down in Los Angeles, that you would confront something very old."

I lower my voice. "Then you know who she was?"

She shakes her head. "I have a feel for her, that is all." Reaching down, she touches the clear water, then feels John's feet to see if they are getting cold. She adds in a serious voice. "Interesting how she mentioned the harvest."

"Yes. I didn't understand that. What harvest was she talking about?"

Paula is thoughtful, her eyes focused far away, as Suzama often was.

"There is a time coming soon," she says, "when everything

will change. I have seen this in what people call visions, but which aren't visions at all. People will either move forward or else repeat what they have already done."

I have to think about this.

Suzama never made casual prophecies.

"What will people move forward to?" I ask.

"An entirely different type of life. One we cannot even imagine as we sit here. Those who do go forward will live in light and bliss."

"But Heidi was wicked. Why would she want to increase such a harvest?"

Paula wipes the water off John's feet and warms them in her lap. "There are two kinds of harvests," she says. "There are two kinds of people. Those who serve others and those who serve themselves. You know this—it is nothing new. Of course, no one is one hundred percent one way or the other. No one is a perfect sinner or a perfect saint. But where there is a dominance of self-interest, a negative harvest will come about for that person. Where there is a dominance of love, a positive harvest will happen."

"You know these things for fact?"

"Yes."

"Suzama . . . ," I begin.

She smiles. "Paula. Please?"

"Paula. When will the harvest occur?"

"The date is not set. But some time in the next twenty-five years the change will occur."

"Will everyone be harvested?"

"Not at all."

"What is the criteria?"

"I knew you would ask that. The criteria, I believe, is the same for both sides, positive and negative. Yet it has nothing to do with religious persuasion, higher learning, physical health or beauty, relative importance in society. None of these qualities will matter."

"Then what will the criteria be?" I repeat.

"It is difficult to describe."

I am frustrated. "Try."

Paula laughs, and so does her child. John is for the most part a happy baby, but he can cry in the middle of the night with the best of them. Many times I have changed his diapers to allow Paula to sleep. Since drinking my daughter's blood, I seldom need to rest.

"Life is the criteria," she says finally. "Who is alive, who is not. Remember, those who are negative can be more full of life than the most positive of people." She punches me in the arm. "Take you for example."

I am her naive student, from long ago, and her remark wounds. It strikes me then how much our relationship has changed since we met. Then I was the sole knower of profound secrets. Now I truly feel I am her student and study at her knee. Mystery surrounds her like a halo. I love her so much, but she scares me.

"Am I only fit for the negative side?" I ask quietly.

She laughs more. "Silly vampire. No, don't be ridiculous. Who more than you is ready to give her life for others?"

I gesture helplessly. "But I have killed so many over the years."

She is compassionate. "It doesn't matter, Sita. Really, I know this for a fact."

I have to smile. "I suppose you would since you have such a special child."

"You understand what I am saying. The issue of harvest is separate from the type of harvest. Whether a person will go forward is dependent on his or her life vibration. Whether he or she will enter a positive realm or a negative one depends on the quality of his or her heart."

"Tell me more about this next realm?"

"I cannot."

"But you see it?"

"Yes. But words do not describe it. The next dimension is even beyond the realms souls encounter when they die." She pauses to run her hand through John's silky brown hair. How will the world react, I wonder, to a brown messiah? Of course, no race would satisfy everyone. Paula adds, "The coming harvest will affect heaven and earth."

"Is that why John was born? To increase the positive harvest?"

"Yes. But . . ." She does not finish.

"What?"

Paula frowns and then sighs. "Something is wrong. The plan is off."

"What are you talking about? What plan?"

"God's plan."

"He makes plans? Are you sure about that? I always thought he just rolled the dice when it came to us."

Paula smiles again, but the expression is short-lived. She continues in a serious tone, hugging her baby to her chest. John yawns and closes his eyes, ready for a nap.

"Every individual affects the world, but it is difficult for so many to go forward, the way we would wish them to, when there is so much evil in the world." She pauses. "Yet this evil is there for a reason. It plays its part. You remember Ory?"

"Yes. How could I forget? I just killed him last month. Why do you ask?"

But Paula is evasive, as Suzama often was. "He played his part" is all she says.

"Paula," I say. "I described to you what happened to me that night in the desert, when I confronted Ory. It seemed as if for a time I was not physical, that the very matter of my body had changed into light. Is that related to this harvest you describe?"

"Yes."

"But when I changed, it seemed that I entered a spaceship from another world. But it wasn't a spaceship. I don't think anyone could see it but me, in my changed condition. There were beings aboard. Beings like demons, and I entered the mind of one. At least I think I did. But as time goes by, I begin to doubt that any of this happened, that I didn't just dream it all. Does that make sense?"

Paula nods. "That is why I can't describe what is to come next. It would just be a dream to us, the way we are now."

"But were these beings from a negative harvest?"

She touches my knee. "Sita. You want to understand everything with your head. You ask me to describe what you call my visions with words. But neither thing is possible. Even your brilliant mind cannot reach beyond concepts. Even your vampire eyes cannot see beyond this world. I don't know who they were, these friends of Ory. I don't know who this Heidi was. I only know that she did not lie to you when she said she met you long ago." Paula pauses and she raises her eyes to the water, to Lake Tahoe beyond the sheltered bay. "And that it was long ago things went wrong."

"Went wrong? For whom?"

"For all of us."

"I don't understand," I complain.

"Did Suzama ever just explain things to you?"

"Sometimes."

"No. She would take a lesson only so far because she was not omniscient. She saw a portion of the mind of God, but no mortal can see all of it. Suzama was not infallible."

"Is John?"

The boy sleeps soundly. Paula speaks with love. "John's a baby."

"But who was he in the past?"

Paula pauses. "I don't know."

"Suzama said this child would be the same as the others: Jesus, Shankara, Krishna. She wrote that—I saw her words with my own eyes."

"Then why are you asking me?"

"To know if it's true."

"Ah. That is the question, isn't it? What is true? But didn't Suzama also write that faith is stronger than stone?"

"But I ask you these things so I will know what to have faith in."

"Have faith in yourself, Sita. These strangers have come for you for a purpose. It does not sound as if they have the welfare of mankind at heart. You must seek them out, learn what they want and how they hope to accomplish it."

"You have seen this in a vision?"

Paula turns her head away. "I have seen too many things."

I have to wonder if she has seen my death.

"You can tell me," I say carefully.

"No."

"I am not afraid to hear what is to be."

Paula lowers her head. A tear runs over her cheek.

"I am afraid," she whispers.

"Suzama," I say, and stop myself. But Paula is already looking at me and shaking her head.

"I didn't call you as I promised I would after I fled from Kalika," she says. "Do you know why?"

"I meant to ask you. I assume you had a vision that it would be better to keep your distance. At least for a time."

"No. I didn't talk to you because I began to understand your destiny—destiny itself. It can only be lived, it cannot be explained. It is like a mystery, which ceases to exist the moment you explain it. The same with a magic trick. When you are told how it works, it loses all its charm."

"What you're saying is that you'll tell me no more of what you've seen?"

"I have seen no more, and for that I am glad."

"You look more sad than happy."

Paula smiles sadly. "Because I know you'll be going away soon."

I thought the same thing. I am anxious to return to Los Angeles to trace Heidi's background. "But I will keep in touch," I say. "I will see you soon."

Paula doesn't say anything more. She glances at the vase containing Kalika's ashes.

"Why did you bring that here?" she asks.

"To put the ashes in the water."

She nods. "It is time to move on."

Sorrow washes over me. "I still think of her all the time."

"She lived the life she was born to live." She pauses. "I never told you what she said to me when she burst into my house and grabbed hold of John. She said, 'Hello, Paula. I have no friends but I am a friend of your son's. Tonight everything will come together in a wave of blood. But don't worry, he is stronger than this night.'"

Now I am close to tears. "Her life was so short."

Paula comforts me, rubs my arm. "She couldn't stay too long. She was a star that burned too bright. The strength of her soul would have made us all go blind." Paula gestures to the vase and stands, John still asleep in her arms. "Say your goodbyes. I will wait for you at the house."

I ask weakly. "To say goodbye?"

"Yes."

My voice cracks with emotion. I need her to understand why. "I loved Suzama. I loved her with all my heart. When she died, I almost died."

Her voice is soothing. "You were younger then. You are stronger now."

I look up at her. "Will I see you again? After today?"

Suzama stares at me for a long time. It is Suzama, yes, and she stares with the eyes of humanity's greatest clairvoyant. Her eyes are dry now; she has no tears, as she slowly shakes her head.

"I don't think so, Sita," she says.

She turns and walks away.

I am left alone with my daughter's ashes, and soon these are gone, too, on the gentle ripples of the bay. I poured them from the vase without words, but with great nostalgia and love. True, she was an avatar, a creature of the divine, yet even Kalika's ashes dissolve in water. My memories are strong then, my pain nailed to a bloody past. But strong also is my vision of the future. It is true what Suzama says. I will leave this place, leave my few friends, and confront an enemy I know will kill me. Kill me because I crave love instead of power. But this I have lived five thousand years to learn. Power is as cold as forgotten ashes. Only my love can keep alive the memory of my daughter, the stories of Ray, Arturo, Yaksha, and most of all the grace of Krishna.

My blessed Lord—how he must laugh at me when I sing him to sleep in the middle of the night. Sing him songs from the holy Vedas that he himself wrote when he walked under the trees of ancient India. It is the divine child I will miss the most. Not to see him grow old, to hear him speak wisdom. I fear I will be ash before he even utters his first words. And I have to wonder who will remember me when I am gone. I worry that even Suzama and Seymour will forget me. Me— Alisa, Sita, or a thousand other names that I have been called by strangers who became friends or lovers. I fear it will be as if I never was. Never a vampire. The last vampire, whose long life now comes to a close.

Death does not scare me, but oblivion does. There is a

difference. In my daughter's ashes I see my own bright star sink beneath the surface and go out. My end will erase my beginning. I don't know how but I know it is true. And I must choose that end because it is my destiny.

THREE

The wallet and the passport from Heidi's pockets identified her as a certain Linda Clairee. I know her address, her bank account number, even her supposed birth date. She is supposed to have lived in a house not far from where I lived when I gave birth to Kalika. I am very curious as I drive to her house after flying into LAX.

The place is modest, nondescript even, stucco walls with a wooden fence surrounding an uninspired yard of grass and a few bushes. Slowly I walk toward the front door. There is someone inside watching TV and drinking what smells like beer. The sounds and odors drift out through a torn screen door. I knock lightly and brace myself for instant death. Yet I have a matrix in my pocket, and I have finally figured out how to operate the ray gun. It is a totally cool weapon.

A bearded fellow in a frayed T-shirt answers the door.

He looks as if he's on his second six-pack. Twenty-five, at most, his gut hangs over his belt like a sausage off the side of a breakfast plate. But I warn myself that Heidi—Linda—appeared to be very ordinary until her psychic force field went up. This guy might be more than he appears, but it's hard to believe.

"Hello," I say. "Is Linda home?"

He burps. "She's out of town."

At least he doesn't know she's missing her head.

"My name is Alisa," I say. "I'm an old friend. Do you know when she'll be back?"

"She didn't say."

"Okay." I catch his eye through the screen door and squeeze his neuron currents. "Would it be okay if I come in and search through her personal things?"

His brain is soft mud, easy to impress—I think. "Sure," he says, and opens the door for me.

"Thank you," I respond.

I leave him in the living room, watching a baseball game. But my ears never leave him. If he tries to sneak up on me, he'll fail. But I won't kill him, if he shows strange powers, not right away.

Linda's room is neat and tidy. She seemed to enjoy sewing and the Dodgers. And if I begin to think I have the wrong house, there are pictures of her and Brother Bud on the mirror on top of the chest of drawers, cheap Polaroids shot with a camera with a dusty lens. Heidi is Linda and I am in the right bedroom. In each of the pictures Linda smiles as if someone just told her to.

I search the drawers and find nothing important. Even the closet is boring—clothes and baseball caps, shoes and socks. And this is the creature who said we all have powers? Talk about a double life. I am on the verge of leaving when a stack of papers under the bed catches my eye.

They are all about UFOs.

Specifically, newsletters from a UFO foundation.

FOF—Flying Objects Foundation.

What happened to the unidentified? I don't care. All the newsletters are addressed to Linda Clairee. She was definitely a member of this group, and it is the only wrinkle in her ordinary life that I have found. Holding the papers in my hand, I return to the living room and Bud. He is, in fact, finishing a can of Budweiser as I walk in. I turn off the TV without asking his permission and sit down across from him.

"Hey," he says, annoyed.

I catch his eye and burn a tiny hole in his frontal lobes. It will probably do him good, in the long run.

"Where did Linda say she was going?" I ask.

He replies in a flat voice, staring straight ahead. "Phoenix."

"What's in Phoenix?"

"A convention."

"A UFO convention?"

"Yes. FOF."

"Did Linda often attend such conventions?"

"Yes."

"Why?"

He could be hypnotized. "She likes UFOs."

"Why?"

"I don't know."

"Are you interested in UFOs?"

"No."

"Does Linda believe UFOs exist?"

"Yes."

"Is she an alien?"

"What?"

"Is Linda an alien creature?"

"No."

"Are you sure?"

"Sure, I'm sure."

"When did you meet Linda?"

"Three years ago."

"Where?"

"In a bar in Fullerton."

"What does Linda do for a living?"

"She works as a secretary."

"Have you ever been to her place of work?"

"Yes."

"Where is it?"

"In Fullerton. On Commonwealth and Harbor. Crays DP Office."

"What is Linda like?"

"Nice. Boring. Sexy."

"What is it like to have sex with her?"

"Fun. Always the same."

"What's your name?"

"Bill."

"What do you do for a living, Bill?"

"Drive a truck."

"Have you ever noticed anything unusual about Linda?"

"What do you mean?"

"Besides attending UFO conventions, does she do anything else odd?"

"Yes."

"What?"

"She stares at the sky at night a lot."

"How often?"

"Every night."

"Does she tell you why?"

"No."

"Do you ask?"

"No."

"When do you expect her back?"

"In two days."

"The convention runs until then?"

"Yes, I think."

"Does Linda have any family?"

"No. They are all dead."

"Every one of them?"

"Yes. Everyone."

"Bill, I am going to leave now but I might be back later. Until I return, I want you to forget I was ever here. I never existed. If someone should ask you if a stranger was here, just say no. Do you understand?"

"All right."

"Also, if Linda should fail to come home, don't worry about her. Get yourself another girl. She is not so important. Understand?"

"Yes."

"Good." I stand and step over and turn the TV back on. "Goodbye, Bill."

He glances up from the game. He doesn't even realize I interrupted it. "Goodbye," he says.

There is a plane leaving for Phoenix in fifty minutes and I get on it. Linda's newsletters have told me where the FOF convention is being held—a Holiday Inn beside a busy freeway. Once in Phoenix, I rent a Jeep and drive to the hotel, but all the rooms are taken. Taking a room at a nearby hotel, I shower and then go for a walk in the desert. Perhaps the UFO freaks took a hotel near the edge of town so they could look at the night sky.

It is late—I study the stars as I walk, but nothing flies down from the sky to whisk me away. Yet I feel no pleasure beneath the heavens. A past I cannot remember haunts me.

"We are of an ancient tradition. Our line is mingled with yours, and with that of others. We hold all powers."

Still, Linda wanted more of my blood, if she had any of it to begin with. Yet she must have had something unique. She was fast and strong, more powerful than virtually any vampire Yaksha made. Plus she had technology that put the government's most secret toys to shame. But so many of her answers had made no sense. What did she want to initiate me into?

"But to join us you must sacrifice him. It is part of your initiation."

It was almost as if she wanted to introduce me to the black mass.

I know about such things, sexual magic, from the past.

The torture and the blood, the sudden awakenings.

But I have not thought of them in a long time.

I find a sandy bluff and sit atop it to mentally survey my life, trying to find a point where my blood could have been taken without my knowledge. But except for Arturo and his alchemy, I think, my blood has always been mine to do with as I chose. Yet a faint feeling of dread sweeps over me as I look back. My shadow is long and dark. In it could lie secrets, hidden from even me, where blood was exchanged and vows were pledged that my conscious memory never recorded. It is as if

I sense a blank spot, a place of reality that wasn't real after all. But I only sense its existence—I don't see it. I have to wonder if my imagination leads me to a wall of illusion. My thoughts are never far from those I left behind in Tahoe: John, Seymour, Paula. But Paula swears they are safe there, for now, and she should know. She who has deep visions.

A shooting star crosses the sky and I make a wish.

"Krishna," I whisper, "don't let me die until I have set right what I made wrong."

Suzama's words are with me. God's plan.

Somehow I know it was me who messed it up.

Maybe that's what she had been trying to tell me.

Maybe that was why she sent me away.

FOUR

The next morning I am at the FOF convention in the Holiday Inn, milling around the many booths, poking my head in on lectures. The attendance is substantial, at least two thousand people. The crowd is pretty evenly divided between males and females, but otherwise the cross section is peculiar. There are, for want of a better expression, a lot of nerds here. Many are overweight and wear thick glasses. These are true believers, no doubt about it. The saucers are coming and they are prepared. In fact, they believe they are already here. Eavesdropping on their jumbled thoughts, I soon get a headache.

I sense no superbeings in the vicinity, yet I don't drop my guard. If this convention was important to Linda, there is somebody significant here. If only I knew who. Besides thoughts, I listen to heartbeats, trying to find physiologies that mimic mine. But there is nothing here but pure humanity.

The talks are boring, discussions of different sightings that have about as much credibility as reports of Santa Claus or the Easter Bunny. As I sit through one, yawning, I think about what I should have done with my life. Retired to a remote spot to spend a year building toys and baking goodies, which I would deliver once a year to the needy. At least then I could have given vampires a better name.

Yet there is a lecture at the end of the day that catches my eye. It is entitled: "Control Versus Anarchy—An Interstellar Dilemma." The speaker is to be Dr. Richard Stoon, a parapsychologist from Duke University. He has a list of impressive academic credentials beside his name, but it is really the buzz of the crowd that draws me to the talk. They have been waiting for this guy. I hear them whispering to one another. Dr. Stoon is supposed to be brilliant, charismatic, unorthodox. It is the last lecture of the convention, and I take a seat at the back of the audience and wait for Dr. Stoon to enter.

Beside me sits a pale blond woman, with a waist as small as my own, and clear blue eyes. She has a kind smile and I quickly scan her mind, detecting nothing more than a day job at a boring office, and a husband who has just been laid off. She appears to be in her early twenties but could be older. Noticing my scrutiny, she glances over and brightens.

"Hello," she says with a southern accent. "It's been a fun convention, hasn't it?"

"I haven't been here for the whole thing. I just caught today."

"Have you heard Dr. Stoon speak before?"

"This will be my first time. What's he like?"

"Very forceful, opinionated." She pauses. "He's interesting but to tell the truth he is awfully arrogant."

"Why don't you leave then?" I ask.

She makes a face. "Oh, I couldn't do that. I'm one of those people who has to see everything." She pauses and studies me. There is a sparkle in her eyes; she is far from stupid, but she doesn't want people to know. She offers her hand. "I'm Stacy Baxter."

I shake. "Alisa Perne. Pleased to meet you." I give one of my more common aliases because I'm no longer trying to hide. I want to draw the enemy out.

"Very pleased to meet you," Stacy replies. "I don't think I've seen you around before?"

"This is my first UFO convention."

"So what do you think?"

"It's all very interesting."

Stacy laughs. "No, you don't! You think we're all crackers."

Crackers. I haven't heard that expression in forty years.

I have to smile. "I don't think you're crackers, Stacy."

She's pleased. "Maybe we can have coffee together after Dr. Stoon's talk."

"I'd enjoy that," I reply.

Dr. Stoon enters a short time afterward. He is a big burly man, of Slavic descent, with dark piercing eyes. His age, like Stacy's, is difficult to pinpoint. He could be thirty-five, or ten years older. He moves as if he owns the room, as if every eye should be on him. After a brief introduction, he is at the podium, overpowering it with his bulk and attitude. His voice, when he speaks, is gruff and unpleasant. Yet he sounds smart, like someone who knows more than he is saying.

And his words sound strikingly familiar.

"There are two kinds of beings in this creation," he says. "Those who strive for perfection and those who submit to chaos. It is the same in outer space as it is on this world—there is no difference. We either choose to be masters of our destinies, or we let the fates rule us. I am speaking now about power, and you might wonder what power has to do with a lecture on UFOs. I tell you it has everything to do with our space brothers. Each night we look to the heavens, waiting for them to arrive. But why should they come if we haven't made a choice in our own lives? But when we do make the choice, the right choice, to be important in the galactic scheme of things, then they will know. They will come to us at the most unexpected time, and fill our hands and minds with knowledge we cannot begin to imagine."

Stacy leans over and speaks in my ear. "Sounds like a bit of an evangelist, doesn't he?"

"Yeah. He talks without saying anything specific."

Stacy nodded. "But look at the people in this room. They are spellbound. Dr. Stoon doesn't have to say anything to have the effect he wants."

Stacy misunderstands me, but her point is well made. Dr. Stoon is one of those people who draws others in, smothers them. Even though he's not being specific, he touches on issues Suzama—and that's who she will always be to me—also explained. Yet his bias is from the other side, even though nothing he says sounds intrinsically negative.

He continues in a loud voice.

"We have to open our minds fully to the truth that we control our own futures, while at the same time we must accept that there are powers above us that are willing to help us if we align our thinking with theirs. Who are our space brothers? They are us a thousand years from now. They are strong. And for us to be strong we must cut off all that weakens us as a people. Here I have to speak on a matter that is almost considered a blasphemy in our society, and yet it is the single most important issue regarding our survival. We are literally drowning in the shallow end of our gene pool. Who is reproducing at the most rapid rate in our world? The uneducated and the foolish. But how did our space brothers reach their exalted state? By casting out the foolish. Our genes are our only treasure. We must plan their use, and use the plan—the plan our brothers are waiting to give us."

Again Stacy leans over and whispers in my ear.

"Sounds like Hitler to me," she says.

I smile. "But he's not blaming any specific group for mankind's woes."

"Isn't he?" Stacy asks, and her question is worth contemplating.

Dr. Stoon speaks for another half hour, and at the end of that time he doesn't accept questions—probably because no one would know what to ask him. I certainly wouldn't. Yet his words have affected me, not so much by their content, but by their resonance. I don't know, however, if the effect is a good one. His lecture was divisive; nothing he said could be used to bring people together for the common good. Another might say that was not true. Such was the strength and weakness of his talk.

When he finishes I wander toward the front, where he stands chatting with what appear to be old friends. But when his eyes meet mine, he momentarily freezes, and then quickly turns away. He excuses himself from his group and walks briskly toward the exit.

I walk after him.

In the parking lot he climbs in his car and races out onto the road, heading for the desert. Naturally I follow him. He must know I am tailing him. At this time of day, a half hour after dusk, we are the only ones on this narrow road that runs perpendicular to the main highway. Within twenty minutes we are deep in the desert, with the city only a glow on the horizon. The stars come out. Dr. Stoon is driving fast, but now it is possible he may not know I am behind him. I have turned off my headlights. I don't need them, of course, but maybe he doesn't either.

Ten minutes later he suddenly swerves off the road and drives across the sand toward a massive hill that is more reminiscent of Utah's Zion National Park than Phoenix's backyard. The hill is more a stone cathedral, built around a symmetrical interior. The rough terrain is hard on Dr. Stoon's BMW but my Jeep loves the challenge.

He drives his car as close to the hill as he can, then stops and gets out.

What do I do? I realize I could be walking into a trap. If he has a matrix, as I have, he could incinerate my Jeep from a distance. I have experimented with the weapon—it has a substantial range. The way he fled from me, for no apparent reason, indicates he is more than he seems. Yet his exit was obvious as well. But I sense no one else in the area, and I can hear a snake slither at a distance of five miles in such a desert.

I decide to risk direct confrontation.

Dr. Stoon stands with his arms at his sides as I drive up. Slowly I climb from my Jeep, the matrix in hand. I do not wish to waste time on pretense. If he is like Linda, he is going to do some talking. If he is human, he has a funny way of showing it. Either way I believe he will die in this desert tonight. I may even drink his blood, although I have not fed from anyone since Kalika brought me back from the edge of death. My hunger simply seems to have vanished. I gesture with my weapon. A million stars shine down on us. I see them all, more than a mortal can see with a medium-size telescope.

"Move away from the car," I say. "Put your hands in the air."

He does as I command. "What do you want?" he asks in a much softer voice than he used at the convention. I step closer.

"I should ask you that question, Dr. Stoon," I say. "What do you want?"

He does not hesitate. "We told you."

"You told me little. Who are you people?"

He smiles slightly, cocky bastard. "Who do you think?"

"Extraterrestials."

"You are partially right, and partially wrong. We have been here a long time."

"How long?"

"Don't you remember?"

His question disturbs me, his voice. I realize he is trying to overpower me with his eyes. His are at least as strong as Linda's. Try as I might, I cannot pierce his aura to read his mind.

"I remember nothing of you. Answer my question."

"Over a thousand years," he says.

"Where did you come from? Originally?"

"There is no simple answer to that question. We move in space and time, through dimensions and distortions."

"Are you here to distort humanity?"

"We are here for the harvest."

"For which side of the harvest?"

"There is only one side—the expansion of the self, the growth of self-awareness."

"Sounds nice. But at whose expense?"

He snorts. "The expense of all those too weak to move forward. Why do you ask these questions? We know you are a vampire, the most powerful vampire on Earth. We have watched you for centuries. You do what you wish; we do as we wish. We are brothers to you, sisters. Why don't you join us?"

"It doesn't sound like you want me as a brother or sister. It sounds like you want me as a blood bank." I pause. "Or do you already have some of my blood?"

He makes me wait. "We do," he says finally.

I stiffen. The confirmation wounds me.

"When?" I ask. I feel violated.

"Over a thousand years ago."

"When?" I demand.

He gloats. "Kalot Enbolot. Chateau Merveille." He pauses before he says the next words. "The Castle of Wonder."

I tremble, not just in my body, but in my very soul.

In all my long life, there had never been darker days.

Yet I thought I had escaped his aerie unscathed.

"Landulf," I whisper. "Oh God."

Dr. Stoon grins. "Landulf took the best you had to give,

now we will take it again. With or without your assistance."

I back up involuntarily. "You lie!" I gasp. "He never touched me!"

Dr. Stoon speaks with scorn. "He did more than touch you. He bled you, used you, and then twisted your mind so that you didn't know. But don't you remember now, Sita? As you swam through the waves away from his castle? Swam to what you thought was freedom? Even the ocean water could not wash off the contamination you felt then. Yet you thought you had won, defeated him. Just as you think you will defeat us now."

I cannot stop shaking. The images his words invoke—I cannot bear to see them in my suddenly shattered mind. Landulf and his sexual magic, satanic practice that used terror and pain for fuel. The human sacrifices, bodies split open with dirty knives, and worst of all the spirits that would appear at his bidding, vicious creatures from an astral hell buried beneath unheeded cries. From the Temple of Erix at which the Priestess of Antiquity had once guarded the Oracle of Venus, in southwest Sicily, he sent forth these unclean spirits and dominated the minds and hearts of men and women throughout southern Europe. Inviting the hordes of invading Moslems, showing them the weaknesses in the Christian world's defenses and so betraying his own race, Landulf had changed the course of history in the ninth century. And so he had changed my life, putting a stain on it that more than ten centuries had not totally erased. I tremble for many reasons, all of them unbearable, Landulf had indeed touched me, I remember, kissed me even, with lips that often enjoyed raw human flesh.

Yet I still thought I had tricked him.

"I will defeat you," I whisper without conviction. "If you have anything to do with him, I will not rest until all of your kind are wiped out. Landulf was a demon, and you use his name as if he were a hero. Your power is a travesty." I aim the matrix. "You will all die."

Dr. Stoon grins and lowers his hands. "We are not alone."

I glance left and right, see nothing, hear only the desert.

Yet I sense the truth of his words, sense a presence.

"Tell them to show themselves," I say carefully. "If you want to live one second longer."

"Very well." He bows his head slightly.

Suddenly there are three figures in red robes, one on each side, another at my back. Each carries a matrix in his or her hand, although their faces are shadowed, as are their minds. They are humanoid but that is all I know about them. They have me in their sights. There seems to be no escape. Dr. Stoon sticks out his hand.

"The matrix, please," he says.

I shake my head. "I will vaporize myself before you will have my blood."

He is amused. "Try."

I try the weapon on him. But it doesn't work.

"We neutralized it at the convention," he explains.

I throw the weapon aside. "You don't want me dead."

"True," he says. "But we will kill you before we allow you to kill us. Lay facedown on the sand."

"I hardly think so," I say, and my attention goes to the figure on my right, the one whose hand shakes ever so slightly. This person—I cannot even see his eyes—but I know it is a male, weaker than the others that guard me. Even though I cannot read his mind, I can sense the general character of it. This is an important assignment for him, one that he has had to struggle to win. If he completes it successfully, captures the vampire's blood, he will receive some type of advancement. But if he fails, he will be killed. Indeed, he is especially fearful of Dr. Stoon. He wishes the doctor dead. That is the chink in his psychic armor. He does not care for his associates, hates them in fact, wishes they all were dead so that all the glory could be his. My eyes fasten on his hidden face, my thoughts drill into his cranium.

Kill them. Burn them. Vanquish them.

The man's arm trembles more.

"It is not wise to refuse us," Dr. Stoon says.

"Do you still give me a chance to join you?" I mutter, stalling for time. Never before have I focused so hard, called upon the depths of my will. The strain is immense. For even though this one is the weakest, he is still strong beyond belief.

"Perhaps," Dr. Stoon says. "Lay facedown or die. Now."

"Die," I repeat softly, to the man. "Die."

His aim shifts slights. The finger on the button on his matrix twitches.

Dr. Stoon is suddenly aware of the danger. He whirls on the man.

"Kill him!" he screams.

There are two bursts of red light, one from behind me, one from my left. My victim vaporizes on an ear-piercing scream. But I do not pause to mourn the sound. I am already in the air, flipping backward in a curving arc, my legs going over me, carrying me over the assailant at my rear. There is another burst of red death—the one on my left tries to shoot me out of the sky. But already I have landed, behind the one who moments earlier stood behind me. In a matter of microseconds I seize his matrix and break his arm. Without speaking, I blow away the red robe on the left. Dr. Stoon reaches into his coat pocket but I caution him to remain still.

"Don't," I say.

The figure I have disarmed groans, moves.

I shoot him and he is no more.

Dr. Stoon has stopped grinning.

"How many more of you are there?" I ask.

He pauses. "There is just me."

"And when you die, you die?"

He hesitates. "We prefer not to surrender this form."

I chuckle. "I do believe there is a note of fear in your voice, good doctor. For a moment there, you know, I thought you were Landulf himself. But Landulf was never afraid."

"Not even of you," he says bitterly.

"Yes," I say sadly, thinking of what he has told me. "Perhaps I was tricked. What did he use my blood for?"

"Is it not obvious?"

"Only your death is obvious. Answer my question so that death won't catch you asking."

He is defiant. "I will not be your puppet. We are alone for the moment, but others of my kind are coming. And if you should slay me, their treatment of you will be that more hideous."

I shake my head. "Nothing can be hideous to me. Not after Landulf."

He speaks arrogantly. "You will not escape us."

"Really? You thought I wouldn't escape you."

He doesn't have an answer for that.

I shoot him and he troubles me no more.

FIVE

I return to my Jeep and drive back toward the road. When I reach it there is another car waiting for me, another person. She stands by the side of the road looking up at the stars. She hardly seems to notice my approach, and only glances over as I park and walk toward her, the matrix in my hand.

Stacy Baxter. She finally glances at me and smiles.

"Hello, Alisa," she says, and the southern accent is gone.

My finger is on the fire button. "What are you doing here?" I ask softly.

She shrugs and gazes back up at the sky. "Just enjoying the night. Isn't it beautiful?"

"Yes. Did you follow me out here?"

She pauses. "Yes."

"I see." I am a moment away from killing her. "Do you have anything else to say, Stacy Baxter?"

She looks at me again, not smiling now, just watching me, very closely. "No, Alisa Perne," she replies quietly.

I shift uncomfortably. This death does not feel right

"Are you one of them?" I ask finally.

She shakes her head. "Not me."

"Who are you?"

"A friend."

"No. I don't know you." I shake the weapon. "Why are you here?"

"To help you, if you want my help."

"What's your real name?"

"Alanda," she replies. "Sita."

My heart pounds. "And you are another incantation of Lundulf's?"

Sorrow touches her face. "You suffered there."

I bite my lip. "Yeah, I suffered. But what's it to you?"

She lowers her head. "Everything you have experienced—it means a lot to me."

My voice is hard. "Why? Because you know me from long ago?"

"Yes."

I fidget on my feet. I want to kill her. Logic dictates that I should. This desert is filled with monsters. Chances are she is one, too. Certainly she is not normal, and knows too much about me. Yet she does nothing to defend herself, even to plead her case, and I find it difficult to strike down the helpless.

"Do you know this weapon I carry?" I ask.

"Yes."

"I know how to use it." I pause. "I will use it."

Alanda is staring at the stars again. "Then use it."

"You are impossible. I will kill you, just as I killed the others out there minutes ago. You saw that, didn't you?"

"Yes."

I am sarcastic. "Why didn't you come to my aid? Friend?"

"It was not allowed."

"By whom?" I demand.

"You had to refuse them. To offer to end your life before they would take it from you." She adds, "You did these things."

"I did nothing but kill. Because they answered me the same way you do, with vague mumblings." I pause and sweat over the trigger. "I think you are one of them."

For the third time she looks at me, and for the first time I really see her. Her blue eyes—they are very much like my own. I could be staring into a mirror. Yet it is more than a physical resemblance. The person behind the eyes, the soul within the body, seems to reach out and touch me in a way I cannot explain. For a moment—from this unassuming person I am threatening to destroy—I feel profoundly cherished. Suddenly she is more than a friend to me, she is a part of me. Sometimes when I looked at Suzama, I would feel this way. Occasionally,

gazing at the divine child, I would sense this same expansion of consciousness, as if my mind were only a portion of a much greater mind. It is only in that moment that I realize Alanda is a spiritual being of great stature, someone who loves me more than I am able to love myself.

The matrix slips from my fingers, lands in the sand. A tear rolls over my cheek and joins it in the dust. I don't know why I cry, perhaps because I am happy. Alanda is an old friend.

Yet I don't remember her.

As I don't remember Landulf stealing my blood.

"I don't understand," I whisper.

She comes to me and hugs me, stroking my face. "Sita," she says over and over again. "My Sita."

But I am not a child. I am a monster. I cannot be comforted even if the space between us is suffused with the vitality of reunion. I cannot turn to this creature that I do not know for help or solace. In a swift move, I brush her off and step away, turning my back on her. If she wanted, she could pick up the matrix and vaporize me. But I know that is not her intention. She lets me stand silently alone. Nothing is hurried in her, I realize. She has waited long for this encounter, and I feel I have as well. Yet I feel exposed before her, and that is a feeling I have never enjoyed. I have always been the master of my own destiny, and now this angelic being comes to me in the night to tell me that I have been fooling myself. Truly, she is an angel to me, a being of light from a distant world I cannot imagine.

"There is no need for imagination," she says quietly. "Those worlds belong to you as much as to me."

I draw in a tight breath. "You are telepathic then?"

"Yes. As are you."

"No. I cannot read your mind."

"You can. You're just afraid, Sita."

"How do you know my name?"

"Because I know you."

"From when? From where?"

"From before. From the stars."

A smile cracks my face, involuntarily. Turning, almost mocking her, I say, "Where's your spaceship?"

"It's coming."

That remark makes me take a step back.

"Are you here to take me away?" I ask, and I hear the hope in my own voice. For five thousand years, I have lived a glorious life, yet there has been too much pain. Alanda's love seems to flow to me in waves. The desert is dry, her eyes are moist. I cannot help but be mesmerized by them, by all of her. She is shimmering now with a faint blue light.

This blue glow, it reminds me of Krishna.

The stars. How bright they shine above us.

Almost as if they have moved closer to Earth.

But Alanda's face is both blissful and concerned.

"No," she says. "You cannot leave this world now, not until what has been ruined has been set right."

"Suzama said as much. Do you know her?"

"Yes. She is a sister, like you."

"Suzama is much more than I am."

"You are fond of denouncing yourself."

"I haven't been a saint exactly. You must know that."

"Yes. But that is past. You are here with me now, and I am with you."

My throat is constricted. "I feel you with me, yes."

"Why are you afraid of love, Sita? Because it has hurt you?"

I nod weakly. "It hurts all of us. Sometimes it seems that is all love is good for."

Alanda shakes her head. "Love is good for many things. You have just forgotten. The veil has to be lifted."

I am curious. "What is this veil?"

Alanda turns away and walks on the sand, between the weeds. She is barefoot—I only realize that now. The way her soles touch the ground, it is almost as if they caress the Earth. Gesturing at the desert, the stars, and playing with her long blond hair, she enchants me as she speaks. The communication may even be telepathic, her voice is so soft. But it is easy to understand her.

"This galaxy is ancient, as you know," she says. "Your sun is old, but the stars at the center of the galaxy were there first. The planets circling them gave rise to civilizations. So life evolved. First plants, then animals and finally, what you would call people arrived. Some of these people looked like us, but not all. They became conscious. They knew all that the people of this world know, and more. For there was at that time no veil between the conscious and the unconscious, no loss of the awareness that we are all a part of the creation. The gods of those suns did not desire this veil to confuse their children, and therefore everyone on those ancient planets lived in light and peace. Do you understand?"

"I'm not sure," I say. "Continue."

"Suzama has told you about the coming harvest, on this world. These ancient people also arrived at a point when it was important for them to move on, to move into another realm, a fourth dimension if you like. But then there was a problem. All these beings from the central suns of this galaxy were positive—what you would call good-hearted. But because they had always lived in bliss, they had no incentive to grow. Therefore, for many billions of years, from the third dimension to the fourth, there were few harvests. Such people were a rarity." Alanda pauses. "Do you understand?"

"Yes. The source of pain for us—here on this world—is the veil between the conscious and the unconscious. Yet this pain acts as a catalyst for us to grow."

"Precisely. People of your world often speak of good and evil. But what you call evil goads you onto the greatest good. This is necessary for you, and all people of your world. That is why it is there. That is why the great being within your sun

allows the veil to exist. The story from the Garden of Eden—
the knowledge of good and evil that your ancient ancestors
received—that was not a curse but a blessing. It only seems a
curse to you at times like this, when you are in doubt."

"But to some extent we live our whole lives in doubt." I pause.
"So you're saying the devil wasn't such a bad guy after all?"

"No. I am saying there is a place for negativity—as much
as there is a place for goodness—in the great scheme of things.
There is no hero without a villain, no peak without a valley.
But our path, the path of love, demands that we overcome
negativity. But we do not overcome it by resisting it. That is an
illusion. What you resist will persist."

"Why are you telling me this?" I ask, and there is suddenly
fear in my voice. But I know what she will answer. For I knew,
personally, the greatest evil that ever walked the Earth. Still,
Alanda's words chill me to the bone.

"Landulf cannot be overcome by force," she says.

My lower lip trembles. "Landulf is dead. He died a long
time ago."

"Perhaps. Perhaps not. But certainly his work lives on. You
met a sample of it tonight in the desert. There are more of
them emerging at this time, and they possess a sample of your
blood." She steps toward me, looks at me. "Do you know what
that means?"

I snort. "Yeah. It means they're tough sonsofbitches."

Alanda is serious. "Yes. They are tough. And it was never

intended that the negative side of harvest should possess such a powerful army of warriors. In the coming years they will over-whelm your people, turn virtually everyone toward fear. This will be the downfall for all who aspire to the light This fear will cause the negative harvest to be larger than it would have been. In other words, your world is out of balance."

"And I caused this imbalance?"

Alanda sighs. "This must be difficult for you to hear."

"The truth is always better than illusions." I pause. "Is it true?"

"Yes. You are the ultimate source of this cancer, and it must be rectified."

"Are you so sure?" I ask, trying to deny what I just heard. It's too much for me, to be told that I am the scourge of man-kind. I feel as if I must run away. Only my irrational love for her makes me stay.

Alanda is gentle. Her next word is not. "Yes."

"But how can you be sure?" I demand.

"Because my old and dear friend, I am from your future."

I take a moment to absorb her statement "What is it like?"

Now she stutters. "In ruins."

I am shocked. "This world?"

The life leaves her voice. "This entire sector of the galaxy. When so much of Earth fails, much else fails later." Alanda steps close to me, puts her hands on my shoulders, her eyes in my soul. "We have come back for you, Sita, to ask you to help us. To ask you to go back to the days of Landulf. To relive those days, and keep him from doing to you what he desired."

The prospect fills me with horror. "But I can't remember what he did to me!"

"You will, I promise, when you travel back to that time."

"No." I shake my head, feeling my guts turn to ice. "That is one thing I cannot do. Ask anything of me but that."

Alanda strokes the side of my face. "You are afraid."

Again I brush her off and turn aside. "Yes," I say in a shaky voice. "And I don't understand why. I can't understand why the simple thought of seeing him again overwhelms me."

"It's because of what you can't remember."

I whirl around. "Then tell me what happened?"

"I cannot. You must face the memory when you are once more in his castle. It is the only way. It is why he was able to block your memory in the first place. At that time you refused to face what happened."

"Did he torture me? Did he mutilate me?"

She nods reluctantly. "In his own way. But there is more than that to the puzzle—you will see."

I am sick at the prospect. "Is your spaceship a time machine as well?"

Alanda glances up. "Not exactly."

"But how can I go back to those days? How can I meet myself?"

She stares at me. "Physically you will not journey in time. Only your mind will go back."

"I don't understand?"

"As our ships approach light speed, we are able to jump into a realm that exists outside time and space. In that realm we can cross many light-years in a moment. The enemy also has this technology, and that is how they were able to surround you in the desert tonight. In that realm, the laws of physics as you understand them do not apply. For a few seconds you will cease to exist in a particular time and place. Therefore, you will have the freedom to be where you wish to be. If you focus all your will on that ninth century vampire, you will become her. Do you see?"

"No. Will both our minds be in the same body?"

"No. There is only one of you. You will become her, and she will become you. There is no question of two."

I am still confused, but dread continues to dominate my mind. "I can't see him again," I plead. "You don't know what he was like."

Alanda is sad. "But I know his kind well. He is not from the dimension beyond this one, but from the one even beyond that. He is negative fifth density—not merely a sorcerer, but a master of sorcerers. Above his head the vipers hiss, and before his vision all wills turn to stone. Those you met tonight are only his minions. But he is not greater than you, Sita. I know you, old friend, know of your extraordinary origin. You cannot directly resist him when you confront him, for in doing so you will become him. That is his special power, the spell he cloaked you in before. Yet you can defeat him." Quoting Suzama, she adds, "'Faith is stronger than stone.'"

"But you will not tell me how to defeat him?"

"No. You must find the way. It is your destiny to do so."

I don't want to ask the question but I do anyway.

"Is it also my destiny to die? Alanda?"

She shakes her head. "I cannot say."

"But you come from the future. You know. Tell me."

"I know that you will rewrite our future. Please do not ask me to say more." Her eyes return to the heavens and she points. "Behold, Sita. Our ship comes for you."

SIX

*T*he funny thing is, I don't see anything. Alanda explains that the ship will land deep in the desert, beside a clear pond. She offers to drive me there, but I prefer to take the Jeep, so she goes with me instead. We cut directly across the sand, murdering more than a few tumbleweeds in the process. Yet the ground is not excessively bumpy, and we soon reach the pond. After parking, I climb out and stare at it in amazement.

The pond appears to be natural—Alanda assures me it is even though it is a perfect circle. A hundred feet across, the water lies so still that it could be a polished mirror set to reflect the stars. Indeed, as I approach the edge of the pond, I see more stars in the water than I do above. I see the approach of the saucer in the water before I see it in the sky, quite a few seconds before. It makes me wonder, yet I say nothing.

The saucer is blue-white, and the light from it slowly begins to flood the area and my eyes, wiping out any chance of my making out the details. If I weren't dreading seeing Landulf, I would be thrilled by this moment. But I can only think of Landulf's devishly handsome face, his deep laugh, and the way he would make an incision in an abdomen with his long sharp nails and slowly pull out the victim's entrails while the victim watched. I feel I must resist Landulf with every fiber of my being. Yet Alanda says that is the way of failure.

I have no idea what I'll do that is different from what I did the last time.

I stare up at the saucer.

"This is incredible," I whisper.

"This is but a beam ship," she says. "Our mother ships are a thousand times this size."

"And I have been on these before?"

"Yes."

"When?"

"Another time."

"Are you sure the brakes work? The ship looks as if it's going to land on us."

"It will land over this pool."

"Then we should move?"

"No. We're fine. It will move right over us."

The light grows dazzling, and I have to shield my eyes.

"This must be visible from a hundred miles away," I gasp.

"No one sees it but us," Alanda replies.

I glance at her. "Is it physical?"

"What is physical in one density is not physical in another."

I have to laugh. "One of these days, Alanda, I am going to ask you a question and understand your answer."

The water of the pond seems to glow as the spaceship settles over us. One moment it is above us, the next we are inside it. The translucent floor, I assume, now covers the pond. During the move to the interior, we have had our clothes changed. We now wear long white robes. I don't even bother asking—the night is so weird already.

A gentleman waits for us inside. He is tall and bearded—like a child's drawing of a Biblical character. His robe is the color of the outside of the ship, blue-white. The interior of the vessel is in various shades of gold, and the ceiling is a clear dome, that opens to the sky. There appear to be no controls. Alanda introduces her friend as Gaia. He smiles and bows his head but doesn't say anything. His eyes are liquid green and very lovely.

"Gaia is from a race that doesn't speak," Alanda explains. "But he understands your thoughts."

I nod in his direction. "I appreciate your coming for us, Gaia. I hope it was not too long a journey."

He smiles and shakes his head. No, not too long.

There is a faint humming.

"What is that?" I ask.

"Our engines," Alanda says.

"Will we leave soon?"

"We have already left." Alanda motions with her arm. "See, we are in orbit."

The floor of the craft turns clear as glass, and I jump slightly, momentarily afraid I am going to fall. Below our feet is the black-blue Pacific, and the glittering coast of California. I spot Lake Tahoe, and think of my friends. We seem to be moving westward, at considerable speed. Yet the hum has stopped, and all is quiet. The view takes my breath away, it is so beautiful, and yet it also makes me sad. To see the Earth from such a vantage point, to realize it is all I have known. Never before did I realize how much I thought of the Earth as my mother.

"She is a strong woman," Alanda says softly, reading my mind. "But delicate as well."

"Can a planet be alive?" I ask.

"Can a sun?" she replies. "I told you that it was the god within your sun that decided that humanity should live with the veil—until this time."

"Are you from a world that experienced such a veil?"

"Originally, yes."

"Can you tell me about that world?" I ask.

"Not at this time."

"But I lived there before I came to Earth?"

"Not precisely. Before you came here, you existed in a realm of great glory."

"You're saying that I was in a higher dimension?"

"Yes," Alanda says. "A higher density."

"Why did I decide to come to Earth?"

"To serve, to grow. The two are the same in the creator's eyes."

"Why did I chose to be a vampire?"

Alanda hesitates. "When you came here, you were not a vampire."

"I had a life before this one?"

Her voice is abruptly filled with melancholy. "Yes. Very long ago."

She is trying to tell me something without saying it.

"I made a mistake when I returned?" I say. "Is that why I had to be reborn as a vampire?"

Alanda reaches over and touches my face. "You returned to this third density out of love. If you made a mistake, Sita, it was only out of love. You mustn't blame yourself."

Already we are over India. I nod to Rajastan, desert meeting green.

"I was born there five thousand years ago," I say. "I am sure you know that. But what you might not know is that I feel I never left that tiny village. I am still that young girl spying on the Aghora sacrifice that invoked Yaksha into Amaba's dead womb." I pause. "I held him as an unborn infant in my hand. He was just a trace of movement beneath the hard skin of a corpse. I had a knife in my hand, and my father gave me the choice of ending his life before it could begin." A wave of weariness sweeps over me and I lower my head. "But I couldn't kill Yaksha."

Alanda hugs me. "Because of love, you see. You must let go of the past."

"But you are sending me into a past I want to let go of."

"But this is the only way you will be able to be finished with it. Trust us, Sita. We do this for you as much as for ourselves. Our futures are entwined."

I look up and smile. "Just because I almost killed you doesn't mean I believe you would lie to me." I pause. "You risked your life meeting me like that."

"It was the only way to meet you."

"It was a test?" I ask.

"In a manner of speaking."

"You could have defended yourself from me."

Alanda turns back to the view. "I counted on your compassion."

"The compassion of a murderer?"

"Of an angel."

I have to laugh. "You are as bad as Seymour. He sees me that way, no matter what I do."

"He is wise."

I sigh. "I would love it if he were with us now."

Alanda is thoughtful. "In a sense, he is. He is always with you."

Her remark strikes deeply into me. "Why is that so true?"

Alanda stares at the Earth, India. "You will see."

A short time later the Earth begins to shrink as we pull away from it at a tremendous velocity. Soon it is only a blue ball, falling into a well of blackness. The floor turns solid as the sides become clear. The rays of the sun stab through the saucer's view screens and I feel their warmth. There is no sense of acceleration, however. I see the moon, but only for a few seconds, and then it is lost in the glare of the Earth. But then that planet, the only home I can remember, is also lost in the rays of the sun. The sun begins to diminish in size and brilliance. Alanda turns away and strolls to the center of the craft. But my eyes are gripped by the stars ahead of us.

"I've had these dreams," I say to Alanda and Gaia both. Gaia stands at a respectful distance, silent, peaceful, absorbed in a contemplation I cannot imagine. Yet I know he watches me and listens to my thoughts. I continue, "In them I would be in a spaceship flying through the galaxy toward the Pleiades. Ray would usually be with me, but sometimes it would be my husband, Rama. Never were both with me, but I think that's because—in my dreams—they were always the same person. Anyway, we would be excited and filled with a sense of adventure. We would know, when we reached the Pleiades, that all our friends would be waiting for us. We even knew that

Krishna would be there, to welcome us and to heal the many injuries we had received living on Earth. Most of all, in these dreams, I would be happy, and it would be hard to wake from them." I pause. "Were they just dreams, Alanda?"

"Or were they real?" she asks. "Maybe they were a little of both."

I look at her. "Are you from the Pleiades?"

"It is a place I know." She shrugs. "We are each from God."

I listen to the silence. "It's time, isn't it?"

"Yes. In a few minutes, we will make what you might call a hyperjump. At that time, as I explained before, it is important that you focus your entire being to a time just before you traveled to Landulf's castle."

"It was Dante who led me to the castle," I say, stepping toward her. "Should I think of him?"

Alanda pauses. "The moment you reappear is entirely up to you."

I force a smile, although the dread weighs on me like a stone in my heart.

"It will be good to see Dante again," I say. "A little comic relief before I descend into hell." I gesture to the center of the floor. "Should I sit down and close my eyes?"

Alanda takes my hand. "Lie down and close them, Sita."

I do as she says, but she continues to hold my hand. I open my eyes and smile at her. "Don't worry," I say. "It is just my mind that is going back in time."

She shakes her head slightly. "But if you die back then."

I understand. "I won't exist today?"

She sighs. "There is something else. These fifth density negative beings—they can imprison you."

"I'm pretty good at breaking out of most prisons."

"They can imprison your soul, in their realm. Make you one of them."

Somehow that doesn't sound fair. "For long?"

"Billions of years. You would only be set free when they are set free."

"Negative beings attain freedom?" I ask.

"Yes. Far up the ladder of evolution, the negative path meets the positive. In the end, all find God." She squeezes my hand. "But you could be lost for the life of this universe."

I cannot conceive of anything worse.

"How can he trap me?" I ask.

"He is subtle, and we cannot penetrate his mind. But he acts much as a mirror does. He stands before you. He shows you what you are. But only the parts of you that can be used to destroy you."

"He can cause me to destroy myself?"

"Exactly. Be wary. He can kill you without your permission. But he can only pervert you to his cause if you enter into an agreement with him out of free will."

"But I would never do that."

Alanda seems unsure. Her expression is anxious.

She leans over and kisses my cheek. There is a tear on her face and I reach up to wipe it away but she grabs my other hand.

"You are loved," she whispers. "Don't forget that."

"I know. I know you." I close my eyes. "Goodbye, Alanda."

"Sita. My Sita."

She lets go of me. The ship darkens.

I hear the strange hum again, a shift inside.

But inside, outside—they have lost their meaning.

We are beyond space and time, and I am falling.

Into horror unspeakable, yes, and maybe hope unimagined.

SEVEN

*T*he collage of colors and shapes that I now see is my life. Yet the different scenes from it are not arranged in a linear fashion, more in the form of a hologram, a pictorial dimension of time that encircles me like a living sphere. I have only to focus my attention on a particular event and I am there. But perhaps because my mind is used to dealing with sequential events, I take myself back in order. This is my deliberate choice, not the choice of the creation. To the creation, I realize, everything is happening in the same eternal moment.

I am with my daughter, Kalika, holding her as she bleeds from devastating chest wounds. Her smile is gentle and I am crying. She tells me she loves me. Then I cry over Seymour, beside his funeral pyre, because Kalika has killed him. Yet a few drops of the divine child's blood and he is alive again. Then I am laughing. Tears are connected to laughter in my life. One seems to bring the other, and that in itself is a great mystery to me. Blood, also, is everywhere. I see the night my daughter was born, in pain and love. The opposites of all life fly before my expanded vision, yet they now seem to be in harmony with one another.

Arturo and Joel are beside me. They tell me they love me. There is a flash of blinding light. They die, their love kills them, I destroy them. But a moment later I am saving Joel by making him a vampire, and a moment before that I am reviving Ray by the same process. Then I take a leap and I am sitting beside Ray's father as he dies from a ferocious blow I have struck to his chest. He perishes with the fear that I will harm his son, the son I love. Again and again, my love brings danger and death.

The hologram of my life seems to spin. In quick succession I see Hitler screaming at his troops, Lincoln ordering General Grant to take up the Union's moral cause. Then I am in a castle in the highlands of Scotland, defending it from an evil duke. Once more my lover dies, and in the next instant I stand before the Inquisition, condemning Arturo to death. Arturo, who has meant more to me than practically anyone I have ever known. I see his eyes as I curse him, but I do not see his heart, do not know that he has already tricked me. I ensure his death but he does not die.

Finally I am walking in the dry hills of Sicily outside Messina, eating a bunch of purple grapes and wondering where

I am heading. It is the ninth century and even the evening air is hot. This is my first visit to Sicily; the previous day I took a sailboat across the straits from Italy. Something about the land has drawn me to this spot in particular, but as of yet I don't know what. My long blond hair is pulled up under a cap, and I wear gray hose and a short linen tunic. I could be a pretty young boy, with my baggy white shirt and long steel knife tucked in my belt. The sun is in the sky, but it bothers me just a little.

Then I am not watching this other self.

I am her, and it isn't easy for either of us.

There is a moment of duality. She does not know me.

I feel as if I bump heads with a shadow, and yet my shadow thinks she is the real one. and that I am the ghost. It takes me a moment to explain, and the moment almost cracks open into an insane fissure of delusion. This Sita does not have a volume of my memories, and certainly does not know about flying saucers and the possibility of mental time travel. I am forced to impress these possibilities on her through a wall of internal resistance that threatens to explode both our minds. Then I realize it is hopeless, that I cannot force myself on myself. I relax, and back off, and then suddenly she is curious about me. She knows me even when she doesn't know all of me. I was always one for a new experience, and meeting myself along an empty road is about as weird an experience as I have ever had. My younger self calls to me.

"Ritorna da me," she says. Come back to me.

"Fa bene," I reply, aloud. All right.

Sita is startled. Who is talking to whom?

Her curiosity is greater than her fear.

I am able to get inside and there I stay.

Finally she understands. The duality ceases. I am Alisa Perne of the twentieth century, in the ninth century, here in Sicily to defeat a monster. There is only me but I am now of firm resolve. Landulf had better beware.

Around the bend of the next hill, I hear cries. Dante.

Before I had not known I would meet him, but now it is as if he is calling my name. Tossing aside my grapes, I run to an appointment I have with the past. Yet already I am not thinking of myself as from the future. Perhaps the other Sita is there as much as I. Yet I do notice that I am not nearly so fast as I was before. This body has not had the last infusions of powerful blood. I am just an ordinary vampire—I can't even read minds. All that I have, that I didn't have before, are memories of things that have not yet happened. They are my only new weapons against Landulf.

As I come around a hill, I find Dante naked and bleeding, strung up to a skeleton of a tree by a rope tied to his right arm and right foot. Gathered around him are two men and a woman, the two men holding swords and poking at poor Dante, encouraging him to sing. There is another rope around Dante's neck. The meaning is clear—if Dante stops singing, they will cut the other ropes and he will be hung.

Dante is not in good shape. At a glance I realize he has severe leprosy of his left arm and leg. The disease has actually eaten away portions of his bones, and I know he must live in terrible pain. He has also been castrated, but by the sweetness in his voice I recognize that he is no ordinary eunuch. He is a castrato, perhaps of the Holy Father in Rome, whom I despise. The castrati make up the greatest choirs in the Catholic Church. Their manhood is sacrificed to maintain their magical voices in a preadolescent range. There are few things the Church will not do, I realized long ago, to petition the angels in heaven. Dante cannot be more than twenty years old.

"Ciao!" I call as I stride up. *"Che cosa fai?"* What are you doing?

The men hardly look over, they are having so much fun. But the dark-haired woman with the cleft palate eyes me suspiciously. *"Stai zitta!"* she calls. Shut up. "He is a leper. He is to be killed."

"Penso di no." I don't think so. I slowly draw my knife as I move near. "Release him now, and I will spare your lives."

Dante stops singing and the two men with swords now give me their attention. One is a clumsy brute, dark featured, the other, the fair young one, appears quick on his feet. They eye my long narrow knife and chuckle to themselves. But the young man spreads his feet slightly, readying himself for combat. He is an experienced swordsman, although he is not sure yet if I am a boy or a woman. My skin is darker than usual from the sun, the gloss of my red lips partially hidden by my tan. Hanging half upside down, Dante stares at me in wonder, his face a mess of blood and tears. Incredibly, he has hope that I will be able to set him free. Naturally I will, in a few minutes. The brute gestures with his sword.

"Vattene dia," he says. Get away. "Or it will be you we string from the tree."

"It won't happen," I reply, and in a fast move I step forward and cut the top of the woman's left arm. The wound is not serious, it will heal, in time, but I want it to serve as a warning that I am skilled with a blade. Blood springs from her flesh and soaks her peasant clothes. The three hardly saw me move. Yet I know they will need more persuasion than this to back off. Of course I have been here before. A part of me knows that even though it is becoming easier to forget that I have. Surely I will kill them all, for the sake of poor Dante.

The woman screams in pain. "She has cut me! Kill her!"

"You foul creature!" the brute shouts as he dashes forward and tries to run me through. But I have sidestepped his lunge, and tripped him. As he tries to raise his head from the ground, I kneel beside him and pull his head back by the hair. My blade rests across his exposed throat, and I speak to the ugly woman and the fair man, who at least has had the wits to wait to see what I can do.

"If you leave now," I say. "I will let this man live."

"He is no friend of mine," the fair man says. "Do with him what you wish."

"No!" the woman cries. "He is my husband!"

"Then you agree to leave?" I say.

The brute, my knife scratching his trembling throat, is agreeable. "We will be gone," he says.

"*Bene.*" Good. I smash his face in the dirt and then release him. But he is no sooner back on his feet than his dull eyes flash with anger and he makes another try for me. Once again I sidestep the thrust of his sword, but this time I sink my blade deep into his heart and withdraw it before he can take it with him to the bloody ground. His wife cries as he lands facedown. She jumps toward me, her arms flailing, and I kill her as I killed her mate. Now there is only the fair-haired man left. Dante is muttering prayers to heaven and drooling all over his wretched face. Wiping off my knife on the sand, I stand and pull off my cap, letting my blond hair fall. It shines in the last rays of the evening sun. Fair head smiles and nods in appreciation.

"My compliments," he says.

But since he now knows I am a woman, he cannot walk away. Sicilian pride—he finally draws his sword and points it in my direction.

"I have been trained by the Vatican guards," he says. "You may submit to me now, or I will have your head."

Pointing my knife at him, I laugh. "I have been trained by

far more experienced teachers. Leave here this instant or I will cut you badly."

He takes a step closer. "My name is Pino. I would take no pleasure in killing such a beautiful woman as you. Drop your knife, and let us take pleasure in each other."

"No," I say. "I would rather kill you."

He moves closer still. The tip of his blade dangles three feet from my face—I could almost reach out, without moving my feet, and take it from him. But I am too much the good sport, and I don't want Dante to see me as a supernatural being. Then I might have to kill him as well. It is funny, how I know Dante, without even being introduced to him.

"You are young," Pino says. "Why make such a rash decision?"

"You are proud," I say. "You have seen my skills. Why not withdraw? Your death will prove nothing here."

He smiles but I have angered him. He takes a swipe at me with his blade, trying to cut my left shoulder. But he misses, and another smooth swipe also fails to draw blood. He appears more puzzled than worried.

"You move well," he says.

"Last chance," I say. "Leave or die."

"All right, cold woman," he says as he turns to leave. "I am no match for you." But he has hardly turned his back on me when he spins and tries to take off my head with his sword. Ducking, I thrust forward and plant my blade in his abdomen. There I leave it as I back off a few steps. He is still regaining his balance from his failed attack. He stares down at my knife in amazement. I don't know if he understands yet that his wound is fatal.

"What have you done?" he gasps as blood begins to show around my knife. Dropping his sword, he reaches down and pulls out the knife with both hands. Bad move—now the blood spurts out, over his hands and onto the ground. He still cannot comprehend that I have defeated him. "You witch!"

"I am not a witch," I say casually. "I am a good Samaritan. This man you torture has done nothing to hurt you."

Pino drops to his knees, bleeding over everything. "But he is a leper," he gasps.

"That is better than a corpse." I come closer so that I stand above him. I stick out my hand. "May I have my knife back please?"

He stares at me, incredulous. But he hands me back my knife, as if I might now help him because he is cooperating. But he is beyond a cure. I take a step toward Dante, whose head bobbles like that of a puppy dog.

"Oh, my lady," he gushes. "God has sent you."

I begin to cut him down. "Somebody did," I say.

Pino cries out to me as he slumps to the ground. There is great sorrow in his words, but I have heard it all before over the centuries. *Non voglio morire.* I don't want to die.

Dante answers for me, giving me a future favorite line.

"Then you should never have been born," he says.

EIGHT

Later, at night around a fire, I muse to myself that I killed the two men and the woman exactly as I had killed them before. The knowledge that their deaths were certain did not affect my actions in the slightest. Not even a single word that was exchanged between us was different. It makes me wonder whose future I'm from.

Dante sits across from me, wrapped in the swordsman's finery. He has washed out Pino's blood. My new friend is busy gloating over a rabbit I caught for him. A stick skewered through it, the meat hangs in the fire growing more tasty by the minute. The dripping grease crackles in the flames. Dante licks his diseased fingers and his dark eyes shine with joy. He has been muttering prayers to himself since I saved him.

"Tis a wonderful eve, I know," he says. "The light of heaven follows our steps. There can be no other way of explaining how a helpless maid was able to rescue me."

I laugh. "Dante, please don't call me that. Or I will show you again just how wrong you are."

He is instantly apologetic. "I meant no offense, my lady. I intended only to praise the grace of God. You are his instrument in this world, I know that in my heart." He adjusts the rabbit in the fire and licks his cracked lips. "We can eat soon."

"You can have it all," I say. "I have already eaten today."

He is offended. "If you will not feed with me, my lady, I myself will go hungry. It is not right that I should keep taking from you."

I continue to smile. "There is one thing you can give me—information. I have never been in Sicily before. Tell me about this land?"

He brightens. "It is a beautiful land, my lady, filled with sweet orchards and tall trees that cover the hills. You stay around Messina and wander not too far from the well-traveled roads, and you will have a pleasant visit."

"If I had not been far off the well-traveled roads this evening, I would not have been there to rescue you. But I am curious why you say I should stay close to Messina. Surely the Moslems have not landed on Sicily's southern shores?"

His face darkens. "But they have, my lady. A force of them is camped on the beaches in the southwest. Have you not heard?"

"No. I heard that the Duke of Terra di Labur is strong in the south, with many armed knights."

Dante trembles. "Do not speak that name, my lady, for he no longer goes by it. He has turned against the Christian God, and has murdered his own knights. It is by his power and with his protection that the heathens have managed to land their forces on Sicily."

I am surprised, even though I know all these things deep inside. Yet the future becomes more a dream to me with each passing hour. I know it exists, I know I am from there, but I have to focus to maintain this knowledge. Yet this does not worry me. It seems entirely natural that I should be one hundred percent in the present moment, with Dante, and the cooking rabbit, and his stories of the evil duke. But I have spoiled Dante's appetite by asking about the latter. Dante stares miserably at the fire as if he were staring at a picture of hell. He scratches at his lepered arm and leg—my questions bring him pain. Yet I know I must ask all about the political details.

"What does the duke call himself now?" I ask.

Dante shakes his head. "It is better not to repeat it in the night lest he hear us talking of him. For the night is his cloak, and shadows flow around him."

I laugh again. "Come on, he can't be that bad. I must know his name."

Dante is adamant. "I am sorry, my lady, I will not talk of him. To do so is a sin to your good company."

"My good company will not be so good if you do not answer me. What is the Duke's name now?"

Dante speaks in a whisper. "Landulf of Capua."

I have heard the name before, of course. But now it rings in my ears with less potency and more harmless connotations. Myth surrounds the title, not remembered agonies. Yet I know Landulf is the one I have come for—from the stars, for the stars—even if the flames that sparkle before my eyes blot out most of the nighttime sky. I do not want to focus on future facts—it is another choice I make. I am more intrigued than scared. Capua is tied to Landulf's name because he was originally from there.

"I know this name," I say. "Even in Italy, the farmers in the countryside speak of him. They say he is an evil wizard, capable of performing magical acts." I pause. "Dante, why are you crying?"

He is really devastated. "It is nothing, my lady. Let us talk of another person." He pokes at the rabbit with another stick he has found. "Or we can just eat, you can have some meat. You must be hungry after such a long day."

There is something in his tone that catches my attention. "Do you personally know this Landulf of Capua?" I ask.

He stiffens. "No."

"You must know him to be so frightened of him."

He rubs at his leper arm. Actually, the disease has spread so far, he has only a stump left. His left leg is also little more than a stump; he walks with the aid of a wooden brace I found not far from where he was strung up. His sores are open and fluid oozes from them. He must be near death, yet he has energy. But now his strength is in a whirlwind of constant motion. His eyes are moist and he cannot stop shaking.

"I cannot talk about him," he begs. "Please do not force me to say his name."

"Dante," I say. "Look at me."

He raises his head. "My lady?"

"Stare deep into my eyes, my dear friend," I say gently, carefully bending his will to mine. "You need not be afraid to speak of this duke. He cannot harm you now."

Dante blinks and his tears begin to dry. "He cannot harm me," he whispers.

"That is true," I say. "Now tell me about him, how you came to know him."

Dante sits back and stares at the fire again. He has forgotten the rabbit. He is half in a trance, half in a dream. I know I am asking him to repeat a nightmarish section of life. For even though I have calmed him with my power, his withered leg and arm continue to twitch. It is almost as if his leprosy was given to him by the duke, but that I find hard to believe.

Yet I do believe it. I *know* it.

What do I know? The stars are far away.

Dante's face holds my attention.

"My duke was not merely a duke, but an archbishop and a

special friend of the Holy Father," Dante says, in a clearer voice than usual. "It was to Rome my duke brought me at the age of ten to serve as his personal attendant and to sing in the Vatican choir. The Holy Father said my voice was a sacrament, and I was allowed to join the privileged castrati and sacrifice my manhood to the Church. This I did not mind, as long as I was allowed to stay close to my duke. For five years I was at peace within the holy walls, and I thought of nothing but my duty and my vows." He pauses and sighs. Even though he is partly hypnotized, his pain comes through. "Then, it happened, one terrible day, that my duke was falsely accused."

"What was he accused of?"

Dante hesitates. "I thought it was a lie."

"Did the pope accuse him?"

"Yes. The Holy Father himself."

"Of what?" I repeat.

Dante pauses before he answers. "Of invoking the spirit of Satan."

I do not believe in such nonsense, nevertheless, his words are chilling. "Was he cast out?" I ask.

Dante coughs. The smoke of the burning logs has entered his lungs. The agony of remembering suffocates him, too. "There was a trial," he says. "The cardinals and the Holy Father were present. Accusations were made, then witnesses were called—I had never seen these people before. Each one came forth and stated how my beloved duke had poisoned their minds with demonic spirits. Even I was called to denounce him. The Holy Father made me swear to tell the truth and then—in the same breath—-told me to tell lies." A tear rolls over Dante's ruined face. "I did not know what to say. But I had never seen my duke commit any of these sins. I was afraid but I knew in my heart I could not lie." A hysterical note enters his voice. "Jesus never lied, even when he stood before his accusers."

"Be calm, Dante," I say soothingly. "That was long ago. None of it can hurt you now. Just tell me what happened."

He relaxes some, but shifts closer to the fire, as if chilled.

"The pope grew angry at me, and accused me of being in league with Satan and my duke. I was chained to my seat and more witnesses were called, more people I had never seen before. These spoke against me as well as my duke, while the cardinals whispered among themselves. I was very afraid. They were talking about burning us. I did not know what to do!"

"Peace, Dante, peace. Continue."

Dante swallows thickly before continuing. On top of everything else, he seems to have trouble breathing. A frown wrinkles his features and he blinks, trying to remember where he is, or where he has been. Yet his voice remains clear.

"We were led away, my duke and I, and thrown into a stone cell where criminals were normally taken. We spent the night together in that stinking place. My fear was great—I knew we were about to be killed. But my duke acted pleased.

He said nothing could harm us, that the Holy Father would be forced to release us."

"Were you released?" I ask. My knowledge of the inner workings of the Vatican is extensive. No one accused by the pope of consorting with Satan ever survives. Such mercy would set a poor precedent. Yet Dante nods in response to my question.

"The next morning the jailer came and opened our door. There stood the Holy Father. He said the judgment of the holy council was that we were to be let go, but to be banned from the city of Rome. My duke's titles and properties were not confiscated, and I was amazed. My duke knelt and kissed the pope's ring before we were led away, and then he stared into the pope's eyes, and for the first time I saw the Holy Father afraid." Dante pauses. "I was afraid as well."

"Of your duke?"

"Yes."

"Why?"

He gestures with a stump. "Because it was as if a black snake reached out from his eyes and touched the Holy Father between the eyes. A snake the others could not see."

"But you saw it?" I ask

"Yes."

"How?"

He speaks with conviction. "It was there!"

"I understand." I have to calm him again, not allow him

to come out of his trance. "What did you and your duke do next?"

"Traveled to Persida."

The name is not familiar. "Where is that?"

"Not far."

"Where?"

"Near. Hidden."

I find it strange he is able to avoid answering me directly, and wonder if powerful hypnotic powers have already been brought to bear on his memory.

"What is special about Persida?" I ask carefully.

He coughs painfully. "It is where magic was first invented."

"By your duke?"

"Yes."

"Why did you stay with him in Persida?"

Dante struggles. "I had to."

"Why?" I insist. "Did he use magic on you?"

He bursts with memories. "Yes! He called forth the great serpent! The living Satan! He invoked it in pain and blood and it poured forth from his navel. I saw it again, the snake—it grew from his intestines and screeched when it saw the light of the world. He poisoned my soul with its filthy powers, and then he poisoned my body."

"That's when you started to get sick?"

He calms down, so sad. "Yes. In Persida, where magic lived, I began to die."

"Why did he make you sick?"

"For his pleasure."

"But you were a loyal subject?"

More tears. "He did not care. It pleased him to see me eaten away."

I want him to go on. "What did he do next?"

"He went to Kalot Enbolot. That is the door to Sicily. He has a castle there. It was given to him by the Holy Father. He wanted to open the door to the heathens."

"To let the Moslems overrun the Christian world through Sicily?"

"Yes."

"And it was there he took up the name Landulf?"

"Lord Landulf of Capua."

"How did he slay his knights? At the castle?"

"He made them slay one another. The demons summoned by the sacrifices always demand betrayal."

"You keep saying he invoked demons, that he summoned them. What proof do you have of this other than the snakes you thought you saw?"

"I did see them!"

"Fine. But what was Landulf able to do with these demons?"

"He used them to torture men. To control their wills." Dante stops and glances away from the fire, into the dark, and his whole body shakes. "Distance does not matter with these demons. They can cross water and bring death. In the fair land of England, my duke boasted, knights in search of the Holy Grail wander lost because of the spells he cast over them. They will never find the Grail, he said. Forever, they will be lost."

I was familiar with this mystical quest. But it was hard for me to imagine that Landulf had a hand in it. "Why does he bother with these knights?" I ask.

Dante speaks with pride. "Because they are righteous, and the light of God shines before them."

"But you say Landulf is stronger than they are?"

Dante hangs his head, as if ashamed. "I am afraid that he is the strongest."

"But you are a Christian. Your Lord Jesus Christ says no demon can stand before the name of Christ."

Dante continues, dejected, "Landulf cannot be defeated."

"Surely he is not all powerful. You escaped from him. How did you manage to do that?"

But Dante shakes his head. "I did not escape. He sent me away."

"Why?"

Dante looks me straight in the eye, and I believe my power has finally failed. He is no longer in a trance, but he is still frightened, more so than ever—terrified of what he has already told me, what I may do with the knowledge.

"My lady, he told me to find him an immortal ruby beyond all worth. And bring her back to him."

An immortal ruby? My vampiric blood?

It sounds as if Landulf of Capua already knows about me.

That is fair. I intend to know a lot more about him.

I will go to his castle, I decide.

Dante will lead me to the black wizard.

NINE

It takes a week to walk to Landulf's aerie, which stands in the heights of Monte Castello, in southwest Sicily, where, Dante tells me, the Oracle of Venus, the Goddess of Love, once stood. Dante knows a tremendous amount of Roman and Greek history and mythology. He is much more educated than I would have guessed. I begin to understand that one of the reasons Landulf kept him around was because of his powerful story-telling abilities. Even the evil duke loved a good tale, and when Dante starts on a story, his whole demeanor changes, as if he were hypnotized, and he speaks with great eloquence. But the moment the tale is over, he reverts. The sudden personality changes are disconcerting, but I am sympathetic to him because he has obviously been warped by his exposure to Landulf. I feel guilty that I am manipulating him further. Only by dominating him with my eyes, by soothing him several times a day, am I able to persuade him to lead the way to the castle. The thought of the place fills him with dread and he must be wondering that his legs continue to carry him in that direction.

Yet he doesn't seem to wonder about me. His affection for me is genuine; it pains me to use him so. And it is obvious that he is more concerned about me than about himself. When my influence on him wanes, he begs me to turn back. The human sacrifices he tells me about as being commonplace at the castle fill me with doubt. It is hard to believe there could exist such evil as he describes. Of course that is Dante's point. Landulf is no longer human. He has become a beast he invoked. The devil lives and breathes on a peak once considered sacred in ancient Rome. Before resting each night, Dante recites the entire mass in Latin, praying to a small copper cross he hides during the day in the wooden brace that supports his leper's stump. At night I see him scratching at his sores, and his suffering weighs on my heart. Only a devil, I think, could have cursed him so.

Yet I still do not believe in his Christian demons.

But what draws me to meet Landulf is the chance to witness his magic, whether it be white or black. Although I know for a fact it will be black, that I have visited the cruel wizard already. But what I remember of the future grows more abstract with each passing day. The dirt paths of old Sicily are my only guides. I remember Alanda's name but I cannot imagine her face. At night, though, I stare for hours at the stars, trying to convince myself that I was once there, in a mysterious ship, with creatures from another world.

And perhaps with the gods of ancient myths.

Dante wants to tell me about Perseus as we walk.

I am familiar with the mythology, of course, having lived in ancient Greece for many years. But Dante insists I have not heard it properly, and it seems to be one of his favorite stories, so I let him speak. But talking as he walks is a luxury Dante can ill afford. Often he must stop to lean on me for support, but now he is remarkably energetic. He has found a stout walking stick that helps him walk as he speaks with loving enthusiasm about the ancient hero. Obviously Dante worships such characters, and wishes he were one, instead of the crippled leper he is. A handsome young god who could sweep away a beautiful princess such as me. I know Dante is more than a little in love with me.

"Perseus was the son of Zeus and Danaë. His grandfather was Acrisius, a cruel king, who visited the oracle at Delphi and learned that his daughter's child was destined to be the instrument of his death. Perseus and his mother were therefore locked in a chest and set adrift on the ocean. The chest floated to Seriphus, where it was found by a fisherman and brought to the king of the land, Polydectes, a generous man who received them with love. When Perseus had become a young man, Polydectes sent him to destroy the Medusa, a terrible monster that was laying waste to his land and turning men to stone.

History has it that Medusa had once been a beautiful maiden whose hair was her chief glory. But she dared to compare herself to Athena, and in revenge the goddess changed her wonderful curls into hissing snakes and she became a monster," Dante pauses. "But that's not what happened."

I have to smile. It is only a story.

"What *really* happened, my friend?" I ask, a mocking note in my voice.

Dante is not dissuaded. "The Medusa never compared herself to anyone. She thought she was beyond comparison, beyond all the gods and goddesses. It was only her hair that became monstrous—her face remained beautiful."

I laugh. "That is good to know."

"It is an important point. One never knows if it was her beauty or the serpents on her head that were able to turn men and other creatures to stone. But I must continue with the tale. Perseus, given a divine shield by Athena, and winged shoes by Hermes, approached Medusa's cave while the monster slept. Perseus took special care not to look directly at her. All around him in the cavern were the stone figures of men and women and animals who had chanced to gaze at the evil creature. Guided only by the Medusa's image reflected in his bright shield, he cut off her head and ended the threat of the monster."

"Then he gave the head to Athena?" I knew the end, I thought. Dante shook his head and spoke seriously.

"That is not true. He kept it for himself. It was with the

Medusa's head that he was able to defeat Atlas, and steal the gods' golden apples. It was only with the Medusa's head that he was able to turn to stone the Titan that was threatening to eat Andromeda, who would later become his wife." Dante shook his head again. "Perseus never gave up the severed head of the Gorgon. It was too valuable a weapon."

I continue to smile, even though I know we draw close to Landulf's castle. The forest has changed, become wilder and darker, filled with trees that have twisted arms for branches, sharp nails for leaves. A gloom hangs over the land and it depresses even me, me who is usually not affected by subtle elemental vibrations. Even the sun's rays are dimmed by a gray overcast that appears made more of dust than water vapor. There is a constant odor of smoke, and I believe I detect the stench of burnt bodies. Still, I think I am an invincible vampire, no easy victim for Landulf and his black sorcery.

"That is only one version of the story," I say.

Dante regards me with disappointment.

"It is the correct version, my lady," he says. "It is an important story. Hidden within it are many great truths."

"You will have to explain them to me another time." I pause and survey the land ahead. We are in rugged mountains made of hard rock and dry riverbeds. In the distance hangs a black mist that even my supernatural vision cannot pierce. This unnatural cloud clings to some kind of massive stone structure, but I cannot discern the details. I point and ask, "What is that?"

Dante is suddenly the cowering fool again. He clings to my arm and the fluid from his open sores stains my white shirt. "It is our death, my lady. There is still time to turn back. Before his thralls come for us in the black of night."

"Who are his thralls?"

Dante speaks in a frightened whisper. "Men who have no hearts, and yet still live. I swear to you I have seen these creatures. They see without eyes and have no need to breathe fresh air."

"How many men does Landulf have at his command?"

Dante is animated. "You don't understand, my lady. His power is not in strength of arms. Had he not one man, he could still hold off the full might of Rome, and the Moslems for that matter. Even they fear him."

I grip Dante's shoulders. "Tell me how many men he has under his command. Even an estimate will help me."

Dante is having trouble catching his breath. "I never counted them. It must be several hundred."

"Two hundred? Eight hundred?"

Dante coughs. "Maybe five hundred. But they are not important. It is the spirits that haunt this land that will kill us. They are in the trees, the rocks—he sends them out to spy on those who dare to challenge him. He must already know we are here. We have to go back!"

I am gentle, but I do hold his eye. "Dante, my friend, you have done me a great service. I know you didn't want to come here but you have. And I know it was out of love and respect for me. But now you have repaid your debt to me. You are free to return the way you have come. I want you to return to Messina, and save yourself. There is no need for you to go any farther along this road."

To my surprise, my power over him is outweighed by his love for me. He shakes his head and pleads with me. "You do not know what he will do to you. He has powers you cannot imagine. A lust for cruelty and pain that cannot be spoken. He rips the eyes from his victims and stores them in jars to later feed to caged rats he keeps in his personal quarters. He pulls the bones from slaves before their very eyes and munches on them at gruesome suppers. All this he does to set the stage for his satanic invocations. But when the spirits come, there is nowhere to hide." Dante weeps and grips my arm fiercely. "Please don't go there, my lady! In God's holy name I beg you!"

I kiss him, stroke his face, and then shake my head.

"I must go," I say. "But I will go in the name of your God, if it comforts you, and the name of my God as well. Wish me luck, my dear Dante, and take care of yourself. You are a precious soul, and I have known so few in my life."

He is in despair. "My lady?"

"Goodbye. Do not worry about me."

I turn and walk deeper into the gloom.

I do not hear him follow.

Yet all around me darkness deepens.

The sun still shines.

TEN

This castle and its enclosure are built at the top of a cliff. Coming within a mile, I am able to see through the mist enough to know that the rear of the castle is unapproachable. The drop down the back is virtually straight, a thousand feet easily. Unable to see beyond the drop, I know that the ocean must lie not far beyond that—two miles at most. With such a commanding view of the sea and coast, Landulf would be able to spot enemies approaching at any point along southern Sicily. His home is strategically placed—as Dante said—as a doorway to the Christian world.

Outside the castle proper but still within the high stone wall are many small houses, some for living, others military structures where horses and arms are stored. Soldiers with swords wander around small fires, cooking meat, talking among themselves. Over them hangs the bulk of the castle—much larger than I had imagined it. These fires, I see, could not be responsible for the strange mist. Yet I no longer smell cooking human flesh and have to wonder if I imagined it.

I glance behind me. The shadows have grown long, the day is almost over. Dante is nowhere in sight. Yet I hear horses approaching from behind me, where I left Dante. They have a cart of some kind—its wheels creak on the rutted path. Above, a thick branch hangs over me and in a single leap I am cloaked within the leaves of the tree. The castle will have to wait for a moment. I want to see what these men are up to.

Minutes later I receive partial verification of Dante's wild tales.

On the cart is a cage, with metal bars. Three desperate females are locked inside. They are naked, but the four soldiers who have captured them are in full battle gear. Two drive the horses, while the other two are on horseback, one at the front, the other at the rear. The men are young but appear strong and battle tested. The females are each about eighteen. There is, of course, no way I can allow them to be taken into Landulf's castle, even if my intervening might upset my plans.

Vaguely, I remember I have rescued them before.

My plan of attack is simple.

As the first horse passes beneath me, a hundred feet in front of the cage, I drop down and land on the animal right behind the soldier. He is surprised to have company. I don't give him a chance to experience the wonder. Reaching up, I grab the back of his head and twist his skull. There is an explosion of bone and cartilage in his neck. He sags to the side, dead, and I shove him from the horse. Behind me, the two horses pulling the cage rear up. My horse I bring to a halt, and turn to face the others.

Already my long knife is out. Whipping my arm through a blinding arc, I let go of the hilt and plant the blade in the forehead of one of the drivers. The other driver draws his sword. I am forced to run toward him empty-handed. But I receive unexpected help from one of the females. As the soldier raises his sword to strike me, a girl with long hair gives him a swift kick in the back. He loses his balance and topples toward me. Before he hits the ground I relieve him of his sword and cut off his head.

There is still the fourth soldier, the one bringing up the rear. He has drawn a bow and arrow and is taking aim at me. He is an excellent shot. In the blink of an eye I see an arrow fly toward my head. Ducking, I realize that even though it will miss me, it will strike one of the girls. I am reluctant to show too many of my powers, but I have no choice. As the arrow flies by, I reach up and grab it and then break it over my knee.

The fourth soldier is worried.

"I am going to release the women," I say to him, staring. "They will ride back the way they have come."

The soldier just nods.

There are keys to the cage tied to the belt of the soldier who has my knife in his forehead. I relieve him of these and open the cage, marveling at the intricacy of the lock. The craftsmanship is far beyond anything I have seen before. But the keys work fine and a moment later the women are free. I give the reins to the one who assisted me, and throw the cloak from a dead soldier over her.

"Ride fast from here," I say, catching her eye. "Do not speak to anyone about me."

She nods. I step from the cart as she turns it around. In seconds the women in the cart are out of sight. Slowly I walk toward the remaining soldier, who has moved aside to let the women pass. I admire his courage, that he has not tried to bolt. But he is still a kidnapper, and I am thirsty. The soldier draws his sword as I approach but I shake my head.

"You are going to die," I say. "It is better not to resist."

He swings at my head, misses. Stepping forward, I grab the hand that holds his sword and look up into his frightened eyes. "Who sent you to capture those women?" I ask. "Was it Landulf?"

He shakes his head. "No."

"Who then?"

He refuses to answer me, even though I press him with my eyes. He continues to shake his head, and I am puzzled. I finally pull him from his horse and throw his sword aside. Drawing his face near, I let him feel the warmth of my breath.

"What is he like?" I ask.

The man is resolute. "He is my lord and my master."

"Is he evil?"

He sneers. "You are evil!"

I have to laugh. "I suppose I am—to you."

He dies, in my arms, from blood loss. Afterward, I feel refreshed, ready for more action. The bodies I hide in the bushes beside the path. The blood, even, I cover over with mud. I wash and dress like a young boy again, my hair under my cap. Then I walk toward the castle and boldly knock at the iron gate that guards the entrance in the wall. A host of soldiers answer and I am stern with them.

"I am here to see Landulf of Capua," I say in a powerful voice. "Bring me to him."

They lead me through the courtyard filled with soldiers and smoke to the castle door. A servant comes, and then another. They all seem fairly normal, although I obviously make them nervous. Finally the woman of the house arrives, Landulf's wife, Lady Cia. A striking woman, she wears a high-necked, tight-sleeved, long tunic belted at the waist. Many jewels adorn her hair and elegant fingers. Her hair is black and worn up and her eyes are dark. She is not Mediterranean but English. Her smile is welcoming, yet it doesn't reach her eyes. She is exceedingly thin, and holds herself under rigid control. I cannot say I warm to her, but she is anything but threatening. Certainly she does not seem afraid of me. I have left my long knife with the bodies of the soldiers.

Lady Cia invites me in without many questions. I don't ask why a man who used to be an archbishop now has a wife. Since the pope doesn't want him, I think, he may have decided to enjoy good company.

"It is seldom we get visitors from Greece," she says, when I explain where I have just come from. "But that is not your home, is it, Sita?"

Removing my cap, I shake out my blond hair. "No. Like you, I am from England."

She is pleased. "You are perceptive. But surely you are not traveling through the country by yourself?"

I act sad. "No. I was with my uncle. But there was an accident on the road, and he was killed."

She touches her heart. "I am so sorry. What was the accident?"

"His horse threw him. His neck broke."

She shakes her head and leads me deeper into the castle. "You poor dear. You must be devastated. Let us give you food, shelter."

"Thank you."

The castle is magnificent, and although my eyes strain to detect anything odd, the only unusual thing I see is an excess of wealth, even for a Sicilian aerie commanded by a duke. Landulf has sculptures from all along the Mediterranean. The marble on his floor is inlaid with gold, and the plaster ceilings are warmed by wooden beams. Everything is tasteful, not an offense to the eye. I compliment Cia on her home.

"My husband prides himself on his collections." She points to a marble statue from ancient Greece. "Since you were just in that part of the world, I am sure you would appreciate our hero."

I approach the statue, touch it, think of Dante, and pray he is all right. Perseus holds the head of the Medusa in one upraised hand, a sword in the other. His head is slightly bowed; his great exploit has not made him proud. But the face of the Gorgon is a horror; even in death she finds no peace. A feeling of disquiet sweeps over me, but I push it away. I have seen this statue before, of course I have. Lady Cia stands by my side.

"Can I have a servant show you to your room?" she asks. "You can rest and wash. Then perhaps you can join us for supper."

"You and Lord Landulf?"

She does not flinch at the name. "Yes. We would both enjoy the company." She snaps a finger and a chubby maid appears. "Marie will show you to your room."

I grasp her hands. They are cold, although the castle is warm, with fires burning in most corners. She trembles at my touch but I steady her with my strength. Staring deep into her eyes, I notice nothing supernatural.

"You are most kind," I say.

Marie leads me up three flights of stairs before we come to my quarters. Along the way we pass a window covered with iron bars, and I see that night has firmly arrived. Marie is dressed in a long black tunic over a white chemise. With a rosary around her neck, she could have been a nun. A few of Landulf's walls are covered with frescoes, paintings done directly on fresh plaster. Most of these have a spiritual theme. He seems to have an obsession with the Old Testament. The God that looks over his household is often angry.

Marie opens a door onto a small room. There is linen on the straw mattress and a bowl of water. Marie lights a row of candles and asks if I need anything else.

"No thank you," I say.

She leaves and I am alone. Washing my hands in the water provided, I am at a loss to explain why I keep looking around for a faucet with running water. Then I remember there are such niceties, in other places. The water is cold but seems fresh. I drink some and it rinses away the blood in my mouth. I do not understand how the soldier was able to resist my questions.

ELEVEN

A short time later I am at Lord Landulf's supper table. An old spear is fastened to the wall. It is this spear that the room seems to be designed around. From the massive stone fireplace logs crack and shoot showers of sparks out into the room as I am introduced to Lord Landulf by Lady Cia.

"This is the young woman I told you about," she says. "She came to our door not more than an hour ago, seeking asylum. Her traveling companion, her uncle, has just been killed on the road. Sita, this is the duke and my husband, Lord Landulf."

He is not a tall man and looks frail, which surprises me, after all the gruesome stories I have heard of him. Yet his delicateness is not necessarily a sign of weakness. He appears to be physically agile, and I suspect he is an accomplished swordsman. He wears a neatly trimmed black mustache and a pointed graying beard. He has oily smooth skin, and is dressed impeccably in a dark red silk chemise with long, tight sleeves, black hose, and a red and gold embroidery tunic, which comes down past his knees. His hands, like those of his wife, are decorated with many uncut gems and pearls. A ruby on his left middle finger is the largest I have ever seen. His voice, when he speaks, is cultured, educated and refined. His large dark eyes are warm but shrewd. He clicks his soft, heelless leather shoes together and bows in my direction.

"Lady Sita," he says. "It is a pleasure."

I offer my hand. "The pleasure is mine, Lord Landulf."

He kisses my middle finger, and glances up at me. "Surprise visitors are always the most enchanting."

"Hidden castles are always the most exciting," I say with a smile.

We sit down to a vegetable soup. Lady Cia leads us in a brief prayer. There are only us three at the table; we have four servants waiting on us. The soup is finished when Landulf inquires about my travels. Considering the expansion of the Arab World, it is impossible to talk for more than a few minutes without the subject turning to the invading Moslems. At this Landulf's mood turns foul.

"Six of those heathen ships tried to land on a beach not five miles from here," he says bitterly. "They came in on a wave of fog, but my scouts were wary. We were able to set fire to their sails before they reached land. All their people were lost in the tides."

His remark stuns me. "You fight the Moslems here?" I ask.

"Of course," he says, and there is a gleam in his eye as he studies me. "Have you heard different?"

I lower my head. "No, my lord."

"Come," he says with force, "we are sharing food. Why have secrets between friends? You have obviously traveled far and wide with your uncle. You know more of Greece than I do. What have you heard of my relationship with the Moslems?"

I hesitate, then decide I may as well dive in. "The word is that you are in league with them."

He does not lose his temper as I fear. But the air chills. "It is only in Rome they would speak such lies," he says.

"I have been in Rome," I say. "Not three months ago."

"Oh dear," Lady Cia mutters anxiously. "We did not know you had been exposed to such matters."

Landulf raises his hand. "It doesn't matter. In the short time I have known Sita, it is obvious to me she is not taken in by every story shared by every frustrated priest and nun."

"That is true, my lord," I say.

Landulf pulls his chair back from the table and sighs. "It is true that the Holy Father and I have gone our separate ways. But our differences were and still are more political than spiritual. Nicholas believes we should fortify our defenses, and wait for the Moslems to break against our walls. But I know this foe too well. I have met these bloodthirsty monsters on the battlefield. If we do not attack, push the war back into their own lands, they will see us as weak and never leave us in peace." Landulf stands and steps away from the table. "But all that is a question of strategy, and in my own land I pursue my own counsel. But to hear the talk in Rome I have denounced the Church and turned against Christ himself." He pauses. "Is that what you have heard, Lady Sita?"

I have already taken the plunge. The wild tales I may as well validate, or else put aside. "I have heard worse, my lord," I say. "The peasants say you conjure evil forces. That you are a master of the black arts and able to raise demons from the depths of hell."

Landulf is momentarily struck, then laughs long and hard. His wife joins him after a tense moment. "I would like to meet one of these peasants and ask him where he gets his information!" he exclaims. "That is the trouble with lies. They are perpetually pregnant. At every turn they give birth to more lies."

"There was a peasant I met along the roads," I say carefully. "He acted as if he knew you. His name was Dante. You've heard of him?"

Lady Cia gushes. "Dante? My lord has known him since he was a child. Pray tell us where you met him?"

I am evasive. "When I was lost in the woods, after my uncle died. But that was three days' journey from here." I add, "Dante seemed lost as well, and I shared food with him."

"I pray you did not share anything else with him," Landulf says darkly, referring to Dante's leprosy.

"I was careful always to keep a safe distance," I say. "But when he spoke of this place, it was with fear. I couldn't understand why."

"Surely you must know," Lady Cia says. "It is his illness. Since he became ill, he has spoken of nothing but demons that chase after his soul."

Again Lord Landulf raises his hand. "It is not so easy as that. I am partly to blame for his condition. When I brought him to Rome, as a boy, the Holy Father became enamored of his singing voice. Without my consent or knowledge, the pope had him castrated, so that his voice would remain high. Dante took the loss of his manhood badly, and I think he never ceased blaming me for the disfigurement. Since I was the cause of one physical aberration, when the illness came over him, he blamed me for that as well."

"But we tried to keep Dante here, and comfortable," Lady Cia says. "It was just that our servants feared his illness and he himself felt he needed to be free to roam the world."

Landulf shakes his head. "It pains me to know that my own friend has joined the chorus against me. Very well, leadership has its price. I cannot turn from the task I have set before me, to protect the underbelly of the Christian world. If I go to my grave cursed by every cardinal in the Vatican, at least I will still be able to hold my head up high when I meet my Lord in heaven."

"That is all that matters," I mutter.

Landulf steps closer to the fire, to the spear, and points out the aged iron tip to me. "Sita, do you know what this is?"

I stand and join him near the object. There is a single crude nail bound to the spear by circles of wire. The black shaft, I see, has more recently been joined to the tip—it is not nearly so old. Landulf touches the metal spear tip lovingly, running his fingers over the tapered edges, which are surprisingly sharp given the spear's obvious antiquity.

"I have never seen it before," I say.

He nods. "Few people have, except those who have been chosen to lead the fight against unrighteousness. This is the Spear of Longinus, sometimes called the Maurice Spear. It is this very spear that Gaius Cassius, a Roman Centurion under the command of Pro-Consul Pontius Pilate, used to pierce the side of the blessed Lord himself. Thus he put an end to Jesus' suffering on the cross. The final prophecy from the Old Testament that Jesus had to fulfill to prove that he was the true Messiah was that of Isaiah, who said, 'A bone of Him not be broken.' You see, Sita, at the time Jesus suffered on the cross, Annas and Caiaphas, high priests of the Sanhedrin, were trying to convince the Romans to kill Jesus before the Sabbath began. It was the priests' hope that the Romans would mutilate Jesus' body, and therefore prove that he was not the chosen one. But Gaius Cassius, although a Roman soldier, was devoted to Jesus and his teachings, and did not want to see

Jesus' body defiled. He took up this spear of his own free will, and in that moment all the prophecies of the world were held in balance in his hand. But at the moment this spear pierced Jesus' side, all the prophecies were fulfilled. For that reason, it is said that whoever holds this spear commands the destiny of the world." Landulf paused and smiled slightly. "It is the story that is told about it."

And a fascinating one, too. I reach out and touch the spear, and feel a strange power sweep over me. It is unlike anything I have ever experienced before, at least none that I can remember. But vaguely the thought of a brown-skinned child comes to my mind. The spear is a weapon of war, yet somehow it comforts me. I touch the tip and think of the blood that once spilled over it. The blood that supposedly had the power to wash away all sins. Standing beside Landulf, I feel the weight of all the people I have murdered for their blood. He seems to sense something odd because he stares at me intensely.

"Sita?" he says.

"But you believe this story?" I say in an unsteady voice.

He continues to watch me. "I do, but then I am a romantic at heart." He leans close and whispers in my ear. "What do you feel when you touch it, Sita?"

I momentarily close my eyes. "I feel the child," I whisper.

"The baby Jesus?"

"John."

He moves back. "The Baptist?"

I open my eyes, confused. For an instant the face of Suzama flashes in my mind. But she had no children, I think. Suzama was celibate. Yet the name of John haunts me, as does the face of a child I cannot quite pinpoint.

"I was not thinking of the Baptist," I say.

"What then?" he insists.

In that moment, in that castle, I cannot remember.

"I don't know," I say.

He gestures to the table. "Why don't we finish our meal?"

"Thank you."

He takes me by the hand and leads me back to the meal.

TWELVE

*L*ater, in my room, I feel dull and tired. I am four thousand years old, I do not normally need much sleep. Yet my vision is now blurred with fatigue. Staring in a mirror surrounded by candles, I feel as if my face changes into that of a person from another time and my blond hair turns dark red. The candles grow to the size of the flames that burned in the fireplace. Splashing water on my face, I feel some of the illusions leave me, but they do not go away. There is an unpleasant taste in my mouth that the water cannot wash away.

Then it strikes me.

I have been drugged.

Landulf, perhaps with his wife's knowledge, had something put in my food. There is no other explanation for my lethargy. But it is unlikely that the drug was administered for my benefit—a good night's sleep in a castle rumored to be filled with demons. If he has drugged me it is because he wants me unconscious so that he can do something awful to me. All of Dante's tales come back to me in a haunting wave, and I am amazed at how I have dropped my guard. But could my carelessness have something to do with Landulf's magic?

For all I know, his drug was poison and I am already doomed.

I force myself to vomit. Then I drink the water left in the bowl and vomit again. Within seconds my head clears, but I am still far from being at full strength. Moving to the door, I find it locked by a device as sophisticated as the one I found on the cage that held the young women. The metal parts are made of a peculiar alloy—stronger than anything I have ever encountered. Fortunately the door, although thick oak, is only wood. Leaning hard on it, and taking deep breaths to clear my system of the lingering effects of the drug, I am able to break it open without much noise.

Marie stands outside my door.

I grab her and pull her inside.

"What are you doing here?" I demand.

She is frightened. I have a strong grip on her neck.

"I was coming to see if you needed anything, my lady."

"You lie. You were waiting outside my door. Why?"

She wiggles her head. "No, my lady, I am here to serve you."

"You are here to spy on me." I choke her. "Did Lord Landulf send you?"

She gasps. "No. Please? You are hurting me."

I tighten my grip and she begins to lose color. "You feel how strong I am? I have the strength of a dozen men. Tell me the truth now or you will die in pain. Were you spying outside my door?"

She can hardly get the word out. "Yes."

"You had been told I was drugged?"

"Yes."

"Who told you?"

"Lady Cia."

"You were waiting by the door for me to pass out?"

"Yes."

"What were you going to do with me then?"

Marie turns blue. But she has enough will left to struggle. "No!" she gasps.

I dig my fingernails into her neck, drawing blood. "You answer me or I'll rip your head off!"

She moans. "I was to take you to the sacrifice."

I loosen my grip and frown. "What sacrifice? Where?"

She struggles for air. "It is below—in the hidden chambers."

I point my finger at her. "You will take me there, through

a back way. I want to see this sacrifice but I do not want to be seen. Do you understand?"

She coughs weakly. "I don't want to die."

I am grim. "You keep thinking that way."

Marie leads me through a dark passageway unconnected to the hallways and rooms of the public castle. We hardly leave my bedroom when we enter a narrow tunnel opened by touching a stone with a series of special pressures. The entrance closes behind us, and I wonder if I would have the strength to reopen it. The effect of the drug continues to plague me. Colored lights flash and trail at the corners of my vision. My heart pounds in my head and I cannot stop yawning. Cramps grip my spine. The power of the poison stuns me. Ordinarily, my system is immune to any kind of busive substance.

We reach steep stairs and start down. The walls continue to press in on us. The stairs are seemingly endless. I carry a torch in one hand, grip the back of Marie's neck with the other. "If you cry out at any time," I say, "that cry will be the last sound you hear in this world."

"I won't betray you," she whispers.

"I can see you are very loyal."

We continue to go down for the next twenty minutes, and I begin to believe Landulf has fashioned his castle over a natural cave. It is ridiculous to think he could have carved away so much stone with human hands. Yet somebody must have built this passageway, and I have to wonder if it is older than I imagined. The surrounding stones appear ancient. I remember Dante's remark, that this spot used to shelter the Oracle of Venus.

Eventually I detect a red glow ahead. At the same time the temperature increases sharply. Putting out my torch, I stop Marie and question her.

"Lord Landulf performs sacrifices down there?" I ask.

"Yes."

"What kind?"

"All kinds."

I shake her. "Does he kill humans? Torture them?"

"Yes. Yes."

"Why?"

She weeps. "I don't know why."

"Then why do you stay here? Are you not a Christian?"

She trembles beneath my gaze. "If I do not serve, I will be sacrificed."

"Is that the law?"

"Yes. Please let me go."

"Not until I am finished with you. Is there a place from where we can watch these sacrifices? And not be detected?"

She glances in the direction of the red glow. It is as if the light of hell beckons us. I smell burnt flesh again, and it has the odor of fresh meat. Marie is having trouble breathing.

"There is a passageway off to the side and above," she whispers. "But it is not all stone."

"What do you mean?"

"It is a metal grill, set in the ceiling. If they look up, they will see us."

"Why should they look up?"

"The eyes of my lord are everywhere!"

"Shh. Don't call him your lord. He is a perverted human." I turn toward the red glow. "He will die this very night." I grab her by the neck again. "Come, you will see."

The passageway Marie speaks of comes well before we reach the cavern. I feel and hear the hot tension in the cavern, the sound of many people whispering among themselves, the moans of a few unfortunates, the faint clash of metal. Even before I see, I know Landulf has brought his devotees as well as his soldiers to this accursed hole. I have to wonder if they're not all Satan worshippers.

Marie leads me into a tunnel where we have to get down on our hands and knees and crawl. The way is hot and soon I am drenched with sweat. But below our hands and knees the stone finally turns to wire mesh. We have reached the grills from which we can peer down at what is to be.

The ceremony is about to begin.

We are directly above the altar. It is circular, surrounded on all sides by rows of pews that lead up and back one hundred feet. There are approximately six hundred people present. Each person wears a red robe, except for a few soldiers at the doors, who have on metal breast plates and helmets. The altar is black and polished; it appears to be made of marble. Inlaid is a silver pentagram. The five tips of the stars dissect the room into five sections. Landulf sits on the floor with his wife. He is the only one wearing a black robe, and I can't help but notice the small silver knife resting in his lap.

Candles surround the altar. They are black and very tall, but what is most remarkable is that they burn with purple flames. The sober light spills over the marble and the silent participants like a glow from an unearthed volcano. The tension in the air is palpable and it is not something I would wish to touch. I sense that Landulf strives for tension in his rites.

Landulf stands and walks to the center of the pentagram. He raises his hand with the knife.

The group begins to sing, and for a moment I am bewildered. For it sounds to me as if they are singing the Catholic Mass in Latin. But then I realize they have started at the end, and are working their way toward the beginning, moving verse by verse through the litany. And the knife Landulf holds—the handle is shaped like a crucifix, yet he grasps it by the blade, upside down.

Everything they are doing is backward.

Landulf's grip is tight on his blade. Blood runs down his arm as his worshippers sing, but he doesn't seem to mind. In all of this, the most amazing thing is that their voices are quite beautiful. They remind me of Dante, who never went to sleep without reciting the Mass. Yet their motives are clearly the opposite of Dante's. He implored God for forgiveness for sins he had never committed. These creatures implore another power to accept their sins and reward them for them.

After forty minutes the twisted mass ends. A wooden cross is brought out by soldiers and laid in the center of the pentagram. Clad in a white robe, a bound female is carried out next. Her mouth is tied, she cannot cry out. But I see it is one of the girls I thought I had saved. That must mean the other two did not escape either. The girl is spread out on the cross but her white robe is left on. Finally the material stuffed in her mouth is removed and she cries out weakly. Landulf stands over her like the Grim Reaper, or worse. He has exchanged his knife for a small hammer and a bunch of nails. His intention is painfully obvious.

He is going to crucify the young woman.

I cannot watch this. I cannot let it happen.

But I have to watch. And I know I can do nothing.

Landulf holds nails and hammer up for all to see. So far the group has been fairly sedate, but now they leap to their feet and start screaming and jeering. I cannot tell if they are experiencing pain or pleasure. It seems a perverse mixture of both. Landulf kneels beside the girl and the soldiers who hold her down as the noise of the group reaches a frenzy. The very air is now vibrating. I find myself panting hard, on the verge of vomiting. I am a vampire who has killed thousands, yet I cannot bear that they should do this *thing* to such innocence, and enjoy it, and still remain human. It doesn't seem as if God should allow it.

I have to remind myself that God allowed it long ago.

Landulf begins to hammer in the nails.

The blood flows over the silver pentagram.

The girl's screams rend my soul.

Then I cry out, and the group falls instantly silent.

Plump, frightened Marie has stabbed a knife in my lower back. Put it in deep, cut a few arteries and important nerves. My blood seeps over the wire mesh and spills onto the altar below. Directly on to Landulf's face. He stares up and hungrily licks it as it drops—rain from hell. There is poison on the tip of Marie's blade; it mingles with the drugs already racking my system and causes havoc with my reflexes. Straining to pull it out, I feel my wound being licked by this docile servant girl. She has been told something about my blood, and thinks it will grant her immortality and great powers. She is like a giant insect sticking a needle in my vital organs. But apparently she takes the feeding ritual too far. Landulf suddenly shouts at her.

"It is for me!" he yells.

I am in such agony. Without wishing it, my weight and Marie's weight sag onto the wire mesh. It breaks. We fall like creatures cast down from heaven. Marie lands on her head and her skull explodes in a gray mass. I land on my back and the knife rams so deeply into me that it pokes through my liver and out my front. I have crashed beside the half-crucified woman, and Landulf steps over her to get to me. His face is smeared with blood, yet incredibly he appears sad, as if he wished it could have ended another way. I feel I have reached the end.

My strength ebbs rapidly; I cannot get the knife out of my back, so that I may heal. The tortured girl screams at me as if I were a demon. Her mind is shattered. On the cold black altar our blood mingles and flows over the silver star as the crowd cheers. All this had been entertainment to them. Landulf puts a foot on my bloody hair and stares down at me.

"How do you feel, Sita?" he asks with feeling.

I cough blood. "Wonderful."

"You have come to where I always wanted you to be."

I try to roll on to my side, still trying for the blade.

He steps on my free arm with his other foot.

"I am happy for you," I gasp.

He grins slowly. "You are very beautiful, your body, your spirit. This agony is unnecessary. Join me, I will remove the knife and you will be better."

The pain is unbearable. "What do I have to do to join you?"

He presses hard on my arm, grinding the bone into the floor.

"A small thing," he replies. "Just finish nailing these stakes in this young woman you foolishly tried to save."

I think about it for a moment.

A long moment considering my situation.

"My lord," I say. "Go to hell."

He laughs and raises his foot and puts it over my face.

Darkness comes. It is especially dark.

THIRTEEN

When I come to, I feel as if I am being crucified. There is pain in my arms and chest,
and I can hardly breathe. Opening my
eyes, I find myself chained in a cell, deep in a black dungeon.
My arms are strung above me, spread out like the wings of a
bird, pinned to a dripping stone wall with locks similar to the
ones I saw on the cage. This metal is a special alloy that I am
unable to break, at least in my present condition. I struggle
with the binds and only end up exhausting myself further.

Naturally, I can still see in the dark. From head to foot,
I am covered with blood, but I see that it is not my blood,
but that of the girl they were sacrificing. The knife has been
removed from my spine and that wound has healed. But there
is no relief for me. Crucifixion brings death by slow suffoca-
tion, and the position of my arms and legs mimics that of the

Roman style of execution. My feet are also bound to the wall, but they are slightly above the floor so that all the pressure of the metal anklets is on my calf bones. Remnants of Landulf's poisons continue to percolate in my system. I have to wonder if he siphoned off large amounts of my blood while I was unconscious.

Yet I do not think so.

How long I have been hanging there, I do not know. But steadily my pain grows so great that I begin to cry quietly to myself. Yes, even I, ancient Sita, who has faced the trials of four thousand years of life and survived, feel as if I have at last been defeated. Each breath is an exercise in cruel labor; the air burns my chest as it is forced in, and each time I exhale, I wonder if I will have the strength to squeeze in another lungful. My cries turn to feeble screams, then moans that reverberate deep in my soul, like the solemn laminations of the dammed already sealed in hell. I feel I have been forced beneath the earth, into a place of unceasing punishment. Landulf's face swims in my mind and I wonder if I see a vision of Satan.

Yet in my suffering, on the verge of final unconsciousness, something remarkable happens. My mind begins to clear, and I remember Alanda and Suzama, Seymour and the child. I see the stars and recall how I floated high above the Earth, and swore to do everything I could to protect my mother world. I am five thousand years old, not four thousand. I am from the future and I have returned in time to defeat Landulf. And I will defeat him, I tell myself. He will come for me, I remember he did before. I just have to hang on a little while longer.

I remember other things as well.

The Spear of Longinus.

I remember it from twentieth century Europe.

In Austria, in the year 1927, in the capital city of Vienna, I saw Richard Wagner's opera *Parsival*, which portrayed the adventures of King Arthur's knights in search of the Holy Grail, in a mythological setting. Historians claimed at that time that there was no historical basis for the events in the opera. Still, Richard Wagner's masterpiece was very moving, the powerful music, the tragic plot of how the knights struggled against the evil Klingsor, who obstructed them at every step from behind the scenes. Most of all, I was intrigued by Wagner's use of the Spear of Longinus—which I had seen in *my* past—as a magic wand in the hands of the evil Klingsor.

It made me realize, *then,* that Klingsor might have been Landulf.

There could be historical accuracy in the opera, after all.

After leaving the theater, I researched Wagner's source material and read Wolfram von Eschenbach's *Parsival,* upon which the opera was based. I was intrigued to see that the spear played an even more central role in the actual tale, and was stunned to learn that Eschenbach had lived eleven generations after the time of Arthur and Parsival, and yet had managed to write a thrilling story even though he was supposedly an illiterate imbecile. From what could be gleaned from the old texts, it seemed that Eschenbach had simply cognized—out of the thin air—the mystical tale.

Even then, in the twentieth century in Austria, that fact had made me wonder if perhaps Eschenbach's story was symbolic of deeper truths. Because by the twentieth century, history had all but forgotten Landulf. Yet even Eschenbach, a wandering Homer of little reputation, a *minnesinger,* had named him the most evil man who had ever lived. Who knew better than I why Eschenbach should condemn the duke so? Chilled by my own memories, I became convinced that Klingsor was indeed Landulf.

In the story, Klingsor had been an archbishop who lived at Kalot Enbolot, in southwest Sicily, where he summoned demons and sent them forth to torment the world. But most important, Eschenbach had described Klingsor's most important identifying mark and the basis of his evil.

Yet, in Landulf's dark prison, I cannot remember that mark.

From far away, as I become more delirious, I hear a sound. Knights and lords approaching from above, slowly winding down to my black cell. My torment is unbearable—for it to end, it seems, is all I can hope for. Yet I force in a shuddering breath and steel myself to fulfill my promise to those who sent me back in time. I recall Krishna's promise to me, that his grace shall always be with me. But I do not ask God to save me, only to give me the strength to save myself.

The door opens and in strides Landulf.

Alone. His men wait outside.

He brings a clean damp towel and wipes at the blood that has dried on my face. Then he touches my cheek, and before I can react, leans forward and plants a kiss on my cracked lips. I try to spit in his face, but there is not enough moisture in my mouth. Landulf stares at me with such compassion that I have to wonder if I have slipped into a dream where demons are angels and the future is already burned to ash by our ancestors' sins. For moment I am in more than one time, but then Landulf slaps me hard on the cheek, even as he pretends to bemoan my torment, and then I am alone with him, only him.

"Sita," he says with sympathy. "Why do you do this to yourself?"

I strain to moisten my swollen throat. "I could swear, my lord, that I did not climb into these chains while I was unconscious."

He enjoys my gusto. "But these chains are of your own making. I have offered you another way. Why don't you take it? What is the sacrifice for one such as you? We are already old partners in this war."

"I didn't know that this was a war?" I say honestly.

He is serious. "But it is—a battle far older than even your nonperishable body. It goes back to the birth of the stars, to the dropping of the veil, and of the opening of the two paths back to the source. You see me as a monster but I tell you I am God's greatest devotee."

"Aren't you exaggerating just a little?"

He slaps me again. "No! It is the truth you refuse to see. Will is stronger than love. Power lasts longer than virtue. My path is left-handed, true, but it is the swiftest and the surest." He pauses and comes closer. "Did not your friends tell you that all roads lead to the same destination?"

His question stuns me, the implications of his insight. "What friends are those?" I ask innocently.

He nods to himself as he studies my eyes. "I have seen you before on the path."

I force a smile and know it must more closely resemble a grimace. "Then you must know I will never join you. Because although I may be a sinner, I am also a servant. I love virtue, I love human love, even if I am not human. These are the things that bring me the most joy. Your path may be swift and sure but it is barren. The desert surrounds your every step and you walk forever a thirsty man. You may leave me to rot in this cell, but I am not forsaken. When I leave this body I know I will drink deep of Christ's and Krishna's fathomless love, and I will be happy while you crawl on your hands and knees to invoke your miserable demons. Whom you send out to perform deeds you are too frightened to perform in person. You sicken me, Landulf. Had I a free hand, I would tear your tongue from your face so that you could no longer spew lies in my direction."

He is unmoved by my speech.

"You will beg for my mercy, Sita. You will kill at my bidding."

I snort. "You will not live long enough, my lord, to see me do either."

He holds my eye. "We shall see." He raises a hand and snaps a finger and two armor-clad soldiers with torches, a prisoner between them, waddle into the cell.

They have brought Dante.

"My lady!" he cries when he sees me and tries to run to my side. But he trips and falls facedown on the damp floor, and is only able to rise when Landulf pulls him up by his hair. The black lord shoves my friend in my direction and Dante cowers and prays at my feet, weeping to see me in such a desperate condition. I would weep for my friend if there were any tears left in my body. But all I can do is sigh and shake my head.

"Dante," I say. "I told you to go back to Messina. Why are you here?"

He clasps my foot. "I could not leave you, my lady. I will never leave you."

Landulf is grim. "We caught him outside the castle walls, groveling like an animal." He grabs him by the neck and picks him all the way up off the floor with one hand. The demonstration of strength disturbs me. Perhaps he did take my blood, and put it into his veins, while I was unconscious. Yet Landulf does not show the signs of being a true vampire. He dangles Dante in front of me. "Will you not beg, Sita?" Landulf asks me.

I am fearful. "For what?"

"You know, my proud ruby."

I sneer. "Why beg for that which does not exist?"

In response Landulf throws Dante down in a heap and takes a torch from one of his men. Knocking out the flame on the damp wall, he steps toward Dante with the embers of the torch top still glowing. Seeing what Landulf has in mind, Dante tries to scamper to me but is kicked aside by Landulf. The evil lord kneels by my friend and points out to me Dante's sores.

"These wounds are infected," Landulf says. "They must be cauterized and sealed. Don't you agree, Sita?"

I stare in horror. "He served you loyally for many years."

Landulf eyes Dante, who trembles in anticipation. "But he betrayed me in the end," he says. "And it is only the end that matters, not the manner of the path."

"Landulf!" I cry.

But he ignores me, and then Dante is crying, screaming for me to save him as if I were his mother. But even though I have returned in time with the wisdom of the ages, I can do nothing—cannot keep Landulf from pressing the embers into Dante's oozing sores. Landulf first does my friend's deformed hand, and then he moves toward Dante's leg, where the damage is even more extensive. Dante howls so loud and hard it seems as if his skull will explode. Certainly the sound threatens to rupture my own heart. As Landulf moves forward with the torch again, I hear myself cry out.

"Please?" I yell. "Please stop!"

Landulf pauses and smiles up at me. "You beg me?"

I nod weakly. "I beg you, my lord."

Landulf stands. "Good. You have passed the first step of initiation. The second step will come later, and then the final and third step." He gestures to Dante, on the floor, who appears to have gone into shock. He speaks to his knights. "Chain this bag of garbage up beside her. Let them keep each other company, and let them talk together about the redeeming and saving power of love and mercy." Landulf winks at me as he leaves the dungeon. "I will see you soon, Sita."

FOURTEEN

*M*ore time goes by and with each passing minute I die a little more inside. Crucified alone in the dark, I could imagine no crueler torture, yet I had not known the half of it. Dante is largely unconscious, but still he moans miserably. For a time I pray that he does not wake again, that he simply dies, and so ends his suffering. But then the curse of all who suffer comes to me.

I glimpse a faint ray of hope.

I have to wake Dante, bring him back to the nightmare.

Calling his name softly, he finally stirs and raises his head and looks around. It is so dark; it is obvious he cannot see a thing. But I can see his ruined expression and it pierces my heart. He is hung up on the wall right beside me.

"Sita?" he whispers.

"I am here," I say gently. "Don't be afraid."

He is having trouble breathing. Landulf's knights have tied him up like me, his arms pinned by unbreakable chains. Yet his feet are not bound; they manage to touch the floor. But I know soon he will begin to smother. He coughs as he tries to speak.

"I'm sorry, my lady," he says. "I disobeyed you."

"No. You have nothing to be ashamed of. You are a true hero. Even when the situation appears hopeless, you plunge forward. Perseus himself, I would guess, would be envious of your stout heart."

He tries to smile. "Could it be true?"

"Oh yes. And you might yet save us both." He is interested. "How, my lady?"

"I need you to shake free of your leg brace and push it over here."

"My lady?"

"Your tiny copper crucifix, the one you pray to before sleeping each night. I need it."

He is worried. "What are you going to do to it?"

"I am sorry, Dante, I am going to have to ruin it. But I think I can form the cross into a narrow instrument that I can use to pick these locks."

"But, my lady, your hands are bound!"

"I am going to use my toes to mold it into a proper shape. Don't worry about the details, Dante, just push your brace over here. Is it easy to slip out of?"

"No problem, my lady." I see him struggle in the dark. "Are you on my right or on my left?"

I have to smile. "I am on your left, two feet away."

"I feel you near," he says with affection as he slips out of the brace and pushes it toward me with his stump. "Do you have it?"

"No. My feet are pinned together. You will have to give it a shove, but not too hard. The brace must come to rest against the side of my legs."

"But I can't see your legs."

"They are pinned to the wall. Lay the brace against the wall and just give it a slight nudge forward."

"Are you sure this is a good plan?"

"Yes."

"I am not sure."

"Dante?"

He suddenly hyperventilates. "I am afraid, my lady! Without my brace I will be a cripple!"

I speak soothingly. "I will not damage your brace, Dante. Only the cross you keep hidden in it. When I am free, you will have your brace back and we will escape from here."

He begins to calm. "We will go back to Messina?"

"Yes. Together we will travel to Messina, and there we will stay in the finest inn, and order the best food and wine. You will be my companion and I will tell everyone how you rescued me from the evil duke."

Dante beams. "I will be like Perseus! I will slay the Gorgon!"

"Exactly. But let's get out of here first. Push the brace closer to me."

"What if I push it too far?"

"You won't, Dante. You are a hero. Heroes don't make mistakes."

Dante pushes feebly at the brace with his leper stump. "Is that all right, my lady?"

"Harder."

"I am trying, my lady." He strikes the brace with his stump and the wooden leg bumps up against my calf. "You have it?"

"I have it," I quickly reassure him. "You relax and catch your breath. You don't even have to speak to me. I will concentrate on getting us out of here."

He groans. "Hurry, my lady. I am in some pain."

"I know, my friend."

Even for a vampire, what I plan to do next is not easy. First I have to let the top of the brace slide down to where I can reach it with my toes. This I do without much effort, but Dante's cross is not stored at the top of the brace. It is fastened somewhat deeper inside the wooden stump. After fishing for it with my toes for ten minutes, I am no closer to reaching it, and even more weary, if that is possible.

Then it occurs to me that I must invert the brace. This is tricky, because if the copper cross slips past my toes, it will land on the floor and be out of reach. What I do to add a safety margin to my plan is to raise the brace up with just one foot, catching it between my big toe and the toe next to it. Then I plug the end of the brace with the bottom of my other foot. Shaking the brace upside down in the air, at a ninety-degree angle to my calf, I feel the cross touch the sole of my free foot. In a moment my toes have a grip on the crucifix and I let go of the brace.

"My lady?" Dante cries.

"Everything is all right."

"My brace is not broken?"

"It is fine. Be silent and conserve your strength. We will soon be free."

"Yes, my lady."

Both my feet grip the copper cross. I will keep plenty of toes wrapped around it at all times, I tell myself. There is no way it is going to spring beyond my reach. As I work to mold the copper, I pray Landulf's *soon* did not mean in the next few minutes. I have prayed many times since entering the castle.

The crucifix is relatively thin, little more than a stamped plate, and this is fortunate. It does not take me long to squeeze the lower portion of the cross into a stiff wire. True, it is a rather plump wire but the key holes in the locks that bind me are far from tiny. Clasping the wire in my right foot, and holding still the key hole with my left foot, I slowly glide the cooper toward the inner mechanism.

"My lady?"

"Shh, Dante. Patience."

"My hand pains me."

"We will make it better soon. Please do not speak for the next few minutes."

The wire enters the lock and I feel around to get a sense of its design. My mind is very alert now. The traumas I have suffered—I put them all behind so I can focus on the inside of the lock. It does not take long before I have a complete mental picture of how it was built, and when I do, I know precisely how to move my wire.

There is a click and the lock springs open.

I kick off the chains. My feet are free.

"My lady!" Dante cheers.

"Quiet. Let me finish."

He gasps. "Oh, yes, hurry. I cannot breathe like this."

Now comes the hardest part. I cannot pull either hand chain down close enough to my face so that I might work the locks with the wire between my teeth, assuming I could get the copper in my mouth. No, I have to reach up with my right foot, stretching my leg to a next-to-impossible length, and attack the *left* lock that way. My muscles are stiff so the task is doubly hard. Yet I can taste freedom now, and it gives me fresh strength.

Clenching the wire in my toes, I kick up.

My hamstring muscles scream.

I fail to reach the lock. I have to kick up a dozen times before I even approach it. But steadily my joints limber, and finally I am steering the wire into the lock that grips my left wrist. Since I already know the internal design of the mechanism, I take only a second to trip it. My left hand is now free, and I immediately transfer the wire from my toes into my fingers. Two seconds after that, I have sprung the right lock and am able to stand and stretch. But Dante has gone downhill. He doesn't even realize that I am free. I step to his side and caress the top of his head. He looks up without seeing me in the pitch black and smiles.

"Are we safe?" he asks softly.

"Almost," I say, and I use the wire to open his locks. But his arms don't come down when they are free, his limbs are so damaged. I have to draw them down, and this makes him cry out. He buries his face in my chest and I comfort him. "Dante," I say. "This dungeon will not hold us."

He lets go of me, but he is lost in the dark and he cannot stand without support. "Where is my brace?" he asks. "Will it still work?"

"Your brace is here and it is undamaged, as I promised." I slide his stump back into it but cringe at the smell of his burnt flesh. Taking his wounded left hand, I study the sores. Landulf took his cauterization too far; he burned into the healthy tissue beneath Dante's wounds. Later, I swear to myself, when we have time, I must sprinkle a few drops of my blood on the sores to ease his agony.

"It is best you don't touch me, my lady," Dante says in shame.

I squeeze his arm. "You are my hero. Of course I will touch you."

He is happy, for the moment, but he is also close to death.

"My lady," he gasps as he continues to struggle for air, despite his release from the bonds. "I know a secret the duke might not even know." He taps the wall behind his head. "There is a passageway back here, if we can get to it. The way leads under the farthest wall and out into the woods."

"Can we reach this passageway from the tunnel beyond this cell door?"

"Yes, my lady. But how are we going to get through the door?"

Good question. After studying the door, I see that it is made of the same alloy as the locks and chains. I cannot break through it. But I have come to this dilemma before. My awareness of the future is still present, but still somewhat cloudy. For several seconds I cannot remember precisely what I did next. Then the water dripping from the wall against which we were imprisoned catches my attention. The mortar between the stones must be weak, I reason, to allow so much moisture to seep through it and into the cell.

"Dante," I say. "Is this secret passageway of yours flooded?"

"Sometimes, my lady. At certain times of the year."

"Is this a certain time of the year?"

He hesitates. "There should be some water in the passage, yes. But I do not think it will be flooded. I hope it is not."

"Does the water run out into the forest?"

"The passageway leads in two directions. The water runs out to the cliff, in the direction of the sea."

"Stand away from this wall, by the door. I am going to work on these stones."

"Yes, my lady. Where is the door?"

I have to lead him to it. He slides down, weakly, with his back to the exit. He cannot stop moving his left hand, and I can only imagine the pain it must be causing him.

Landulf has removed my shoes, but this does not stop me from leaping in the air and kicking at one of the stones with my right heel. It cracks with a single hard blow, and a series of kicks crush it. I pull out the chunks of stone and mortar with my hands, and soon I have a small river running through my fingers and over my lap. Yet I see the passageway is slightly above us, and that there is not more than a foot of water passing through it. Dante shivers and cries out as the cold water touches him and I have to talk to reassure him. My hands are frantically busy, pulling out pieces of stone. My strength level has gone up another notch. We were both so close to death, everything was hopeless, and now we stand on freedom's door.

Soon there is a hole large enough for us to crawl through. I help Dante into the passageway, and then I follow him. Soon I am standing beside him, steadying him with my hand. The water current is feeble; even Dante is able to stand against it. He grabs my arm and points upstream.

"This way is the woods, my lady," he says. "Soon we will be free of this unholy place."

I stop him. "I can't go with you, Dante, not yet."

His exhilaration turns to distress. "My lady? Why not?"

"I cannot go from here and leave Landulf alive."

Dante is devastated. "But if you go after him you will die! He is too strong!"

"I am strong, Dante. You have seen that. But I need your help to find him. Where does he spend most of his time in the castle?"

Dante is animated. "No, my lady. I don't know. He is like most people and moves around from place to place. You will not find him before his knights find you. Please, we must escape now while we have a chance."

I clasp his shoulders. "But I have to try to find him, Dante. Landulf may have taken something from me, something very precious, and I cannot leave this castle without knowing that he has been destroyed."

Dante is confused. "What did he take from you that is so precious?"

"I cannot explain that to you. I just need you to trust me that I speak the truth. Come, you spent many years with him. Where is the most likely place he will be right now?"

"But I don't know when right now is, my lady. All is dark in here."

I stop and concentrate. Even though I have been unconscious much of the time, my very cells remember the passage of time. "It is the second morning after I came here, not long before dawn." I pause. "Where does he spend his mornings?"

Dante's face twitches. "If I tell you, will you do what you did last time? Will you go to him?"

I stroke his head and speak in a gentle hypnotic voice. "You have to tell me. You are my friend. You are the only one I can trust. It is imperative that I destroy Landulf before I leave here. Not merely for the safety of you and me, but for the well-being of all people everywhere. You can see that, can't you? His evil has spread far and wide. I must stop it here at its source."

My words go deep into Dante. "He causes much suffering in many lands," he whispers as he nods to himself.

"And that suffering can stop today. Tell me where in this castle he spends his mornings?"

"But, my lady, if you leave me now, when will I see you again?"

I continue to stroke his head. "Remember the pool of water where we slept the night before we came to the castle?

It was off the road. Do you think you would be able to hike back there?"

He nods vigorously. "I can do it. I know these woods. When will you meet me there?"

"This evening. I can get there by then. Can you?"

"I am sure of it, my lady. If I do not stop to rest."

"You can stop to rest. If I get there before you, I will wait."

He grips my arm fiercely. "Do you promise, my lady?"

"I promise you, Dante. With all my heart." I pause and sharpen my tone. I know my next words must feel as if they cut right through him like knives but the time has passed for gentle persuasion. "Now tell me where Landulf is."

Dante speaks quickly, startled. "He is probably not in the castle now. He spends most mornings at the ancient oracle, where Venus was long ago venerated."

"Where is this spot?" I demand.

"It is a stone circle built into the side of the cliff at the back of the castle." He gestures downstream. "That way opens onto a stream that falls not far from the place. But it is a dangerous spot, my lady. His power is greatest there, and the spirits protect him. You will not be able to get to him. You have to wait until he leaves the circle."

"We will see." I pat Dante on the back. "Before this day is through, you and I will meet again. It will be a time of rejoicing. The evil enemy will be defeated and good friends will be together and free to go where they wish."

"To Messina?" he asks excitedly.

"Yes, we can go to Messina." I hug him. "Take care of yourself, Dante. You are much loved by me."

He hugs me in return and speaks in my ear.

"You are my love, my lady."

FIFTEEN

*T*he dark path leads to light, but the sun is not yet up when I exit the underground passageway and stand on the edge of the cliff and look out at the vast panorama. A large section of the south shore of Sicily is indeed visible. The sea is purple and there are few clouds. The closest beach—far below and perhaps three miles distant—is occupied by a large contingent of soldiers. I can see the color of their skin, their black and green flags that wave in the morning breeze.

Arabs. Moslems.

They could not be so near without Lord Landulf's consent.

The duke is not far away, off to my left, down about five hundred feet. As Dante warned, he sits in the center of a circle of stones—denned by the shape of the ledge and the pointed rocks that enclose it—in another pentagram. This five-pointed star appears to have been drawn by blood, and there is something red and slimy in his hands. He sits on his knees with his back to the cliff and I do not know what thoughts run through his corrupt mind. I only know he will be dead in a few minutes.

I start down the cliff.

Venus shines bright in the eastern sky.

I take her white light as a good omen.

I come within fifty feet of the stone circle before I pause. There is a young woman chained to the cliff just below me, and I see Landulf has the Spear of Longinus with him at the center of the pentagram. I find it odd that I did not see it at first since I have not let him out of my sight on the hike down the cliff. But the fact does not concern me; the girl does. She is the one who assisted me when I rescued her and her friends from the cage. Like her friend, who was sacrificed at the black mass, she wears a white robe and looks terrified. Yet except for the three of us, I sense no one else in the vicinity. I descend another thirty feet, silently, staring at Landulf's back. I know it is him. The girl sees me and I motion for her to remain silent. Her eyes are suddenly wide with hope, and I have to wonder if that is good. This all seems too easy.

Then I pause again. Something makes me sick.

Lady Cia lies not far from the chained girl.

Her heart has been cut from her chest.

Now I know what Lord Landulf holds in his hands.

He continues to sit with his back to me. Defenseless.

"It was necessary, Sita," he says softly.

That he knows I am here stuns me.

"Why?" I ask.

He glances over his shoulder.

"The sacrifice demanded the ultimate sacrifice," he says.

"To achieve what aim?" I ask.

"To bring you here, to this spot."

I snort. "I brought myself here, thank you. None of your demons assisted me."

He stands and stares at me. His wife's heart continues to drip in his open palm. His eyes are so dark. "That's what you think," he says quietly.

I gesture to the girl. "Why is she here?"

"For you. For the next step in your initiation."

I point to my ears. "I have sensitive hearing. The three of us are alone on this cliff. Not that it matters. You would need an army to protect you from what I am going to do to you now."

He gestures to the circle, using the heart. "You say your ears are sensitive. What about your eyes? Can you not see what you are up against?"

Now that he mentions it, I do notice a peculiar vibration in the air. It's as if we're surrounded by a swarm of insects, yet there is no sound. The sensation of the swarm is psychological. Now I feel as if something foul picks at my skin. I start to brush it away, but stop myself. I fear to show weakness in front of him. Yet a faint thread of fear has already entered my mind, and slowly begun to wrap around the center of my brain. However, I still feel I have the upper hand. I am an ancient vampire of incredible strength. He is just a man. Why, he doesn't even have his spear in his hand to protect himself.

I step toward the stone circle and bump into a barrier.

It is invisible but palpable. A wall.

Or a magnetic force that resists physical contact.

I pound on it with my fist to no effect.

Landulf grins at me from inside the circle.

"To enter," he says. "You will have to sacrifice an innocent."

The girl cries behind me. I silence her with a gesture.

"That will never happen," I say as I slowly probe the perimeter of the stone circle, seeking for a weak spot. But the force field is uniform, and I am amazed that it even exists. My memories of the future are back again, clearer than ever. I have to wonder if the shield is of extraterrestrial origin. The last time I confronted Landulf on this spot, I defeated him by using his wife as a shield. This is the first event that is being played out differently from the last time. So I know I must have come back in time for this final moment.

Yet I do not know what to do.

Landulf follows my movements and does nothing to thwart

me. I complete my inspection of the circle and pause to consider the possibility of jumping into the circle from the side of the cliff. Landulf reads my mind, or perhaps he logically figures out what my next move must be.

"You can try it," he says. "I would enjoy watching you bounce off the edge of the cliff."

"You cannot stay in there forever," I reply.

"Dante cannot stay in the underground passageway forever."

I freeze. "You bluff. You cannot stop him from here."

In response Landulf raises the heart toward the sky and to my amazement it starts beating. The blood squirts on his face and he licks it. Then he lets out a high-pitched cackle, and I hear a loud shifting of stone far above. Glancing up the way I came, I see that the exit to the cliff has been closed over with a fallen boulder. Landulf lowers the heart.

"That is one end," he warns. "I can close the other end the same way. If . . ."

He doesn't finish. He wants me to.

"If I don't come get you," I say.

"Exactly." He gestures to the chained girl, who is not enjoying the display of the duke's powers. "The life of your friend for the life of a stranger."

I glance at the girl and she shakes her head slightly.

"Don't worry," I snap at her.

"You need to rip out her heart," Landulf explains. "Quickly.

While it still beats, you will be able to penetrate the circle."

"I do not barter in human lives," But sudden doubt plagues me. If I do not kill him, he will kill the girl anyway. And I will not be able to take her with me down the side of the sheer cliff. Dante's innocent face haunts me, as do Landulf's hypnotic eyes. I just want to get to the duke and scratch his face off to put an end to his circus. He moves to the edge of the circle, comes within five feet of where I stand. Once more I pound on the barrier but my fists rebound against my chest. His dead wife's heart continues to beat and now the sound is in my ears. I do not understand how his palm can animate it. How a wizard, no matter how powerful, can infuse life into what should be dead.

"You will barter," he promises. "Fool! There is no part of you I cannot touch. No aspect of you I cannot defile." He stops. "Hear something, Sita?"

The beating of the heart grows louder in my ears.

In my head. Even when I cover my ears it doesn't help.

He shoves the heart toward me and I am forced to stare at it.

This is madness—I cannot even close my eyes.

"Kill her and it will stop," he says.

"No!" I cry.

"Kill her and your friend will live! Kill her and you can kill me!"

The blood of the pounding heart splashes through the barrier and catches my face. I taste the waste of Cia's perverted life on my lips and the pounding in my head increases ten-fold. Surely I will go mad if I do not stop it in the next few seconds. Whirling toward the chained girl, I do not know what she hears except that she suddenly screams. Maybe the sight of my crazed expression makes her scream. What is one human life, I think? In four thousand years I have murdered thousands, ripped the lives from a parade of innocents. I need her heart, just for a second. Her sacrifice is necessary to spare the torment of billions in the future. She should be happy to die for such a noble cause. God should see that I have no choice in the matter.

But he will not see that and I know it.

Because I am five—not four—thousand years old.

I know to murder innocents is to murder my own soul.

But the pounding grows louder.

It is a miracle Landulf's voice can be heard above it

"You can rip out my heart when you are done with me," he says. "And then you will finally be at peace. Peace, Sita!"

My body balls up in pain.

I squeeze my ears between my knees.

The beat of the dead heart. Nothing can stop it.

Tears run over my face. Bloody tears.

The girl swims in my red vision.

My head will explode, I know.

"Kill her, Sita!" Landulf implores.

My mission will fail. Billions will burn.

"Rip out her heart!"

In my head. The pain. The pounding. Please.

"Do it!"

I do it. Finally, just this once, I listen to him.

Leaping toward her, giving her almost no time to react, I thrust my left hand into her chest, smashing through her white gown and her pale ribs. Yet for a fraction of a second, she knows what I am going to do. She feels the absolute horror of the ritual execution. That is what Landulf wants, what he needs, to activate his black sorcery. The battery of the bastard is tied to perversity and pain. The girl's heart is in my hand. I feel its life, and still I yank it from her chest and leap toward the circle. Out the corner of my eye I see her staring at me, and understand the betrayal she is feeling deep in my soul. Her eyes are as blue as mine. Even in death, they could be mine.

I land inside the circle, at the tip of a point on the pentagram.

The pounding stops. The agony in my head.

The dead girl's heart seems to melt in my hand.

Landulf has picked up the mystical spear.

"They are always hungry," he explains as he nods toward the heart vaporizing in my left palm. In moments it is entirely gone. There is not even a stain of blood left on my hand. Landulf raises the spear and takes a step toward me. He is pleased with me. "You have passed the second step," he says.

I ready myself for his attack. I shift to the right side.

My foot touches fire.

I whip my foot back. There are no visible flames.

"You are now in hell," Landulf says. "You are required to stay inside the lines of the pentagram. But I am free to roam where I wish, all over the circle."

He lunges at me with the spear. He is fast.

I leap over to the adjacent star point.

He barely misses me. He flashes me a smile.

"Isn't this fun?" he asks.

"Delightful," I say.

"There is one other rule you should know. Don't jump or walk through the center of the pentagram. There is an invisible being waiting there that might consume you alive."

"You expect me to believe you?" I ask.

"You don't have to. But then, I will lose you forever, and you will be trapped in a dark place forever." He raises the spear once more. "But do what you want. You may even try to escape from the circle, but you won't be able to. Once you are in here with me, you will stay in here."

He makes another stab at me. I leap to the next point on the star. He misses, but I realize that I cannot keep on like this forever. His freedom of movement gives him a devastating advantage. His speed and strength are a mystery to me. But perhaps they come from the sum total of all the demons he carries in his heart. He is not necessarily as strong as I am, but his strength is close. I can tell by the power in his physical bursts. And he has the mystical spear, and I have to wonder if Christ's dried blood is an advantage or disadvantage in this cursed place.

"The spear is neither negative or positive," he says, maybe reading my mind, maybe guessing. "The tip is simply a point around which destiny turns. In the hands of a saint, it could be used for great healing. In my hands, it is merely a tool for my immortality."

"You are not immortal," I snap.

"But I will be, Sita. In a few moments. As soon as I pierce your side with this spear and channel your blood into my body."

"You could have done that when I was unconscious."

"No. To get the full benefit of your blood it is necessary that I drain you in my place of power. And you had to enter here of your own free will, after executing an innocent. Everything that has happened to you has been planned to bring you to this precise point." He pauses. "You see, Sita, I know you are from the future."

He continues to shock me.

"How do you know?" I gasp.

"Because I am from the same future."

"Did I know you?"

"Yes."

"Who?"

"Linda's boyfriend. I was the one who sent you into the desert."

"That fat slob?"

He is not offended. "I was in disguise."

I nod in admiration. "You are clever. More clever than any foe I have ever encountered."

My remark pleases him. He lowers the spear.

"Thank you. You have also been a worthy adversary. Why don't you let this end with dignity? I will give you that if you stop resisting me."

I sigh. "What do you want me to do?"

"Stand still for a moment. I do not need a lot of time."

"What will you do to me?" I ask.

"I will take your blood. I need your blood. But you will not have to suffer. You have my promise on that."

I consider. "All right. I will surrender on two conditions."

"What are they?"

"I want to open my own veins. And I want to use the nail that was on the cross, the one now tied to the tip of your spear."

"Why the nail?" he asks.

"Because you say it was pounded into the hand or foot of Jesus. If I am to die, I want that nail to pierce my own flesh." I add, "It will make me feel closer to him as I die."

Landulf is thoughtful. "That will not save you from what

is to follow. You are already in my circle. No works of Christ function here. I am not lying to you."

"Perhaps. But those are my conditions." I shrug. "I don't ask much."

He is wary. "You could try to use the nail as a weapon. You could throw it at me."

"Would you be able to block such a throw?"

"Yes."

"Then what do you have to fear by tossing me the nail?"

"Nothing. I fear nothing in my place."

"Then toss me the nail, O Fearless One."

"You mock me?" he demands.

"Well, in the future it might be called flirting."

He hesitates. "I don't have to do this. I will get you eventually."

"Probably. But you never know."

"You believe the talisman will protect you? Despite what I say?"

"No. You are wrong there."

"Then you lie to me. You will not keep your side of the bargain."

I laugh. "You call me a fool? You have nothing to lose by trusting me." This time I catch his eye, and put all my will behind the gaze. "You will never be successful as an immortal if you live in such fear, Lord Landulf."

I have pushed the right button.

Perhaps his only button.

He hates to be called a coward.

He begin to undo the wire holding the nail in place.

"When you have the nail, you open your veins immediately," he says. "I will tolerate no delay."

"I will not waste your time," I promise.

The nail is free. He tosses it to me.

"Christian paraphernalia," he says bitterly.

I place the nail in my right palm, the tip pointed toward Landulf, and stare at it. Neither Yaksha's nor the child's nor my daughter's blood is in this present form of mine. I am strong but still only a shadow of what I will be in the future. Since returning to Sicily I have felt no power of psychokinesis, the ability to move objects with my mind. It was Kalika's blood alone that gave me that ability, and my daughter hasn't even been born yet. Still, my daughter gave her life to save the child, paid for his life with her own. And the child's blood, in an earlier reincarnation, was once on this nail. There is a connection that can reasonably be made here, or else mystically contrived. No doubt a particle of Christ's blood still remains on the metal, deep in the folds of the atoms that bind it together.

It is on this invisible blood I focus. I still believe in the miracle of this blood. My belief is born of experience. I have seen it bring a friend back to life. My belief is stronger than evil incantations spoken to cruel spirits, and bloody pentagrams drawn on forsaken cliffs. I made a serious mistake by stealing the girl's heart, but now I will give my own heart in exchange for hers. And in exchange for my life, for just a second of time, I ask for the power that my daughter already gave to me. I ask it out of favor to Kalika, whom I am sure would not want her mother to go down without a final chance of victory. Yes, I have the nerve to remind God that he owes me for my daughter's sacrifice. But I also have the faith to believe he hears me.

And my faith is stronger than stone.

Landulf lifts the spear. "You had better hurry."

I feel my mind touch the nail.

"Yes," I whisper. "Hurry."

I feel my heart touch it. Caress it.

And I know beyond all doubt it once touched Christ.

Landulf shoulders the spear. "You die now, Sita."

The nail trembles. My hand remains firm. My gaze.

Power sweeps over me from way beyond the circle.

"No," I say. "Evil one, you die."

Landulf starts to let the spear fly.

The nail flies out of my palm and is impaled in his forehead.

Between his eyebrows. He stares at me through a red river.

"You," he says, and drops the spear.

I leap to his side and catch the spear before it lands.

The nail has plunged all the way in.

"I take back what I said a moment ago," I say. "You are not so clever."

I stick the spear in his heart, and his blood spurts out, even into the center of the pentagram, where it is mysteriously consumed in midair. He tries to speak one last time, probably to curse my soul for all of time, but he is staggering blindly with a long spear thrust through him and a nail in his brain. He makes the serious mistake of stumbling into the center region of the five-pointed star he has drawn with his wife's blood, and there something truly awful happens. In a sickeningly wet sound, his clothes and flesh are simultaneously ripped from his body. For a moment he is a carved cadaver risen from an autopsy table. Then invisible claws go around his head, and he is pulled down and backward, into a pit of nothingness. He just vanishes and I am so grateful that I fall to my knees and weep for a long time.

The spear and nail remain where they have fallen from his body. They lie in the center of the circle. And I know the power of the circle has been broken.

Eventually I climb down the cliff, and walk toward the ocean. I swim away from the hordes of Moslems, who only stare at me as I step onto the beach covered with blood from their dead benefactor. Perhaps they are afraid to touch me, I don't know. But they must have heard stories about Landulf's castle.

The place where magic was performed.

I swim through the waves beyond the invading army.

Beyond reason. The water is clean and stretches forever.

Yet I feel as if I will never be clean again.

SIXTEEN

When I reach the clear pool of water that same evening, Dante is not there. His absence hits me like a wall. It was too much to hope, I know. But as I sit exhausted beside the pond and stare at the reflection of the vanishing sunlight and the slow emergence of the stars, I ponder the unfairness of life. Here was Dante, a simple man who would give his life for a just cause, killed out of love for me. And here am I, a monster, who will easily kill, and I am still alive. God had granted me a miracle that very morning, yet I feel I would trade all of his grace just to see my friend for a few minutes.

But the night grows darker and still Dante does not come.

He is dead, I know. Death is all I know.

There is blood on my left hand.

The hand that stole the girl's life.

Funny I hadn't noticed it before. Leaning over the pond, I place my hand in the water and try to wash off the dark red stain.

But it does not come off. I wonder why.

"Good. You have passed the first step of initiation. The second step will come later, and then the final and third step."

Killing the girl had been the second step.

Or so he said. That Prince of Lies.

He is dead now. He will say no more.

Not to me. There will be no third initiation.

I scrub my hand fiercely. To no avail.

I have never seen a stain like this before.

"But I am sorry for what I did," I tell the starry pond. "You know I had to do it. I had no choice."

If I am explaining to God, he does not answer me.

But once more my memory of the future is clear. Perhaps the pond acts as a catalyst. It is every bit as clear and round as the one Alanda led me to. And as I could at that watery oasis, I imagine that I can see more reflected stars than I can in the sky itself. My sudden grip on reality makes me marvel at how much my memory faltered while I was embarked on my dark adventure. Maybe Landulf had been blocking me. Maybe my deep-seated fears distorted my memory. I could have tricked myself into not knowing the horrors that awaited me. Or perhaps it was all a function of coming back in time.

I feel as if all my powers, the ones I left behind in the

twentieth century, have returned to me. Come back just when I no longer need them. I am surprised, now that my mission is complete, that my staring at the stars does not bring me back to Alanda and Gaia and their spaceship. But maybe I don't want to leave yet. I promised Dante I would wait for him and I am determined to wait. I don't care how long it takes, long past hope I will sit here. Or, indeed, I even consider the possibility of returning to the castle to see if he has been taken captive once more. I could free him, save him.

But the latter is all bravado.

I will not go back to that castle.

I swore it once before and I swear it again.

The stars, as they are reflected in the pond, move lazily on the faint motion of the water. They are beautiful and I feel as if I can stare at them forever. Yet my mood is not peaceful. There is music in my head and it will not go away. I hear a strident refrain from Richard Wagner's *Parsival*. It is almost as if, staring at the heavens, I look upon a vast stage where Wolfram von Eschenbach's *Parsival* is still being played out. I see the knights striving to fulfill their quest for the Grail, and then, Klingsor, in the background, always out of sight, obstructing their every move with his magic wand, the Spear of Longinus. I wonder if I should have left it in Landulf's body. The sacred stabbed through the sinful. But I had feared to approach the center of the pentagram to retrieve it.

Even when he was dead, I was still afraid of him.

It is a truth I have trouble accepting.

I am afraid even now. The stain bothers me.

How was Klingsor stained? What was his mark?

The play explained it all. If only I could remember.

Something about a certain kind of smoothness.

But I cannot remember. No.

Nor can I understand why Dante was so insistent that I understand the meaning of the Medusa story. He was such a simple fellow, full of phobias and goodness, but when he spoke of mythology, he spoke with great authority. Almost as if another personality used his mouth and lips. I keep feeling as if Dante had been trying to warn me of a deeper threat. One that could not be seen because the true power of the wizard was that he was able to control one's will. Capable of turning whomever he wished to stone, so that he or she did not move unless the wizard wished it.

Could that be the real meaning of the Medusa tale?

The Gorgon did not merely kill her enemies.

She placed them under complete mind control.

Doubts continue to assail me. Questions that are more like ancient riddles. What about the snakes in the hair of Medusa? What about her fair face? Dante had emphasized that the latter was crucial. And I had laughed and told him it was time to concentrate on what was real. But I of all people should have known that reality was not always what it seemed.

A profound certainty sweeps over me.

Dante had been trying to warn me of something *unseen.*

Then I see him. And it is a miracle.

He is struggling up the path to the pond, limping badly, gasping for breath. In a moment I am by his side, helping him to sit down on a large rock not far from the water. He is in worse shape than when I saw him last and is already babbling about how sorry he is that he is late, and why he is late. I can't get a word in, but I am so happy to see him that I weep. Really, it is one of the most wonderful moments of my life. God has heard all of my prayers.

"The passageway was blocked," he says rapidly, with hardly any air in his lungs. "There was a large stone. I had never seen this stone before. Never! My lady, I didn't know what to do. I tried walking back in your direction, but I couldn't find you, and I kept slipping in the water. My brace kept falling off, and once it almost floated away. I would have been crippled! Then I took another path that I know but no one else knows and I went back into the castle and by all the saints in heaven I knew I was going to be put back in the prison. But everyone ignored me! The knights were running all over the place and the servants were crying and it sounded as if something horrible had befallen Lord Landulf." He pauses to breathe and his eyes shine with hope. "What befell him, my lady?" he asks.

I have to smile. Yet there is no joy in it and I wonder why. My happiness is tempered with regrets I can hardly explain to myself.

"He died," I say. "I killed him."

Dante bursts out with laughter. But then he catches himself and quickly does the sign of the cross. But his relief is not to be contained and a moment later he is howling in pleasure again. He jumps up from his rock and hugs me and shakes like a child. Yet the news is too good for him. He is having trouble believing it.

"Is he is really dead?" he keeps asking. "Are you sure it was him? Did you see his body? Are you sure it was his body?"

I strive to calm him. "It was him, I swear it. I put the Spear of Longinus through his evil heart. He died like any other man."

Dante is smiling. "Did you burn his body? Did the smoke stink?"

I shake my head. "No. I didn't burn him. There wasn't time."

His smile falters slightly. "But what did you do with his body, my lady?"

I shrug. "Nothing. I left it. Don't worry, he will not return to haunt us. I am sure of it."

Dante seems reassured. "Then we can go to Messina now and tell everyone that the world is safe?"

I force a laugh. "Yes. We can tell everyone that there is nothing left to worry about." But my laughter soon dies because that is not the way I feel. I add softly, "We will tell the whole world."

Dante is uncertain. "Is something wrong, my lady?"

I turn away. "No. I am just worried about you. You need to eat, to rest and regain your strength."

He stands and steps to my back. "Something weighs on your heart. Share it with me, my lady. Perhaps I can lighten your burden."

My eyes are suddenly damp. I am ashamed to look at his face.

But I feel I can tell him. He will understand.

"When I found Lord Landulf," I say, "he was in the stone circle as you said he would be. But I did not do what you suggested. I did not wait for him to leave the circle to attack him. I was too impatient. He was simply sitting there—I thought I could just kill him and then it would be all over with."

Dante speaks sympathetically. "But you could not penetrate the circle."

My hands clasp each other uneasily. I cannot stop moving them. "Yes. There was an invisible shield around it. Landulf had created it, I believe, by employing a sacrifice that required him to cut out the heart of his own wife."

Dante gasps. "Lady Cia!"

"Yes. She was dead when I arrived. But there was a young woman chained nearby who was very much alive. Landulf told me if I wanted to get to him, I would have to rip out the girl's heart. At first I refused, but then this pounding started in my head, and it wouldn't stop, and I didn't know what to do. In a moment of pain and anger I reached for her . . ." I have trouble finishing. "I reached for her and I—I killed her, Dante. I killed her with my own hands, and she had never done anything to me."

Dante is silent for a long time. Finally I feel his good hand touch my shoulder. "You did what you had to do, my lady."

I clasp his hand but shake my head. "I don't know. Sometimes I think I just did what I have always done in the past—kill. That has always been my ultimate solution to every problem." I gesture weakly. "But this girl—she was praying for me to save her."

"But you saved the rest of us."

I am emotional. "Did I? Did I do what I was supposed to do? If I did then can you explain to me why the stain of this girl's blood refuses to wash off my hand?"

Dante grabs my left hand and stares at it anxiously. "Perhaps we only need to wash it in clean water. Come, my lady, a quick wash in the pond and everything will be all right."

I take back my hand. "No, Dante. I have tried washing it a dozen times. The stain will not come off."

He is confused. "But why?"

I lower my head. "I think it is because I listened to Landulf, in the end."

"No!"

"Yes. I performed the ritual murder of an innocent. That's all that was needed to be initiated by him." I pause and stare at my left hand. There is only the stars for light, but I see the stain well. It is almost as if I see my whole life expressed in the red of the mark. "I have become one of them," I whisper.

Dante is adamant. "No! You are the opposite of them! You are an angel! You bring light where there is darkness! Hope where there is despair! A dozen times you have come to my rescue! A dozen times I would have died without your courage!"

I turn and force a smile. "Oh, Dante. I had to keep saving you because I kept putting you in danger." I raise my hand as he tries to protest. "Please don't look upon me as an angel. When you get to heaven, you'll see real angels and they'll look nothing like me."

He pauses and seems to think hard for a moment. But his eyes never leave my face. "You have too much love in you to be hated by God," he says finally. "When we get to heaven, you'll see that."

I have to laugh and hug him again. "My friend! What would I do without you? No, wait, don't answer that question. There is something I want to do for you. Something I have been planning to do for the last few days. But before I do it I want you to know that it is entirely safe. That no harm will come to your body or soul by the change I am going to bring."

He is curious. "What is this wonderful thing you are going to do?"

I hold his shoulders and stare into his eyes, trying to bring calm and understanding into his excited mind. "You saw how

Landulf was anxious to get my blood? There was a reason for that. Long ago a mysterious man gave me some of his blood, and that blood changed me in a way that made me both strong and resistant to disease. It is impossible for me to get sick. And just a few drops of my blood is able to heal others." I pause. "Do you understand what I am saying, Dante?"

He shakes his head. "I am not sure, my lady."

"I want to cut myself and sprinkle a few drops of my blood over your sores. I know they hurt you terribly, but when a little of my blood touches them they will close and heal. It will be almost be like you never had leprosy. No one will be able to tell by looking at you."

He frowns. "But it is God's will that I am sick. My disease is a punishment for my sins. We cannot change the will of God."

"Your disease is not a punishment. It is not from God. It is something you caught from another person who had the same disease."

He blinks. "From the other lepers in Persida?"

"Exactly. They gave you the leprosy."

He protests. "But I never did anything to them. I only tried to help them."

"But you were around them. You touched them. That is how you got sick."

His confusion deepens. "But Landulf wanted to use your blood, my lady. I should not use it. I should not do anything he wanted to do."

"There is a difference, Dante. Landulf wanted to use my blood to hurt people. I want to use it to heal you."

His superstitions are deep. His disquiet remains.

"But blood should not be shared," he says. "That is what heathens do. When the Holy Father accused my duke, he said that he had been sharing blood with children. I thought at the time that it was lies but it came to pass that it was true. And it was a great evil that Landulf did that. With blood he invoked the demons from hell. The pope saw clearly."

"The pope did not see clearly. Good God, Dante, the pope had you castrated."

His face twitches and his lower lip trembles. I have wounded him with my words and feel ashamed. He drops his head in humiliation.

"I wanted only to do God's will," he moans. "That is all I want to do right now. But I do not know how your blood can make my disease disappear."

I feel I have no recourse. We can argue all night, and get nowhere, and I believe it is possible that he could die this very night. From the burning and the other abuse, his sores are even more inflamed. Half his body is infected tissue, and I feel without even touching him the fever that cooks his blood. The effort it took him to reach me has drained what reserves he had left. His breathing is a perpetual wheeze. If I do not give him my blood soon, I will not be able to return to the future with a clear conscience.

"Dante," I say, meeting his gaze again. "Look at me."

He blinks rapidly. "My lady?"

"Look only at me, my friend. Listen only to me. You do not need to be afraid of my blood. It is a gift from God. Just a few drops of it will make you feel better, and God wants you to feel better after all that you have struggled do in his name."

He is suddenly dreamy. "Yes, my lady."

"Now close your eyes and imagine how nice it will to have your sores healed. How good it will be not to have people run away when they see you because they see you only as a leper. Dante, my dear, I promise you the leprosy will be gone in a few minutes."

"It will be gone," he whispers to himself with his eyes closed.

"Good." I stretch out my hand. "Now keep your eyes closed but give me your hand. I will lead you to the pond and we will first wash your sores and then I will sprinkle something on them and they will be all better."

"All better," he mumbles. But he stiffens when I try to lead him toward the pond even though his eyes remain closed. He is still under my spell, at least I think he is. "No," he says.

I have to speak carefully. "What is the matter?"

"I cannot go in the pond."

"You will not go in the pond, only beside it. I need to wash you off."

"I can drown in the pond," he says.

Now that I think of it, I have never seen Dante wash beside a pond. It is probably one of the reasons he smells.

"I will not let you drown. There is no way you can fall in."

"No," he says.

He appears to be under my spell, but he is resisting me as well. I am reminded of an earlier time when I pressed him for information he knew and yet he managed to evade me—even while in the midst of a powerful hypnotic trance. There is still something in his mind, a psychic aberration of some type, that makes it impossible for me to read him clearly. Even with all my powers now at my disposal, I cannot read what he is thinking exactly.

And I should be able to read his mind completely.

"What if you rest on the rock you were sitting on a moment ago," I suggest. "And I bring you water to clean you. Would that be all right?"

He nods with his eyes closed. "I'll rest on the rock and be all right."

I lead him back to the stone where he initially rested. As he sits, I stroke his head. "I will moisten my shirt," I say. "Then I will touch your sores gently, to clean them. There will be no pain. You will feel nothing but relief. You understand, Dante?"

"I understand," he whispers.

I let go of him. "I will be gone a few seconds. Remain at peace."

He sighs. "Peace."

At the pond the water is very still, more so than ever. Like the pond in the desert, it is a perfect mirror of the heavens. There are so many stars on its delicate surface, so many constellations that it seems almost a sin to disturb the cool liquid. Yet I have stood here before. Last time I also gave Dante my blood and sent him on his way healed of his horrible disease. Like now, and then, I felt moved by love to give him what I could. Certainly he has earned my blood and my trust.

I bend to dampen my shirt and then pause.

I cannot stop staring in the water at the sky. There is the familiar constellation, Andromeda, and I can't remember it ever looking so clear. Why, I can almost imagine that I see Perseus' wife, chained to the rocks as the Titan slowly approaches, bound as a human sacrifice to appease an evil monster. Much as Landulf chained and sacrificed young women to appease his own wickedness. It is incredible, as I look closer, to see Perseus creeping closer to her side, to rescue her, with the Medusa's head hidden in his bag, out of sight. He will only show it at the last moment, when the Titan has exposed himself. Perseus was wise to keep his weapon hidden. It was Dante who suggested that Perseus would have been a fool to part with such power.

Medusa. Perseus. Dante.

"My lady," Dante whispers at my back.

"Coming," I say.

I kneel to wet my shirt.

But once again I pause.

Richard Wagner's opera returns to me on the silence of the night air. The music echoes in my mind with rhythms older than man. Again it is as if I am watching the opera, *Parsival,* being staged against the majestic background of the constellations. Each of the principal characters could be a mythological being. King Arthur could be King Polydectes, who sent Perseus after the Gorgon. Parsival could be Perseus, who slew the Medusa. But who would Klingsor be? Why, of course, the Medusa itself. The one who appears fair from the outside, but whose hair—whose *aura*—is filled with hissing snakes. I understand in that moment that the serpents are symbolically placed above the Medusa's head. They are there so her true identity cannot be mistaken.

"Hurry, my lady," Dante whispers.

"I will," I say. But I cannot move, or breathe.

Klingsor and the Medusa. Klingsor and Landulf.

They had so much in common.

Except for one little thing. The play spoke of this "thing."

Wolfram von Eschenbach's *Parsival* told of this "thing."

Klingsor had a special mark.

He was smooth—in a delicate spot.

I remember now. Everything.

And I am sick because the truth is horrible beyond belief.

I am turned to stone. Tears cannot help me. They will not come. Not before a pain beyond all measure comes. Because even though I know the truth, I refuse to accept it. My faith may be stronger than stone, but in time all stones are worn away by water. Or tears—it doesn't matter. All I can do now is force my stone body to face what waits behind me.

Wetting my shirt, I stand and spy a lizard that slithers near the side of the pond. In a moment he is in my hand, in my pocket, and I casually walk back to Dante, who sits expectantly on the rock where I left him. A smile springs to his face as I approach even though his eyes remain closed. Leaning over, I begin to gently wipe at his burnt and diseased hand and arm. My touch pleases him.

"Oh, my lady," he says.

"Just relax, Dante," I say softly, "I have to clean you and then I can cure you. You want me to cure you, don't you?"

"Oh, yes."

"Good." I momentarily close my own eyes and bite my lower lip. "That's good."

Seconds later his hand and arm are clean. I stand and reach for the lizard in my pocket. "Now don't be afraid," I say.

"I am not afraid," he whispers.

Placing the lizard behind my back, I pulverize it in my hands. I crush it so hard all the blood squirts into my palms. Then my hands are over Dante's leper sores, dropping the reptile's blood over his wounds. The lizard was cold-blooded; its blood is not so warm as mine would have been. But Dante doesn't seem to notice and for that small favor I am glad. I cannot take my eyes off his face. I am looking for something there, a faint change of expression as his system soaks up my blood. An expression I have not seen before. An expression of triumph, perhaps, or maybe even arrogance. I need to see such a thing to dispel all my questions.

But what I see is much worse.

As the blood sprinkles over him, his lower lip curls ever so slightly. Curls in an unpleasant manner, and I believe deep in my heart that he is reacting to my great sacrifice with all but disguised contempt. I pull my hands away.

"Open your eyes, Dante," I say.

He opens his eyes and beams. "Am I cured, my lady?"

I grin with false pleasure. "Almost, my friend."

Then I grab him by the collar of his filthy shirt and, before he can react, I drag him to the edge of the pond. The water has not completely settled since I touched it, but it is flat enough to show his reflection. No wonder he did not want to stand next to the pond with me by his side. For in the water, Dante's supposedly ruined and pained expression is extraordinary.

Literally, he is more beautiful than a man should be.

He could almost be a goddess.

I leap back from him and tremble.

"Landulf," I gasp. "It was you. All along, it was you."

The other Landulf was just a puppet. Just a disciple of the real master, Dante. The duke in the castle was just a minion.

Dante was the real power behind the throne.

Dante *was* Landulf.

He stares down at his face for a long time before responding. Perhaps he has not seen his reflection in a while—I don't know. When he finally does speak, his voice is remarkably gentle, not unlike it was before, yet with more power, the confidence of a being that has for a long time been master of his own destiny. He straightens as he speaks, as if his physical disease has no real hold over him. But I am not sure if that is the case. He speaks with authority but there is disappointment in his tone.

"I should have guessed you would return with greater wisdom," he says. "Last time you were easily tricked. But now I am the one who has been fooled." He sighs. "You have grown, Sita, in the last thousand years."

"Because I chose wisdom over compassion?" I ask.

He glances at me. "In a sense. It is easier for humans to pass a test of love than a test that requires wisdom. Because even love often obscures wisdom."

I am bitter. "You do not have the right to speak to me of love."

He has been tricked but he still has the ability to smile. "But I do admire you even if I don't love you," he says. "Admiration is the closest my kind gets to love. It serves us well. I never feel the lack of this love you constantly crave."

"You imply that I need something from you. You're wrong."

"Yet you cherished Dante's love," he says.

"I was merely bewildered on the path. You are lost here at the end."

"Perhaps." He pauses. "How did you guess?"

"*Parsival.* I saw it in Vienna before World War Two. The character of Klingsor was Landulf. He had been castrated by the pope." I mock him. "In the play, they said he was smooth between the legs."

A wave of anger rolls over his face but he quickly masters himself. "You have an excellent memory. No doubt I made other mistakes with you as well."

"Yes. But I am puzzled. Why did you give me the clue of the Medusa's head?"

"It was necessary. For you to be totally mine, you had to be warned by me in advance. Free will operates on both paths, the right and the left. When you intentionally killed that girl, then and only then were you made ready to meet me here."

"It was all just a setup? The whole thing?"

"Yes."

"And had I willingly given you my blood, I would have completed the third step?"

"Precisely. Then your blood would have been of the most use to me."

I sigh. "Well, I guess now you're not going to have it."

He stares at me. I see him clearly now, his supernatural beauty, even the faint tendrils of black that crawl around the field above his head. Yet I realize he still has leprosy.

"You are wrong on that point," he says softly.

I take a step back. "You are still about to die. You need my blood to live even a few more days. Your evil invocations really did give you leprosy."

He takes a step in my direction. "That is correct. The work has its price. But I need your blood to sustain this physical body, and continue my work in this third density. But unlike last time, I will now be unable to pass my blood onto others. You can no longer be convinced to be my initiate and undergo a shift toward negative polarization. Still, your blood will be useful to me for a long time." He removes a dagger from under his dirty shirt. It is the same one that the maid stabbed me with. It is stained with my blood. "There is no point in trying to run from me, Sita, or in trying to harm me. My psychic powers are beyond yours."

I find it impossible to turn away from him.

Indeed, I cannot even move my arms or legs

The Medusa. My body has turned to stone.

"It doesn't matter what you do to me now," I say, thankful to be able to use my tongue. "I have defeated you and the rest of your kind. In the future there will be no army of invincible negative beings to confuse humanity. Your cancer has been cut from society. The harvest will go forward the way it was intended. You have lost, Landulf, admit it."

He steps to within two feet of me. He brushes my long hair with his knife. Then he licks the tip of the blade, the dried blood, and smiles sadly.

"It is not my nature to admit anything," he says. "But I will say that I would have enjoyed your continuing adoration almost as much as your body, and the immortal blood that pumps through it." He scratches the skin below my right eye and a red drop runs over my cheek. The sight fills him with pleasure. "A vampiric tear, Sita. Cried for me? I must still be your hero."

I am defiant, and no longer afraid.

The stain on my left hand has vanished.

"My only regret is the tears I cried for you," I say. "Other than that I have none. I am at peace. And you are still a monster. One day you will be forced to look in Perseus' mirror, and you will see your own reflection, and see just how foul you are to behold. And on that day you will turn to stone, Landulf. You will die and rot, and the world will be relieved of a great burden." I stop. "Kill me now and get it over with. If you have the nerve, you disgusting creature!"

I spit in his face. He does not like that.

He wipes the saliva away and raises his knife.

"I was going to kill you quick," he says. "But now, Sita, it may take all night."

He moves to slit open my side and then pauses, puzzled.

I am confused as well, for a moment. My body has begun to glow. The pond shines as well, with the light of the heavens. It is as if the constellations in the sky have been awakened, and been inspired to send down their light to Earth. The white light that fills my body comes from the direction of the pond as well as the sky. Landulf seems to recognize the transformation I am undergoing and is filled with dismay. But this stellar current fills me with euphoria. I have experienced it before, just before I rescued the child from the Setians. Landulf is like one of those creatures, I see, only worse. He struggles to cut into my flesh as I grow brighter. His frustration makes me laugh.

"I guess you're going to have to remain a leper," I say in a voice that grows faint. "But don't take it too hard. You're not going to be around much longer. Yaksha is still somewhere on this planet and you might try to find him, but I don't think that you'll get to him in time. As far as you're concerned, I am the last vampire. Your last chance, Landulf. How does that feel?"

His rage is incredible to behold. The fair face of the god is transformed into a demon. The all but invisible serpents above his head hiss poisonous vapors. They surround him in a noxious cloud. It is as if his whole body has been swallowed by his leper's sores. He tries to grab me but his fingers pass through me. Seeing his efforts are useless, he strains to regain his pleasant demeanor, to make one last stab at my soul. But he still has the knife in his hand and in either case I will never be fooled by him again.

"Sita," he says. "Our offer is still good. We can grant you powers unimaginable. You have only to join us, and we will rule this world together."

I am practically a ghost but I can still laugh.

"You shouldn't have mentioned the togetherness part," I reply. "I can't think of anything more dull."

SEVENTEEN

There is a brief moment when I am lying on the floor of the interstellar craft. I feel Alanda and Gaia close. It is possible Alanda even calls my name. She must know I have successfully completed my mission. She must be waiting for me, to smile at me, to take me to other worlds, into a glorious future.

But my battle with Landulf has taken something from me.

Finally I am tired of such adventures.

As Yaksha finally grew weary, I also crave a change.

Before Alanda can call me back to the present moment, I focus my entire being on another page of history. I return to the first vampire, the strange night Yaksha was born, five thousand years ago in India, when I was a girl of seven years. The Aghoran ceremony has ended and the evil priest has been killed by Amba's animated corpse. The corpse finally lies down but there is movement inside Amba's belly, which is still swollen with the nine-month-old fetus she was carrying when she died. My father takes his knife and goes to cut out the unborn child trapped in the womb. I leap from my hiding place behind the bushes.

"Father!" I cry, as I reach for his hand that holds the knife. "Do not let that child come into the world. Amba is dead, see with your own eyes. Her child must likewise be dead. Please, Father, listen to me."

Naturally, all the men are surprised to see me, never mind hear what I have to say. My father is angry with me, but he kneels and speaks to me patiently.

"Sita," he says, "your friend does appear dead, and we were wrong to let this priest use her body in this way. But he has paid for his evil karma with his own life. But we would be creating evil karma of our own if we do not try to save the life of this child. You remember when Sashi was born, how her mother died before she came into the world? It sometimes happens that a living child is born to a dead woman."

"No," I protest. "That was different. Sashi was born just as his mother died. Amba has been dead since early dawn. Nothing living can come out of her."

My father gestures with his knife to the squirming life inside Amba's bloody abdomen. "Then how do you explain the life here?"

"That is the yashini moving inside her," I say. "You saw how the demon smiled at us before it departed. It intends to

trick us. It is not gone. It has entered into the child."

My father ponders my words with a grave expression. He knows I am intelligent for my age, and occasionally asks my advice. He looks to the other men for guidance, but they are evenly divided. Some want to use the knife to stab the life moving inside Amba. Others are afraid, like my father, of committing a sin. Finally my father turns back to me and hands me the knife.

"You knew Amba better than any of us," he says. "You would best know if this life that moves inside her is evil or good. If you know for sure in your heart that it is evil, then strike it dead. None of the men here will blame you for the act."

I am appalled. I am still a child and my father is asking me to commit an atrocious act. But my father is wiser than I have taken him for. He shakes his head as I stare at him in amazement, and he moves to take back the knife.

But I don't give the knife to him.

I know in my heart what I must do.

I stab the blade deep into Amba's baby.

Black blood gushes over my hands.

But it is only the blood of one. Not thousands.

The creature inside Amba's body stops moving.

Alanda turns to Gaia after studying her friend's body. They are not in a spaceship, but stand in the desert at night beside a clear pond. Many stars shine overhead.

"She is not breathing," Alanda says. "Her heart has stopped."

"But she stopped him," Gaia says, who actually can speak in his own way. "The path is now clear for many."

Alanda glances down at her friend. There is sorrow in her voice. "But she was coming back to us," she says.

Gaia comforts her. "She always went her own path. Let her go this way."

Yet Alanda later sheds a tear as they slide her friend's body into the pond. For a moment her friend floats on the surface of the water, and the reflection of the stars frame her figure. And when Alanda glances up, she sees the same outline in the heavens. For a moment her friend is constellation and it gives her a measure of comfort. But when Alanda looks back down, her friend has sunk beneath the mirror of the water and is gone.

"It is like she never was," Alanda whispers.

"It is like that for all of us," Gaia says.

One moonless night, when I am twenty years of age, I am awakened by a sound outside. Besides me sleeps my husband, Rama, and on my other side is our daughter, Lalita. I don't know why the sound wakes me. It was not loud. But it was peculiar, the sound of nails scraping over a blade. I get up and go outside my house and stand in the dark and look around.

For a long time I stand there, expecting to meet someone.
But there is no one there.
Finally I return to my bed and fall asleep.

The next morning I am playing with my Lalita by the river when a strange man comes by. He is tall and powerfully built. In his right hand he holds a lotus flower, in his left a gold flute. His legs are long and his every movement is bewitching. I cannot help but stare at him, and I am delighted when he comes and kneels beside me on the bank of the river. For some reason, I know he means me no harm.

"Hello," he says, staring at the water. "How are you?"

"I am fine." I pause. "Do I know you, sir?"

A faint smile touches his lips. "Yes. We have met before."

I hesitate. He does seem familiar but I cannot place him.

"I am sorry, I don't remember," I say.

He finally looks at me and his eyes are very blue. They remind me of the stars at night; they seem to sparkle with light from the heavens. "My name is Krishna," he says.

I bow my head. "I am Sita. This is my daughter, Lalita. Are you new to this area?"

He turns back to the water. "I have been here before."

"Is there anything I can do for you? Would you like some food?"

He glances at me, out the corners of his eyes, and I feel a thrill in my heart. There is such love in his glance, I don't understand how it can be so. "I was wondering if I could do anything for you, Sita," he says.

"My Lord?" I ask, and I feel he is deserving of the title.

He shrugs faintly. "I merely came to see if you were happy. If you are, then I will be on my way."

I have to laugh. "My Lord, I am not long married. My husband is a wonderful man whom I love dearly and God has seen fit to grace us with a beautiful child. We are all healthy and have plenty to eat. I cannot imagine being any happier than I am right now."

He nods briefly and then stands. "Then I will say goodbye, Sita."

But I jump up. "You came all the way here just to see if I was happy?"

"Yes." His eyes are kind as he looks at me for the last time. "Your happiness is all that matters to me. Remember me, Sita."

Then he walks away and I never see him again.

But I never forget him. Krishna.

EPILOGUE

Seymour Dorsten sat at his computer in his bedroom and stared at the words on the screen. It was late, close to dawn, and he had been writing most of the night. For the last six months, in fact, he had worked almost every night without rest. But it didn't matter how much sleep he missed. He could always sleep during the day. Because he was very sick with AIDS, he no longer attended school, or even went out of the house. Indeed, his personal physician thought he wouldn't live out the year, and it was almost Christmas. Yet the tragedy of his early demise did not disturb him, at least not at the moment. Like his imagined heroine, he was happy in the end, to have even reached the end.

He had just finished his story. *Her* story.

About Alisa Perne, his Sita. The Last Vampire.

Seymour felt as if he had taken her everywhere she could go, but at the same time he knew that it was *she* who had led him on the adventures. Lifted him up to heights he could not have imagined if not for his serious illness. For him, the constant experience of his waning mortality had been the greatest muse. She had never said who she was sending her thoughts out to, but it was to him, always to him. But *he* had made her immortal, and himself, so that he wouldn't have to be afraid of his own death. He knew, in the end, that she had not been afraid, and that her only regret had been that she had not been able to say goodbye to him. But at least he could say goodbye to her.

Seymour leaned forward and turned off the screen.

There was a noise outside his window.

He glanced over. Quickly, he always did.

But it was nothing. A cat, the wind.

But such sounds, this late at night, always made him think of her. Ageless Sita coming through the window to give him her magical blood. To save him from his illness. But she had chosen the only destiny worthy of her. She had simply decided to vanish, to exist only in his heart.

Seymour coughed weakly and brushed away a tear that came to his eye. He should be in a hospital. His lungs were half-filled with fluid, and he couldn't draw in a full breath without pain. Still, he thought, it was better to be at home with his computer and his story. He just wished his heart could beat for her forever.

Seymour was going to miss her. Yeah.

"Goodbye, Sita," he said to the empty screen.

He thought he would miss her forever.

ABOUT THE AUTHOR

CHRISTOPHER PIKE is the author of more than forty teen thrillers, including the series Remember Me, Final Friends, and Chain Letter.

SHADE

BY JERI SMITH-READY

Don't miss this sexy paranormal novel!
COMING IN SUMMER 2010

"You can hear me, can't you?"

I punched the green print button on the copier to drown out the disembodied voice. Sometimes if I ignored them long enough, they went away—confused, discouraged, and lonelier than ever. Sometimes.

Okay, almost never. Usually they got louder.

No time to deal with it that day. Only one more set of legal briefs to unstaple, copy, and restaple, and then I could go home, trade this straitjacket and stockings for a T-shirt and jeans, and make it to Logan's before practice. To tell him I'm sorry, that I've changed my mind, and this time I mean it. Really.

"I know you can hear me." The old woman's voice strengthened as it came closer. "You're one of them."

I didn't flinch as I grabbed the top brief from the stack on the conference room table. I couldn't see her under the office's

bright fluorescent lights, which made it about one percent easier to pretend she wasn't there.

Someday, if I had my way, none of them would be there.

"What an intolerably rude child," she said.

I yanked the staple out of the last brief and let it zing off
in an unknown direction, trying to hurry without *looking* like
I was hurrying. If the ghost knew I was getting ready to leave,
she'd spit out her story, no invitation. I carefully laid the pages
in the sheet feeder and hit print again.

"You can't be more than sixteen." The lady's voice was close,
almost at my elbow. "So you were born hearing us."

I didn't need her to remind me how ghosts' ramblings had
drowned out my mother's New Agey lullabies. (According to
Aunt Gina, Mom thought the old-fashioned ones were too
disturbing—"down will come baby, cradle and all." But when
dead people are bitching and moaning around your crib at all
hours, the thought of falling out of a tree is so not a source of
angst.)

Worst part was, those lullabies were all I remembered of her.

"Come on," I nagged the copier under my breath, resisting
the urge to kick it.

The piece of crap picked that moment to jam.

"Shit." I clenched my fist, driving the staple remover tooth
into the pad of my thumb. "Ow! Damn it." I sucked the pinpoint of blood.

"Language." The ghost sniffed. "When I was your age,

young ladies wouldn't have heard such words, much less murdered the mother tongue with . . ." Blah blah . . . kids these days . . . blah blah . . . parents' fault . . . blah . . .

I jerked open the front of the copier and searched for the stuck paper, humming a Keeley Brothers song to cover the ghost's yakking.

"They cut me," she said quietly.

I stopped humming, then blew out a sigh that fluttered my dark bangs. Sometimes there's no ignoring these people.

I stood, slamming the copier door. "One condition. I get to see you."

"Absolutely not," she huffed.

"Wrong answer." I rounded the table and headed for the switches by the conference room door.

"Please, you don't want to do that. The way they left me—"

I flipped off the light and turned on the BlackBox.

"No!" The ghost streaked toward me in a blaze of violet. She stopped two inches from my face and let out a shriek that scraped against all the little bones in my ears.

Cringing? Not an option. I crossed my arms, then calmly and slowly extended my middle finger.

"Don't you look at me!" Her voice crackled around the edges as she tried to frighten me. "Turn on the light."

"You wanted to talk. I don't talk to ghosts I can't see." I touched the BlackBox switch. "Sucks to be trapped, huh? That's how I feel, listening to you people all day."

"How dare you?" The woman slapped my face, her fingers curled into claws. Her hand passed through my head without so much as a breeze. "After all I've been through. Look at me."

I tried to check her out, but she was trembling so hard with anger, her violet lines kept shifting into one another. It was like trying to watch TV without my contacts.

"Those shoes are beyond last year," I said, "but other than that, you look fine."

The ghost glanced down at herself and froze in astonishment. Her pale hair—gray in life, I assumed—was tied in a bun, and she wore what looked like a ruffle-lapelled suit and low-heeled pumps. Your basic country-club queen. Probably found her own death positively *scandalous*.

"I haven't seen myself in the dark." She spoke with awe. "I assumed I would be . . ." Her hand passed over her stomach.

"What, fat?"

"Disemboweled."

I felt my eyes soften. "You were murdered?" With old people it was usually a heart attack or stroke. But it explained her rage.

She scowled at me. "Well, it certainly wasn't suicide."

"I know." My voice turned gentle as I remembered to be patient. Sometimes these poor souls didn't know what to expect, despite all the public awareness campaigns since the Shift. The least I could do was clarify. "If you'd killed yourself, you wouldn't be a ghost, because you would've been prepared to die. And you're not all carved up because you get frozen in the happiest moment of your life."

She examined her clothes with something close to a smile, maybe remembering the day she wore them, then looked up at me with a sudden ferocity. "But *why?*"

I ditched the patience. "How the hell should I know?" I flapped my arms. "I don't know why we see you at all. No one knows, okay?"

"Listen to me, young lady." She pointed her violet finger in my face. "When I was your age—"

"When you were my age, the Shift hadn't happened yet. Everything's different now. You should be grateful someone can hear you."

"I shouldn't be—this way—at all." She clearly couldn't say the word *dead*. "I need someone to make it right."

"So you want to sue." One of my aunt Gina's specialties: wrongful death litigation. Gina believes in "peace through justice." She thinks it helps people move past ghosthood to whatever's beyond. Heaven, I guess, or at least someplace better than Baltimore.

Weird thing is, it usually works, though no one knows exactly why. But unfortunately, Gina—my aunt, guardian, and godmother—can't hear or see ghosts. Neither can anyone else born before the Shift, which happened sixteen and three-quarters years ago. So when Gina's firm gets one of these cases, guess who gets to translate? All for a file clerk's paycheck.

"My name is Hazel Cavendish," the lady said. "I was one of this firm's most loyal clients."

Ah, that explained how she got here. Ghosts can only appear in the places they went during their lives. No one knows why *that* is either, but it makes things a lot easier on people like me.

She continued without prompting. "I was slaughtered this morning outside my home in—"

"Can you come back Monday?" I checked my watch in ex-Hazel's violet glow. "I have to be somewhere."

"But it's only Thursday. I need to speak to someone now." Her fingers flitted over the string of pearls around her neck. "Aura, please."

I stepped back. "How do you know my name?"

"Your aunt talked about you all the time, showed me your picture. Your name is hard to forget." She moved toward me, her footsteps silent. "So beautiful."

My head started to swim. *Uh-oh.*

Vertigo in a post-Shifter like me usually means a ghost is turning shade. They go down that one-way path when they let bitterness warp their souls. It has its advantages—shades are dark, powerful spirits who can hide in the shadows and go anywhere they want.

Anywhere, that is, but out of this world. Unlike ghosts, shades can't pass on or find peace, as far as we know. And since they can single-handedly debilitate any nearby post-Shifter, "detainment" is the only option.

"I really have to go," I whispered, like I'd hurt ex-Hazel less if I lowered the volume. "A few days won't matter."

"Time always matters."

"Not for you." I kept my voice firm but kind. "Not anymore."

She moved so close, I could see every wrinkle on her violet face.

"Your eyes are old," she hissed. "You think you've seen everything, but you don't know what it's like." She touched my heart with a hand I couldn't feel. "One day you'll lose something that matters, and then you'll know."

I ran for my car, my work shoes clunking against the sidewalk and rubbing blisters on my ankles. No time to stop home to change before going to Logan's. Should've brought my clothes with me, but how could I have known there'd be a new case?

I'd wussed out, of course, and let the old woman tell my aunt her nasty death story. The ghost was angry enough that I worried about what she'd do without immediate attention. "Shading" was still pretty rare, especially for a new ghost like ex-Hazel, but it wasn't worth the risk.

The leafy trees lining the street made it dark enough to see ghosts even an hour before sunset. Half a dozen were loitering outside the day care center in the mansion across the street. Like most of the buildings in the Roland Park area, Little Creatures Kiddie Care was completely BlackBoxed—its walls lined with the same thin layer of charged obsidian that kept ghosts out of sensitive areas. Bathrooms, military base buildings, that sort of thing. I wish Gina and I could afford to live there—Roland Park, I mean, not a military base.

I stopped for a giant Coke Slurpee and guzzled it on my way toward I-83, wincing at the brain freeze. I usually prefer to use the spoon end of the straw, but after ex-Hazel's intake session, I desperately needed the massive caffeine-sugar infusion that only pure, bottom-of-the-cup Slurpee syrup could provide.

The long shadows of trees cut across the road, and I kept my eyes forward so I wouldn't see the ghosts on the sidewalks.

Lot of good it did. At the last stoplight before the expressway, a little violet kid waved from the backseat of the car in front of me. His lips were moving, forming words I couldn't decipher. An older girl next to him clapped her hands over her ears, her blond pigtails wagging back and forth as she shook her head. The parents in the front seats kept talking, oblivious or maybe just unable to deal. *They should trade in that car*, I thought, *while that poor girl still has her sanity*.

The on-ramp sloped uphill into the sunshine, and I let out a groan of relief, gnawing the end of my straw.

After almost seventeen years of hearing about grisly murders and gruesome accidents, you'd think I'd be tough, jaded. You'd think that ghosts' tendency to over-share would eventually annoy instead of sadden me.

And you'd be right. Mostly. By the time I was five, I'd stopped crying. I'd stopped having nightmares. I'd stopped sleeping with the lights on so I wouldn't see their faces. And I'd stopped talking about it, because by that point the world believed us. Five hundred million toddlers can't be wrong.

But I never forgot. Their stories are shelved in my mind, neat as a filing system. Probably because I've recited many of them on the witness stand.

Courts don't just take *my* word for it, or any one person's. Testimony only counts if two of us post-Shifters agree on a ghost's statement. Since ghosts apparently can't lie, they make great witnesses. Last year, me and this terrified freshman translated for the victims of a psycho serial killer. (Remember Tomcat? The one who liked to "play with his food"?)

Welcome to my life. It gets better.

I pulled into Logan's driveway at 6:40. I loved going to the Keeleys' house—it sat in a brand-new development outside Hunt Valley on what used to be woodlands. No dead people ever lived there, so it was one hundred percent ghost free. At the time, anyway.

I checked my hair in the rearview mirror. Hopelessly well-groomed. I pawed through my bag to find a few funky little silver skull-and-crossbones barrettes, then pinned them into my straight dark brown hair to make it stick out in random places.

"Yeah, you look totally punk in your beige suit and sensible flats." I made a face at myself in the mirror, then leaned closer.

Were my eyes really that old, like ex-Hazel said? Maybe it was the dark circles underneath. I licked my finger and wiped under my brown eyes to see if the mascara had smeared.

Nope. The gray shadows on my skin came from too little sleep and too much worrying. Too much rehearsing what I would say to Logan.

As I walked up the brick front path, I heard music blasting through the open basement window.

Late. I wanted to hurl my bag across the Keeleys' lawn in frustration. Once Logan got lost in his guitar, he forgot I existed. And we really needed to talk.

I went in the front door without knocking, the way I had since we were six and the Keeleys lived around the block. I hurried past the stairs, through the kitchen, and into the family room.

"Hey, Aura," called Logan's fifteen-year-old brother Dylan from his usual position, sprawled barefoot and bowlegged on the floor in front of the flat-screen TV. He glanced up from his video game, then did a double-take at the sight of my Slurpee cup. "Bad one?"

"Old lady, stabbed in a mugging. Semi-Shady."

"Sucks." He focused on his game, nodding in time to the metal soundtrack. "Protein drinks work better."

"You bounce back your way, I'll bounce my way."

"Whatever." His voice rose suddenly. "Noooo! Eat it! Eat it!" Dylan slammed his back against the ottoman and jerked the joystick almost hard enough to break it. As his avatar got torched by a flamethrower, he shrieked a stream of curses that told me his parents weren't home. Mr. and Mrs. Keeley had apparently already left for their second honeymoon.

I opened the basement door, releasing a blast of guitar chords, then slipped off my shoes so I could walk downstairs without noise.

Halfway to the bottom, I peered over the banister into the left side of the unfinished basement. Logan was facing away from me, strumming his new Fender Stratocaster and watching his brother Mickey work out a solo. The motion of his shoulder blades rippled his neon green T-shirt, the one I'd bought him on our last day trip to Ocean City.

When he angled his chin to check his fingers on the fret board, I could see his profile. Even with his face set in concentration, his sky blue eyes sparked with joy. Logan could play guitar in a sewer and still have fun.

Logan and Mickey were like yin and yang, inside and out. Logan's spiky hair was bleached blond with black streaks, while Mickey's was black with blond streaks. Logan played a black guitar right-handed, and his brother a white one left-handed. They had the same lanky build, and lots of people thought they were twins, but Mickey was eighteen and Logan only seventeen (minus one day).

Their sister Siobhan—Mickey's actual twin—was sitting cross-legged on the rug in front of them, her fiddle resting against her left knee as she shared a cigarette with the bassist, her boyfriend, Connor.

My best friend, Megan, sat next to them, knees pulled to

her chest. She wove a lock of her long, dark red hair through her fingers as she stared at Mickey.

The only one facing me was Brian, the drummer. He spotted me and promptly missed a beat. I cringed—he was sometimes brilliant, but he could be distracted by a stray dust ball.

Mickey and Logan stopped playing and turned to Brian, who adjusted the backward white baseball cap on his head in embarrassment.

"Jesus," Mickey said, "is it too much to ask for a fucking backbeat?"

"Sorry." Brian twirled his stick in his thick hand, then pointed it at me. "She's here."

Logan spun around, and I expected a glare for interrupting—not to mention leftover hostility from last night's fight. Instead his face lit up.

"Aura!" He swept the strap over his head, handed his guitar to Mickey, and leaped to meet me at the bottom of the stairs. "Oh my God, you won't believe this!" He grabbed me around the waist and hoisted me up. "You will *not* believe this."

"I will, I swear." I wrapped my arms around his neck, grinning so hard it hurt. Clearly he wasn't mad at me. "What's up?"

"Hang on." Logan lowered me to the floor, then spread my arms to examine my suit. "They make you wear this to work?"

"I didn't have time to change." I gave him a light punch in the chest for torturing me. "So what won't I believe?"

"Siobhan, get her some clothes," he barked.

"Choice," she said. "Say please or kiss my ass."

"Please!" Logan held up his hands. "Anything to keep your ass in the safe zone."

Siobhan gave Connor her cigarette and got to her feet. As she passed me, she squeezed my elbow and said, "Boy thinks he's a rock god just because some label people are coming to the show tomorrow."

My mind spun as it absorbed my biggest hope and fear. "Is she kidding?" I asked Logan.

"No," he growled. "Thanks for blowing the surprise, horse face!" he yelled as she slouched up the stairs, snickering.

I tugged on his shirt. "Who's coming?"

"Get this." He gripped my shoulders. "A and R dudes from two different companies. One's an independent—Lianhan Records—"

"That's the one we want," Mickey interjected.

"—and the other is Warrant."

I gasped. "I've heard of Warrant."

"Because they're part of a major, major, *major* humongous label." Logan's eyes rolled up in ecstasy, like God himself was handing out record contracts.

"We'll use Warrant to make Lianhan jealous," Mickey added. "But we're not selling out."

Logan pulled me to the back side of the stairs, where the others couldn't see us. "This could be it," he whispered. "Can you believe it? It'd be the most amazing birthday present ever."

I steadied my breath so I could get the words out. "Hopefully not the best present."

"You mean the Strat from my folks?"

"Not that, either." I reached up under the back of his T-shirt and let my fingers graze his warm skin.

"Is it something you—wait." His eyes widened, making the silver hoop in his brow glint in the overhead light. "Are you saying—"

"Yep." I stood on tiptoe and kissed him, quick but hard. "I'm ready."

His gold-tipped lashes flickered, but he angled his chin to look at me sideways. "You said that before."

"I said a lot of things before. Some of them were stupid."

"Yeah, they were." His eyes crinkled, softening his words. "You know I'd never leave you over this, either way. How could you even think that?"

"I don't know. I'm sorry."

"Me too." He traced my jaw with his thumb, which always made me shiver. "I love you."

He kissed me then, drowning my doubts in one warm, soft moment. Doubts about him, about me, about him *and* me.

"Here you go!" Siobhan called from the stairs, a moment before a clump of denim and cotton fell on our heads. "Oops," she said with fake surprise.

I peeled the jeans off Logan's shoulder and held them up in salute. "Thanks, Siobhan."

"Back to work!" rang Mickey's voice from the other side of the basement.

Logan ignored his brother and gazed into my eyes. "So . . . maybe tomorrow night, at my party?" He hurried to add, "Only if you're sure. We could wait, if you—"

"No." I could barely manage a whisper. "No more waiting."

His lips curved into a smile, which promptly faded. "I better clean my room. There's like a one-foot path through all the old *Guitar Worlds* and dirty laundry."

"I can walk on a one-foot path."

"Screw that. I want it to be perfect."

"Hey!" Mickey yelled again, louder. "What part of 'back to work' is not in English?"

Logan grimaced. "We're switching out some of our set list—less covers, more original stuff. Probably be up all night." He gave me a kiss that was quick but full of promise. "Stay as long as you want."

He disappeared around the stairs, and immediately Megan replaced him at my side.

"Did you make up? You did, didn't you?"

"We made up." I sat on the couch to remove my stockings, checking over my shoulder to make sure the guys were out of sight on the other side of the stairs. "I told him I'm ready."

Megan slumped next to me and rested her elbow on the

back of the sofa. "You don't think you have to say that to keep him, do you?"

"It's something I want too. Anyway, who cares, as long as it works?"

"Aura . . ."

"You know what it's like, going to their gigs." My whisper turned to a hiss. "Seeing all those girls who'd probably pay to get naked with Mickey or Logan. Or even with Brian or Connor."

"But the guys aren't like that—well, maybe Brian is, but he doesn't have a girlfriend. Mickey loves me. Logan loves you."

"So?" I slipped on the jeans. "Plenty of rock stars have wives and girlfriends, and they still screw their groupies. It comes with the territory."

"I find your lack of faith disturbing," she said in her best Darth Vader impression, forcing a smile out of me.

I unbuttoned my white silk blouse. "What should I wear?"

"Same stuff as always, on the outside. That's the way he likes you." Megan snapped the strap of my plain beige bra. "But definitely do better than this underneath."

"Duh," was my only response as I slipped Siobhan's black-and-yellow Distillers T-shirt over my head. I'd made a covert trip to Victoria's Secret weeks before—the one way up in Owings Mills, where no one would recognize me. The matching black lace bra and underwear were still in the original bag, with their tags on, in the back of my bottom dresser drawer.

"The first time doesn't have to suck," she said, "not if you go slow."

"Okay," I said quickly, in a deep state of not wanting to talk about it.

Luckily, at that moment Brian tapped his sticks to mark time, and the band launched into one of their original tunes, "The Day I Sailed Away."

The Keeley Brothers wanted to be the premier Irish-flavored rock band in Baltimore. Maybe one day go national, become the next Pogues, or at least the next Flogging Molly, with a heavy dose of American skate-punk 'tude.

As Logan began to sing, Megan's face reflected my bliss and awe. With that voice leading the way, the Keeley Brothers didn't have to be the next anyone.

Two record labels. I closed my eyes, ignoring the way my stomach turned to lead, and savored the sound that Megan and I would soon have to share with the world.

I knew then that everything would change the next night. It was like time had folded in on itself, and I could remember the future.

A future I already hated.

Her death will not go unpunished. . . .